after the
leaves
fall

after the
Leaves fall

nicole baart

Tyndale House Publishers, Inc., Carol Stream, Illinois

Visit Tyndale's exciting Web site at www.tyndale.com

Visit Nicole Baart's Web site at www.nicolebaart.com

TYNDALE and Tyndale's quill logo are registered trademarks of Tyndale House Publishers, Inc.

After the Leaves Fall

Designed by Jessie McGrath

Edited by Lorie Popp

Scripture quotations are taken from the *Holy Bible,* New International Version®. NIV®. Copyright © 1973, 1978, 1984 by International Bible Society. Used by permission of Zondervan. All rights reserved.

Library of Congress Cataloging-in-Publication Data

Baart, Nicole.
 After the leaves fall / Nicole Baart.
  p. cm.
 ISBN-13: 978-1-4143-1622-2 (pbk.)
 ISBN-10: 1-4143-1622-4 (pbk.)
 I. Title.
 PS3602.A22A69 2007
 813′.6—dc22   2007011431

Printed in the United States of America

13 12 11 10 09 08 07
 7 6 5 4 3B

For Dad

(I've waited twenty-four years to write that.)

Many heartfelt thanks . . .

To Todd Diakow, my writing partner, encourager, friend, and first-draft editor. This book would not be without you.

To both of my lovely grandmothers. Your courage, beauty, and strength is on every page of this book.

To Toni Tweten, for inviting me in. You are truly my esteemed friend.

To Arlana Huyser, for calling me from a bus on some back road in Nebraska halfway through reading the first manuscript. You renewed my energy.

To Jamin and Kate VerVelde, for being more than just good friends. I couldn't ask for better cheerleaders.

To Bruce and Sue Osterink, for being the hands and feet of Christ better than anyone I've ever met.

To my parents, for never once laughing at the countless poems, short stories, and sorry attempts at literature that I proudly brought home from kindergarten on.

And to my family: To Aaron, for your patience and loving support. To Isaac, for your three-year-old wisdom and never-ending supply of puppy kisses. To Judah, for keeping this all in perspective. Knowing you waited for me half a world away realigned my every priority.

God has blessed my life far more than I could ever claim to deserve. The debt of gratitude I owe my Master defies explanation.

part 1

WAITING IS A COMPLICATED LONGING.

I lost my father when I was fifteen, and I've been waiting ever since.

He was buried on a rainy day in October, and I remember the sound of the raindrops on the lid of the sleek black casket and how it seemed like music to me. The pastor was doing his best to make sorrowful an occasion that seemed anything but—the leaves on the trees above us were burnt amber, the consoling sky around us was velvety gray, and the rain was singing softly. I didn't feel sad. I felt expectant.

My father had been in pain. There was so much pain. It had seeped out of his limbs and crept hauntingly into my blood and bones. My grandmother and I carried pain from his bed every time we walked away from a failed attempt at getting him to eat. We steeled ourselves against the ache that slowly invaded when we sat by his side and held his cool hand, his fingers dry and fragile in ours as if this small part of him were already gone. Even walking the few steps past the living room, where he lay entombed in an impossibly narrow hospital bed, to the dining room, which was the only way into the kitchen, was a staggering experience. I'd pause imperceptibly in the hallway, gather myself, and walk with purpose and more than adequate speed until I was wrapped in the warmth of the kitchen, where the oven was baking something that he would never eat.

Sometimes he cried, but the tears just gathered in the corners of his eyes and pooled there like so much dark water lost among the black-brown of his gaze. I wasn't always sure if he was even aware of his crying, but those tears called out of their own accord, and the reverberation would echo through the house until it drowned out all else. I felt I would go deaf from it. *Stop. Oh, please, God, make it stop.*

When it stopped it was as if the world was filled with air again. I breathed again. Great gasping lungfuls of air that left me dizzy and panting. And weeping. The night after Dad died, Grandma found me in the grove behind the old chicken coop, gulping that glorious, rich air and sobbing without making the tiniest sound. She knelt beside me in her housecoat, letting the damp grass soak her arthritic knees, and pounded me on the back until all that good air took and my tears could be heard as well as seen. *I'm dying too*, I thought when I heard the keen that could only be coming from my own mouth. What but death could possibly feel like this?

But I wasn't even close to dying. Fresh air was new life that filled my veins. Grief was so quickly and yet so incompletely replaced by something that felt like relief that I careened from guilt to repose and never became fully settled with anything I felt.

After he was gone, I would find myself in the darkness of the living room in the middle of the night, standing where his bed had filled the space in front of the picture window. The October sky would be cold and clear, and from the farmhouse window the stars would shimmer like something otherworldly. *Thank You, God, for taking him.* I would breathe the half prayer over and over, and for those minutes in the newly quiet house, I would feel something close to peace. Then the very next morning the lack of his presence across the table would choke me until my tongue was thick and threatening in my mouth, and I promised God my soul if only I could have one more day with Dad.

It was in this new living that waiting became so complicated.

I began to exist in a tension between wanting and not wanting—waiting for something I couldn't even pin down in my most naked and honest moments. Waiting for a balance where I neither ached nor forgot, regretted nor accepted. Waiting for my heart to be light again yet fearing the implications of that same lightness. I suppose I waited for peace—an end to my own personal warfare.

The imbalance struck me for the first time immediately after I threw a fistful of sodden dirt on the box in the ground that contained his body. I was torn between laughter and tears. Feeling that something big and incomprehensible had just happened, Grandma and I stood hand in hand until the graveyard was empty and the rain had all but ceased to fall. Her lips moved faintly, and I knew she was whispering prayers for me. I couldn't join her—I had forgotten how; the ability to pray had slipped out of my soul like the dirt had tumbled from my fingers. I wasn't angry at God or anything—that would have been far too clichéd. He just seemed irrelevant.

When Grandma spoke, it was unexpected. "You know what my favorite time of year is?"

I blinked for the first time in minutes and looked up at her. "Huh?"

She continued without looking down at me. "I love it best when the leaves fall."

I didn't know what to say.

"Lots of people like autumn because the leaves turn such pretty colors." Grandma smiled at this as if she had a secret, something sweet and unforeseen that she was going to share with me. I watched the familiar, wrinkled profile soften. "I like it when all those leaves fall because it's such a small thing that means so very much." Pulling her hand out of mine, she turned to me and tilted my face toward her own. "Do you know what I mean?"

I didn't.

She searched my face. "There's this subtle sadness—winter is coming, and it's going to be hard and cold. And there's a feeling of good-bye. But there's also . . ." She searched for the right word. "Suspense? Maybe hope? Because it's not *over*; everything is just waiting for spring. Do you know what I mean?"

Grandma sounded expectant, and I smiled at her because I loved her better than anyone else in the world now that Dad was gone. "I think so," I said quietly.

"You can see more clearly when it's all stripped bare. You can see that everything gets to be new." Grandma smiled at me with every hope for our future shining in her eyes. "That's the good part."

A gust of wind from the southwest shot through the trees and showered us with cold water and soggy leaves that were anything but hopeful.

I've been waiting a long time for the good part.

janice

My MOTHER LEFT when I was nine. It wasn't as traumatic as it probably should have been because I had considered her gone well before she actually packed her bags and vacated our house on Pearson Drive.

She didn't pay much attention to us, to Dad and me, and I guess we didn't take the time to notice her much either. It had always been that way. She was my mother—the woman who had carried me inside her and nursed me from her own body and given me the slant of my hazel-green eyes—but she didn't do a lot of mothering. I called her Janice from kindergarten on.

Janice was the receptionist and secretary in a dentist's office. She worked eight to five Monday through Friday and every other Saturday morning, and while she was gone, I went to Grandma's house. Grandma was far more of a mother to me than Janice ever was.

I don't remember Janice cheerfully asking me about my day while she checked a casserole in the oven or making supper at all, for that matter. I can't recall a single bedtime story. She wasn't one for hugs. We never giggled over a secret joke. Dad did those things, and Janice was the woman on the periphery, watching reruns of *Bewitched* on Nick at Nite and laughing on the telephone with her friend from high school who didn't have a husband or a daughter and who had moved to Chicago after graduation to be a waitress in some restaurant where she was supposed to be rude to the customers. Janice thought this was hilarious. I thought that if Ellen at the China Blue Café was rude to me, I wouldn't let her tug my braid when she gave me my fortune cookie.

Once I got up in the middle of the night to go to the bathroom and through the kitchen window caught a glimpse of Janice standing on the front porch. She was holding something mysterious and glowing and was studying it carefully with her shoulders hunched and her head at an attractive tilt. The dim light played with the honey-colored highlights in her hair, and the easy angle of her jawbone slanting away from me was so pretty and relaxed that my breath caught in my throat. It filled me with a warm, hopeful feeling, like I was witnessing something beautiful and secret and profound. I didn't know what the object she held was, but something so lovely and orange and unexpected could only belong to someone who was similarly lovely and mysterious.

I adored her for a week—my remote, ordinary mother was not who I thought she was—until I caught her in the act a second time and watched her raise her glowing hand to her mouth, pause, and then slowly blow a transparent, silvery white cloud into the air. She wasn't *mysterious*. She was a *smoker*.

I hated smoking. It smelled gross. It made me cough. I couldn't possibly have a mother who smoked. And on the sly, too!

Janice always said I had a mouth on me, and although I didn't exactly know what that meant when I was younger, I felt a certain rush when I saw her smoking that prompted me to use my mouth to the best of my ability. I'd confront her—that would get us somewhere. Even if she raged at me and grounded me for a month, she would have to see the reason in my argument and eventually come around.

I found her stash of cigarettes. It wasn't hard. She always wore Dad's red and navy blue checkered corduroy jacket if she had to go outside after dark. It was a far cry from the faux fur–lined, hip-length coat she wore everywhere else, but I suppose she figured no one could see her in the dark. Sure enough, when I checked the pockets of that ratty old jacket, I found a mostly full pack of Marlboro Lights in the left side and a neon yellow lighter in the right. I had hoped to burn the cigarettes—she'd never be able to rescue them after that—but I didn't know how to work the lighter, and I wasn't allowed to touch the matches in the junk drawer in the kitchen.

So I had to improvise. Since I didn't want her to be able to find the cigarettes and finish smoking them, I decided destruction was the only possible method of elimination. Taking the kitchen scissors—a risk well worth it, I thought, even though, like the matches,

I wasn't supposed to use them without supervision—I painstakingly cut cigarette after cigarette into tiny shreds. I tried not to make a mess—I cut above the garbage can—but the little flakes of tobacco inside each stick exploded in a muted poof every time I made a cut. The lightest breath of air carried the debris away from the garbage can and all over me and the floor where it stuck with determination. I gave up trying to brush it away and continued methodically cutting, not budging an inch when I heard the garage door open and Janice's rusty Caprice pull inside and choke to a stop.

"Excuse me?" She raised an eyebrow at me as she trudged into the kitchen and deposited two brown grocery bags on the counter with a distinct thump. "What are you doing, Julia?"

"Cigarettes cause cancer, Janice. And they make your teeth brown and your breath smell bad. You shouldn't smoke them." I looked her in the eye and beheaded another little stick. *Snip*.

For a moment, she looked at me uncomprehendingly. Then she laughed. A short, sarcastic grunt that told me she didn't think this was very funny. "That's ridiculous," she said, wrenching the scissors from my hands with more force than was necessary. "You're not allowed to use these, you know." She waggled the blue-handled scissors under my nose.

"I'm sorry I used the scissors, but it was the only way to get you to stop smoking," I explained, still confident that this conversation would go the way I wanted it to, even though she had already turned her back to me as she put a gallon of skim milk in the refrigerator.

"How do you know I smoke, Julia?" Janice shut the refrigerator door with her hip and, without looking at me, began to dig groceries out of the bags on the counter.

"I saw you one night."

"Spying is a nasty habit," she said, making her voice sound creepy on the word *nasty*.

I rolled my eyes. "I wasn't spying. I saw you on accident. You should have tried to hide it better if you didn't want me to know."

"Now I have to sneak around my own house?" She slammed a box of Alpha-Bits on the cupboard shelf, and I knew I was getting to her.

"If you're doing something you shouldn't be doing."

"Whoa, Julia." Janice turned to me full-on for the first time since she entered the kitchen. Leveling her finger at my face, she spoke carefully. "Don't you tell me what I should and should not be doing, little girl."

I stared back. "Does Dad know you smoke?"

"Unless he's stupid, I can't see how he missed it."

She knew that comment would hurt me, and for a moment I was derailed from my original intent. "Don't say that about my dad!"

Janice sighed. "I didn't call him stupid. I said if he didn't know—"

"I know what you said. I'm mad about what you *meant*." I still had three cigarettes in my left hand, and with a flourish I cracked them in half in my palm and, rubbing my hands together, discarded the pulpy contents in the garbage can with a distinct gleam in my eye.

Janice was watching me from five feet away with her hand still on a jar of spaghetti sauce as it rested in the pantry.

In the time it takes to inhale, my mind flipped the scenario, and I imagined she was about to take out the sauce and hand it to me, ask me to empty it in the little pot while she got water boiling for the pasta. I was in a different kitchen, with a different mother, one who didn't smoke on the back porch when everyone else was asleep. We played the parts we were supposed to play.

Then her eyes got hard and the image vanished. She banged the pantry door shut and covered the floor in two strides. For a second I thought she was going to hit me, but she swept right past me as if I didn't exist. From the depths of one of the grocery bags she produced another pack of cigarettes, identical to the one lying in the garbage can in front of me. "Lucky for you, I have more." She breezed out of the kitchen, leaving the groceries half put away and me standing in my mess by the sink.

The back door slammed, and a moment later I could see her outlined in the laundry room window. She put a cigarette to her lips, lit it, and turned her face so I could see her blow the smoke out in profile. It was nowhere near glamorous.

After that, she didn't smoke at night anymore—she smoked all the time. Dad drew the line at letting her smoke in the house, and she obeyed him, but she made it seem like he was actually doing her a favor. Like when I got invited to a slumber party and didn't want to go, so I got grounded instead and had an excuse to stay home. Janice took the phone outside with her when she smoked and talked to her waitress friend. She seemed to have more fun doing that than hanging out with Dad and me inside.

I didn't talk to her for a week and felt very sanctimonious in my innocence. *I* would never smoke. I was only nine but I knew better.

Dad, for his part, didn't ask what happened, and if Janice ever told him, he never let on. He most likely guessed, though; the haughty looks I shot Janice and her obvious disregard for me must have been revealing. It wasn't until years later that I wondered how he weathered the animosity between his wife and his daughter. But then, maybe the passive-aggressive, just-below-the-surface scorn she had for him was more prominent in his mind.

There had been a lot of power struggles like this between Janice and me but none that had such lasting repercussions. A few months later, when Dad assured me that it wasn't my fault Janice had left us, my mind replayed the scene with almost garish clarity—the wicked little smile dancing on my face as I snipped each cigarette—and I knew that every word was a lie. It was exactly my fault. The cigarettes were the beginning of the end. They were the reason that the Sunday after I destroyed her pack, Janice didn't go to church with Dad and me.

Sundays were the only sacred day in our house, and even Janice in all her surly splendor took care to get her lipstick just right and sometimes joined us in the kitchen for a cup of coffee before we left. It was the one day we acted like a normal family and managed to pull it off, even if the normalcy wore off on the drive home. Our wood-paneled station wagon turned back into a pumpkin long before we pulled into the driveway.

Sunday morning meant cinnamon rolls from the bakery, a knee-length pale pink dress paired with white leather shoes, and hymns on the local radio station as we got ready for the nine-thirty service. It did *not* mean strawberry Pop-Tarts in front of the TV in your pajamas, which was exactly how I found Janice when I emerged from the bathroom.

"What are you doing?" I asked quietly from behind the easy chair that marked the division between the family room and dining room.

Janice made eye contact with me and shot me a look that said, *Are you* really *asking me something so obvious?*

I rephrased my question when she turned her attention back to the TV. "Why aren't you ready for church?"

"Not in the mood," she answered, licking her fingers as she stuck the last bite of Pop-Tart into her mouth. There was red filling under her fingernails, and she ran them over her eyetooth one at a time.

I didn't know what to say. There were lots of times when I wasn't in the mood for church, but that didn't mean I didn't go. Weren't you supposed to go whether you wanted to or not?

"You have to," I said eventually, unsure myself if what I said was true.

"No, I don't," she countered, and again I was speechless.

We remained like that for a minute, Janice watching something that I didn't recognize on TV and me gaping at her from in between the dining room and the family room.

Finally she hit Mute and flung an arm over the back of the sofa to study me. "You better hurry," she said with concern. I couldn't tell if she was sincere or not. "You don't want to be late."

I walked slowly through the dining room and into our little kitchen, where Dad had already smeared butter all over an icing-topped cinnamon roll for me. "Dad . . . ?"

He smiled sweetly at me and patted a stool. "She's not feeling well today," he offered, and the discussion was closed.

He always did that. He always stuck up for Janice—or at least he didn't speak ill of her even though she deserved every hateful word that was coming to her. Sometimes he even lied for her, and this morning was an example so heartbreakingly clear that I felt the burden of her sacrilege fall on my shoulders with a staggering weight. I had done this, and I had to make it right. Janice as an unwilling accessory in our family was one thing, but Janice as a willful outsider was a whole new world. It wasn't right.

Throughout the entire church service, I stood and sang and read when I was supposed to, but my mind was on autopilot. I've always been good at acting the appropriate part, and although my heart thumped crazily all morning and my hands were cold as ice, Dad never suspected a thing. Even when I stumbled over the words to the confessional litany, he didn't glance at me.

As Pastor Trenton delivered his standard twenty-five-minute sermon, I ran down a dozen rabbit trails and imagined each scenario with my mother. I could apologize and beg for her forgiveness. Nope. Been there, done that, and it just made her feel justified and possibly even more bitter. I could appeal to her sense of obligation to our family. That *might* work—I knew better than to play an emotional card, but a feeling of duty could potentially set her back in line.

I could tell her how much I loved her and how much I needed her to be a part of my life. Not in a million years. She knew that wasn't true—at least, not *exactly* true. I didn't want a sappy reunion; we were too far past that. All I needed was for things to return to the pattern we'd established years ago: Janice with us but not of us.

By the time I stood for the doxology, I had narrowed my options down to one practical choice. I was going to track down Lane Williams and ask him what to do.

Lane was the youth leader at Fellowship Community Church, and although I was still three years away from the youth group, I knew exactly who he was and had the same crush on him that every girl at Fellowship, no matter what age, indulged in. He was fresh out of college and so confident and idealistic that it was hard not to imagine that God Himself sat down for espresso and theological debate with Lane.

Surely Lane with his longish brown hair and crystalline blue eyes would lean earnestly over the table and ask the Lord flat out every question that the rest of us hardly even dared to think. But for all his handsome intensity, Lane was also authentic and sincere, and he loved God with a passion that made everyone around him want to fall in love as deeply and genuinely.

I didn't understand his fervor or even how someone so beautiful could effectively point to God without becoming a god himself, but I did believe that if anyone knew how to get Janice to come back to church, it would be him. Janice would never respond to the boring, balding Pastor Trenton, but who wouldn't respond to Lane?

I found him hanging out in the hallway by the youth room. Sunday school was after church, and I had to get to my own classroom, but I was willing to be late if only Lane would give me a few minutes of his time. The hallway was full of teenagers, and they all high-fived Lane as they ducked past him into the couch-lined room. He spoke to each one by name, and I realized that if I didn't know who he was, I would assume he was another high school student. Or a Gap model who just stepped away from a photo shoot. He was wearing khakis and a button-down, blue-striped shirt that he hadn't tucked in. He was the only grown man at Fellowship who didn't tuck his shirt in, and the effect was that he appeared even more approachable and handsome up close.

I took a deep breath. "Pastor Lane?"

His tousled head swiveled around, and he fixed his exquisite eyes on me. I'd say that he smiled at me, but his smile was as permanent a fixture on his face as his nose, so it wouldn't be fair to say that I incited any such thing. "Hi!" he fairly shouted and extended his hand to me.

Nobody had ever shaken my hand, so I placed mine in his tentatively. My fingers disappeared, and he gave my arm a few hearty pumps.

"Are you a new member at Fellowship?" he asked cheerfully, still holding my hand.

"No, I was pretty much born here," I said. His enthusiasm begged to be countered by some mediocrity. I found myself speaking quietly. "My name is Julia DeSmit." I pulled my hand out of his, and he let go, giving one last squeeze as we broke contact.

"What can I do for you, Julia DeSmit? You look a little too young for youth group."

"I just have a question for you, Pastor—"

"Lane," he interrupted. "Forget the pastor part—just call me Lane."

"Okay . . . Lane. Um, I have a question." He was disarmingly difficult to talk to. I hadn't asked him a single thing, and he was already nodding as if he knew the answer.

"We all have questions, Julia. What we need to ask ourselves is if the true answer lies in the journey." His smile radiated benevolence.

What on earth was that supposed to mean? "My question is about my friend," I continued, somewhat confused and a little concerned that he had some sort of spiritual power that would let him see right through my lie. I almost expected him to say, "Come now, Julia. We both know you're talking about your mother."

But he was silent. He nodded for me to go on and arched an eyebrow.

"My friend has stopped going to church, and I was wondering how I could convince her to come back," I said. Even as the words slipped out of my mouth, I wondered if there was anything that could change what I knew was the end of my life as I knew it.

Lane obviously felt differently. "Oh, Julia, of course, *of course!*" He beamed at me. "What a gentle heart you must have to want to save your friend."

I didn't think I had a very gentle heart—more like a selfish, pragmatic heart—but he made me feel special, so I gave a little sigh.

Lane misinterpreted it as a cry of the heart and slipped his arm around my shoulders in a friendly hug. "Don't worry. God is using you to call her back. And it's really quite simple." He let go of me and fished in his back pocket for a moment. Taking out his wallet, he removed a little card and held it out to me.

"What's this?" I asked, accepting it hesitantly. I didn't think a business card would fix what was wrong in our house.

"It's a cheat sheet, but I'm going to tell you what it's for and how to use it." Lane was fairly hopping with excitement. "You're going to be an evangelist, Julia. People respond to truth when they hear it, and you are going to put the truth front and center in your friend's life. Ask me the first question on the card."

I stared down at the card and found that it was blank except for five numbered questions neatly typed in bold black print. Locating number one, I read, "'Have you ever stolen anything?'" I paused. "Lane, what does this have to do with it?"

"Just ask me the question—you'll see."

"Okay. 'Have you ever stolen anything?'"

Lane screwed up his mouth as if thinking and then said, "Yes." In a different voice he added, "Ask me the second question."

"'Have you ever lied?'"

"Yes," he said emphatically.

Tracing the third question, I continued. "'Have you ever said anything hurtful to anyone?'"

Again, Lane responded with a resounding "Yes."

I started to read the fourth question, but he stopped me. "Wait, after the third question you're supposed to say something. When your friend has said yes to the first three questions, you say to her, 'So, you're telling me that you are a thief, a liar, and a murderer?'"

I almost dropped the card. "I'm supposed to say that to her?"

"Well, yeah. That's what she's saying. I mean, I can see how the murderer part is a bit hard to follow, but the Bible does say that we don't have to physically murder someone to kill their spirit with our words." He seemed altogether too pleased with himself.

"I don't get it," I said. "I don't think I can insult her like that."

"You're not insulting her. You're opening her eyes to the truth. Sometimes the truth hurts, but we're better people when we accept it and change our lives accordingly," Lane argued. "Seriously, it works. I once converted a guy on a flight from Minneapolis to Seattle. We talked the whole way, and he gave his life to Christ before we landed at Sea-Tac."

Miraculous airplane conversion or no, I didn't want to use this method on Janice. My sharp tongue had already gotten me into enough trouble with her, and the last thing I wanted to do was make matters worse. "I don't think this is going to work for me, but thanks anyway," I said and tried to hand his card back to him.

He held his palm up and refused to accept it. "Julia, it'll work. I know it sounds harsh, but sometimes the only way to get people to see the light is to show them how truly dark their world has become."

He was so persuasive. I tried to imagine if he asked me the questions. What would I say? I wouldn't run away from him. I couldn't imagine anyone running away from Lane. But would I be insulted? Probably. More importantly, if I were asking the questions, would Janice run away? Would she be insulted? Definitely. The thought of asking her those questions—and worse, accusing her of those things—made me sick to my stomach. I couldn't do it. Absolutely no way.

I couldn't hold the card a second longer. Just having it in my hand made me fear Janice's reaction. Lane's fingers were still poised as if in salute, and I tried to place the card in them, but it slipped and drifted slowly to the floor.

"No, thank you." My voice was small as I backed away. I was angry at myself for not faking it, for not staying and listening to the rest of what he had to say. Just because I listened it didn't mean I had to follow through with what he told me to do. I could have hidden the paper in my palm until I was out of sight, then dropped it in the nearest garbage can. *Why didn't I do that?* I begged myself, but the card with its five insidious questions was already lying on the floor between us.

Lane was looking at it with a mixture of confusion and hurt on his face. He looked different without the smile. "Julia, just—"

"Thank you very much," I said again. "I'm going to figure it out for myself." I slipped around the corner and he was gone.

I never spoke to Lane Williams again, and the following year he fell in love with the new church secretary. Apparently they did nothing wrong—they waited to officially date until after his contract with Fellowship ran out—but it was scandalous all the same. He stopped showing up at youth functions and gave lame excuses like he was in the middle of "Kingdom work" and couldn't get away. He was nearly nonexistent at anything church related. People started grumbling that he was no longer doing his job, and indeed, when I saw him for the last time at a church service in June, he did not even appear to be the same person. Their relationship was public, and Samantha sat still and solemn, staring straight ahead next to him in the pew while he gazed at her with a slightly sick and longing look on his face. It was obvious she consumed him even more than God had. He wasn't smiling.

I heard much later that they were married by early fall and moved to Florida to start over. I couldn't help but hope that things went well for them, although the yearning ache in Lane's eyes as he studied her seemed like too high a cost for any earthly love. Even Samantha's charcoal curls would fade to gray. And then what?

For some reason, when I discovered that Lane was human, no more, no less, I finally felt at peace with dropping his evangelism card on the day my mother left us. Before he ran off with Samantha, I always wondered if things would have gone differently if I had been as forward as he prodded me to be. Would Janice have stayed if I'd called her a thief, a liar, and a murderess? Maybe I should have thrown in *deserter*.

As it was, I called Janice a different name altogether.

When Dad and I returned from church around lunchtime, she was still in front of the TV. Her pajamas were rumpled, and her hair looked greasy. She was watching an old Western with one foot on the coffee table as she painted her toenails fuchsia. Nail art was all the rage, and as she finished each toe, she carefully placed a tiny silver rhinestone in the center of the wet polish. An open bag of devastated cheese curls announced that she had already eaten lunch, but she didn't say anything about that to us.

Not breaking the silence, Dad went into the bedroom they shared to change clothes. He emerged minutes later to find the two of us in exactly the same positions—Janice finishing her pinky toe and me on the arm of the couch, alternating between staring at her and the TV.

Dad touched my head as he passed and asked quietly, "Pea soup or chicken noodle?"

"Pea," I responded, although he wasn't actually waiting for an answer. He knew.

"Ten minutes," he informed me, and suddenly the countdown began. I had ten minutes, minus the time it would take to change out of my Sunday dress, to make everything all right with Janice. To convince her to come and have a bowl of canned soup instead of continuing to take up space in front of the TV. It was excruciating. I didn't know what to say or where to begin, and all the while Lane's questions were burning in my mind. Maybe I should try one, test the waters?

I opened my mouth, and the words stuck fast to my tongue. The only one that would come out was one that I hadn't used in a very long time. "Mom?"

She looked up immediately, and I knew the word had touched a nerve somewhere, but when her eyes caught mine, they were cool and blank, and I understood there was nothing I could say that she wanted to hear. I wanted to repeat the word so she would know that I hadn't said something else, hadn't made a mistake, but once it was out of my mouth, it flew out of reach and I couldn't form it again.

"You may smoke if you want to," I finally said. It was the best I could come up with, and a small shiver ran down my spine when I realized its insignificance.

"You think this is about smoking." It was a statement, so I didn't respond. Janice was still eyeing me offhandedly.

The silence stretched, and in a detached part of my mind I thought that the soup must be almost ready and Dad would come in to tell me so before I could fix this. "It's okay, really," I continued quickly. "You can do whatever you want, and I won't boss you anymore. I promise."

"Promises don't keep, Julia," she said. "And I'd like you to call me Janice." She bit her bottom lip and gave a helpless shrug as if to say, *Oh, well; what do you do?* Then she turned back to the small, pink fingernail polish bottle and screwed the lid on tightly. Leaving the cheese curl bag and the TV on, she palmed the bottle and left the room without a backward glance.

As Dad and I ate our pea soup, we heard the shower running and then the blow-dryer. Janice emerged from the bathroom as we were putting away the clean dishes from the dishwasher. She was wearing a pair of snug jeans and a lavender sweater that made her eyes look the same color. She looked fresh and clean and happy.

"I'm going out," she said cheerfully and waggled her fingers in a little wave.

Dad looked at her across the room, and I knew that he knew she wouldn't be coming back. He lifted his hand and waved at her, but he didn't say good-bye and neither did I.

It was the last time we saw Janice. She took the rusty Caprice, the clothes on her back, and her purse, which contained a joint credit card in the names of Daniel and Janice DeSmit. Dad didn't cancel the credit card, but she put only two purchases on it: one for gas and food at a Shell three hundred miles away and another for more gas and food at a Phillips 66 just outside of Chicago.

We didn't try to find her.

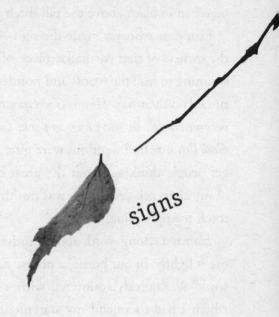

signs

THERE WAS A sign in a farmer's field a few miles away from Grandma's acreage. It was obviously homemade, with letters that got smaller and more cramped together as they reached the right side of the piece of plywood they were painted on. Whoever made it did a poor job of planning ahead and didn't take the time to measure out how much space each letter would take. It was big and bold though, and in spite of any artistic oversights, it got the message across.

Heaven? Or Hell? the top line proclaimed unflinchingly. *Heaven* was lettered in a gaudy turquoise green that I assumed was meant to invoke a feeling of cool, inviting newness. *Hell* was a rich scarlet that I far preferred to the green-blue of heaven, but who would ever admit that? Under the curlicue question marks another line marched in black above the tall ditch grass: Are You Ready?

I suppose whoever made the sign—Grandma and I didn't know the owners of that particular piece of property—imagined drivers straining to read the words and pondering their depths as they continued on their way. *Hmm. Good question. Am I ready? How does one become ready? Are there bags to pack? Oh, boy, I'd better get right with God!* I'm sure his intentions were pure, and maybe his questions did get people thinking about the great beyond. But for the summer of my sixteenth year, there was nothing I wanted to do more than torch the ugly thing.

Hate is a strong word, and Grandma always advised me never to use it lightly. In our home, a phrase as innocuous as "I hate homework" was quickly countered with a gentle, "Really, Julia?" After which I had to amend my statement or be ready to defend why I violently disliked something that would make me more studious, intelligent, and well-rounded. Grandma was big on dictionary definitions, and words were to be used intentionally and—more importantly—properly. But *hate* accurately described the way I felt about the hell sign, which is what I began to call it after it started making me crazy with disgust.

Every time I drove past it, I envisioned new ways to bring it down. I was never very clever when it came to retorts, but for months I tried to come up with the perfect thing to write over part of the sign. I'd leave the top line or the bottom line, but I'd spray paint over the other and write something that would make people laugh. Like, "Bedtime. Are You Ready?" But that was just plain stupid.

Or "Heaven? Or Hell? Northwest Iowa." Get it? Oh, forget it. Just as stupid. Maybe I would sneak up in the night and light a match to it. But then again, that could be disastrous—all that grass and surrounding crops? *Poof.* Maybe I'd go to juvie hall.

I was trying to ignore the sign one afternoon as I was driving home from school, and an idea flitted into my head without a single prompting from my conscious mind. It was *perfect.* I would drive my car into the sign with a giant *yes* painted on the windshield in black letters. Of course, it would only be cool if they had to pull my limp and lifeless body from the wreckage. Otherwise it was pointless. If I were dead, then everyone would wonder what I meant by *yes.* Yes, I was ready for heaven? But how could that be? I had committed suicide, and if my final act on earth was a sin that I could not ask forgiveness for, how could God possibly forgive me and accept me into heaven? So then the *yes* meant I was ready for hell? How frightening and unexpected and mysterious! Why? Why would this sweet, young, innocent girl be ready for hell? The whole scenario would drive people nuts. I loved it.

But I wasn't suicidal. After all, it was just a sign.

I never told Grandma about my obsession with the sign because I knew she wouldn't understand, and more than anything it would only worry her. Once I casually mentioned it as we were driving past, and she absently said, "Makes you think, doesn't it?"

No, it did not make me think.

I did, however, share my fixation with Thomas, and he offered to take his father's ax and chop it down one night. The sign was at the far edge of the property and nowhere near close enough to the house for anyone to hear wood splintering.

I had to ponder that one for a few days, and when Thomas saw me in the hallway at school, he would grin and make a sweeping arc with his arms as if he were landing a huge blow with an imaginary ax. I loved him for his willingness, but in the end I told him that I was fine with it and the sign could live on.

"Whatever you say," Thomas said when I told him, wrapping his arms around my shoulders from behind and nuzzling the top of my head with his chin. "If you ever change your mind . . ."

I pulled away from him and punched him teasingly in the stomach. "Yeah, I know who to come to."

The first time I ever spoke to Thomas was the same night that Dad and I moved onto the farm.

It had been three years since Janice left, and Dad and I made a sorry pair of castoffs. He was so busy that laundry piled up, food went moldy in the fridge, and dust bunnies collected under nearly everything. I never blamed him and even tried to help, but I was only twelve.

Even though we lived in town, Grandma cooked supper for us every night those first bewildering years we were without a wife and mother. Usually cooking was Dad's job, but with so much to juggle, he found little time for culinary artistry. I think Grandma felt sorry for us. Once, over steaming plates of roast and mashed potatoes, Grandma casually mentioned that her house was too big for one lonely woman, and Dad's face lit up as if she had presented him the moon. It was an unspoken but impossible-to-ignore offer, and within six weeks we had become a party of three. Though Grandma's farmhouse was small and we would be living on top of one another, you couldn't find three happier people.

The night that we moved, it was cold outside, cold enough to warrant my winter parka and the thick mittens that Grandma had knit for me a month previous. Even bundled so, I hunched my chin down into the tall collar of my coat and covered my numb ears with my mittened hands. The wind whipped the few remaining leaves on the trees into an eerie, spinning frenzy, and in the moonlight I could see the occasional leaf give up the fight and escape across the yard into the darkness. The air smelled of snow, and in the perfect rectangle of light cast by the picture window in the living room, I could dream about how high the drifts would reach this winter. To the windowsill? Beyond?

I was waiting for Dad to come back with the truck. We had already eaten supper—fried chicken and new potatoes from the cellar with lots of hot mustard—and although it was time for reruns of *Seinfeld* and Grandma's air-popped popcorn, Dad wanted to make one last trip to our old place.

Everything we truly loved or needed had already been sandwiched in Grandma's house, and the remaining items that we simply couldn't part with had been put into storage. Appliances and several pieces of furniture had been written into the deal when we sold the house, but there was one object—an old, teak writing desk—that Dad had decided over supper he couldn't live without. Adam, the guy who bought our house, was over there turning my bedroom into a nursery for his soon-to-be-born first child, and when Dad called him on his cell phone, he must have conceded the desk.

Dad punched the air in triumph and winked at me with the phone still cradled against his shoulder. "Julia, I'm going to get the desk," he whispered with his hand over the mouthpiece. "Adam'll help me put it on the truck, but I want you to put your coat on and meet me outside in ten minutes."

Into the phone he said, "Thanks so much, Adam. This whole thing has been a really pleasant experience." He meant no one had gone into hysterics over drapes and light fixtures and little fixer-uppers. Adam was almost as easygoing as Dad, and his wife was too pregnant to care. "I just want to be out of the trailer before the baby is born," she had said to me conspiratorially at the paper signing.

I didn't know where Dad planned to put the desk once he had it in the little farmhouse, but I didn't question him. Ten minutes after he left, I dutifully pulled on my coat and went outside to kick at the gravel in the driveway while I waited for him to show up.

"Wait inside!" Grandma yelled from the living room. She was knitting a hat to match the mittens I was wearing. "It's too cold!"

"I want to see the stars!" I yelled back and didn't wait for an answer before swinging the door shut.

There were a million stars on such a clear, cold night, and they trickled so far down the horizon that they seemed to nestle between the tree branches like tiny Christmas lights. I traced Orion and the Big Dipper, then tried to make up my own constellations because I didn't know any more. I found a snake and a stick that looked a lot like the snake I had just discovered. Ashamed at my own lack of creativity, I gave up.

I was just about ready to give up on Dad, too, and go back into the living room to wait with my coat on. It was so cold I didn't dare breathe with my mouth for fear the wetness on my lips would freeze if I so much as parted them.

And then, in the stillness, I heard someone walking across the yard. The moon was not quite half full, and the light it cast was shimmering and imperfect; I had to strain to see in the darkness. But he was obvious even in the shadows: a tall, lone figure carrying something bulky and clearly cumbersome. He walked with his head hunched over and his arms akimbo around the object that was twice the size of his chest and as tall as it was wide. I didn't recognize him at a distance—he was halfway between the house and the barn, a hundred feet easy—but I wasn't afraid, and it never crossed my mind that he would be anything but harmless and ambling through our property with very good reason. It occurred to me that I should be neighborly.

He hadn't seen me standing near the front porch, and he was too consumed with his task to notice when I began making my way to intercept him. The frozen grass crunched beneath my feet, and my nose was making diaphanous little clouds of steam that looked remarkably like the smoke that curled out of Janice's mouth all those years ago.

I expected him to look up at any point and see the telltale clues that would notify him that he wasn't alone on this frigid night. He'd probably smile at me knowingly, the conspiratorial smile of strangers who share nothing but the weather in common, and comment, "Cold one." And I'd agree. But he didn't look up, and he didn't know I was there.

When we were fifteen feet apart, I found myself with nothing clever to say. "Looks heavy," I managed.

The boy—now that we were close, I could tell he was not much older than me—swung his head around, searching for the source of the sound, and leaned forward slightly as if ready to run. He looked confused when he caught sight of me, and I was surprised to realize that he was scared. "What?" he said.

"Your . . ." I gestured at the thing in his arms. "It looks heavy."

Afterward, I looked back on this moment and held it gently in my mind as if it were precious and valuable, though I didn't understand its worth.

The boy was silent for a few breaths, and skepticism was etched in a deep line across his outlined forehead. And then, out of nowhere, the line disappeared and he smiled at me.

The smile broke luminously across his face, and the white of his teeth reflected the moonlight as he began to laugh. I think I fell in love at that instant.

"It is heavy," he said, still laughing. Carefully, he set the object down and turned it bit by bit along the ground until it was facing me.

"It's a stop sign," I said. My voice didn't sound like my own.

"Yeah, we ripped it off the B-level road intersecting Highway 2. You know the one?"

"I know the one," I repeated and wrapped my arms around myself as if for protection.

He continued to smile but didn't say anything more.

I could barely look at him but was less able to tolerate the stillness, so I asked, "What do you want with a stop sign?"

He shrugged. "It's cool. I don't know. I'll hang it in my room, I guess. I already have a yield sign."

I was looking at the sign, but I snuck a glance at his face as he was talking. The thought crossed my mind that stealing road signs might be a federal offense or at the very least not legal, but that would be a stupid thing to say. "How did you get it?" I eventually asked.

"Oh, you know, a bunch of guys, a truck with a winch . . ." He trailed off, and I caught his eye for a second. "You're Nellie's granddaughter, aren't you?"

"Yeah." I untangled my arms and held out my mittened hand. "Julia."

"Thomas. I belong over there." He hooked his thumb over his shoulder in the direction of our neighbors to the north. He gave my outstretched hand a friendly shake.

"You're the oldest Walker," I said as it clicked into place. I knew Thomas's little brothers and sisters—there were four of them—quite well. They were always playing in our grove. I knew they had an older brother, but I had never met him.

"Yup," Thomas said.

"Yup," I repeated.

"Well . . ." Thomas looked over his shoulder, and I understood for the first time that I was a huge impediment to whatever plan he had for the sign. "I'd better get going."

"Me too," I said as if I had something equally interesting and inexplicable to do. "Nice meeting you."

As I turned away, headlights swung down our long driveway.

Thomas froze. Giving the sign a hard push, he let it fall flat to the ground and thrust his hands into his coat pockets. "Who's that?"

"My dad," I guessed, and the silhouette of Dad's little pickup confirmed it.

I watched the truck pull onto the cement pad by the front porch. Dad was far enough away that I was sure he couldn't see us standing in the shadows, and somehow I was thankful for that.

Thomas grabbed my arm and spun me around, catching me completely by surprise. I held my breath.

"Keep the sign for me," he said quickly. "I can't exactly be caught with it." He flashed another stunning smile, and his mouth was so close to me that I could see each perfectly straight tooth. "Just pull it into the grove before morning, and I'll come back for it later, okay?"

"Okay," I echoed.

"You're a good girl, Julia," he said, squeezing my arm. And then he turned toward the grove and took off at a light jog.

I watched him go.

When I turned back to the truck, Dad was standing on the tailgate watching me watch Thomas. "Who was that?" he yelled as he hopped out of the pickup bed.

"Thomas Walker!" I yelled back. Looking down at the sign, I realized there was no way he could see it lying there in the dark, but I nervously scuffed at it with my foot anyway.

"Get over here! You're supposed to be helping me with the desk!" Dad waved me over with both arms.

"Coming!" I shot back. I peeked once at the grove, where Thomas had disappeared, but he was long enveloped in the darkness and the trees. The only movement left was the wind.

"What was Thomas Walker doing out here in the freezing cold? It's almost nine o'clock," Dad commented as we lugged the desk— which was far heavier than it looked—into the front entryway.

"Drop it here," he added, and I gratefully slid my fingers out from under the hefty piece of furniture.

"He was on a walk," I improvised.

Dad cocked an eyebrow at me but only said, "Kids are so weird."

I followed him out when he went to pull the pickup into the detached garage and managed to drag the sign into the grove while he was busy. I left it facedown and kicked some leaves and branches on top to hide it.

Before school the next day, I went to make sure no one had found the stop sign. It was gone.

good
girl

AFTER DAD DIED, I became a bit of a celebrity. I had always been the object of peripheral pity as the little girl whose mommy had left, but when I became an orphan, the sympathy that flowed out of people was almost tangible.

In the grocery store, one woman would whisper something to another, and the two would fix me with looks so equally compassionate and voyeuristic that I hardly knew where to turn. At first I shriveled beneath their concern and avoided going out alone where I could be cornered and gently ministered to by every well-meaning stranger who believed they had some insight to offer me. But I soon found it easier to disappear inside myself and ignore them altogether.

"Pray to Jesus," one woman advised me as she clung to my arms and blinked back tears. "He'll carry you through this."

I nodded faintly and tried to look grateful as the latest Green Day song played in my head. I just couldn't stand any more tears.

Unfortunately, church was the worst, and I began to dread going to Fellowship Community. It seemed that if I wasn't on the verge of weeping, some people thought I was a callous and unfeeling little girl who didn't fully grasp the loss of her father. On the other hand, if a song did touch me or I found myself unwillingly emotional, somebody would approach me and righteously explain that if I only had more faith in God, I would be able to accept that my father was in a better place.

A man my father had worked with before I was born cornered me after church one Sunday and laid his hands on me to pray for healing. I guess he was trying to heal my broken heart—to my own deep consternation I had cried when we sang the doxology, and a number of people noticed. His prayer was bold and punctuated with amens, and his hands were so heavy on my head that I actually slumped against the wall.

"How do you feel?" he asked expectantly when the final amen had hung meaningfully in the air for a few breaths.

I stopped myself from saying thankful that his arms were finally at his side instead of weighing down my head. But I didn't want to insult him, so I thought for a moment and tried to probe myself to see if anything felt different. Nothing did.

"I feel fine," I answered when I could come up with nothing else to say.

"Has the Lord taken away your pain?"

It was easy to answer that one. "No," I said, and I imagined that the rest of my life would probably be filled with a myriad of different answers to that question. *For now. A little. Maybe. I feel better but not whole. . . .*

He stared at me with a bewildered look on his face. Finally he raised a finger as if to scold me and said, "Then you don't have enough faith." And he walked away.

Thomas was the only one who understood—or at least didn't plague me with misplaced good intentions—and his even, uncomplicated acceptance of however I was feeling allowed me to experience a freedom with him that I felt nowhere else. He'd let me rage and cry or laugh and be caustic, and then he'd pretend that nothing at all had happened and act like life was perfectly normal and sane.

I spent innumerable hours on the couch in his basement, spread out beneath an array of road signs that he somehow convinced his parents he'd achieved by innocent means. There was a yield sign, a street sign lettered Bottom Drive—Thomas thought it was funny—and my favorite, the fire-engine red stop sign that had spent the night in our grove.

"I'd get another one for you if it would make you happy, Julia," Thomas would say with a phony smile as he motioned to the collection. "It's just that I'm past all that foolishness." He winked because I knew better than anyone that Thomas would never be completely past his endearing foolishness.

"You're so mature," I'd groan.

Then Maggie, Thomas's youngest sister, would bound down the stairs, launch herself onto the couch where I was still lying, and demand that we turn the channel so she could watch *Dora the Explorer*.

We learned a lot of Spanish that way.

Thomas always complained about his younger siblings—Simon, the closest in age to Thomas, was six years his junior, and the rest of the Walker clan spread out at one- or two-year intervals all the way down to the baby, four-year-old Maggie—but I adored them and kept coming to the Walker house partly because they were there. I had never had a brother or sister, and there was something so comforting about a preschooler cuddled up on the couch beside me that I felt like this was the home I was meant to be a part of; somehow I'd gotten switched out along the way. They treated me like family, and although I went home to eat every meal with Grandma, I was worked into the fabric of their lives with complete acceptance.

Sometimes on Friday nights Thomas would have impromptu parties, and a bunch of people from his class would come over to hang out and trash-talk the latest PlayStation game. I was two grades behind Thomas, and no senior in their right mind hung out with sophomores, but because of who Thomas was—and in part because of who I was— nobody seemed to mind. I became a pet of sorts, but a very protected pet because everyone knew that to Thomas I could do no wrong and to insult me in any way was to wound Thomas deeply.

For my part, I didn't necessarily know which way was up or down on any given day, and Thomas was the savior who kept me afloat. I was vacant, waiting to be filled, and Thomas offered me a place to rest in the meantime.

Thomas also offered me Brandon. Or offered me *to* Brandon. I never really understood which.

The night I met Brandon, Thomas's basement was full of people, and I sat curled in a corner of the couch, watching the action from a safe vantage point. Thomas didn't usually invite this many people over, and we were draped on every available piece of furniture and flowing over onto the floor and even the basement steps, where two girls sat head to head, giggling.

The topic of conversation among most of the groups seemed to be graduation in the spring and what everyone planned to do after they achieved their freedom. Coldplay was on in the background, and it gave the room a feeling of dreamy contemplation. I felt like I was caught in a scene from a movie—the moment of epiphany when the main character finally realizes whatever it is she needs to realize. The moment when everything makes sense at long last, and it is both poignant and bittersweet because it is altogether different from what was hoped for. I felt like I was on the verge of the moment that would make everything clear. But my mind was blank.

"Bored?" Thomas asked me, sitting on the arm of the couch and offering me a bottle of Coke from the antique pop machine his parents kept in the basement.

I shook my head but didn't have anything witty to say.

We sat in silence for a moment.

"What will you do after graduation?" I finally asked, wondering what life would be like when he was gone. It was hard for me to see past tomorrow, but I had the vague feeling that a day without Thomas in it was something I simply couldn't take.

He looked bemused when he answered, "I don't know. Will you miss me if I go?"

I rolled my eyes, and he brushed a strand of hair from my forehead as if it were the most natural thing in the world. "Have you ever met Brandon?" he asked absently.

When I looked up at Thomas, he was gazing across the room at a guy who frequented his house. I had never talked to Brandon before, but once he sat next to me on the couch while we watched *The Empire Strikes Back*—Thomas loved campy movies and owned every eighties classic from *The Breakfast Club* to *Sixteen Candles*, for which I teased him incessantly. He subjected us to corny classics, and we provided sarcastic feedback. It could get pretty ugly, but I remembered that Brandon hadn't joined in the teasing that night and in fact seemed completely drawn in by the movie. I recalled wondering what his story was.

Brandon was skinny like skeletons are skinny, but he had a striking face and big, brooding eyes. I wouldn't say I was necessarily attracted to him, but I wasn't repelled either, and there was something about his look that made me feel simultaneously sorry for him and a little afraid of him. His baggy clothes and direct gaze seemed a contradiction in terms, and I couldn't deny that at the very least I found him intriguing.

"He's such a great guy," Thomas said, searching my face. "I know he looks kind of goth, but he has an absolute heart of gold." He paused. "He thinks you're . . . well, he didn't actually use the word *cute*, but I think that's what he meant."

I didn't know what to say. Boys had never really entered the picture before. It wasn't that I didn't like them; I was just preoccupied. And now it was impossible for me to imagine a boy coming into my life with any intention other than rescuing the damsel in distress. I had no desire to be the object of pity—or the object of any delusional hero fantasy, for that matter.

But Thomas would think I was being too serious if I offered my psychological evaluation of Brandon's motives. He was expecting a normal response from a normal girl. What exactly did normal girls say when they found out a boy was interested in them?

"That's nice," I eventually said because it was the most normal thing I could think to say.

"That's nice?" Thomas laughed. "Julia, you can do better than that." He gave me a significant look. "He's *interested* in you. Would you at least like to meet him?"

"Are you setting me up?" I asked, and my stomach did a flip-flop that I couldn't interpret. "Do you think that's appropriate?"

Thomas's eyebrows knit together as he regarded me. "What do you mean? Do you think that because your father died, you shouldn't date? It's not like you need his permission."

"I know that," I said quickly. "But isn't there a mourning period or something? It hasn't even been four months."

Thomas pulled me into an affectionate headlock and whispered in my ear, "He'd want you to be happy. Stop moping."

"Okay," I said softly.

He let me go. "Come on. I'll introduce you."

Turned out, Brandon wasn't about to try to rescue me, and I got the impression early on that maybe I was the one who should be saving him instead.

I don't know if *boyfriend* is really the right word to describe what Brandon was to me, but he was the first boy I kissed, so I suppose that title would fit the bill in most people's minds. I always imagined my first kiss would be this sweet, intimate memory that I would think back on fondly for the rest of my life, but kissing Brandon—or rather, having Brandon kiss me—on a gravel road half a mile from my house wasn't exactly a memory I treasured.

It should have been memorable. It was a gorgeous night. The black sky was filled with snow, and the flakes were falling so slow and heavy that you could single out one diminutive snowflake, watch it drift from above your head, and follow it until it landed in your outstretched hand. Six spires shone silver against the dark sleeve of my coat, and try as I could to find one that matched any other I had seen before, I failed. The moon was full and glimmering brilliantly off the snow already collected in the fields, and Brandon and I were wandering down the middle of a gravel road and talking earnestly. It was simply beautiful and would have been the stuff storybooks are made of if not for the topic of conversation.

Brandon was a Chernobyl baby. Or at least that's what he claimed. I knew for a fact that he was adopted from Russia, but I couldn't help thinking that if his mother had been affected by the fallout at Chernobyl, there would have to be something obviously wrong with him—I half expected him to glow in the dark. But then again, maybe the scars were deeper than that. Could nuclear radiation cause emotional damage?

I think because my parents were both gone, Brandon felt some sort of connection to me. Never mind the fact that his adoptive parents—the only parents he had known from two years old on—were the sweetest, kindest, dearest people you could ever meet. Brandon was hardly an orphan. But he was disturbed and lonely, and I couldn't help imagining this skinny little baby in some orphanage being ignored twenty-three hours every day and how those solitary weeks and months and years must have shaped the almost man who now walked beside me. I don't know if Brandon trusted anybody, even though he had been given no reason I could see to distrust anyone this side of the Atlantic.

Brandon's adoptive parents went to the same church we attended, and when Brandon turned sixteen, they allowed him to decide if he would continue to join them there or not. He opted for not. He said he had issues with a God who could let such awful things happen, but he loved talking about his faith or lack thereof.

I fell into the role of defender even though I wasn't that defensive in the first place—if given the option, I would join Brandon in the "not" category. But it worked for us, and it kept Brandon talking as long as I wanted him to. Our theological and philosophical debates were the heart and soul of our relationship—if the limping excuse for a friendship we had could be considered a relationship at all.

That snowy night, on the gravel road in the darkness, I tried to convince him that God was like a father.

"If God is a father," Brandon said, stopping at an intersection and standing in the middle of the four corners, "then I'm not interested."

"I'm not interested if He's anything but," I countered. "Besides, you love your dad. What are you talking about?"

"I guess it depends on your definition of father," Brandon said, and he took a step back from me. I always wondered why he did that. One minute he'd be holding my hand and the next he'd let go and put distance between us.

"I have a good definition," I said with a smile.

"I have a good definition too—clear good, not happy good."

Brandon started ticking off on his fingers. "Controlling, manipulative, selfish, uninterested, uninvolved—"

"Brandon, seriously, your dad is none of those things."

"I'm not talking about Norm," he said irritably.

"Well, I imagine God is a father exactly like Norm." I paused and then added more quietly, "Or like my dad."

"Look, Julia, if God was like Norm, He wouldn't let all this horrible stuff happen. Do you know what goes on in this world?" Brandon was getting worked up, and our conversations never went nicely after he got too emotionally involved.

"I don't think it's like He *wants* those things to happen . . . ," I said slowly, trying to gauge how he would respond. "It's just that sin—"

"Oh, don't give me that!" Brandon exploded. "The universal struggle between good and evil," he mocked in a sickening, singsong voice. "You buy into that Star Wars nonsense?"

I didn't feel like fighting with him, and even more importantly, I couldn't form the thoughts to articulately dispute him. I wasn't in the mood. Instead I arched my eyebrows at him and tried to smile playfully, tried to defuse his anger before it ruined the snowy night. "Well, if you don't like to think of God as a father, He is apparently much, much more," I offered. "What does interest you?"

Brandon opened his mouth to spit a retort back at me but thought better of it and stood in silence for a minute. I watched him wrestle with himself as he tried to find his way back to less somber ground. Finally he looked up at me with a faint smile.

"You said you're not interested in God as a father. What does interest you?" I repeated.

"Buddhism."

"What do you know about Buddhism?" I laughed.

"I don't know—it's trendy. Wouldn't it be cool to say, 'I'm a Buddhist'?"

I just stood there and giggled at him. Brandon had tried before to convince me he was an atheist, but I didn't believe it any more than I believed he now wanted to convert to Buddhism.

"What do you believe in, Julia?" he asked, and his voice was very serious.

I had to think about that one. After a moment I said, "I believe there's a God."

"And . . . ?"

"And . . ." The smile slipped off my face. "I don't know."

In one motion, Brandon closed the distance between us and kissed me on the mouth. At first he didn't touch me, but then he tangled his hands in my hair and kissed me as if it would save his life. As if I had answered his question with much more than an "I don't know."

I wasn't sure how to kiss him back, and I didn't particularly want to. I didn't understand why we were kissing at all. What did Buddhism have to do with my first kiss? But I closed my eyes, which seemed proper, and waited for him to be done. At some point, though, I became aware of the smell of his clothes and the feel of his body pressed lightly against the length of mine. I actually felt his lips, warm and insistent, and it flooded me with something so deep and overwhelming that I started to tremble.

When Brandon finally backed away, he left his hands around my head and studied my face for what felt like forever. Then he let go and turned around to walk back the way we came. He didn't say anything and I didn't either, and for an eighth of a mile or so we just walked in silence. I was a step or two behind him, and he never glanced back at me.

Still trembling, I stared at his feet, clad in chunky, black army boots, and watched them ruin the clean, smooth surface of the powdery snow blanketing the road. It was hard to know what to think and even harder to know how to act. A part of me wanted to feel his hand in mine since we had just shared something that in sixteen years I had never shared with anyone else. Another part of me never wanted to see him again because I was inexplicably, uncontrollably embarrassed.

Before Grandma's farm came into view, Brandon stopped and searched in his pocket for a second. To my utter surprise, he pulled out a pack of cigarettes and a lighter. "Do you mind if I smoke one before I go home?" he asked, and his voice was as flat and normal as if he had never kissed me at all. "I can't smoke in my car—my parents will smell it."

"I didn't know you smoked," I said and looked at him closely because it was as if we were strangers.

"Just to relax," he explained. "Not that I'm addicted or anything. Not all of the time." He seemed different to me, aloof, and I wrapped my arms around myself in confusion.

"Okay," I managed.

Brandon carefully lit the cigarette. Looking past me, he took a long, hard drag and then, with perfect deliberation, as if it were something we shared all the time, he held out the cigarette to me.

I don't know why I did it, but I reached for the stick and held it gingerly while he lit another one for himself.

Without saying a word, he looked at me and raised it slowly to his lips as if to say, *This is how it's done.*

I did the same and put the cigarette in my mouth but didn't do anything with it. A cloud of smoke encircled my head, and in spite of everything I had been told, it wasn't necessarily unpleasant. I just held my breath.

"You're supposed to inhale," Brandon said. Each word was punctuated by a little puff of smoke.

I put the cigarette to my lips again and took the tiniest, shallowest breath I could. The smoke hit the back of my throat like vaporized fire. Gasping and coughing, I doubled over and in the process dropped the cigarette in the inch of accumulated snow.

When I straightened up, I expected Brandon to be laughing at me, but he smiled gently and said, "Try again." He offered me his cigarette. "Thomas told me you were a good girl. I should have expected that to happen."

Brandon taught me how to smoke the night of my first kiss. It was almost as if the latter act replaced the former because he never kissed me again. We did, however, continue to get together and talk, and each time I had a smoke or two with him. I felt a little cold-blooded, but when he graduated early two months later and left to get a job in the city, I was far less than heartbroken.

I never saw Brandon again, and I *almost* never smoked again. Once or twice I imagined what it would be like to see my mother after all these years and light up a cigarette in her company. I wondered if she'd appreciate the irony.

consumed

Dear Julia,

I heard about what happened to your father. I
am very sorry for your loss. I would have written
sooner, but I did not know that it happened until
a few weeks ago. Please let me know if there is any
thing I can do.

Yours truly,
Janice

I received the card from Janice six months after my dad passed away. It was postmarked Milwaukee, Wisconsin, and the envelope was ragged and smudged, with a torn corner that someone had tried to fix with Scotch tape. The card itself looked expensive with a little brass-colored cross attached to the front and a perforated bookmark on the back flap that contained the Twenty-third Psalm. Janice's handwriting was the same flowing cursive that I remembered—beautiful to look at but hard to read. I had read the card at least a dozen times before I could decipher every word.

It was the first correspondence from her since she left—I had to take a moment to calculate it—seven years previous. Dad had been in contact with her parents in Arizona a few times, and I vaguely remembered a man delivering a large brown envelope to our house and waiting while Dad signed his name on a clipboard. But I had never spoken to her since she walked out of our lives in her fuzzy lavender sweater, and I had certainly never received a card or letter.

Papa and Gram, her parents and our only connection to her, lived in Tucson, and I hardly ever saw them even when Dad and Janice were together. After the divorce, it was almost as if Janice was entirely wiped from our lives. She was obviously gone, but Papa and Gram were pretty much out of the picture too. They were young grandparents, and when I was old enough to understand, I got the impression that they had wished I would have waited to make my appearance in the world until they had a few more gray hairs. Occasionally I would receive a late birthday card from them with a crisp five-dollar bill tucked inside. But Janice never sent a thing.

Until the sympathy card.

I opened the card without looking at the return address, and although I was curious who had sent it, I wasn't prepared for her name in willowy black pen at the bottom of the page. I put the card down without reading it. It took two days for me to be able to pick it up again and scan the few lines she had penned.

For all my hesitancy, though, I couldn't really begin to explain what I was feeling as I held something that she herself had held so recently—something that she had intended for me. Each emotion jostled for attention, and in the ensuing confusion I had to be content with momentary sparks of anger, longing, helplessness, and even fear.

What bothered me even more than the fact that she had reached out of her self-inflicted exile and made a pathetic attempt at sympathy was what every word of her letter seemed to imply. Every word of every sentence told me unmistakably that she cared nothing for me or even Dad, the man she had married. Didn't you have to feel more than a negligible amount of affection to have a child with someone? Clearly we were nothing more than a blip on the radar—people who barely registered on the compass of her life. *I'm so sorry for your loss*, she had written, and the whole world would have been a very different place if she had left the *y* off *your*. Wasn't his death her loss too? Hadn't she cared for him even a little? Didn't the memory of him conjure up a hint of regret? Apparently not.

"Who signs a letter to their daughter *yours truly*?" Thomas asked with disgust when I showed him the card. I had been hiding it in my drawer for two weeks before I couldn't stand it anymore and had to share it with him. I needed the catharsis of hating her with someone.

"Janice does," I said bitterly. "I didn't expect *love* from her, but maybe *sincerely*. *Yours truly* is downright laughable. She's not mine and she's certainly not true."

Thomas laughed. "It's like some Elizabethan love letter—unrequited love and all that garbage." He turned the card over and detached the bookmark. It made a satisfying zip. "Do you want to keep this?" he asked, offering me the pocket-sized psalm.

"Of course not."

"It's a Bible passage, Julia!" he exclaimed, feigning shock.

"It's from her."

"In that case, I'll be right back." Thomas took off toward his house, and I was left alone on the cold seat of the wooden swing beside the barn.

It was April, and the snow was melting furiously in the tepid fifty-degree sunshine. My shoes were caked with dirt and grass, and the lawn beneath me ran with little rivulets of water. There was a cool breeze from the west, and my cheeks were numb and cherry colored, but the sun was warm on my back and I had taken off my coat to absorb it. Spring was always beautiful in the Midwest, and this one was particularly spectacular—lots of late snowstorms and then crocuses poking their purple, turtle-shaped heads out of the disappearing white blanket.

Dad had been gone for over six months.

I would have been passably content if Janice hadn't disturbed my world.

I kicked my feet off the ground and began to pump the swing as high as I could. The wind whipped my hair around my face, and I closed my eyes to let it wash over my cheeks. I swung in the darkness, clinging tightly to the cold chains, until I started to get dizzy. When I opened my eyes, Thomas was back.

"Trying to fly away?" he quipped, taking a seat on the swing next to mine and hooking his arms lightly around the chains. I didn't respond, and he watched me for a minute before saying, "Hang on." Then he shot out an arm as I swung back, and I felt him push my shoulder. I went spinning out of control and couldn't stop a breathless giggle from escaping when my stomach sank away.

"You're such a jerk," I reprimanded him when I had slowed to a gentle sway. But I didn't mean it and he knew it.

Getting off his swing, he came to face me and grabbed my knees to stop my movement completely. "I have something for you," he said with a glint in his eye.

"What?" I demanded, because Thomas was the kind of guy who would make you guess until you didn't care anymore. "I'm not guessing," I added.

"Here." He handed me the bookmark from Janice's card. "Wait a second. . . ." He rifled in his coat pocket and, emerging triumphant with a little book of matches, placed them in my other hand.

I looked at him expectantly.

"Burn it, sister."

I didn't question him. I laid the little slip of paper on my lap and carefully took a matchstick from the book. Flipping the cover over, I placed the match between the green strip and the cardboard and pulled. It sputtered for a moment, and a few sparks skipped off the end. Then a flame engulfed the short stick, and without hesitating, I grabbed the bookmark and held the flare to the lower right-hand corner. Orange fingers tentatively licked up the side of the glossy

paper before grabbing hold and consuming the entire thing in dancing fire. Slowly, ashes began to fall away, and I watched the Twenty-
third Psalm disappear. *"Surely goodness and love will follow me all the
days of my life. . . ."*

"Forgive us, Father, for we have sinned," Thomas prayed when I
had finally dropped what was left of the bookmark.

"You're not Catholic, Thomas. And I wasn't burning the Bible.
I was . . ." I stopped, not knowing how to articulate what I had
done—not wanting to even *try* to articulate what I had done. I
closed my eyes on the hot tears that came from nowhere and managed to stop them before they spilled.

"God knows, Julia," Thomas said, and his voice was achingly
sincere. "Here, finish it off." He handed me the rest of the card.

The tears were gone as quickly as they had come, and one more
match reduced Janice's words to smoke. The little cross didn't burn,
but the heat melted the glue that held it on, and it fell into a puddle
at my feet.

Thomas picked it up and wiped it off. "Do you want to keep
this?" he asked, offering it to me.

"Not particularly," I answered, but a part of me wanted to reach
for it. I stopped myself.

"You know what really gets me," I said a few moments later. "I
really can't stand it that she wrote 'please let me know if there is
anything I can do,' but she didn't leave any information. No address,
no phone number, not even an e-mail address."

"Would you contact her if she had?" Thomas didn't look at me
as he asked the question but cocked his arm back and prepared to
launch the little brassy cross into the alfalfa field. I watched his

arm swing in a perfect pitcher's arc. But he kept his fist closed and without looking at the cross again stuffed it absently into his pocket. "Well, would you?"

"No."

"Then why do you care?" His eyes bored into mine.

I fumbled. "Because . . . because she *should* have."

"She didn't do a lot of things she should have."

"I know," I said, and I couldn't stop myself from sounding miserable. Then, before I could think about it, I blurted out, "She should love me—at least a little."

"Your dad loved you enough for both," Thomas said quietly.

"I know," I whispered. I sounded even more miserable.

"I love you, Julia," he said. Then he stepped close to me and, sliding his hand under my chin, lifted my face and placed a solemn kiss on the highest curve of my cheekbone. His lips brushed the farthest tips of my eyelashes.

"I love you, Julia," he said. And I took him at his word.

decrescendo

THOMAS HAD BEEN a freshman at Glendale Hill University for all of two weeks when she stole his heart. It made my pace quicken and my blood simmer to even think of it that way, but try as I might to reframe the context of their newborn relationship, it could be considered nothing less than a brazen, outright, unrepentant theft. Thomas was mine as much as the hand on the end of my arm belonged to me and me alone, and the intensity with which I loathed her for the way she sidled up to his life and made it a part of her own was matched only by the inexpressible fear I felt as I watched him slip away. Although, if I was brutally honest with myself, I couldn't describe Thomas as *slipping* away—he fell away from me like a rock flung carelessly over the side of a cliff. He plummeted.

Glendale Hill was less than a half-hour drive from Grandma's farm, and if I was really eager to get there, I could make it door to door in exactly twenty-one minutes. I had already visited Thomas three times and would have gladly gone every single day if Grandma hadn't sat me down and earnestly outlined her expectations for me in my junior year of high school. I had a job taking tickets at the local movie theater—a small, two-screen affair with ancient red brocade carpet and a candy counter that was polished so smooth I could accidentally sweep a bag of M&M'S right off the edge as I shoved it toward a customer—and, more importantly, I had grades to maintain. Grandma had visions of scholarships dancing in her head, and although Dad's life insurance could easily carry me through as much schooling as I could ever want, she had no inclination to pay full tuition when the day eventually came.

Besides, as Grandma so candidly put it, "Thomas needs some space. He's in college now." As if college were an alternate universe where Thomas would shed his old life to morph into something entirely new and different.

I ignored her as much as I could and dropped in on Thomas whenever I wasn't working and he had visiting hours—no girls in the guys' dorm rooms and vice versa except during a rigid and incomprehensible schedule that I kept tucked in my purse.

The first three times I saw Thomas in his new context had been great. He welcomed me with a bear hug and introduced me almost proudly to his roommate, a slightly chubby guy from Texas who had a drawl as slow and sweet as the smile that curled leisurely across his face. I liked him instantly, and the three of us sat on the ratty old sofa tucked under the loft that contained their beds and drank copious cups of coffee. We played Mario Kart because it was cute to be impish and playful and because anything that was not the norm was cool, as everyone had spent the first eighteen years of their lives trying to fit in and was just plain sick of it.

I loved it. I loved this relaxed, happy Thomas, who laughed easily and who seemed to have grown up and become more childlike simultaneously. I loved to peer around the open door of his room and see him hunched over a book so immense and burdensome it could contain nothing less than the secrets of the universe. Mostly I loved it that he still had time for me. His eyes lit up when he saw me, and he seemed eager to make me a part of his new world. Grandma was wrong. Thomas didn't need or want an ounce of space from me.

The sun was just resting on the tops of the trees when I pulled into the visitors' parking lot outside Thomas's residence building late one uninspired afternoon. The greenbelt between the squat, brick structures of the old part of campus was filled with students lounging in the shade as they tried to stay cool. The little park was dotted with blankets and bodies, and where there would normally have been Frisbees and footballs and laughter there were only sun-lazy conversations and often closed eyes and no conversation at all. It was so humid the grass was damp, but since the dormitories had no air-conditioning, the sticky moistness of the sun-scorched fall ground was far preferable to the suffocating heat of the seemingly never-ending floors of tiny rooms.

I stayed on the sidewalk so I could browse the faces as I walked by. Thomas didn't know I was coming, and I didn't want to miss him if he was anywhere but in his room. The brief walk to building D—a piece of unimaginative, weak-tea brown architecture that was aptly named after nothing more creative than the next letter in the alphabet when *A*, *B*, and *C* had been used on the surrounding dormitories—revealed no languishing Thomas and no faces I could recognize.

Some of those blank faces watched me as I walked past, and halfway across the open space I was suddenly so self-conscious that I had to force myself to maintain the relaxed pace I had set. They were looking at me as I naively paraded myself down the center of the lawn, and as their eyes traced my steps, it struck me that they knew—they had to know—I was just a little sixteen-year-old high school student. I didn't belong here. I looked downright silly walking across the campus like I owned the place. I was what people needed space from when they went to college in the first place.

Building D was no more inviting than the student-lined greenbelt had been, and the stillness of the stagnant air slowed my steps—I had to wade through the thickness. Feeling defeated and obtuse and ridiculous for even being here in the first place, I would have gratefully returned to my car and cranked the air-conditioning if I wouldn't have had to face the gauntlet of college students to do so. But I had made it this far, and Thomas was the closest oasis to provide a soothing balm for my heat-exhausted soul, so I climbed despondently to the third floor.

His door, like every other door along the nearly abandoned hallway, was open, but it was impossible to tell if he was in his room or not. I didn't really care either way anymore. I just wanted a place to escape for a moment.

When I reached the room that had *Thomas* and *Chris* written on red construction paper beside the door, I didn't knock or even pause. It was only when I was poised to throw myself down on the couch that I realized Thomas was here too.

He was kneeling on the floor with his back to me as he fiddled with the dials on the stereo beneath his desk. There were speakers in each of the four corners of the room and a subwoofer behind the couch—status symbols for any self-respecting college boy—and as I stood in the middle of the room, soft music began to drift over me as if Thomas had known I was coming and had arranged this calming breeze of song. I listened for a moment and watched his back—he hadn't yet noticed that I was here—and the sweet, soulful strains of something I didn't recognize hung mournfully in the air between us. It made me feel strangely shy.

"It's pretty," I whispered. "Who is it?"

Thomas's head whipped around so fast it was obvious I had scared him half to death. "Julia—" He spat out my name like a curse and took a deep breath to steady himself. "What in the world are you doing here?"

I came to see you was the obvious answer, but it was a difficult thing to say because it was clear that he was very surprised and not necessarily happy to see me. He was looking at me with an expression I had seen many times before, but it had never been directed at me; the mixture of annoyance and displeasure in his eyes was usually reserved for his siblings when they had done something unforgivably obnoxious.

Thomas blinked quickly and the expression disappeared, but I didn't find the ensuing blankness in his gaze any more comforting. His look had paralyzed me, and when I didn't answer him right away, he stood up and waved a hand at the speakers, answering my question instead. "Norah Jones." Then he began to pick up stray clothes and dump them in the hamper in his closet.

I had to force myself to breathe around the pounding heart that had found its way into my throat. Something felt very wrong, and not knowing what it was only gave me a false hope that I was misunderstanding the way he turned his back to me. I'm not sure there is anything more agonizing than empty hope.

"I like her voice," I finally said, trying not to sound strained.

"It's Chris's CD—it's not something I would normally pick up." I didn't say anything more, so he continued, "I like it, though."

"Me too." I stood stock-still in the middle of the room and watched him as he avoided looking at me.

"Sure is hot," he tried again, and although he attempted to do it casually, I saw him glance at his watch.

"Yeah," I replied, wishing with every fiber of my being that I could erase my steps and forget I had ever come to see Thomas today.

We didn't say anything for a few minutes, and in those seconds, the months and years of our relationship were diminished into something that carried none of the weight and significance that I knew in my soul they had. It felt worse than death. It felt like everything good that we had ever been was being carried away with each faint note that floated from the room and disappeared into the stillness. He was slipping further away with every breath we took in silence. When I lost my dad, at least I'd lost him loving me.

After the last wrinkled shirt had been deposited on the wash pile, the dorm room was neat and there was nothing left for Thomas to do. He stood for a moment surveying every aspect of the room and avoiding my gaze. Everything must have met his approval because he glanced at his watch again—not even trying to hide it this time— and then put his hands on his hips, squared his shoulders, and turned to the one thing he had left to address: me.

"Look, Julia," he started, "it's nice to see you and all, but I've got someone coming over in a few minutes. . . ." His eyes dropped away from mine as he trailed off.

"It's okay," I blurted out. "I was just out for a drive and thought I'd stop by." The lie sounded pathetic even in my own ears.

He seemed relieved that it was going to be easy to get rid of me. "I mean, I'm not trying to kick you out or anything—"

Two short raps on the open door behind me caused us both to whirl around.

She was standing in the doorframe, knuckles still suspended against the wood and smiling beguilingly at the two of us. She was bright and vibrant with eyes so brown and rich they looked like the last swallow of a cup of hot, black coffee. Her teeth were dazzling against her skin, and everything about her seemed luminous.

I turned to Thomas.

He had taken a step back from me as if he had been caught doing something he shouldn't, even though we were easily ten feet apart. "Francesca," was all he said.

It was the way Thomas looked as he watched her that told me everything I believed to be true was not and may have never been. He loved the girl in the door with more than just his eyes, and my mouth went dry as I realized that if he'd ever loved me at all, it was nothing compared to this.

But it was worse than that. As I stared at Thomas, his eyes darted back to mine, and the guilt written deep within them told me that he knew. He knew—he had probably always known—that I loved him, and in his face I read that he also knew he could never love me like that. And he didn't stop me. He had never once even attempted to stop me.

"Who is this, Thomas?" Her voice was light and cheerful, begging to be answered, but he didn't say a word.

I tore myself away from Thomas in time to meet her as she walked up with her arm outstretched. I was hardly even aware of doing it, but I took her hand, and it was as smooth and dark as toffee and cool in spite of the heat.

"I'm Francesca," she said with a smile, and although I hated her, her eyes were warm and genuine. "Thomas apparently has no manners." She gave him a look that was both soft and mischievously stern. She held my hand a second longer, waiting for me to introduce myself.

When I didn't, Thomas finally stepped forward. "I'm sorry, Francesca. Julia and I were just talking, and . . . I guess I just wasn't thinking." He looked back and forth between us. "Francesca Hernandez, Julia DeSmit. Julia, Francesca." He paused before adding, "Julia is like a little sister to me."

"Oh, that's so sweet!" Francesca gushed.

"She lives on the farm next to ours; don't you, Julia?" Thomas prodded.

I opened my mouth and when nothing came out, nodded slightly.

"You're so lucky to have family nearby," Francesca said, shaking her head to get her chin-length chocolate curls off her cheeks and forehead. It hurt to watch her.

Now that Francesca was in the room and the worst of it was already over, Thomas seemed more relaxed, and he gave me an almost-normal smile as he said, "Francesca is from California."

"My family has been in the San Diego area for four generations, but whenever somebody hears my last name, they think I don't speak English!" Francesca laughed as she took the spot on Thomas's sofa that I had intended to occupy. She spread out her arms and looked meaningfully at me as if she were about to confess an unpardonable sin. "Funny thing is, I don't speak Spanish!"

Thomas joined in laughing with her.

I still hadn't said a single word, but Francesca didn't seem to notice. "I came to Glendale Hill because my aunt came here . . . and I wanted to get away from home," she offered, winking at me. "Everyone asks that question within five minutes of meeting me, so I've decided to get it out of the way early on in the conversation."

I don't care, I thought, and for a heartbeat I was sure that I had said it aloud. But she was still smiling, and when I looked at Thomas, he was too. Apparently I hadn't said anything nearly so impolite. In fact, I hadn't said anything at all, but somewhere in the back of my shock-numbed mind I knew that at some point I would have to speak. I could not simply walk away. Yet what could I say to her? It was impossible to even formulate a coherent thought, much less carry on a conversation with the girl who made Thomas look at me that way. More than anything, I wanted to run, to pretend that I had never heard the name *Francesca*, but wasn't that what they were expecting? After all, I was little more than Thomas's baby sister.

The music in the background faded to silence during a pause between songs. It couldn't have lasted for more than the span of a breath, but to me it stretched unbearably.

"What's your major?" I finally asked. The numbness faded slightly.

Although my words were hardly audible, Francesca was prepared for the question. I hadn't impressed them with my witty resilience or buoyant spirit—it was the quintessential inquiry on a college campus.

"I'm in nursing," she answered, wrinkling her nose as if it was a distasteful occupation to her. "My mom is a nurse, two of my aunties are nurses, and my grandmother was a nurse. . . . You get the picture." Directing her attention to Thomas, she said demurely, "I didn't know you were a Norah Jones fan."

I had never seen Thomas blush—unless you counted the time that we walked in on his parents kissing in the kitchen—but with Francesca's words his ears turned pink, and he tried somewhat unsuccessfully to hide a little-boy grin. I felt myself disappear from the room.

"I'm a new convert," he said carefully. Only someone who knew him well would understand that he was hoping beyond hope that she wouldn't ask him what his favorite song was on the CD.

"Are you familiar with Diana Krall? She's actually a jazz singer, but . . ." Francesca trailed off as she realized that I was still in the room. "I'm sorry, Julie. We're being rude. What kind of music do you like?"

It wasn't that she called me Julie that made my heart pound twice for every normal beat, although I hated it when people did that. It wasn't the obvious delineation that separated the three of us into *them* and *me*. It wasn't even that Francesca was blinking innocently at me with her stunning dark eyes, and I couldn't meet her gaze in return. It was that they were openly placing me in the role Thomas had so offhandedly designated for me—they were treating me like a little sister instead of an equal. I was an afterthought, a nuisance that they would say good-bye to with relief. And I was supposed to be making small talk about my musical preferences.

"I have really eclectic taste in music," I said after a moment. "I don't think I could name a particular favorite." Speaking had made me finally able to put one foot in front of the other, so I forced a distracted smile and made my way to the door. Composing myself for one last civility, I said, "It was nice to meet you, Fran." I knew I was being childish by refusing to call her by her proper name, but deep inside of my horror was a cool, hard anger, and it felt good to say it wrong.

"Francesca," Thomas corrected.

I just smiled and gave them both a little wave. "Have a good evening."

They each said good-bye, and the last thing I saw as I left was Francesca shooting Thomas a raised eyebrow and a wholesome, confused expression. I didn't buy it. Sweet and wonderful person or not, she knew exactly the dynamics in the room, and she was only pretending to be oblivious. Somehow it suited her purposes to be naive.

Though the music took flight and evaporated into the air around me, my feet felt heavier and heavier with each step farther away from Thomas's room. I took quick, shallow breaths to stop myself from crying—I could not cross the greenbelt with tears in my eyes. I had always been able to turn off my emotions, and I did that now, focusing on the betrayal I felt instead of the pain of losing a friend. Galvanizing my hurt into anger was the only way I knew to preserve myself. I was so absorbed in trying to do so that when Thomas grabbed my arm halfway down the first flight of stairs, I nearly screamed in surprise.

He didn't say anything for a minute, just held on to my arm and looked at me with a mixture of emotions that seemed confusingly incongruous. I could tell he was still annoyed with me, but underneath that he was also upset, and although I wouldn't have believed it thirty seconds ago, he seemed hurt, too.

"Julia—"

"Thomas, don't," I interrupted, trying to pull away.

He let go of my arm but matched my stride as I continued down the steps. "It's not like we ever dated."

"I know" was all I said.

We rounded the landing on the second floor, and Thomas jogged a few steps around the far side of the banister to stay by my side.

"Our friendship was never romantic," he tried again.

"I know."

"I'm allowed to date whomever I choose."

"I know."

He groaned in frustration and jumped down a step to stand in front of me.

I stopped and our eyes were almost level. I didn't avoid his gaze.

"Then why are you being like this?" Thomas's eyes were clear and blue and sad. They sought me out from behind my anger and held me in a place where we were on familiar ground, a place where we felt comfortable looking into each other's eyes. He sighed, and the regret in that one soft sound made the tears I had been holding back fill my eyes so quickly that I didn't even have time to blink them away.

Watching me cry, Thomas said, "Julia, I'm sorry. I'm sorry I was cold to you when you came over this afternoon. I'm sorry I didn't tell you about Francesca sooner." He couldn't stop the words now that they were coming, and he continued as if a string of apologies could repair what had been broken. "I'm sorry that I hurt your feelings. I'm sorry Francesca called you Julie. You know, she really is great. You two have so much in common—you're going to like her so much. . . ."

He stopped and gently reached out both hands to brush them across my cheeks. "Don't cry," he said, wiping my tears away. "I said I was sorry. I'm still your best friend."

I closed my eyes and suffered the warmth of his skin on my face. He was the same Thomas as always and I was the same Julia, but everything had changed. As much as I wanted to, there was no going back. I couldn't pretend that I believed he was anything less than the one person who could save me from myself. I couldn't be his best friend, his sweet little sister, and watch him fall in love with the woman who would take the place that should have been mine.

With my eyes still tightly shut, I whispered, "Thomas, you apologized for the wrong things." And then I pulled away from him and walked down the rest of the stairs and into the fading sunlight.

lessons

As I DROVE away from Thomas the day everything changed, I found myself ensnared in the story of the chick.

It had nothing to do with Thomas or Francesca or what I was feeling, but I replayed the incident again and again in spite of my every attempt to focus on the present, to deal with what had happened. Maybe it was a defense mechanism—my mind was refusing to concentrate on Thomas because it would simply be too difficult. Maybe the stories were somehow connected, and deep down I knew that one would make sense of the other. Whatever the reason, this particular piece of my personal history lived in my mind for the remains of the day, and with it I spent more time thinking about my father than the man who had slipped from me that afternoon.

My dad had loved to tell the story of the chick.

It was less dramatic than downright silly, a childish encounter that left Dad with what he considered to be a meaningful and allegorical little anecdote and me with an acute feeling of repentance that faded with every year that marched between the spring I was six and the present day. While I used to cringe in horror whenever Dad would begin to recall that particular episode of my life, the older I got the less I cared and the less I even bothered to listen to his tender retelling.

But with my sweaty hands wrapped tightly around the sticky steering wheel as the speedometer reached sixty on the gravel roads, I struggled to remember the words he used and the tone of his voice. With a growing sense of almost desperate loss, I found that I had forgotten the story—not the actual events, the skeleton of what happened, but the beauty of what Dad had seen in it. It was a cavernous feeling—a dark and echoless free fall—because who would ever remember with him gone?

It had been early spring and my grandpa, who was only slightly over a year away from the heart attack that would take him peacefully in his sleep, had ordered fifty broiler chicks for the little henhouse he had spent the winter restoring. The building was old and full of cracks and holes, but Grandpa had sealed them to the best of his ability and had bought a few old heating lamps from a neighbor who had once raised golden retrievers.

April should have been a fine month to receive chicks, and Grandpa was confident about the state of his chicken coop. But

after almost two weeks of above-average temperatures in the six-
ties and even seventies, a cold front moved in and brought with it
rain that turned to freezing rain that—against all our most fervent
prayers—turned to snow. Just under a foot fell in the hours between
midnight and 6 a.m., so when we woke in the morning, the world
was a very different place than it had been when we went to sleep.

The warmer weather had encouraged trees to bud and tulips to
leap out of the ground, and now snow was draped like Dutch lace
over the promises of spring that had been so plump and unspoiled
only twenty-four hours before. Everything was soft and blurred, and
the wind continued to shift the landscape by blowing and whipping
the snow into creamy drifts that crept silkily up the sides of some
buildings and left others clean and bare. For December, it would
have been stunning. For April, it was devastating—particularly
to the lemon-colored chicks huddled in Grandpa's drafty chicken
coop.

School was canceled, and since Dad taught science at the high
school, we both had the day off. After scrambled eggs on toast and
hot chocolate for breakfast, he donned his parka and scooped the
driveway while I watched from the kitchen window. We let the car
run for a full five minutes before we got in it and made sure to call
Grandma to let her know we were coming just in case we got stuck
and no one knew where we were. Janice had made it in to the office,
and we didn't expect her to give us a second thought throughout
her busy day.

The roads in town had been plowed and weren't as bad as we
thought they might be, but once we left city limits, the snow swirled
over the road like crystallized fog. Ditch and asphalt became one,

and the only thing that kept us from driving right off the road and into the snowbanks alongside Highway 10 was the fact that the road was straight as a pin—Dad simply refrained from turning the steering wheel. We didn't meet any cars, but it was exhaustingly slow going. I think he would have turned back, but the visibility was so bad he couldn't see a field driveway to pull into.

When we crested the hill above Grandpa and Grandma's farm, the view was spectacular. The sky was blue above the ground-storm, and the sun glared blindingly off the newly covered fields. The whole earth was blanketed in white, and the wind was spinning the snow into swirling funnels of diamond light.

"We may not make it home if this keeps up," Dad commented with a grim smile.

The thought didn't disappoint me.

Grandma was just putting on her boots as we came rushing into the entryway, shaking snow from our coats.

"It's freezing, Grandma!" I yelled, my enthusiasm bubbling over.

She laughed. "I know, but it's *April*—it's not supposed to be freezing!" She cupped my hooded face in her gloved hands and kissed my snow-damp forehead. "Grandpa is with the chicks. You want to come see?"

This was why I had wanted so badly to come in the first place. I was dying to see the chicks that were still tiny enough to hide in my cupped hands. I practically hopped with impatience as I waited for Grandma to tuck her slate and silver curls into the hood of her coat and wrap a hand-knit scarf around her neck and face.

Bundled against the cold, we headed outside again, and I felt Grandma take one of my hands and Dad take the other. The snow barely covered my boots in some places, but in others they had to swing me over drifts that would have engulfed me.

The chicken coop was faded red and often obscured by the swirling whiteness, but we could always make out the shape of it at least, and before my toes got too cold in my boots, we were tromping up the two sagging concrete steps and into the leaning little building.

The atmosphere was warm and dry with an acrid smell that made me skip a lungful of air when it hit the back of my throat. Little puffs of blonde chicks littered the floor, peeping in a chorus of charming soprano notes that sounded remarkably like animated chatter. They ran quickly to wherever they were going on toothpick-size legs and huddled in bunches that seemed to be constantly growing, shrinking, and changing. I loved them all in less time than it took to survey the whole room.

Grandpa was ankle-deep in the thick of it, adjusting one of the lamps. "Cute, aren't they?" He grinned at me.

"May I hold one?" I asked without taking my eyes off the enchanting little birds.

"Of course," Grandma said at my elbow, and she bent down to scoop one up. "It'll probably mess on you, though," she warned with a little knowing smile.

"I don't care," I whispered and pulled my mittens off.

The chick was more delicate than I expected—and more fidgety. I had thought maybe she would curl up in my hand like a contented kitten and fall asleep, but she didn't seem very interested in being held at all. I cupped one hand underneath her and curled the other over the top of her so only her little head peeked out, and after a moment she relaxed enough to let me explore her. Her down was softer than anything I had ever felt, yet it was misleading because it seemed impossible to actually touch. Her downiness simply gave way to the weight of my finger, and underneath was the curve of her firm body, small enough for me to hold completely in my own six-year-old hands. I held her to my face, and she peeped forlornly at me. I kissed the top of her head and put her down.

"I like the ones with a little brown in them," Dad said, picking out a chick with smudges of brown on her head and wings. "They have character."

"I don't," I stated firmly. "I like the really yellowy-yellow ones."

"Perfectionist, eh?" Grandpa teased. "I'll find you the perfect chick." He stooped down and scattered a few of the groups, passing over one, picking up another, and finally emerging triumphant with a chubby chick grasped in his right hand. "Here you are, Julia."

I accepted the chick solemnly and inspected her. She was so softly yellow as to be mistaken for a shimmering white gold and rounder and fuller than the chick I had held earlier. I wouldn't have even cared if she did mess on me like my grandmother predicted. "She's beautiful," I said.

Dad must have seen the longing in my eyes because he put a hand on my shoulder. "They're very fragile creatures, Julia. You must be extremely careful with them."

"I am being careful," I defended.

"How are they doing?" Dad asked, giving me a wink and a squeeze before diverting his attention to Grandpa.

"Well, I lost a few last night, but I hope they'll be okay now. One of the heating lamps wasn't working properly, but I think I've got it fixed. And this snow isn't supposed to last. . . ."

"You lost a few?" I asked, still concentrating on the chick in my hands. "How did they get out?"

Grandpa paused for the space of a heartbeat. "No, sweetie, a few of them died last night. It was too cold."

I don't remember enough of my youth to know what I did and did not understand about death at the age of six. According to how the rest of the story played out, I must have been devastated by the thought that a few of those adorable little chicks had died. Apparently I would not be consoled.

I can't fathom the depths or shallows of a first-grade mind, but when no one was looking, I took matters into my own hands and did the unthinkable. I stuck the chick in my coat pocket—I simply couldn't abandon her to a potentially deadly night in the freezing chicken coop. She fit rather well and didn't fuss too much, and with a deceitfulness that made me blush even ten years later as I drove recklessly home, I zipped the pocket and quickly bent over to pluck another chick from the floor.

This part I can recall quite clearly. I remember that my purple quilted winter coat didn't feel a single ounce heavier for having her in my pocket. I remember that the new chick in my hand squirmed almost uncontrollably and I was thankful when Dad turned around and told me to put her down because it was time to go back to the house. I remember that my heart didn't quicken a single beat when the adults praised me for listening so well and that I smiled politely when Grandpa assured me that the rest of the chicks would be perfectly safe and sound through the coming night.

Dad carried me back to the house since snow had gotten into the top of my boots on the walk out and, after our brief time in the chicken coop, had begun to melt and sting my shins and ankles. I wrapped my arms around his neck and ignored the living creature concealed in my coat because I didn't want anyone to be suspicious. Besides, I imagined the chick warm and comfortable and napping peacefully, knowing she would be well cared for.

At one point, Dad tightened his grip around my waist in a brief, tight hug, and I hugged him back because I knew that he would understand when I showed him the chick later. He couldn't make me take her back when we were home and I had proven that I could be a good mother to her.

Once we got to the house, the mudroom became a flurry of activity as we removed hats and gloves, boots and snow-dusted coats. Grandma unzipped my parka and helped me out of it before I could think of any reason to keep it on. She hung it on the hook next to the door and gave it a few hard pats to shake off the snow.

"Coffee?" she asked the men, and they murmured gratefully. "You may have some too," she said conspiratorially to me. "It's been a pretty full morning for you."

The thought of coffee with the adults erased any worries for my secret chick, and we all ambled into the kitchen to gather around the table as Grandma put the coffee in the percolator. I loved watching the tall pot on the stove and the way the water bubbled up into the glass bulb on the top to release steamy drips and splatters. The smell wasn't necessarily appealing, but the idea was—especially since I had never been offered so much as a sip of anyone's coffee before. Apparently it no longer stunted your growth after the age of six.

Grandma placed a pan of spice cake with maple-butter frosting on the table and set a plate and mug in front of each of us. My mug had a chip on the rim and sported a Farmers Mutual logo that I recognized from a similar magnet on the refrigerator. It was lovely and grown-up and immense to someone who had formerly only drunk out of a miniature juice cup with oranges dancing around the rim. I grasped it tightly in both hands, and my fingers met on the far side.

I was still holding it when Grandma put her hand over mine and poured out a thin stream of the steaming, molasses-colored liquid until the mug was half full.

"Blow on it for a minute," she instructed. After pouring three more cupfuls, she took the milk out of the refrigerator and the sugar bowl from the cupboard by the sink. I watched her unscrew the milk cap and add the whiteness to my mug until the coffee looked like melted caramel. Taking the sugar bowl, she measured out two flat teaspoonfuls and added them to the cup. Handing me a spoon, she directed, "Stir."

No one else added milk or sugar to their coffee, but I didn't mind. Mine was a much prettier color. By the time I took my first sip, Grandpa was already on his second cup. The coffee was luke-warm against my lips and didn't taste at all like it looked. I expected something smooth and sweet, but it was kind of bitter, and the taste stayed on my tongue long after I swallowed. I tried another sip.

"How do you like it?" Grandma asked casually when she noticed me trying the coffee.

"It's good," I said unconvincingly.

"It takes a little while to get used to," she offered.

I sat tall and straight in my seat and drank the entire cup between mouthfuls of cake. Grandma was right—by the end it tasted rather good.

It was an exceptional day because I wasn't offered coffee again for a very long time, and when I did finally become a caffeine addict, I took my coffee black and strong. But for the width of a few memorable hours, I didn't feel like a little girl, even though my feet were tucked beneath me and my coffee was a different color. That morning, they shared their pot of coffee with me and even included me in the conversation from time to time. I was mature and wise, a lady among my peers—or almost.

The coffee was gone and lunch was ruined after too many pieces of spice cake when Dad finally announced that we should try to make it home before the wind picked up or we got more snow. At the mention of the word *home*, the facade of my responsible near adulthood melted to the floor, and the image of the perfect little chick nestled in my coat pocket came flooding back to me.

With a gasp that must have startled my family, I leaped out of my chair and raced to the front porch. Tearing down my coat, I fumbled in one coat pocket and found it empty. Flipping the coat over and ripping open the zipper, I plunged my hand into the opposite pocket and extracted the limp body of a lifeless chick.

Her down was matted against the side of her small body, and her neck sagged against her chest in a drooping curl. The leg that wasn't trapped under my fingers swung slowly back and forth. I screamed and dropped her.

Dad's story never ended with an inconsolable child and an innocent, dead animal. But no matter how earnestly I tried, no matter how many times I relived the story as the sun set in my rearview mirror, I couldn't see past the moment when my six-year-old stupidity had been exposed. It was inane and just plain naive. The story was a worthless reminder of everything that I truly, deeply, madly wanted to forget about myself and a youth that seemed disconnected to the almost woman I was now. What did the little girl I had been have to do with the person I was today?

Yet Dad had made it all make sense; he made it all seem right. He had found beauty in something so senseless and sickening that I would have understood if for the rest of my life he used the incident as a lesson—a veritable guidebook for what not to do, adaptable for nearly any situation: maturity, obedience, caution, sensitivity, common sense, responsibility. . . . He could have had an arsenal of sermons with points of application derived specifically from this one misjudgment in my young life.

But he didn't. He loved the story more with every telling, and against all understanding it seemed to make him love me more too. I needed that love. That unconditional, I-don't-care-what-you've-done love. The love that made me realize from that moment on, no part of me could step outside of it even if I tried.

I needed Dad to teach Thomas how to love me like that.

I had been driving for over an hour when I pulled into a field driveway and shut off the car. The sun had mostly set and the air was beginning to cool, so I rolled down the window and put my head back and looked across the rolling hills. I was overwhelmed by an urge to stretch myself out, to lie facedown on the ground and just give up, to talk to my father as if he were a spirit hovering over me or maybe talk to God, but I fought it. I was a practical girl, and whether or not Thomas loved me or Dad's story had lost all meaning, life would go on. I had been through worse.

As I sat in the silence and listened to the squawking of a flock of crows that had settled on the golden corn in the ditch below me, I determined to derive one lesson, one nugget of truth, from the tale that ran on continuous play in my tired mind. After a day that made little sense to me and that I had yet to deconstruct, it was the least I could expect.

The sky had faded to amethyst and the sweat on my skin was cool and clammy when I started the car and backed out of the dirt driveway to head for home. The story had been drained of all its garish color in my mind, and I was grateful to put it away and leave it in a place where I hoped I would not soon find it again.

If I'd had one wish in that long, agonizing evening, I would have wasted it begging my dad to tell me why. Why did he love the story of the chick so? Why did I think of it so obsessively with Thomas fading to gray in the background? Why did Dad never use it to teach me a single lesson? Maybe I would have learned something. Maybe everything would have been different. Maybe *I* would have been different.

But answer or no, there was one thing I knew. I would not hold on to Thomas. I wouldn't fight it or cry any more tears about it or obsess about what I could have—should have—done differently. I couldn't remember why Dad loved the story, but I was taking a lesson away from it: let go.

As far as I was concerned, I had begun a new life—not shiny new, just new for me. Different.

reconnect

"IT HURTS ME to see you so sad," Grandma said one night shortly after Christmas.

It had been over three months since I had said anything more than a forced hello to Thomas, and as my mind did the calculation, I realized that my life so far had been little more than counting away from the last *since*. Eight years since Janice left. Fourteen, almost fifteen, months since Dad died. Fourteen and a half weeks since I lost Thomas. How do you keep track of time when there is no devastating point of reference to weigh you down like an anchor and keep you from floating day into day with no thought of where you have been? I wondered how long the counts would stay fresh and clear. How long before my mind had to stop and process how many weeks and months and years it had been? *Dad died four, no, five years ago in October. It's amazing how time flies.*

Grandma's lined hands plunged into the now-greasy dishwater and pulled the plug from the deep porcelain sink.

The initial suck of draining water startled me out of my daze, and I considered how long I had stood in silence with my hands wrapped in a flour-sack towel around a bone-dry plate. I added the chipped Corelle dinnerware to its mate and looked at the forlorn little stack of two. Ten of the twelve in Grandma's collection hadn't been touched in more months than I cared to remember.

But she had said something to me and was hoping for a response. Was the correct answer yes or no?

"Mm-hmm . . . ?" I mumbled noncommittally and stole a side-long glance at her sweetly wrinkled profile.

She turned to me and caught me in her sharp brown eyes. They were just like Dad's. "I said it hurts me to see you so sad," she repeated.

Hearing it again I realized that *mm-hmm* had not been an acceptable reply. So I said, "I'm not so sad, Grandma."

Her smile told me that we both knew I was lying, and my lips faintly mirrored hers, if only for a moment.

"What would make that smile stay?" she asked, and I cringed at the concern in her face.

"It's not nearly so serious," I said consolingly. "Life is a series of ups and downs, right?" I attempted a smile again and willed it to be sincere. "Wait until the weather gets nice; I just have a good case of the winter blues."

Grandma looked utterly unconvinced. "It's December, Julia. Spring is a long way off."

"Then I need to spend more time with friends," I quickly replied and immediately regretted it. It would be too pathetic to admit that I didn't have any friends, but the naked truth was that I really didn't.

I hadn't existed anywhere but in Thomas's shadow almost since the night we met over the stolen stop sign. We had had mutual friends, I suppose, but somehow without the person to stand in the light and cast it, a shadow quickly disappears. People I had peripherally known through Thomas either graduated or simply failed to remember me. Not that they were mean—I think they just forgot. And not that I cared. It was hard to cry tears over something that never really was.

School wasn't my only possible outlet. I guess I had quasi relationships with the people at the movie theater, but they were the stunted, shallow friendships of the occasional coworker. The schedule was always changing, and the conversations never progressed past chitchat about the latest movie and gossip about whoever had the night off and wasn't around to defend against the often glitzy accusations. *Did you know Alex caught Meredith and some guy making out in an empty theater after the late show last week? Don't tell anyone this, but Jackson didn't quit—he was fired after someone told Brad that he was stealing candy bars from the concession stand.*

And that was it. My two avenues for friendship were dead ends and my weekends reserved for a good book and *Jeopardy!* with Grandma. Funny thing was, I didn't really mind. But she did, and I had just opened the door to the one conversation I did not want to have.

Grandma was looking at me apologetically, and I knew that she was trying to come up with a way to broach the topic.

I decided to make it easy for her. "I don't have any friends," I said, laying my hand on her arm to let her know that it didn't really matter.

"I wasn't going to say that," she murmured.

"I know. But it's okay. I'm not offended or anything." I shrugged. "I just spent so much time with Thomas I didn't have any left over for anyone else."

"You have time now," she said quietly.

"So I do." I paused, then added, "I'll try." I tried to sound optimistic, like I was genuinely ready to embark on a new journey in my life. One without Thomas and with endless possibilities for other friends and opportunities. But more than anything, I just wanted this conversation to be over. I wanted to retreat to the warmth and comfort of the living room and curl up in the overstuffed armchair with the latest Harry Potter. Never mind that I had already read it twice. But a feeble promise to try harder and simply snap out of the funk I was in was not enough for my heartsick grandmother. It struck me that the lines under her eyes were more likely than not caused by me. Was she losing sleep over me?

"You could have some people over here," Grandma offered hopefully. Her gaze flicked around the kitchen and through the double-wide arch into the living room beyond. It was obvious she was trying to assess it and even more obvious that the sweet little farmhouse built in the late forties didn't pass her scrutiny. Pea-soup green carpet in the living room and brown-striped wallpaper with raised strips of faded velvet were a far cry from the glamorous decor that lit up our television on a regular basis. She sighed, and I knew it meant she never expected to see a laughing knot of teenagers crowded around her table.

She teared up almost instantly. "I don't know how to do this," she whispered.

I hadn't seen her cry since the day of my dad's funeral, and I was suddenly overwhelmed by guilt. I had lived with her for four years and had given between little and no thought to how my presence must weigh on a woman who should be long past worrying about a moody, miserable teenager. I was her granddaughter, not her daughter, yet she had been thrust into the role of sole parent to a social reject who rarely thought past her own selfish desires. How many nights had she cried silently into her pillow over me?

"I don't know how to do this," she said again, and now the tears made two little lines down her cheeks.

I wrapped my arms around her and held her quietly. After a moment I said, "Don't worry about me, Grandma. I'm fine. I'll be fine."

She pulled away from me and looked almost desperately into my eyes. "I don't want you to become bitter. You carry so much for someone so young, and I just don't want you to get cold. . . ."

"I won't—I'm not," I assured her.

Grandma took a deep breath and pressed her hands to her cheeks. "Julia," she began almost shyly, "will you do something for me?"

I answered without hesitation because I would have done almost anything to erase the suffering in her face. "Of course, Grandma."

She nodded gently and stepped around me to reach for her Bible. It was open on the kitchen table, and she picked it up tenderly so as not to disturb any of the scraps of paper that stuck out from between the thin, fragile pages. Her whole life was in that Bible— scribbled prayers and bulletins from special church services and precious black-and-white photographs with brittle, crinkly corners. She even had the program from Dad's funeral with my name typed first among the ones he left behind.

I had peeked in her Bible once and found the family tree among the first stiff pages and seen that next to my father's entry she had put a small, unfinished line through Janice's name. I couldn't decide if she had begun to scratch her name out and been unable to follow through or if because Janice was neither here nor there it was appropriate to mark her only half gone. Janice wasn't dead—Grandma couldn't write a neat date in the "deceased" line—but to simply write *divorced* beside her name didn't seem to quite cover what had happened either. I never asked her about it.

But Grandma didn't have Janice in mind when she took out her Bible that night. I figured we would spend some time sharing memories or that she would flip open that cherished book to a passage and ask me to read with her, but instead she extracted a small blue flyer from the front cover and replaced the Bible on the table. Opening the flyer, she smoothed the center crease and handed it to me tentatively.

The heading read *Thunder Road*, and I cringed inwardly because I knew exactly what it meant. I pretended to read it as my mind worked furiously to find a way out without devastating her. I forced a smile.

"You want me to go to the youth retreat?" I finally asked because it seemed like the safest place to start. Maybe I had misread her intentions, and I didn't want to put any ideas into her head—

I didn't want her to think for a second that it was my idea or that I secretly wanted to go.

My hopes were proven unfounded even before I had the words completely out of my mouth. Grandma was looking at me with thinly veiled expectations, and I could see that in her eyes this weekend away with the church youth group would be nothing less than my very salvation.

When I didn't say anything more, she came to stand beside me and began to point out different things on the gaudy flyer. "It's not so much a retreat as a time of *restoration* and *renewal*," she explained, indicating two buzzwords that jumped off the page in flashy fonts. "It's a time to help you *refocus* and *reconnect*." Two more boldfaced words.

It made me want to *retch*, and the smile that I suppressed at my own private joke was a real one.

"You get to miss school on Friday," Grandma said as if I were a child who could be coaxed with the promise of some tantalizingly proffered treat.

I turned my smile to her, and she read it as acceptance and maybe even excitement about her idea. I let her. She looked so happy and relieved that I heard myself saying, "I'd love to go," though my voice wavered a bit and my smile faltered.

"Oh, Julia, I'm so glad!" Grandma drew me into a quick, delighted hug, and though my heart had sunk into the pit of my stomach, I would have said yes again if only to feel the warmth of her happiness. "You're going to have so much fun," she continued cheerfully. "You'll meet so many new people. . . ."

I began to put the dishes away so I had an excuse to turn from her as my face fell.

❀

Grandma dropped me off at church before sunrise the following Friday morning.

The storm blue church bus was full, and I had to sit next to a girl who perched on the end of the seat and talked to her two friends across the aisle the entire two-hour trip. She would have just sat with them on their own short bench—they were skinny enough to have allowed it—but the bus driver announced that he wouldn't leave until everyone was sitting two to a seat. He stood there with arms crossed and looked over the whole of the bus with a keen, meticulous eye as a few people shuffled and moved. The girl from across the aisle—who had curly brown hair tossed into an updo that was supposed to look thrown together but that I was sure contained enough bobby pins to set off a metal detector—looked over at the empty space beside me, then turned regretfully back to her friends. She grasped their hands for a moment, and they gave her brave smiles as she shouldered her knapsack and shifted her weight across the tiny aisle.

"Hi!" she said brightly, and her smile was so fake that I didn't even attempt to respond. She watched me for a minute, her plastic pink smile frozen in place, and before I could force my mouth to form a polite hello, she had turned away with a distinct huff.

I sighed as I looked out the window because it was clear I had already failed my first entrance exam. At best, I had been instantly labeled weird or a loner; at worst, they would mutter nasty but decipherable words under their breath when I walked by. The retreat was a spectacular train wreck, and the bus hadn't even pulled out of the parking lot. The worst thing was, after sneaking another glance at the girls, I realized that they were a grade below me. At what point did my self-worth become contingent upon what a group of younger girls thought of me?

The weekend hadn't improved any by the time we arrived at the lakeside lodge. It was depressing to step out of the stuffy bus alone and behold the familiar sprawling cabins of Elim Springs Retreat Center obscured by the dismal gray patina of midwinter gloom. I had only ever seen Elim Springs during the prime summer season, when the cabins were full of happy vacationers and the lake was a translucent, pearly blue beneath silver aspen leaves whispering in the perpetual breeze.

Now the trees stood stark, limbs twisted awkwardly as if they were attempting to cover their own nakedness, while the lake was an indistinct, half-frozen mass the lifeless color of cold oatmeal. This dull, cheerless place was hardly recognizable, and I couldn't stop my mind from flickering between what I remembered this haven to be and what I saw before me.

When one of my seatmate's friends bumped into me and knocked the book I was holding into the gravelly snow at my feet, I abandoned any hope of something redemptive coming out of my trip to Elim Springs.

The girls' dorm room in the west wing of the main lodge was freezing, and as I tossed my stuff onto the top bunk of one of the beds in the far corner of the room, I realized that I had not brought warm enough clothes. I stripped off my sweatshirt to add a long-sleeved T-shirt underneath and ended up being late for the camp-style sing-along at the weekend opening.

Pastor Brad and his wife, Jennie, were on stools in front of a stone fireplace—a massive affair that looked as if it should sport a whole hog on a slowly turning spit—and as I tried to slip in the back door, they both caught my eye and smiled.

Pastor Brad was strumming a guitar that rested casually on his knee, and without pausing, he called out, "Come join us, Miss DeSmit. We're so glad that you've come!"

I could tell by the soft way he looked at me that he didn't mean to cause me any embarrassment, nor was he upset by my slight tardiness. But it was hard not to hate him as every head in the room swiveled in my direction.

Sinking deeper into a well of self-pity, I convinced myself that they were all snickering at me—although most of the faces seemed to offer little more expression than mild curiosity. Sometimes I forgot that I was still the lost soul of choice, the orphan waif of the church, the vulnerable recipient of hand-wringing sympathy. But it had been over a year now. My protected status couldn't last forever, and as I tried to avoid making eye contact with anyone and quickly sat down cross-legged in the back, I heard a muttered word that I chose to ignore. To top it all off, the room was stiflingly hot. I stubbornly refused to remove my sweatshirt and admit that I had made myself late for no good reason.

God, get me through this, I breathed. It was the first prayer I had uttered in ages. With a cynical smile, I realized that the weekend had barely begun and already I was talking to God. If nothing else, it would make Grandma happy, and I wouldn't have to lie when I told her the youth retreat had rejuvenated my prayer life.

We sang some praise-and-worship songs, and I moved my mouth without making any sound because I didn't know the words, and Pastor Brad, assuming that we all knew what we were doing, hadn't provided song sheets. One song melted into another, and soon Jennie was lost in devotion and a few kids had followed suit.

I had the perfect vantage point from the very back, so I carefully stole looks around the room as the service dragged on. Most were singing charitably, almost as if they knew this was part and parcel of a youth retreat and they wanted to maintain at least the pretense of interest and involvement. A handful of people seemed to be trying to hide the fact that they were bored by overcompensating with fake enthusiasm.

But there were a few who looked nothing like the rest. They sat straight or curled over with their heads in their hands or with arms outstretched as they looked at something far away, but their faces had the same gentle quality. There was a peacefulness, a look of fulfillment in the wake of deep longing. For a moment, my breath caught in my throat, and I wanted to be where they were.

Then the song was over, and Pastor Brad announced lunch. There was nothing left to do but join the throng of teenagers crowding the tables along the south wall to grab a brown bag and a pink carton of skim milk.

The rest of the day withered away under the emotionally charged testimonies of a few seniors or recent graduates who deigned to leave their post–high school lives to offer us a taste of maturity and erudition. I knew I was being cold—the one thing Grandma was so afraid

I would become—but they were offering quick answers and thrilling conversions, and it was hard to accept their glamorous offer when I was just worried about making it through the next two days.

I didn't want to be this way, but for the duration of an entire prayer, I actually found myself worrying to the point of obsession about the acceptability of my pajamas. I had never given an article of clothing, much less a faded pair of stretchy black yoga pants, so much thought. I was losing myself as I tried to survive this ridiculous retreat.

That night, crawling into the chilly top bunk after scrubbing my face and teeth in the ice-cold water of the attached girls' bathroom, I had to appreciate the fact that at least I had marked my opponent and identified my areas of weakness: the girl with the updo had barely concealed a derisive giggle when she saw me wear the same sweatshirt I had worn all afternoon and evening to bed. Apparently I now had a major fashion faux pas to go along with my earlier social blunder.

I wiggled into my sleeping bag and, though I was exhausted, didn't expect I'd be able to sleep much, if at all. The chatter in the room continued long after Jennie had poked her head in to remind us in a singsong voice that we had a full day tomorrow and it was well past lights-out. Girls giggled in the darkness, moved from bed to bed without touching the floor, and ate cookies pilfered from the kitchen.

I couldn't make out any specific conversation as I lay there quiet and unnoticeable, but I did recognize the occasional name. I didn't know whether to be grateful or disappointed that my name was never mentioned—that I was a nonissue.

I had forgotten my watch at home, so I didn't know what time it was when I snuck carefully out of my bed. It had been quiet for a long time—long enough for me to imagine in great and glorious detail a far-fetched escape from this torturous weekend. Thomas was involved, and I was vindicated in front of Little Miss Updo. As I snapped back to reality when my feet touched the floor, I was a little sickened that I had allowed myself to indulge in such a childish delusion. "Grow up!" I mouthed, chastising myself.

Bags and belongings littered the floor, making it hard to navigate my way through the rows of beds. I almost tripped twice, but the sounds of thirty-odd girls in various stages of sleep muffled the scuff of my feet. If anyone heard or noticed my escape, they didn't let on.

I went to the bathroom because I didn't know where else to go. Standing in front of the mirror, I surveyed myself with a critical eye and found nothing overtly offensive or necessarily attractive in my features. I did have remarkable eyes—my one legacy from Janice— and they were a deep and golden green outlined with a thick ring of brown that was both exotic and kind of mysterious. I wondered if eye makeup would cause them to be more noticeable—I was sure that not many people made it past my nondescript features to admire my pretty eyes. But I certainly wasn't repulsive and was no more or less eye-catching than the most average girl at my school. Only a few stood out as either breathtaking beauties or sadly subpar in the looks department, and I was neither. I had always thought that it was a safe place to be.

And then it struck me. Maybe it wasn't about looks.

If that was true, it made matters painfully, infinitely worse. If it wasn't about looks, that could only mean they disliked me for me—for who I truly was. It meant that what was wrong with me was not something that could be fixed with a little mascara or a new haircut with highlights named after some trendy, earthy shade. Harvest-wheat blonde would not make me popular. It was a staggering realization.

Until now, I had always believed that any lack of popularity or heaps of friends was a direct result of my own inability to be bothered with the trappings of status. What if . . . *Oh, God, if You exist, don't let this be* . . . what if I was a charity case? an object of pity? someone parents encouraged their children to be nice to, but that the kids themselves could barely stand to be near, much less befriend? *Include that little DeSmit girl, honey; she has no parents, you know.* Well-meant sympathy I could handle. Abject pity was beyond tolerance.

It was as if I had looked into that flawed, inadequate bathroom mirror and pierced it with the sharp agony of my gaze. Lines veined across the surface like so many infinitesimal cobwebs, spider-silk fingers that raced to the far corners and sparkled in the light. They shone there for a moment—shimmering, silvered lines that divided my life into meaningless fragments—before crumbling into jagged wreckage at my feet. Although it was less a crumbling than an eruption—a shining wave of spectacular, glimmering beauty, terrible and breathtaking all at once. It was a dangerous collection of brokenness, and I wanted to wade through it and piece it back together, but I feared all those sharp corners. I didn't know who I was anymore, and I didn't know how to begin putting myself back together.

I needed air. Past the point of caring if anyone caught me or paid attention to where I was going, I crept back into the dormitory with less caution than I had left it and collected my coat and shoes. I slung on my coat in the hallway and stepped into my tennis shoes without bothering to tie the laces.

The central meeting room was dark and empty, and the glass wall facing the lake reflected the dying embers of the fire in dozens of different panes. It was warm and still, and had I been in any other mood, I would have found it the perfect place to curl up alone with a book. In my current state, it was oppressive and close. I couldn't leave fast enough, even though I had no idea where I was going. I tried the doors leading out to the lake, but they were locked tight.

Remembering that there was an exit through the kitchen, I started off in that direction but stopped with my hand on the door when I heard voices inside. The leaders were going over the fine details of tomorrow.

I nearly shouted in frustration.

Escaping to the narrow hallway behind the meeting room, I stood with my back pressed against the far wall and tried to pull myself together. I couldn't wander all night looking for a release from this dim prison—especially since I was beyond sure that they had locked and double-checked every door—but I couldn't stand the thought of returning to the crowded dormitory where all those girls lay contentedly dreaming of clothes and boys in the darkness. There was nowhere for me to go.

Had I been a different girl or maybe younger, I might have waited somewhere that the adults could find me when their informal meeting adjourned. They'd discover me wide-eyed and brimming with emotion, and with the enthusiasm of self-appointed saviors they would just *listen*. That was the textbook-approved method, right? Just listen. Except they could only listen for so long before the answer clearly presented itself, and as the proprietors of all that is wise and mature, they would find themselves compelled to pluck the tantalizing nugget of truth as if choosing a ripe apple and share their insight and perspective. Beautifully packaged. Easy to digest.

I wasn't interested.

My head was getting fuzzy and my legs tired when I heard footsteps at the far end of the hallway. I hadn't been standing there very long, but it was late and I was exhausted because every road seemed like a dead end. In spite of myself, I wished I had never left my cold bed. I shrank into the shadows along the wall and held my breath, hoping that whoever was at the other end of the corridor wouldn't notice me. If I could go undetected, I would hurry back to my bed, do whatever was necessary to survive the rest of the weekend, and deal with all of this later. My quick jaunt around the sleeping lodge had revealed that this was not the time or place for me to get dramatic.

But the footsteps had stopped.

"Who's there?" somebody whispered, and the sound seemed loud in the stillness.

I didn't answer.

The figures didn't move.

"You're not a youth leader or you would have said something," the voice came again. And they both started down the hallway toward me.

It wasn't like I could hide or run away, so stepping away from the wall, I said, "It's Julia DeSmit."

"Julia DeSmit," the voice repeated as a boy stepped close enough to scrutinize my face in the darkness.

"You're Thomas Walker's girlfriend, aren't you?" the second boy asked.

I stopped myself from saying I was and tried to be grateful that at least I wasn't the only one who had misunderstood Mr. Thomas Walker's intentions. I decided I could count it a blessing that they first associated me with Thomas instead of the tragedy of my father's death.

"Friend," I finally corrected because I didn't feel like explaining.

"Whatever," the guy responded. He was almost exactly my height, but he carried himself as if he were much, much taller; I felt like I was looking up to him even though our eyes were level. I recognized him as the new transfer. His California tan and longish hair stood out against the pale skin and short cuts of the guys I knew. He was new and enigmatic, and all the girls had been rendered half crazy because of him. His name was Jackson or Donovan or something equally cool and un-Midwesternish. I was shocked he was wasting even a second on me, but his gaze was calculating, and it was obvious he was trying to make a snap decision as he studied me in the shadows.

"Let's go, Jackson," his friend muttered, grabbing his coat sleeve and giving it a little tug. I vaguely recognized him. "We're going to get caught."

"Don't be stupid, Eric," the tall boy said, shrugging off the offending hand and continuing to watch me. "Looks like you're going somewhere," he stated, nodding at my coat, my shoes.

I tipped my head evasively, leaving him to interpret it as assent or otherwise. What was I supposed to say?

Whether he took pity on me or wanted to use me as the butt of some private joke, I'll never know. But his next words caught me so off guard I had no choice but to comply.

"We put a stone in the basement door so we could get out. Come on." He took off in the direction they had come and flicked his fingers at me to follow. At the intersecting hallway, he stopped and realized I hadn't moved. In the light from the glowing exit sign I watched him cock his head at me and make the motion again. *Come.*

I went.

The stone was so tiny that the door sealed almost completely, and I thought for a moment that their plan hadn't worked and we wouldn't be getting out after all. But the boy never paused, walking right through the doorway with utter confidence, then quickly ushering the two of us outside. Replacing the stone carefully, he shut the door slowly and took off at a light jog away from the sleeping lodge.

It was freezing. I balled my hands inside the sleeves of my coat and nuzzled my mouth and chin into the collar. But for all its biting iciness, the air was fresh and clean, and I drank in the feeling of it as it awakened every part of me. The bathroom mirror, the catty girls, and even Thomas seemed very far away as I followed these two strangers around the smaller, family-size cabins and through the thin woods surrounding Elim.

Our feet slipped on hard-packed, glazed snow as we wandered farther and farther away, and once when I almost fell, the boy snaked out a hand and grabbed my shoulder to steady me. I glanced up at him, but he had already looked away, and although I knew it was only instinct that made him stop my fall, I was grateful.

We didn't say a word until we had walked for at least five minutes and the only light was the half-moon reflected on the surface of the lake. I followed the boys down a small embankment to a fallen log near the edge of the frozen water.

The other boy, Eric, the one who had wanted to leave me in the hallway, sat down on the log and patted the space beside him as he looked at me.

I shook my head and instead walked to the beginning of the ice and took a few steps onto it. I could feel the solidness of it and knew that in some places a foot of ice separated me from the glacial water below. Knowing it didn't seem to make a difference though—my heart was beating wildly, as if the ice would crack at any moment. I took ten more steps.

I stood out there on the lake and listened to the sound of the ice shifting and fracturing—a dull, muted call, as if some fallen bird were trapped beneath the surface and crying plaintively to be released—and watched the Milky Way rip a shimmering gash in the black of a midwinter night sky. I stood out there just breathing in the cold and let the last pieces of who I thought I was slip from my shoulders and join the blend of ice and snow at my feet. I felt weightless there, alone in the night, and strangely new—like it was up to me to decide where I went from here.

But I wasn't alone, and before I was done walking over the water of the lake, Jackson called to me from the edge. "Don't fall in," he warned flatly.

I whipped around to look at him. I couldn't read his voice—whether he was mocking me or teasing me or concerned—but I felt like I owed him something for releasing me in the first place, so I walked carefully back over the ice to him.

"It's solid," I said as if I had to clarify that I wasn't suicidal. I doubted that lakes froze over in California.

"It's creepy," he responded. He turned away from me and placed his back between me and his friend on the fallen log. It was almost as if he was trying to pique my interest—he had called me back yet was now excluding me from whatever brought the two of them out here in the first place.

They fumbled for a few moments, and I watched because it seemed like that was what they wanted me to do. When he finally turned to face the lake and I could see past to the boy on the log, I almost giggled. Eric was holding a smoldering cigarette between his thumb and first finger, and his face flashed between smug self-satisfaction at his own rebellion and an almost childish uncertainty that bordered on fear—it was obvious he had no idea what to do with it.

For his part, Jackson looked as if he had been smoking for years. He turned his gaze from the lake and puffed a series of perfect smoke rings in my direction, then glanced at his friend as if encouraging him to do the same.

Eric put the cigarette to his mouth and managed to cough harder than I had the first time Brandon introduced smoking to me.

I couldn't help but laugh.

"Like you could do better," the tall boy murmured with a touch of aggression in his voice.

His friend was still coughing too much to respond.

"Try me." I couldn't keep the smirk out of my own voice. I knew it was an immature thing for me to do, but a rather large part of me that was still vulnerable enough to want to impress this handsome boy was excited at the prospect of being more than he had imagined. It was a stupid act of pretension, yet I was eager to do it; I smiled at him even as he glared with barely concealed hostility at me.

He fished in his pocket again and tossed me the pack of cigarettes and a cheap convenience-store lighter.

I caught them both in my cupped hands and fingered out a cigarette from the Camel box. I put it to my lips, brushed the safety on the lighter, and flicked a tall, orange flame into being. Puffing slowly, I lit the cigarette and threw back the pack and lighter. I took a big drag and blew it all out into a cloud that rested warm and heavy in the air between us before slowly fading to a misty, translucent fog.

It was like riding a bike—as familiar and common as if I had done it every day since the last I shared with Brandon. Part of me wanted to say his name, to invoke the older boy and sound mature, experienced. But I didn't say anything; I just took another puff and arched an eyebrow at the boys in front of me.

Eric glared at me, but the California boy was smiling. It was a bit of an unreadable smile—a one-corner half smile that was both approving and wary—but it was a smile all the same. "Julia DeSmit," he said again, as if cementing it in his mind.

It was like hearing my name for the very first time.

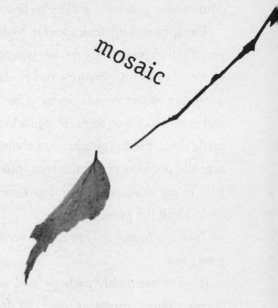

mosaic

I became a thing of mystery—inscrutable, vague, a well-kept secret. Of course, I was none of those things, but after Dad and Thomas—and, I suppose, the miasma that once was Janice—obscurity was a very beautiful thing.

Jackson and Eric played their parts well and created a confusion of tangled stories around me in the days and weeks that followed the doomed youth retreat. I never told them how I learned to smoke, and the half-truths and partially concealed revelations that I carefully doled out for the rest of the year only helped to fortify the allure of my elusive nature. I was the girl in the mask. Always more than imagined. Always deeper than could be probed. It didn't necessarily gain me friends, but it gained me something akin to a reluctant admiration, and I was willing to live with that.

The spring of my senior year in high school I had to take a college-prep English course. My teacher was ripe with creative ideas designed to exercise our imaginations and push us to the limits of our artistic capability. We wrote eulogies for ourselves, odes to inanimate objects, and poetry based on scents that prodded subconscious memories and made them rise to the surface. I thought it was a waste of time. I'm sure she pored over my material looking for hints of the enduring pain in my shadowed spirit, but I resolutely gave her little to work with. Until the proverb.

Take, my friend, only what you need, lest the world see the extent of your greed.

It was undeniably pathetic and I took no pride in it—in the cheesy rhyme, imperfect meter, or archaic language—but it spoke truth to me like little before ever had. My proverb was a given, a big duh when everyone else was trying to be profound.

Only Jackson's eyebrows rose when I stood in front of the class to read and expound on my maxim. Only he, who knew me better than anyone, would wonder at my choice of words when I was obviously the opposite of every conventional definition of greed.

I'm sure my decadent classmates and even the teacher were uncertain of the merit of my proverb because, in my generation at least, greed was presupposed—every person lumped into the same category: greedy, just on different ends of the spectrum. After I handed the teacher the three-by-five note card with my proverb printed in careful, bold letters across the lines, she scanned it, blinked, and read it again as if she had missed something. When she finally looked up at me, she forced a little smile, and I watched with increasing amusement while she did the mental gymnastics necessary to decide how best to handle the burdened, potentially unstable DeSmit girl.

In the end, pity won out and she said nothing, probably because she figured I was intentionally being shallow to protect myself from having to draw a lesson from my heartbreaking life. It was one time I was actually thankful for pity. It kept her from questioning me.

While a part of me wondered if she was right, wondered if I was inventing a theory that served only to soothe my own restless discomfort, I felt there was an entirely dissimilar level of greed that went regrettably unexplored even as we gorged ourselves on it. I didn't fight her, though, nor did I defend my sad little proverb when we presented and elaborated on the wisdom in our sage declarations to the rest of the class. They expected greed to be a wanton lust for the things of this world: the usual vices of cars and money and fame. And I let them believe that their perceptions were right so they could resent me for reminding them of things they'd rather forget.

But I knew that greed could have a very different face.

Pride can come *after* the fall. Martyrdom is a badge that can be worn with as much vanity as the most extravagant success.

I believed my own proverb, and I began to live my days carefully, with Spartan indulgences and self-denial, fearing that the world had already seen me take more than my share—stuffing myself with tears and sorrow that weighed me down and bulged from every pocket, gap, and crevice. Sorrow so big and consuming it begged to be noticed, begged for time and attention, sympathy and pity. I didn't want it anymore. I emptied myself of it. Left it behind when the mirror broke, when I had to reinvent myself one piece at a time. When I finally realized that it was me—not Dad or Thomas or even some impossible, far-flung God—who had to create a stronger, better Julia.

And in the newness of it, in the miracle of learning to create, I made sure to be a careful collector, picking up tiny pieces of life like hard pebbles and tucking them one at a time into the palm of my hand, where no one but me knew that I held them.

My life became a cautious mosaic, slowly taking the form of a shabby mixed media—shattered glass among cool, round stones and tentative, interrupted strokes of inoffensive color. I couldn't see myself as much as I could feel myself in the angles and corners and lines. I was well hidden. Unrecognizable.

I was unfamiliar even to Jackson, Eric, Grandma. It wasn't that I was afraid of getting hurt, of losing more than I had already lost. I wasn't trying to hold them at arm's length or be evasive. The truth was, I didn't know who I was, and I was afraid of being defined by who I wasn't. By what I didn't have. By all the tears that I had cried and the catalog of dates that told me who I could never be. By remembering with predictable, cyclic accuracy all I had lost.

I decided I could do better than that. I could handcraft the life, the person I wanted for myself. I could be my own artist, and I surrendered myself to the creation of a Julia who was too smart to attach, too independent to want to, and so secure as to be untouchable. I wasn't interested in allowing myself to wait a single second longer for something I was convinced I could walk up and take.

part 2

departure

I WOKE IN THE MORNING to the sun filtering softly through the windows and casting a mellow light across the shadows behind my eyes. I rolled over and pressed my cheek into the coolness of an untouched stretch of pillow and allowed myself a contented, sleep-drenched yawn. The room was warm and still, quiet except for the gentle sound of a muted snore coming from somewhere across the room.

It didn't register at first. The snore. But somewhere in the back of my mind it didn't make sense, and although I wanted to crawl back into that sweet, dream-filled, early morning sleep, something wasn't right.

And then she snorted loudly and shifted in her bed.

The shock was so overwhelming I ripped off the sheets and stumbled halfway to the door before I remembered where I was.

"Do you start every morning like this?" the girl mumbled, rolling over and pulling the blankets over her head.

"No—no, of course not," I stammered hesitantly. As I glanced around the box-filled room, the fog began to clear. I repeated her name in my mind to assure myself that I hadn't forgotten it. *Becca.* Not Becky. Not Rebecca. *Becca.* That's what she'd asked to be called, even though the letter I got halfway through the summer was signed Rebecca. Even though the placard on our door said Becky. "Becca," I said aloud, and I wasn't even aware that I had said it.

"Yeah?" came the muffled and slightly prickly reply.

"Nothing," I quickly said. "Go back to sleep. It's only six-thirty." Flustered, I crawled hurriedly back into my own bed and pulled the comforter up to my chin. I could tell by the even hum of her breathing that she had already fallen back asleep. Hardly daring to move lest I disturb her again, I lay in the tiny dorm-issue bed and let my gaze roam around the cluttered room.

Our two beds were pressed against opposite walls with our structurally uninspired desks crammed in between. The massive tables looked like a high school shop project gone wrong, and the wood used in constructing them had obviously been salvage since even the tops and sides of each individual table didn't match. But they were sturdy and currently home to towering stacks of boxes and books. Though the desk touching my bed was technically mine, the waxy fruit boxes proclaiming Washington apples were Becca's. I told her I didn't mind if she used my desk as storage for a day or two, since all my stuff was already carefully tucked away.

According to everything Becca had lugged along, I hadn't brought anywhere near enough junk. My small wardrobe and handful of personal effects didn't fill the closet at the foot of my bed nor take up much space on the shelf beneath the chest-high mirror bolted unattractively to the concrete block wall. I had tried to bring as little as possible—partly because I didn't have much I cared to show off and partly because I wanted to make the right impression and I didn't yet know what things or lack thereof would do that. I had hoped my frugal packing would, if nothing else, gain me an appreciative roommate. Instead, when Becca arrived a few hours after I had settled in to find my stuff already put away and me lounging on my neatly made bed with a novel, she looked at me as if I were from outer space.

"You're done?" she asked incredulously after we had introduced ourselves. I had tried to shake her hand, but her arms were full with a duffel bag and two hot pink pillows—one in the shape of lips and the other an overstuffed heart—and she didn't move to put them down.

"Yup," I said, attempting a light and cheerful manner.

She had a cute face and spiky, russet-colored hair that was too gorgeous to be anything but natural. She was easy to smile at, even though she was still surveying me a bit warily.

"The dorms have only been open for two hours!" Becca accused.

I just shrugged.

She didn't even see it; she had already turned to appraise the bare walls and the bland, khaki-colored duvet that covered my bed. There were no decorative pillows. "No posters?" she asked.

I shrugged again, this time wishing against all logic that there were a roll of fascinating posters—maybe blink-182 to prove I was cool or Che Guevara to make me seem edgy and avant-garde—hiding underneath the seat of my car. But, of course, there was no such secret stash, and my smile faded.

Becca wandered over to my desk and dropped her cargo on the floor in front of it. She picked up the mug that held my assortment of pristine, as-of-yet unused pens and pencils. The mug was the one impractical purchase I had included in my shopping, and it sported a sweeping panorama of the Rocky Mountains. It didn't even say where specifically the picture was taken, just those three words: *The Rocky Mountains*. The peaks were snowcapped and impossible in their height and immensity. I loved it because they took my breath away and because I could hardly believe that they were something more than an outrageous figment of someone's imagination. I had never seen the mountains in all their real-life glory before. They seemed just outside the realm of belief.

"These are the coastal Rockies," Becca commented absently. "The mountains around Spokane look very different."

I had forgotten that mountains were everyday for her—her hometown was right outside Spokane—but I didn't have a chance to respond before her dad and brother stumbled into the room buried beneath dangerously tilting loads of boxes.

I made my polite hellos, then got myself out of the way before I became a boring roommate *and* a nuisance. I hardly saw Becca for the rest of the day.

Listening to the sounds of her sleep, I decided that in spite of our somewhat cool introduction, she wouldn't be a bad roommate.

Not quite what I had in mind, but to be perfectly fair, I wasn't even sure myself of what I had had in mind. I had never had a roommate before. But Becca would be fine. A bit messy and a bit disappointed in me but certainly not as bad as some of the scenarios I'd envisioned. She neither emitted a peculiar odor nor packed a chain saw in one of those overstuffed boxes—not that I could tell, anyway. We would survive each other at the very least.

I didn't move until her alarm clock went off at seven-thirty. By then, the sounds of an awakening dorm had filtered underneath our door, and as footsteps ambled back and forth and pipes creaked and flowed in the distance, I wondered what my chances were of getting a hot shower. I hopped out of bed before she even had a chance to hit snooze on her alarm.

Becca moaned and glanced bleary-eyed at the clock and then at me. "How do you do that?" she muttered reproachfully.

"Do what?" I asked, gathering my clothes and tossing a towel over my shoulder.

"Jump out of bed like that. I've seen you do it twice now."

"I guess I'm a light sleeper," I said, although I had never thought of myself as such before.

By the time I got back from my shower, Becca was just throwing off the blankets. She still looked half asleep, and her hair was kinked out on one side of her head and flattened to the scalp on the other. She sat on the edge of the bed and stretched, moaning and yawning noisily.

"There's no hot water," I offered, pulling the turbaned towel from my head and running my fingers through my cold, damp hair.

Becca yawned so big I could hear her jaw crack. "I didn't expect there to be," she said. "My sister was in this building last year, and she said that there never is. Lesson one: sleep is more important than trying to catch a lukewarm shower." She stuck her finger in the air and looked pointedly at me. I was about to be mildly offended by the unsolicited advice, but she grinned at me and I realized she was parroting her sister. "Claire is so superior. Like I need her to tell me what to do. Do you have an obnoxious older sister too?"

"I'm afraid not," I said.

"Lucky you." Becca slid off the bed and went to stand in front of her closet. "I have two—and an older brother." She shot me a smile over her shoulder. "Nate is great, though. He once beat up one of my old boyfriends." She paused and then amended, "Well, he didn't exactly beat him up. . . . I think he punched him once. Or told him to leave me alone. Whatever. Nate is cool."

Becca was silent for a few moments as she rummaged through the hangers in her closet. I was trying to scrunch some life into my hair when she turned to me with two shirts held against her chest. "What do you think for orientation? Slinky tank top?" She jiggled one of the hangers, and the purple sequins on a lingerie-looking shirt sparkled in the light. Holding the other top forward, she added, "Or something more casual?"

I could tell by her voice that she wanted me to pick the pajama top over the white-and-pink-striped henley, but I couldn't do it. "I like that one," I confessed, pointing to the waffle-weave shirt. It was about five inches wide at the waist and intended to stretch and hug her every curve—it wasn't like she was giving up a single ounce of sex appeal with her more "casual" shirt.

She sighed anyway. "I knew you'd say that. It's exactly what my brother would say." I half expected her to ignore me, but she hung the club shirt back in her closet. "How 'bout you?" she asked after a minute of digging around for the perfect pair of jeans.

"I think I'll stick with what I'm wearing," I said, glancing at my V-necked T-shirt layered over a white tank.

"No, Julia, not your outfit. Do you have any brothers? anyone to tell you what to wear?"

I shook my head and watched her reflection in the mirror behind me.

"You don't?" It was more of a surprised declaration than a question. I didn't offer anything more—it didn't seem that she had left me room to—so she said, "You're an only child?" Another statement masquerading as a question.

Only days before, I had spent hours prepping myself for these sorts of questions and inquiries into my past. I thought I was more than ready to be light and fun and flippant—as if being the only child of one dead and one absent parent were the mark of all things sought after and fashionable. But Becca's surprise—and the turn that I knew the conversation would take—was crumbling all my careful intentions to dust.

I struggled to hold the easy smile on my face. "It's really nice," I said quickly. "No competition, no sharing my room or my clothes, no nagging . . ." I gave her what I hoped to be a friendly wink in the mirror before turning my attention back to my hair. I hoped the conversation was over.

"Must be nice," Becca said finally, and I nearly melted in relief. "Although I think I'd miss it too. Brothers and sisters, I mean. There's always someone to talk to."

I heard her pull the door open and I wished her a nice shower, even managing to put a bit of tease back into my voice. She just moaned and let the door fall shut with a loud bang.

When she was gone, I squared my shoulders and rehearsed the lines that I had practiced to ease the introduction of my unconventional family. I knew it would come up again. I knew that even as Becca struggled to hold herself under that ice-cold stream of water, she was wondering what my home life was like. Whether my parents were superinvolved and overprotective. Whether I was old beyond my years because I had always been around adults and never children. Whether I was rich and spoiled because there was no one else to share my parents' income and attention. And I also knew that she was wondering why mommy and daddy dearest hadn't been around to help move their baby into college. Why my possessions were sparse and my clothes plain. Why I was nothing like the only-child stereotype she had always held in her mind.

My dad died a few years ago, and my mom left when I was nine, I mouthed as I stroked mascara onto my eyelashes. That was way too blunt. She'd pity me before she ever got a chance to feel anything else for me. *My parents aren't very involved in my life.* That was too ambiguous. She'd wonder if they were druggies or in jail and if I was here on a full-ride scholarship because I was some sort of hard-luck prodigy. I wished I could just say nothing.

As it turned out, I could. She didn't ask any more questions on her return, and I certainly didn't offer.

Becca and I went to freshman orientation together even though she had already made friends on our floor. I had anticipated being left alone as she went with them, and when she chose to go with me instead, I didn't fool myself into thinking it was because she liked me better. She had simply taken a long time getting ready, and I was the only one who would wait for her.

We sat together near the back and quickly lost interest as the dean of students droned on about the responsibility that came with the independence of this new life outside our parents' walls. He was stuffy and pretentious and used words that I doubted even he knew the meaning of. It was obvious he cared little for us and lots for the image of his reputable school.

"I wonder if he gives the same speech every year," Becca whispered, leaning into me.

"He certainly knows it well enough," I said. "I think he's on autopilot."

She suppressed a giggle, although I hadn't found my comment all that funny.

We tried to listen for a few more minutes before she tilted her head toward mine and said, "My dad thinks he's a jerk. When we flew out here to visit he was sucking up to my dad so bad—they wanted me to play basketball." I raised my eyebrows at her, so she added, "I told them I wanted to focus on my studies."

We both laughed. After knowing her for just over a day, even I could find the humor in that.

Brighton was a rather prestigious private school, and although Grandma had wanted me to go to Glendale and be closer to home, she was very proud that I had been accepted and especially that I was the recipient of a none-too-modest scholarship. No one had flattered or sweet-talked Grandma or me in an attempt to get me to come, but I couldn't help feeling a bit pleased to be here at all.

In a completely uncharacteristic move, I looked knowingly at Becca and said, "I totally know what you mean. They can be so pushy."

It was obvious she hadn't expected that from me because her eyes widened just a bit. "Really? What sport do you play?"

"I don't play sports," I quickly answered, afraid of starting some awkward rumor. Something told me that Becca would be a good person to spread just such a juicy misconception. "I'm here on an academic scholarship." It wasn't a lie per se, but it sounded a little more glamorous than it actually was because I had left out the addendum—the part of the story that explained how I probably only got the scholarship because I was one of the few girls to apply for it in the engineering college. It didn't take amazing powers of deduction to figure that equal opportunity had played at least a part in my substantial scholarship. But Becca didn't need to know that.

"What's your major?" she asked, her voice tinged with curiosity.

"Engineering," I said a little smugly, holding my breath because I wondered if she would be impressed or if such a confession would cement me as the dull, egghead roommate.

"Cool," she responded immediately, and I could tell she was neither very impressed nor turned off. "I'm undeclared. It makes my parents so nervous!" There was barely concealed glee in her voice, and I decided to try a friendly move, bumping my knee into hers. She smiled, and we diverted our attention back to the speaker.

He was going over curfews. A few soft groans went up from the eight hundred or so students collected in Price Auditorium. The dean just kept right on going. He didn't even seem to notice or mind that people were chatting or napping or barely paying attention to him. It was like watching those poor flight attendants on the one and only flight I'd taken in my life to Florida. They stood in the aisles and diligently went over each and every emergency procedure, even though I seemed to be the only person who listened to a single word they were saying. Apparently, as long as they repeated the right words, they could wash their hands of any culpability in the case of a true emergency. The dean was doing the same thing: washing his hands of us.

I had tuned him out and was trying to discreetly study my diverse classmates when Becca spoke again. "Your parents must be so proud."

It was the comment I had been waiting for, but it still caught me off guard. I didn't say anything for a moment; then, deciding to plunge in and get it over with, I whispered, "My dad died a few years ago."

Becca gasped. She actually gasped. "Oh, my word, Julia! I'm so sorry! I had no idea!"

She was talking too loudly, but I didn't dare shush her. By the sympathetic slant of her eyes I knew she felt compelled to say more, and since I was already cringing from the attention, I quickly hopped in. "It's okay. I'm okay with it now. It was a long time ago."

Becca looked skeptical, but the pained concern in her face had eased just a bit. "What about your mom?" she asked. "It must be hard for her to have you so far away."

"I'm not that far from home," I reminded her. "It's only a two-hour drive." And then, although I hadn't planned it and although

I regretted it even as my mouth formed the words—I could have just left things as they were, vague and uncertain and safe—I said, "Besides, her job keeps her really busy. She's a chef."

The lie slipped off my tongue as easily as if I had practiced it beforehand. I hadn't. I didn't even know where it had come from or why I had made Janice into a chef of all bizarre things. I had always sort of envisioned her working as a waitress beside that friend who took up her every spare minute on the telephone in those days before she left. But the waitress I imagined her to be was trashy, and I could never admit to anyone that that was the picture I carried of her. Maybe my mind had rushed away from that make-believe woman in the too-tight dress with a plunging neckline in a greasy diner to the closest respectable occupation.

But a chef? And how could I undo it now? How could I take it back? How could I say, *No, sorry, that was a lie. My mom actually left when I was a little girl, and I don't know where she is or what she does.* What had been done could not be undone.

Of course, Becca was hooked. "A chef? You mean, like a cordon bleu? Or a cook at a family restaurant?" Her voice took on a different quality with the latter option. She probably thought I was trying to inflate my mother's vocation.

"A chef," I answered defensively without thinking, even though I was defending nothing more than a pathetic mirage. I quickly threw in, "And a sommelier." I had read the word somewhere and hoped I was pronouncing it right.

"That has to do with wine, right?" Becca asked, now completely engrossed.

As my heart sank deeper into the pit of my stomach, I tried to be thankful that at least she wasn't looking at me with those weepy-sad eyes anymore.

"My parents belong to a wine club," she continued. "They would just *love* to meet your mom!"

I nodded and tried to turn back to the orientation. But Becca was taut beside me, and I could almost hear the cogs revolving in her mind. After a minute, she cleared her throat quietly, and I waited for her next question with silent dread. She must have been wondering what a chef and sommelier was doing in itty-bitty Mason, Iowa.

"Does your mom have her own restaurant?" she finally inquired casually.

I must have been subconsciously preparing the lie because nonchalantly, without even bothering to look at her, I said, "She works at a five-star restaurant in Minneapolis. I doubt you'd have heard of it." Burying myself even deeper, I went on, "I lived with my grandmother during the school year because Mom liked the high school in Mason better. She figured I'd get more attention. A better education."

"Ohhh . . . ," Becca breathed. I guessed she was trying to absorb it all and, more accurately, trying to figure out which question she could ask next without sounding too nosy. "What about—?"

"It's complicated," I broke in, cutting her off. I didn't want to be rude, but more than that I didn't want to answer any more questions about my imaginary mother. I went numb just thinking about it. Classes hadn't even started. I hadn't made any new friends. I had just—*just*—begun the life that I had worked so hard to reinvent, and already it was careening so far off course that I wanted to jump ship and start over. Was it too late to enroll in another college?

Thankfully, for the remainder of the day, Becca didn't question me any further about my chef mother, so I didn't have to be curt or provide any more details about my personal life. I had definitely piqued her interest, although not in the way that I had hoped to when I first saw her walk into our shared dorm room. I stumbled through my day half distracted as I tried to remember exactly what I had and hadn't said.

When we split into smaller groups for brief campus tours and introductions to some of our professors and counselors, I played the part of the good girl and went along, even though Becca—and lots of other people—were skipping out to go grab coffee at the nearest Starbucks.

I had thinking to do. I had to live as though my lie were reality. I couldn't backtrack—I could only maintain the pretense of the person she thought I was. It was a mask I hadn't planned on wearing.

I called Grandma as soon as I got back to my dorm room.

When I left home for Brighton, I told Grandma she wouldn't hear from me for a couple of days. We were standing in the driveway in front of my packed, gassed-up, and already-running car. I was leaning against the passenger door, and the morning sun was in my eyes. She stood facing me, and partly because I was blinded in the bright light and partly because she was holding her emotions so very tightly, I couldn't read her expression.

She didn't beg me to call her first thing when I arrived, and she even said, "Okay, that's fine" without a trace of worry or self-pity.

"No news is good news, right?" Then she smiled, and I almost couldn't tell that it was forged sincerity.

"Right," I affirmed, equally as genuine. "I'll call as soon as I can. I just don't want to get caught up in all the busyness and not have a chance to call you earlier if you're expecting it." I was making excuses even though she didn't want or need any. "I don't want you to worry," I added after a moment.

"I'll worry anyway," she murmured.

When we hugged I could feel the tears in her shoulders, but her eyes were clear and her voice steady.

It was my plan to be brave and independent, but the night before classes started—when my notebooks were bought and my backpack ready for the morning, and when the lie that hung between me and Becca threatened to ruin everything that I had worked so hard for—I hauled out my prepaid calling card and, after entering seemingly endless codes, dialed the number that my fingers knew by heart.

Grandma answered on the very first ring. "Hello?" she said expectantly.

"Hi, Grandma, it's me."

There was a little exhale on the other end of the phone line, and it communicated the relief she felt at hearing my voice. *I love you* and *I miss you* and *I pray for you every day* all flooded their way through the line, and I found myself wishing I could say something half as eloquent as her expressive sigh.

In the end, I didn't say anything more, and she jumped in. "How are you doing, honey?"

I started to say, "Fine," but she kept right on going.

"Do you like your roommate? Are classes hard? When are you coming home?"

I laughed and after a moment she did too.

"Sorry," she said. "I promised myself I wouldn't be so overbearing."

"You're not," I assured her, somewhat guiltily loving the fact that she missed me so much.

We were silent for a minute, each waiting for the other to speak. We both started at the same time. And stopped. Silence.

"What—?"

"How—?"

"Go ahead," I said quickly.

"No, you first," she responded.

Because I didn't want to do this all night, I started to talk. I cheerfully told her about Becca and our tiny room, orientation, and my overloaded schedule. It was nice to just talk and to hear the familiar little noises of her surprise, approval, and concern. But it was also somewhat empty. I was telling her all the *whats* of my life without any of the *whys* or *hows*.

It reminded me of the travel journal my dad kept when we went on an elaborate vacation for my twelfth birthday. I teased him about it relentlessly because it seemed so pointless to me—it was nothing more than a list of dates and places. *December 10: Epcot Center. Ate in Mexico on the Plaza of Nations. Watched the fireworks.* There was no feeling, no reaction to what we had seen or anecdotes to reveal telling little snippets of our time in Orlando. Dad told me all of that stuff was forever locked in his memory—the journal was just a way of jogging it.

I was giving Grandma the travel-journal version of my life, and she had no point of reference to flesh it out and give it life. She didn't have the memories to go along with my narration, and she had no idea how I felt about any of the particulars that I was so dutifully recounting. It was a lonely feeling.

I thought about telling her more, about letting her in on some of the confusion and doubt so I didn't have to carry it all myself, but I didn't know how. So I kept listing the facts. If she found our conversation shallow, she didn't say.

Just before we hung up, she asked the expected questions about money, my health, and whether or not the food in the cafeteria was edible and at least marginally nutritious. And then, with the slightest deepening of her voice, she asked, "How are you *really* doing?"

If she noticed my slim pause, she didn't press me, and when I answered her with a considerably too bright "Fine," she let it go at that.

"I love you, Grandma," I said. "Maybe I'll come home next weekend."

"Oh, that would be so nice!" she gushed, then quickly tacked on, "But you do whatever you want to do."

I couldn't help smiling. "Okay."

"Anyway, I love you, too. Be careful, have fun, and—oh yeah, I almost forgot! Would you be open to a visitor this Saturday?"

I didn't really like the idea of her driving the entire four-hour round trip alone, but on Saturday mornings she baked the cinnamon rolls that she had made from scratch on Friday night, and as much as I knew I should say no, the thought of a warm hug and a fresh-baked cinnamon roll were just too tempting to pass up.

"I'd love company," I said sincerely.

"Good. We'll talk to you soon."

"Yup."

"I'll be praying for your first classes tomorrow!" she said cheerfully, slipping in the reminder because it was a part of her language.

I didn't really know how to respond to that. The thought of what was to come momentarily dwarfed any misgivings I had about Becca and my embellished mother. Although I clung to the phone as if it were a lifeline, I couldn't say a word.

When Grandma finally broke the silence and said a gentle good-bye, I mumbled something back, then held the receiver pressed to my face until I heard the dial tone.

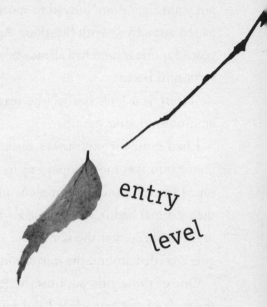

entry
level

THE LECTURE HALL was already packed by the time I squeezed my way through the crowds in the halls. The building where I'd just finished my first psychology class was across campus from the sprawling science building that housed the engineering college, and I had sprinted the last eighth of a mile. I had already had two classes, and they had both been part of my liberal arts requirements.

Becca and I had the same block of Philosophy 101 and had walked to class together this morning at quarter to eight. Following another of her sister's tenets—even though she vehemently attacked Claire for every bit of shared wisdom—Becca rolled out of bed ten minutes before we left and did little more than throw a sweatshirt over the tank top she slept in and brush her teeth. She didn't even bother to put jeans on, opting instead to sport her pastel-plaid pajama pants paired attractively with flip-flops. Apparently the girl who got gorgeous for orientation had already been replaced by a more authentic version of Becca.

"Don't you look spiffy," she teased when I returned from the bathroom to wake her up.

I had gone for my shower early, deciding that making a good impression was more important to me than appearing like a seasoned veteran. And I wasn't alone in my intent. Getting up earlier than normal hadn't secured me a warm shower, but it did put me in the bathroom at the same time as a happy, chattering group of girls crowded around the mirrors and giggling.

One of those girls was finished getting ready and offered to curl the ends of my hair while I did my makeup. It was a completely foreign and intensely girlish gesture, but I said that I would really appreciate it because I didn't want a refusal of her offer to come off like a refusal of her. So I stood stiffly, feeling oddly naked, and listened to her prattle on about a messy breakup with her boyfriend back in Ohio while she worked magic on my hair. The result was, I made a kind of friend and I looked prettier than I probably ever had in all my eighteen years. It made me feel a little taller than I was, like the earth was slightly farther below than it had been before. It was a heady feeling.

Walking to class with Becca diminished everything a bit—partly because I got the strange feeling that she resented my new pink sweater and my softly curled hair, and partly because I felt conspicuous beside someone who was so comfortable in her own skin that she was willing to roll out of bed and half stumble to her very first college class. I wondered if her obvious self-confidence made my insecurities glaringly transparent: the shy, little, unattractive me shining blindingly through the first-day-of-class veneer.

By the time we chose our spots in the two-hundred-seat lecture hall, I had seen enough to realize that no one had the time to notice me. Becca, in her sleep-attired glory, got the occasional laugh and thumbs-up as we made our way to H-117, but I fell uninterestingly into the wallflower category on a campus that was full of Bohemian princesses, ink-stained goths, and trendy piercings in places that made me cringe. When an honest-to-goodness cowboy walked by—cowboy boots, Stetson, and even the infamous Wranglers—I relaxed enough to enjoy the walk and even allowed a secret smile to cross my face as I let anticipation run up and down my spine.

It didn't take long for the excitement to wear off.

The philosophy professor was a diminutive man with a voice to match. Even from the middle of the auditorium, I had to strain to hear his voice as he trailed off, left sentences hanging, and spoke mostly to himself behind half-closed eyes. He asked us impossible questions like, "What is real?" and "What is existence?" which he didn't expect us to answer and didn't answer for us. By the time he started in on Plato's allegory of the cave, I was so far beyond lost I had stopped trying to take notes.

As I glanced back over the five pages of barely decipherable nonsense I had scribbled, Becca leaned over to whisper, "He's just introducing the syllabus. You don't have to take notes."

Psychology was marginally better. Becca had a different class, and losing her beside me made the air slightly more breathable. Without her unwelcome insights and patronizing vibe I felt more like me, but the class itself was heavy and oppressive and no less depressing than philosophy had been. The registrar had informed me that I needed to have one psych class to meet all the necessary requirements for graduation. Since it didn't matter what kind of psychology and since the majority of my classes were locked in because I needed them for my program, I got stuck with the only available class that fit into my schedule: abnormal psychology. Not only was the class morbid—sexual predators had their very own section on the syllabus—it was also filled with upperclassmen who obviously knew each other and even knew the prof. Two girls actually had a conversation over my lap as we waited for the class to begin.

After a long morning of watching my expectations turn to disappointments, I approached the engineering college with more than a little trepidation. "Regular" college courses had proven themselves to be more than a mouthful, and now I was entering territory that was little more than a naive ambition to me.

Grandma had asked me before I left, "Why engineering?" Although I had given her some pat, planned answer, I had thought to myself, *Because it's as far away from me as I can get.*

It wasn't that I didn't have the grades. I did. It wasn't that I didn't have a love for math and science. I had that, too. But to say that I had some deep-seated, all-compelling desire to be an engineer would be a blatant lie. I didn't want to be an engineer any more than I wanted to be a nurse or a teacher or a gas station attendant. I had no idea what I wanted to be. But to pick something and stick with it—particularly something high and unattainable and admirable—that gave me purpose and direction. It gave me a sense of destination. I had no intention of failing. But I hadn't planned on college being another world.

And if college itself was another world, the famous college of engineering at Brighton was a separate universe.

The science building was intimidating enough—three stories of glass-fronted gray brick with greenhouses and enormous labs and corridors ripe with unidentifiable scents of earth and chemicals. As I climbed the steps to the second floor and followed the signs to the engineering department in the far-west cluster, I wished I could tuck into one of the brightly lit chemistry labs and hide, taking everything in tiny swallows instead of all at once. My course list said I had statics in room 224, and I had only a faint concept of what statics even was.

Even more daunting was the fact that the dense crowds of students were thinning out and changing. There was less diversity of dress and demeanor. There was less teasing and laughter. There were fewer girls and those that I did see did not have their hair so prettily curled as mine. Everyone seemed to know where they were going, and they looked at me as if I could be nothing but obviously lost.

That's probably why when I finally arrived, still mildly breathless and undeniably exhausted, the lecture hall was almost full. I paused in the doorway, feeling discouraged and exposed. I checked my watch. Class wasn't supposed to start for another seven minutes. What was everyone doing here already?

"You here for statics?"

I glanced to my left, trying to locate the source of the query.

"You in the pink, are you looking for statics?"

He was sitting in the last row of chairs, a short row with only four seats because the platform for the slide projector jutted out beside it. He was handsome in a sort of severe way—his eyes were a penetrating blue and his features chiseled—and looked to be in his midtwenties. I couldn't tell from the curl of his lip if he was smiling or sneering at me, but it was obvious he was on the verge of thinking I was deaf and dumb.

"Yes," I said quickly, meeting his gaze. "I'm here for statics."

He looked a little surprised but managed an almost-genuine smile as he slid out of his chair and moved over one. "You'd better take a seat. There aren't many left."

"Thanks," I said slowly, descending two steps into the theater and depositing my stuff beside him.

He was silent for a few moments as I unzipped pockets on my bag and extracted mechanical pencils, yellow engineering graph paper, and a graphing calculator big enough to take up more than its share of space on my already overstuffed desktop. I could feel him watching me.

Finally, when all was out and arranged in front of me, he said, "You don't really need all that today." There was amusement in his voice. "We're just going over the syllabus."

On any other day I wouldn't have minded being the object of his entertainment, but not today. I bristled. "I like being prepared," I said icily.

He caught my tone and immediately tried to smooth my ruffled feathers. "Hey, look, I'm not trying to tease you. I just thought I'd let you know."

"A little late," I shot back, disgusted that he had saved his comments until after my bag was unpacked.

"Yeah," he said with a wry laugh. "I'm a bit of a jerk that way."

Because it was the last thing I expected him to say, I stole a look at him out of the corner of my eye.

He was smiling at me, and when he caught my gaze, he extended his hand. "I'm Patrick, but everyone calls me Parker. Sorry I held my advice until it was no longer needed."

I waited a second, then gave him my hand. He squeezed mine and let go. "Is Parker your last name?" I asked.

"No, it's the name of the town where I'm from." He shook his head. "It's not even a speck on a map. When I was a freshman everyone kept asking where I was from. . . . I guess I was saying Parker so much some people thought it was my name. What can I say? It stuck." We were silent for a moment, and then he tapped the corner of my desk with his fingertips. "You didn't tell me your name."

"Julia DeSmit," I said. "But I'd prefer it if you didn't call me DeSmit."

"I wouldn't dream of it," he commented, and though his face was solemn, there was a twinkle in his eye.

A bit confused, I turned from him and tried to take stock of my fellow classmates. The room, which held just over a hundred people at my estimation, was nearly packed. The students were mostly guys, and although I hated to stereotype, knowing that I had been the object of many misplaced labels myself, I had to admit they made up a bit of a different demographic than the other two classes I had just come from.

"Pretty geeky, eh?"

I jumped, startled that my thoughts were so transparent. "Uh . . ." I couldn't think of a single intelligent way to respond.

"Don't worry. We all know it," Parker said glibly. "Geekdom is a small price to pay for the letters that we'll get to put behind our names." He shrugged. "Brilliance has its price."

I forced a little laugh because I didn't know if he was joking or serious, but I felt I had to respond somehow. "Is that a prerequisite?" I asked. "Must one be oblivious to the rest of the world to be an engineer? Sounds pretty ridiculous to me."

Parker sighed. "Julia, Julia. There's so much you have to learn. . . ."

I didn't like his condescending tone. Scanning the room, I tried to locate the professor. Shouldn't class be starting by now? I had hoped to make new friends in college, but between Becca, who seemed uninterested in pursuing a friendship with me, and Parker, who was completely incomprehensible and even a little weird, I hadn't come across many viable options. I didn't even remember the name of the girl who had so generously curled my hair.

Apparently Parker wasn't picking up on my cues because he was talking again. "You don't really fit into this crowd, do you, Julia?"

Whether he was trying to flirt with me or provoke me, I couldn't tell. But I also couldn't sit beside him for the remainder of a one-hour lecture and be rude, so although I wanted to ignore him, I said, "What do you mean?"

Taking my response as interest, Parker leaned forward and put his elbow on my desk, resting his chin on his fist so that our heads were side by side. Six inches was too close for my comfort, and I tried to scoot away imperceptibly. "Look around you," he said, pointing his finger around the room. "How many women do you see?"

I counted a few heads with long hair but lost count when one of the girls turned her head and revealed that she was a he. Likewise, a guy with a crew cut turned out to be female. Or male. I couldn't quite tell.

"Two dozen?" I finally answered.

"A little more than that," Parker acknowledged. "Statistically speaking, women in the field of engineering are steadily gaining ground, but Brighton is one of those prehistoric little pockets where men still dominate this sphere." He again directed my attention to the people below us. "Now, tell me how many of those lovely ladies are . . . well . . . *lovely*."

"What?" I sputtered, totally thrown off guard. "What are you talking about?"

Parker looked straight at me. "We're adults. We can say it like it is." He paused, and for the first time since we met, I believed that what he was about to say was, at the very least, his version of the truth. "People looked at you weird as you walked into this room because A, you're a girl and B, you're attractive."

It was a word that I wasn't sure had ever been used to describe me before. I blushed so red my ears felt like they were on fire. The fact that I knew Parker meant what he said only deepened my embarrassment.

He was still looking at me, and his face had taken on a serious expression, eyes and all. "Can I give you a little advice, Julia?"

"Sure," I said quietly.

"Next class, don't wear pink." He sat back in his chair and

regarded me with his arms crossed. Cocking his head, he nodded at the curls that had fallen over my shoulder. "Don't curl your hair," he said matter-of-factly.

My mind flashed to Becca and her tousled bed head and wrinkled clothes. Maybe I should have followed her lead.

"If you want to be taken seriously," Parker continued, "you have to act the part. Your life is now engineering: Newtonian physics, linear dynamics, calculus, statics—" he gestured around the room—"and mind-numbing discussion hours. You don't have time for makeup or curling irons. I doubt you'll have time to depress the pump on your perfume bottle."

I shrank, hoping he couldn't smell the Clinique Happy that I had generously spritzed on only hours before.

"Don't look so sad." He patted my arm. "You want this, remember? You want to be an engineer."

I tried to smile but it was less than sincere.

Ignoring my obvious lack of enthusiasm, he pressed me more. "What type of engineering do you plan to study? Biomedical? Chemical? Industrial, mechanical, or electrical?"

"I'm thinking biomedical," I managed, though my voice was small.

"Good choice," he affirmed. "Brighton partners with the state university medical school and hospital. You'll be set."

I was grateful when someone brushed past me, and I looked up to see a man who could only be the professor making his way to the podium on the floor of the hall. It meant the beginning of my formal education as an engineering student, but it also meant that Parker would finally have to leave me alone. For someone who asserted that he could "say it like it is," I found Parker to be the most perplexing person I had ever met. He seemed to have struck up some sort of friendship with me, yet I still didn't know if he liked me or regarded me as a bit of a joke. Was he laughing at me or advising me because he wanted to see me succeed? I didn't know how to take him.

Apparently the entrance of our professor wasn't enough to deter Parker's running narrative. "Newbin is brilliant but arrogant," he whispered, motioning to the gaunt, graying man who was almost angrily pulling stacks of papers from a box that he had carried in with him. "He's a chemical guy, but they all take turns teaching the undergrad courses. Newbin just resents it more than most. Don't get on his bad side."

I was past nodding or even acknowledging that he was talking to me.

"Are you smart?" Parker asked.

"What?" I gasped, shocked that his bluntness seemed to have no end.

"I said, are you smart? If you're not, Newbin will know it by tomorrow. He can sniff those things out from a mile away—and he doesn't even have to see your work to make that judgment call."

I tried to gather myself. "I got a scholarship," I finally offered as if it was proof of my intelligence.

"Four thousand dollars every year for the next four years?" Parker asked.

I nodded in disbelief. "How do you know my package?"

"Oh, it's standard. Half the people here got that scholarship. We've got a well-funded program."

I was so dazed I didn't even attempt to respond. When Newbin started talking, my mind was too frozen to hear much of what he was saying.

I was ready to at least try to collect myself and focus when Parker leaned over one last time and, hiding his mouth with the back of his hand, whispered, "I hope I didn't scare you with all the nuts and bolts of engineering. You'll be fine. You have friends in high places." He winked at me.

I looked at him blankly.

"I'm the TA," he said with a smile. "You know, teacher's assistant? You're just lucky I saw you before you start looking the part."

I couldn't decide if I should consider myself fortunate or if I had just made the most problematic connection of my college career.

time and again

THE REST OF THE WEEK was dismal by anyone's standards.

I took Parker's advice, not because I trusted him, but because after studying my peers in the engineering college, it seemed he was telling me the truth on that score at least. No makeup, boring ponytails, and frumpy clothes made my morning routine much simpler, but it made me feel invisible at best and downright ugly at worst. I sat in my liberal arts classes half slouched in my seat. The girls who had majors like education, business, or communications looked nothing like me. They didn't have to stop caring in order to be taken seriously in their fields. And they were the ones the guys brushed past me to notice. They had dates by Friday night.

I told myself that I wasn't jealous. That I had always been—and would always be—just plain *Julia* and that looks and boys were about as important to me as watching grass grow. But things were different here, and although I didn't want to be someone I was not, I did want to be someone I had never been before: intelligent and self-possessed and anything but *un*attractive, *un*desirable, *un*stable.

Even Becca, who maintained the sloppy-cute, I-don't-care-look that she had assumed for the first day of class, informed me that she was going out with some guy named Chet. Apparently, pajama bottoms and sleep-flattened hair aside, she was still attractive, desirable, stable.

"I'm *so* not into him, but Kara likes his roommate, so I said I'd be a pal and double just this once." Her eyes glowed even as she tried to appear blasé and uninterested.

It wasn't just the crummy image that I had to maintain in order to gain credibility in my chosen discipline. Classes were so indecipherable it was as if the professors were speaking in a foreign language. Homework was a steadily growing and seemingly unattainable mountain. And what baffled me more than anything was that Parker hovered between being a thorn in my side and my very best friend. Though I struggled to make sense of exactly which slot he filled in my confusing life, he simply defied explanation.

As Newbin's TA, Parker led our statics discussion group on Tuesdays and Thursdays. I was hopelessly lost and felt I had absolutely nothing to offer or add to the dialogue, but whenever a pause presented itself, eight times out of ten Parker would turn to me. Sometimes he would let me fumble and flounder before turning away almost in disgust, as if he had expected more from me and I had embarrassed him and let him down. Other times he would guide my comments and finish my thoughts so I seemed intuitive, exceptionally perceptive, and bright—capable of seeing things my classmates didn't, though that couldn't have been further from the truth.

I wanted to drop out.

Or at least change my major and get myself out of that suffocating cluster of classrooms where competition, derision, and even fear lurked so close beneath the surface that my heart beat faster with every step that brought me nearer to my next engineering class. But it had been only one week. *One week*, I reminded myself over and over even as I avoided meals because my stomach was too upset to find food appealing. *One week*, I whispered as I stared blankly at page 23 of a textbook that had cost me more than all the books for my liberal arts classes combined. "One week," I kept repeating out loud because it could only get better after this. Things could only go up because I couldn't fathom what it would look like for them to go down from here.

Parker must have read my mind. It was an uncanny ability that he had picked up by midweek. As we waited for the class to begin on Friday, he pressed his shoulder against mine and said, "Hey, the first week is tough for everyone."

I was sitting next to him because I couldn't make it to class any faster to allow myself to choose another seat. I had already decided to ask Grandma for a bike for Christmas.

"Yeah," I responded absently, wishing he would simply leave me alone.

"Everyone thinks of dropping out," Parker persisted.

"What makes you think I want to drop out?" I asked, trying to spice my tired voice with a little indignation.

He didn't say anything, and against my will I looked at him out of the corner of my eye. He was raising his eyebrows at me as if to say, *Please. Don't even try to fake it.*

He was right and we both knew it. I couldn't defend myself, so I cooperated and asked, "So it gets better?" because that was what he wanted me to say.

"No," he replied thoughtfully. "It gets much worse. But you get better at it."

I tried to take at least a little solace in that.

Parker left me alone for a minute, and I thought about asking him to lay off a bit in discussion group. Even though I sat beside him during lectures, I wasn't afraid of my classmates thinking he had found a pet—he was regularly way too nasty to me to make that suspicion seem warranted—but I disliked the attention anyway and hated the way he played me. In the end, I didn't say a word. Mostly because I was a big chicken, and I was afraid a heartfelt plea could have the opposite effect and make everything much, much worse.

When class was over and my mind was full and dizzy, Parker pushed almost rudely past me and started to leave. Turning back quickly, he nodded toward the statics book I was cramming into my bag and offered, "If the homework questions give you too much trouble this weekend, e-mail me."

His e-mail address was public knowledge, and the entire class had been given the opportunity to do exactly what Parker had just invited me to do, but the fact that he singled me out made me feel a bit unnerved. I still couldn't discern if he liked me or if he had it in for me.

"Thanks," I finally said, not meeting his gaze. "I think I'll be fine." When I looked up again he was gone.

I practically stumbled back from class, numb and thankful that for two whole days I didn't have to set foot in a single lecture hall. Although the bag on my back was heavy with obligations to meet and requirements to fulfill, it actually felt lighter when I mounted the steps of my dorm hall because in less than twenty-four hours I would get to taste something familiar and sweet. Grandma was coming to visit.

I had told Becca that my grandma was coming, and she seemed mildly excited to meet the woman who was my sort-of mother. Although we hadn't further discussed my cordon bleu mom at her swanky five-star restaurant in Minneapolis, I did remember to nonchalantly warn Becca not to mention my mother to my grandmother.

"They have a bit of a strained relationship," I explained, trying to give her a consequential look. "I want to have a nice visit with my grandma. It would be best if we didn't mention Janice." Oh no. Now she knew my mother's name.

But Becca didn't seem to register what I was saying. She was picking out an outfit for her not-really-a-date with Chet. "Sure," she murmured noncommittally, holding a pair of dangly earrings against a silvery white blouse.

So I had nothing to worry about. Friday night would be relaxing and quiet with Becca gone; I could get a head start on my homework. Saturday would bring Grandma and some semblance of normalcy and peace, and I didn't even have to be concerned about Becca exposing my stupid lie. Maybe Parker was right. Maybe I was already getting better at this.

I struggled my way through two of the five assigned questions for statics on Friday night. I had used up four sheets of graph paper already, and while I was slightly concerned because Newbin had informed us we would probably fill only four or five sheets in total, I was hesitantly confident that I was at least on the right track. It was a good thing, though, that both philosophy and psychology were only reading assignments and that I didn't have calculus or chemistry until Tuesday—I would need a good portion of the remainder of the weekend to complete my statics homework.

My sleep was the sleep of the exhausted hopeful, and it stretched uninterrupted—save for a brief, half-conscious hello for Becca at close to 2 a.m.—from just after midnight until ten o'clock Saturday morning. I hadn't planned on sleeping so long, but my body must have needed the rest because my alarm clock, which was set for eight, was unplugged and I didn't even remember doing it.

The bathroom was empty, and I crossed my fingers when I stepped into the shower, only to be met with an almost blistering stream of water. I nearly yelled from shock and joy. I took a shower so hot and long that my skin was red and shiny by the time I stepped out to towel off. I finally understood why there was never any hot water. Once you stood underneath that invigorating, scalding spray, it simply wasn't in your power to reach over and turn it off. It was a small, extravagant pleasure.

I was in such a good mood as I brushed my teeth that I ended up taking an extra fifteen minutes to do my hair. Parker wouldn't be seeing me today—it was *Saturday*. Relishing the thought, I tried to make curls like that girl had created almost a week ago. I wasn't quite as accomplished as her, and my hair certainly didn't look as spectacular as she had made it, but I still looked nicer than I had in days. As I left the bathroom, I actually smiled at myself in the mirror.

Thomas was sitting on my bed when I walked into my room.

Something in me detached when I saw him—it was so surreal and improbable that he was sitting only feet from me—and I didn't even react at first.

He had been chatting with Becca, who was sitting up in her own bed with the blankets wrapped around her knees and her sleep-blushed face making the most of the look that she pulled off so well. They had been sharing a laugh, and when I opened the door, Thomas turned toward me and smiled as if this were something familiar and comfortable, as if we three friends talked and laughed together often.

"Your friend is great," Becca piped up. "You didn't tell me you knew such fun people."

I blinked and looked at Thomas, still too stunned to respond to his presence.

He quickly got off the bed and crossed the room in a few strides to stand in front of me. His arms were open, palms up as if in supplication, and he said, loud enough for Becca to hear, "It's so good to see you." Just for me he added, "Your grandma said it was okay for me to visit." Then he wrapped me in a careful hug.

I didn't hug him back.

Thomas must have anticipated a little coolness on my part

because he ignored my slight and took control without pausing. He turned to Becca and asked with an easy smile, "Do you think I surprised her?"

Becca giggled.

To me he said, "I was just telling Becca that you weren't expecting me today."

I wanted to include, "Or ever."

Becca jumped in. "Julia was expecting her grandma today. Seeing you must be such a nice surprise."

Everything clicked. "Grandma's not coming?" I asked, though it was more of a statement to myself. I was still processing the thought that it was Thomas she meant when she so vaguely mentioned a visitor.

"Is that what she told you?" Thomas murmured.

"No," I clarified. "I just assumed that when she said *visitor* she meant herself."

Thomas shrugged with an air of artificial self-consciousness. "Sorry to disappoint."

"I'm only disappointed you didn't bring any of those famous cinnamon rolls I've been hearing so much about." Becca pouted.

I hated her for flirting with him.

"Two strikes," Thomas confessed. "I'm not Grandma DeSmit, and I didn't bring cinnamon rolls. But I will try to redeem myself." He looked at me questioningly. "I was hoping you would let me take you out for a late breakfast. Or brunch. Or an early lunch. Whatever you want."

I was afraid if I said no, Becca would try to take him up on his offer, so I said yes even though I'm sure my eyes were communicating something very different. The single, choked word sounded strained even in my own ears.

Thomas ignored the contradiction in my voice. "Good," he affirmed, clapping with finality and then grabbing my fleece jacket off the back of my desk chair before I could change my mind. "You're going to need this—it's chilly," he said.

I allowed him to hold it for me while I slipped my arms into the sleeves. He lifted the coat onto my shoulders and gave them a little squeeze before he let go.

"Bye, Becca," he called with a friendly wave. "It was nice to meet you."

"Ditto," she said, smiling from beneath her yellow gingham comforter. "Turn off the light on your way out, will you? I'm going back to sleep."

I clicked off the light, and we left the room in silence.

We didn't say much as we crossed through the building, but Thomas kept looking at me encouragingly, almost as if he was trying to ease my discomfort and let me know that he meant me no harm.

For my part, I was convinced he was here to personally tell me that he and Francesca were finally engaged, that we were adults now and should put any childish misunderstandings behind us, and that he wanted me at his wedding because I'd been such a big part of his life for so long. I wondered what it would feel like to hear him say the words.

I didn't know how I felt about him after all this time. Other than brief interactions at church functions or special occasions when his parents had invited Grandma and me to their loud and happy family gatherings, Thomas and I hadn't spoken in two years. Thinking back to the afternoon I first laid eyes on Francesca, I realized it was almost two years to the day.

When we got to his car, Thomas opened the door for me like a gentleman. It was just something he always did, something his father had taught him was important, but it made me feel uncomfortable. It felt intimate, and Thomas only added to my unease by commenting, "You look really pretty, Julia," as I lowered myself past him into the passenger seat.

I didn't say anything in response.

When he slid in behind the wheel, he continued, "You've changed." He was hard to read, but he seemed appreciative of whatever change had occurred in me.

"You have too," I said carefully, noticing how he still made something deep inside me resonate as if he had spoken in a canyon and I was the echo.

"How is college life treating you?" he asked conversationally, apparently unaware of the effect his presence was having on me. "Looks like you're doing great," he added, and the tenor of his words was sincere.

I couldn't tell him that I felt like I was sinking in quicksand, so I made my voice carefree and said, "It's fantastic. I'm having a great time."

"Becca seems nice," he commented.

I nodded because it was true—*nice* was a broad enough word to encompass many different interpretations.

"Are you making a lot of friends?" he asked after a moment.

I was affronted. "Yes, Thomas," I said sharply. "And I eat all my vegetables and stay away from drugs and alcohol."

"Hey, I didn't mean any offense," he quickly defended. "I'm just trying to make small talk."

It didn't feel like small talk. It felt like he was worried about my miserable inability to make friends, but I was probably being over-sensitive, so I let it go and tried to be mature and civil for the rest of the ride to the restaurant. Thomas hadn't asked me where I wanted to eat, but I knew where he was going because there was a Denny's on the way out of town if you were headed home to Mason. We both had a history of loving their breakfast menu.

We were settled into a maroon booth and studying the menu before I dared to get somewhat real again. "Thomas," I started, glancing at him over my fanned-out menu, "what are you doing here?"

I had asked it very casually, and he felt safe enough to answer jokingly. "Deciding between Moons Over My Hammy and a Belgian waffle with strawberries and whipped cream," he said with a goofy smirk.

He had always had a literal sense of humor, and I smiled because I remembered how he genuinely loved and laughed at stupid knock-knock jokes. "Come on," I said gently. "You know what I mean."

Instead of answering, he looked past me, and I realized the waitress had materialized at our table. He ended up ordering the Belgian waffle while I opted for the ham-and-cheese omelet with mush-rooms. We each ordered a tall orange juice to go with our meals, and she refilled our already empty coffee cups.

"You know I'm going to need a bite or two of your omelet," Thomas said when the waitress was gone. "I almost ordered that. You can have some of my waffle, too."

I nodded, feeling a little nostalgic because some things never change. No matter what he or I had ordered, Thomas would end up eating half of mine anyway. He had a bit of an infatuation with breakfast. But I wasn't going to let him distract me. "You were just about to tell me why you're here," I reminded him, pressing on.

He sighed and didn't say anything as he ripped the corner off a packet of sugar and poured the powdery-white cascade into his coffee. I could tell he was trying to phrase it just right, so I left him alone. After he stirred his coffee, tasted it, and added one more packet of sugar, he said, "I'm here to check up on you." He gave me a look that said, *Please don't be mad at me.*

It was my turn to sigh. "Thomas, you don't have to check up on me. Besides—" I shrugged—"we're not even friends anymore. What made you suddenly feel obligated to see how I was doing?"

Apparently it was too honest of me to admit that we were no longer friends. Thomas looked hurt. "Julia, I'm like a big brother to you."

That word again. I had to stop myself from rolling my eyes.

"Siblings aren't always the best of friends," he offered. "But they are always connected. They always love each other."

He could tell by my expression that I wasn't buying it. He dropped his gaze. Quietly, as a man caught in a half-truth that he no longer cared to sustain, he admitted, "Your grandma asked me to come."

Finally. The truth. I wasn't surprised.

"But—" Thomas reached across the table and grabbed my hand. I wasn't expecting it and I didn't know what to do, so I let him hold it as I watched him warily. "Julia, I really do miss our friendship. I really do care about you."

I knew he believed what he was saying. It felt like too little too late, but we had once been close, and although it could never be like it had been, I was not opposed to the idea of having Thomas in my life again.

"Okay," I said, looking him in the eye.

He took it as a definite step in the right direction. "Good," he stated firmly, and we both knew that some sort of unspoken agreement had been reached. He let my hand go and sat back with an air of satisfaction.

By the time our food arrived, I had relaxed enough to enjoy his company. He was still the same funny, sweet Thomas I had known and loved, but he had also deepened somehow. He was more expressive, more sure of himself, a little more of everything that he had always been before. It was as if someone had gone over him with strokes of fresh paint and brightened all his colors.

Thomas must have thought the same of me because he kept looking at me as if he were seeing me for the very first time. I realized with some regret that he had always known me as a sad victim, someone he had to protect and shield. Seeing myself reflected in his eyes across the shabby Denny's booth, I could see just how much I had changed. Here I was, a confident, independent, pretty—all his words—engineering student with the whole world spread out before me like an untouched field of new snow. It was up to me to make the first footprint.

I couldn't help wondering if I really was all his expression told me I was or if I had become a great actor. Was I good enough to fool even this man who had once known me better than anyone else? Or had I truly become a new invention in so little time? Either way, as we pulled into the parking lot of my building, the quicksand that had been threatening to drag me under suddenly didn't seem so ominous anymore.

Thomas got out with me, and we stood by his car for a few minutes. He was finishing a story about one of the middle school students in the classroom where he volunteered. It was part of the graduation requirements for his bachelor's degree in education, but it was obvious that the kids were more than an obligation to him. I was filled with a sort of pride and admiration for this amazing, selfless man, and when he offered his arms for a good-bye hug, I was happy to step into them.

"It was so good to see you," he said sincerely.

I responded with a heartfelt, "Mm-hmm."

I don't know what possessed me to do it, but just as he was letting go, I was gripped by a desire to give him a kiss. Something unexplainable made me brave, and instead of letting the bizarre impulse pass, I turned my head to place a chaste little kiss on his cheek. It would have been over in less than a second, but he had also turned his head to say something, and in the end my lips brushed the corner of his mouth.

Crimson, he pulled away from me. "Francesca and I are still together—"

"Accident!" I interrupted, touching my lips with the back of my hand and forcing a laugh. "It was a thank-you kiss, a sister kiss. . . . I meant to get you here." I poked my finger into my cheek.

He smiled hesitantly and nodded.

If he was skeptical, I couldn't blame him. Deep down, I was a bit skeptical myself. What in the world had made me do that? But I tried to ignore it and keep the light feeling that we had so carefully cultivated all morning.

"Make sure you tell my grandma that I'm doing fine," I said, marching right past what had just happened as if it were nothing at all.

"Beyond fine," he confirmed as he stepped back into his car. He shut the door but rolled down the window.

"I really am glad you came today," I said, hoping he wasn't bemoaning the fact that he had done my grandmother a favor.

"Me too," he said, and he must have believed me when I explained away the awkward kiss because he grabbed a pen out of his console and took my hand. "Do you want my e-mail address?" he asked. When I nodded, he wrote it on my palm, then repeated it so I could remember it properly. I wrote mine for him on the back of the Denny's receipt.

Looking at his e-mail address smeared across my hand, I smiled. "Thanks."

And when he drove away, he was smiling too.

initiation

My relationship with Thomas grew in fits and starts. As I mounted the steps to my dorm room that early September Saturday when he reentered my life over a Belgian waffle, I promised myself that I would not pursue him. I would carefully tuck him into some darkened corner of my heart while I filled my time with classes, homework, study sessions—my present reality. If he emerged as more, if he became a part of me again, so be it. But I wouldn't dwell on some empty hope or delude myself with visions of life as I had imagined it to be when I was a naive little girl.

As it turned out, all my attempts to be cavalier and indifferent proved unnecessary when Thomas continued to seek me.

His first e-mail was waiting in my in-box by Monday morning, and although it consisted of a single, practical line—*Just checking to see if I have the address right*—it was a beginning. More than that, it was a beginning I had not initiated.

I responded on Tuesday, not wanting to seem too eager, with an equally short and matter-of-fact message. *You have the address right.* I debated writing more, sat at the computer typing and retyping innocent little questions and friendly, innocuous banter, but I couldn't get anything to sound right. In the end, I sent only that one impersonal line with my name typed formally at the bottom. No *Bye* or *Sincerely* or *Have a nice day*. Just a short, uncomplicated dash followed by *Julia*: Dash Julia.

Thomas must not have interpreted my briskness as unfriendly because the next day I got a full e-mail from him. It was boring stuff, really, mostly harmless babbling and the running narrative that seems to creep into all instant correspondence: *My roommates are making supper in the kitchen, and it smells awful. I think I'll order pizza. . . .* As if I cared about his dinner menu. But it was nice to hear his voice in the words, and I found myself smiling in spite of my wariness.

I wrote back a quick paragraph that probably came off sounding a little preoccupied—which was accurate—and he responded within hours.

We continued like this for weeks, slowly getting to know each other again—virtual strangers with nothing more in common than a few shared memories—as we played an unhurried game of catch.

He'd throw me a piece of himself and I'd reciprocate, at times matching his offering of familiarity with a small gift of myself and other times throwing him a bit of a curveball just to keep him guessing. Sometimes we wrote every day. Sometimes I wouldn't have a spare minute to check my e-mail for almost a week, and one of his messages would sit unopened in my Hotmail account until whatever it contained was stale and hardly worth reading anymore.

Thomas never wrote directly about Francesca, but occasionally he would slip *Francesca says hi* into one of his e-mails, and I assumed that she had walked into the room while he was writing to me. So she knew about our rekindled connection and apparently had no objections. That meant Thomas's motives were purely platonic and nothing more, and I convinced myself that I was relieved to know exactly where I stood—that friendship was all I really wanted anyway. I found myself politely tagging my notes with *Say hi to Francesca,* because it felt like the proper thing to do. The companionable, the *sisterly* thing to do.

By mid-October Thomas and I were Internet pals if nothing else, and I looked forward to his quirky notes with unguarded anticipation. Becca regularly teased me about "the one that got away," and though I regretted sharing a bit of my Thomas story with her, it didn't stop me from continuing to work at our growing friendship or even deter me from writing to him in our dorm room. It was this almost careless acceptance of our renewed familiarity that changed my communication with Thomas in a way I never thought possible.

When I arrived at my statics study group on Wednesday, Parker was slouched in a desk. He was attending our group as part of his rounds. I appreciated the help that I knew he would be able to offer, but my heart did a little tumble when I realized he was there. I had six weeks of college under my belt, and still Parker was as inscrutable as the first day I met him.

We were friends of a sort, but how he treated me depended on the day and the mood he was in. Mostly he was nice—in his blunt, somewhat uncomfortable way—but he also liked to get under my skin, and discussion groups continued to be an intimidating experience. I had no idea how he would behave toward me or what I should be prepared for when I saw him at my study group.

However, after an hour had passed and we were ready for a break, it was apparent that Parker wasn't gunning for me today. He let me be silent and take notes madly and ask the occasional question to which he did not respond with derision. Knowing that he was privy to my grades made me nervous, but apparently the fact that I was struggling was making him more sympathetic to my cause instead of the alternative.

I gave him a brief, thankful smile when we paused to stretch our legs and rest our minds, and he returned it easily. Pleased, I slipped out of my desk to grab a quick drink and walk up and down the hall a few times. When I returned to the room, it was still half empty, so I settled down in front of my laptop for a peek at my e-mail. I was halfway through a note from Thomas when I felt Parker behind me.

"E-mail from your boyfriend?" he asked, peering over my shoulder.

My hand shot up to fold the screen of my laptop down and shield Thomas's note from Parker's prying eyes. At the last moment before my hand slapped the lid shut, I realized how desperate it would look to Parker, and to avoid piquing his interest, I merely brushed a fuzzy from the glowing monitor.

"An old friend." I faced him and gave him a casual smile. We were having such a good day together, and I didn't want my mistrust to jeopardize that. I put my back to the computer to show him I had nothing to hide, nothing to protect. And I didn't really have anything to hide. Thomas's e-mail was completely innocent—it contained a rather boring rundown of his encounter with a professor—but it felt secret to me, precious somehow. It was mine. Although I tried not to, I flinched a little when Parker's eyes drifted from my face and glanced at the screen.

"Are you sure it's not a boyfriend?" he asked tauntingly. As always, I couldn't tell if he was mocking me or playfully teasing me. "Maybe an ex? That's it." Parker searched the e-mail for a moment. "This *Thomas* is your ex." I didn't like the way he said Thomas's name. It was somewhere between derisive and—though I hardly dared to consider it—jealous.

I laughed. "Yeah, Parker, he wishes."

Parker ran with it. "Ouch, Julia!" He grinned at me. "How can you say that about your long-lost beloved?"

"Oh, please." I rolled my eyes and turned away from him, effectively ending the conversation—in my mind at least—and returned my attention to the e-mail.

But Parker wasn't finished. "You have to be coy," he said, leaning over my shoulder and tapping the corner of the keyboard. "You've got to leave him hanging, keep him wanting more."

I exhaled sharply. He was aggravating me in spite of my every effort to be impenetrable. "I told you, he's not a boyfriend. I don't have to play any stupid games with him." Forcing a smile, I gave him a blithe look and added, "Besides, I don't have *time* for a boyfriend."

"You're a good listener." Parker laughed, patting me almost paternally on the back. "But you've got to loosen up a little. Come on—have some fun. Let's make him jealous." He spun the laptop so he could reach the keyboard. As his fingers picked at the keys, he narrated: *"Hey, Thomas, it's Parker."* He punched a period with his finger. *"Julia says hi. She's a little busy. . . . Can't talk now."* He paused to survey his handiwork.

"Parker, grow up," I said with just a hint of unease in my voice.

"It's funny!" He was smirking at the monitor as he dragged his finger across the touchpad.

I didn't want to overreact, but I couldn't stand the thought of Thomas getting some ridiculous, suggestive e-mail from Parker of all people. Very carefully, I said, "It's not funny; it's stupid. He doesn't even know who you are. What will he think?" I reached for the computer, but he slid it out of my reach.

"He won't know what to think. That's what makes it so fun," Parker stated confidently, and before I could stop him, he had clicked the Send icon.

I froze for a moment. Mentally reading and rereading what Parker had written, I wavered between being angry with myself for even checking my e-mail in such a public place and being angry with Parker for being so obtuse. Things were just starting to feel good between Thomas and me. Had Parker written anything to endanger that? I had never once even mentioned Parker to Thomas—what would he think when a message from my account came written by a stranger?

Parker must have sensed my growing unease because he returned the computer to its spot in front of me and gave my forearm a little brush with his fingers. "Hey, I was only fooling around, Julia. You don't have to look so heartbroken." He was wearing the sincere expression that he reserved for after a discussion group when he had really put me on the spot. I had never known anyone to flip-flop so abruptly, to go from almost merciless, spiteful teasing to seemingly genuine care and warmth. It reminded me of elementary school when boys pulled little girls' ponytails in a poorly chosen display of affection.

When I remained silent, Parker jumped in. "Listen, I'll send him an e-mail and tell him I was only trying to be funny. Would that help?"

There were a dozen things I wanted to say to Parker—none of them nice—but when he stopped his incessant teasing and baiting, there was always a part of me that felt oddly sorry for him. It hit me that he didn't seem to know how to act, and if it was a ploy, it was very convincing. I sighed. "Parker," I said softly, "why are you so mean to me?"

He didn't even pause. "Because I like you," he said. And then he winked and walked away.

Exasperated, I glared at his retreating back even as my cheeks warmed just a bit. Parker was impossible. But because it was habit, as normal to me as blinking, I convinced myself I was more concerned about Thomas. I didn't want him to think I wasn't the person he believed me to be. I didn't want him to think that I was hiding things from him or that this dialogue we had begun was a joke to me. I thought about writing him immediately and trying to explain away

Parker's weird message, but I decided to ignore that it had happened at all. Maybe if I didn't bother to acknowledge it, he would write it off as a silly joke and forget about it.

He didn't.

Who's Parker? was the very first line of his next e-mail.

I nonchalantly clarified that Parker was my joking TA and acted like the whole incident wasn't even worth thinking or talking about. I assumed the subject would be dropped.

But Thomas persisted. *He seems a bit immature for a TA. Shouldn't he have better things to do than bug you while you're e-mailing a friend?*

He was trying to be funny, I responded. *Study groups get pretty intense; he was just letting off a little steam.* I smiled when I realized that I was defending Parker to Thomas. Only days ago, I had been utterly disgusted with Parker for pulling such a stupid move, but when Thomas attacked him, I rushed in to stand up for the one person I couldn't imagine needing any protection at all. It wasn't what I would have expected myself to do. Nor was Thomas's response what I expected it to be. In some incomprehensible way, Parker had achieved his goal—Thomas did indeed seem somehow jealous. Or at least protective, defensive, concerned in a brotherly way. I couldn't understand where that particular emotion had come from. I tried not to dwell on it too much, though. It was such a small thing; Thomas would soon lose interest in Parker, and I'd never have to mention one to the other again.

But Thomas had other ideas. He would not let it drop. For a week he punctuated his correspondence with references to Parker's immaturity or my *annoying TA*.

I ignored it for the most part and hoped that he'd get over it soon so I wouldn't have to be continually reminded of Parker in what I had come to count on as my one safe place. But when Thomas wrote that he hoped I was keeping my distance from *that jerk*, I'd had enough.

You're acting like you're jealous! I accused, upset that he wouldn't let such a stupid incident go and downright angry that he thought he had the right to speak into my life. Whether or not he liked Parker was of absolutely no importance to me, but it irked me that he was trying to tell me how I should feel and who I should hang out with from somewhere far outside a place of trust. We were e-mailing each other. It hardly made us best friends again.

My accusation must have touched a sore spot with Thomas. He didn't respond for a long time, and I stubbornly refused to reach out to him either. I knew I had gone too far—that I had unflinchingly, almost rudely, hit on the issue that tore us apart in the first place—but I wasn't ready or willing to apologize when I had yet to receive a heartfelt apology from him. I remained silent.

Whether or not my boycott of Thomas had any effect on him, it did, strangely, seem to have an effect on Parker. An unwitting participant in my tug-of-war with Thomas, Parker became the means by which I punished my old friend for leaving me high and dry, then suddenly—when my life finally seemed to be going in the right direction—diving back in as if he had a right to tell me what to do. It was misplaced, inappropriate, and infuriating. I couldn't stand it.

Although neither man in my life had any way of knowing what I was doing, I started to be friendly to Parker just to stick it to

Thomas. It was childish and hopelessly ineffective, but as I began to treat Parker better, he became a little more tolerable, a little more worthy of a simple act of kindness in my eyes. I slowly forced myself to give him the benefit of the doubt. Where I would have regarded him cautiously, I smiled. Where I would have rolled my eyes at his seemingly endless advice, I listened—and found that at least some of it was worth taking to heart.

In turn, Parker changed toward me. The sly, half-teasing, half-serious tone that he usually took with me mellowed into an almost softness that began to feel comfortable. He laid off a bit in discussion group, and when he had a sarcastic witticism to direct at me, he tempered it with a smile that didn't leave me guessing as to its meaning. Even his eyes were surprisingly attractive and bordering on warm when seen without the shadow that had often glowered from beneath his furrowed eyebrows.

In this more gracious space we had carved out for each other, Parker seemed to know something was bothering me—and that it was more than just my steadily sliding grades. If he guessed it had something to do with what he had done in study group, he never said anything, but he did make an effort to be gentle with me. I accepted it as an apology of sorts, and though my heart began to feel sick when I counted the days that had gone by since Thomas had last e-mailed me, I didn't blame Parker. After all, I was the one who had written that seditious word: *jealous*. I could only blame myself.

It had been five days since Thomas's last e-mail—three days longer than he had ever gone before responding to one of my notes—when I ran into Parker on campus. I had never seen him outside the engineering college as even our study group met in a classroom after hours. I wasn't prepared to run into him on the sidewalk between the library and my dorm room, and when I brushed past the tall man in the black and charcoal ski jacket, I almost didn't recognize him.

It was dark except for the feeble light from the lampposts lining the walk. A breeze was rustling the crinkly brown leaves and breathing a feel of winter down my exposed neck. I wished I had a scarf or that my hair was not pulled into a high ponytail and bobby-pinned in place. It wasn't bitter cold, but everything feels colder in the fall after a long summer of forgetting what winter is really all about. I balled my hands up in the sleeves of my coat and rushed down the sidewalk for home.

He must have recognized me from a distance because when we were still twenty feet apart he called, "You look cold!"

"I am," I said, barely glancing up. It was a sidewalk conversation: two strangers exchanging pleasantries because it's rude to simply ignore the other's presence. I had spoken out of convention, nothing more, and assumed we would pass each other without another word. But when we met, he switched direction to walk beside me. I looked at him sharply. "Parker!" I nearly shouted his name.

"You didn't recognize me?" he questioned, feigning hurt. "We see each other practically every day. How could you not recognize me?"

"It's dark," I defended with a smile in my voice. "I didn't expect to see you here."

"It's not that dark," he countered.

"I was looking at the ground."

He grinned at me. "You're a bad liar. You just plain didn't recognize me. Admit it."

I threw up my hands in defeat, and the backpack that was slung over one shoulder slipped to my elbow. The weight of the portentous books inside flung me off-balance, and I stumbled into Parker. He didn't even flinch. Snaking his arm under mine, he carefully righted me and pulled the bag firmly back onto my shoulder.

I looked at him sheepishly. "I was going to say, 'You caught me,' but I guess that's a pretty stupid thing to say now."

Parker laughed. "What's this? First you don't recognize me; then you try to tackle me? Not cool, Julia."

"What can I do to make it up to you?" I asked, and I was surprised to hear the flirty tone in my voice.

He didn't even think about it. "Have supper with me."

Automatically, my mouth began to form a refusal, but I stopped myself with my lips slightly parted. My immediate reaction had been to make some quick excuse and say good-bye before things got awkward. But looking at him with his eyes almost bordering on hopeful and the light wind tousling his hair, I found that I actually wanted to say yes.

Parker saw me hesitate, and before I could accept his offer, he clarified. "I'm not asking you on a *date* or anything. I just thought you'd like to eat something other than commons food." He shrugged. "It's Friday night."

I was a little embarrassed that he realized I thought I was being asked out, so I tried to turn the tables. "I've got lots of homework. I should keep going for a few hours," I said, taking a step or two in the direction of my building. "Thanks anyway."

My deferral had the desired effect. Parker followed me. "I could help you." He didn't add, "You need it," and I appreciated his new-found tact.

"Well . . . ," I said slowly, looking at my watch.

"I make a mean plate of spaghetti," he offered convincingly.

It was then that I knew it *was* a date. "Okay," I agreed, although I didn't know if I had gotten what I wanted or not.

Parker's apartment was off campus, so we had to take his beat-up, mustard yellow Chevy truck to get there. It was full of rust spots and missing the tailgate, but inside it was almost uncannily immaculate. It wasn't what I had expected from Parker, and when he was looking at the road, I stole quick glances at his profile. I wondered if we'd end up talking statics all night or if he would let me in a little bit. He was a walking contradiction in terms, and I was just starting to want to unravel the mystery.

The apartment was actually one side of a duplex Parker shared with three roommates. It was a messy bachelor pad, but there were posters of Einstein on the walls and dog-eared math and science books splayed open like some half-finished experiment all over the room.

I had to suppress a little giggle. "You live with dorks," I whispered to Parker as he hung his coat on a hook by the door and then helped me out of mine.

"Hey, it takes one to know one," he shot back.

One of Parker's roommates was out with his fiancée, but the other two joined us in the kitchen when they heard that Parker was making spaghetti. He introduced me to the two slightly disheveled grad school students, but I promptly forgot their names and focused instead on making perfectly rolled breadsticks from the Pillsbury tube that Parker put me in charge of.

It was nice to stand in a warm kitchen and be surrounded by conversation and laughter. I didn't mind that his roommates had joined us or that they were talking over me. In a way, it assuaged some of the discomfort I felt knowing that Parker asked me over because he meant what he had said the day he e-mailed Thomas. *"Because I like you."* Besides, the sauce was beginning to smell wonderful, and I was setting a table for four. It was a good feeling.

Best of all, Parker hadn't been exaggerating when he bragged about his spaghetti. He told us that the recipe was a Holt family secret, and it struck me that I had never even known his full name. I had to think for a moment. Peter? Phillip? *Patrick.* His name was Patrick Holt. Suddenly he looked somehow different to me.

When I used the doughy end of my breadstick to sop up the last of the tomato-rich pools of sauce from my plate, Parker laughed. "Just lick it off and put it back in the cupboard," he joked, obviously pleased that I had enjoyed his pasta so much.

I just smiled.

The roommates disappeared when the spaghetti was gone, and Parker and I were left to clean up the kitchen together. "They always do that," he complained as we loaded dishes into the dishwasher.

I didn't say that it was kind of nice to be alone, but I thought it.

"Cup of coffee?" Parker asked after the dishwasher was running and the kitchen was as clean as could be expected in an apartment filled with four twentysomething guys.

"Sure," I said, pulling a chair out from under the table and lowering myself into it.

"Oh, go sit in the living room. It's more comfortable." Parker motioned me out of the kitchen with one hand as he measured out scoops of coffee with the other.

The living room was furnished with two mismatched sofas and a trio of beanbags that looked like they had enjoyed their prime curved comfortably around my parents' generation instead of my own. I surveyed the room for a moment before deciding on the brown couch with blue flowers and then plopped myself down smack in the middle of it because there was no one to leave room for.

It was a little surreal to be sitting in Parker's living room. At times I had been convinced that he hated me; other times I was sure he saw me as a childish little peon. Watching that change—and more, realizing that at the very least he wanted to pursue some sort of friendship with me—was something I couldn't quite get my mind around.

"I make a mean cup of coffee, too," Parker informed me, walking carefully into the living room with two mugs brimful of coffee. He offered me the handle of an oversize orange mug, and although there was space all over the room, he sat down right beside me. Our legs were touching.

I didn't know what to say, so I warmed my hands on the mug and peered thoughtfully into it. The coffee was the color of homemade caramel, and without thinking I commented, "I take my coffee black."

"You'll like this," Parker encouraged. "Try it."

I took a little sip. It was hot and creamy, and it stung the back of my throat a bit. I had already guessed what it was, but I asked anyway.

"It's Baileys," he said, taking a drink from his own mug. "Not a lot, just enough to relax you after a long week."

I thought about reminding him that I was underage, but it wasn't like he was trying to get me drunk—it was a tablespoon of alcohol in a cup of coffee—so I let it pass. And enjoyed it. It was smooth and light and good.

We talked about college life and making friends as an engineering major. When the conversation turned to classes, I made a move for my backpack and the statics book waiting threateningly inside.

Parker threw a pillow at me. "Not tonight!" he moaned.

"Hey, you said you'd help me!" I complained indignantly.

"Tomorrow," he countered, waving the book away as if it was distasteful.

I sighed, sitting back down on the couch. "Likely story." I was slightly farther away from him than I had been before.

He slid closer to me. "It was the only thing I could think of to get you to come."

"You lied to me?" I punched him playfully on the arm.

"I asked you out and you were on the verge of turning me down. What was I supposed to do? A guy has his pride, you know."

Although I had kind of known all along, I was surprised that he was willing to say it so readily. For all the games he had played in the first few weeks of knowing me, he was being unexpectedly candid now. It didn't feel like another game. Parker seemed incredibly sincere and even a little nervous, but I still wasn't about to wholeheartedly accept him at face value. I didn't say anything.

Parker filled the silence. "You know, I was going to take you out somewhere. Spaghetti with my roommates was plan B."

I laughed in spite of myself. I wasn't convinced that this was a good thing at all, but Parker was being charming. What was the harm in enjoying his company?

With Parker's confession out of the way, we relaxed enough to lose complete track of the clock.

It was after 1 a.m. by the time I finally looked at my watch and noticed how many hours had slipped away as we talked. Parker had proven himself to be a good listener, and when he probed me with questions about my life, I found myself able to confide in him things that I wasn't willing to share with anyone else. I didn't tell him about Janice or my dad or anything too heavy, but I did admit my true feelings about Becca, college life, and the loneliness that seemed to come hand in hand with independence. I realized with a start that he was the first person I had truly and honestly talked to since I left home. I don't know if the words fell off my tongue because they were so eager to be spoken or if something about Parker made me trust him even though he had done so much earlier to make me hold him at bay.

But whatever the reason, as he drove me back to my dorm, I felt oddly satisfied—a sleepy combination of contentment and relief wrapped in the delicate thrill of the unknown, the yet-to-be-explored.

"I don't kiss on the first date," Parker said with a sly smile as he pulled up in front of my dorm room.

Truthfully, the thought hadn't crossed my mind, but as Parker said it, I laughed because I was both relieved and disappointed. "Good. Me neither," I stated resolutely, hoping he wouldn't hear the slight tremor in my voice.

"It's settled then," he said, putting the truck in park and swiveling to face me. In spite of what he had just asserted, he looked like he actually did want to kiss me.

I put my hand on the door handle because I wasn't ready for that yet. "Thanks, Parker. It was lots of fun." I cracked the door open, then turned back to him for a minute. "Can I ask you a question?"

"Anything," he affirmed, and I knew he would tell me the truth.

"Why were you so . . . ?" I trailed off because I couldn't find the right word.

"Impossible? Mean? Sarcastic?" he offered helpfully.

I bit my lip. "Yeah," I said softly. "Half the time I didn't know if you hated me or liked me."

Parker put his hand to his forehead and rubbed it for a moment. "Couple of reasons," he finally said. "I'm a bit blunt, abrupt, harsh, however you want to say it. Always have been, always will be. I think you realized that the first day. And I'm a natural-born motivator—I wanted to see what you were capable of, and when you walked into statics all pink and pretty, I knew you'd be eaten alive. I had to intimidate you a little or you would have dropped out after the first week." He paused. Took a shallow breath. "And I meant what I said in study group. I liked you. I *like* you. I guess I didn't know what to do with that." Parker looked at me pointedly. "You're a lot younger than me. I'm not sure I'm supposed to like you."

I was nonplussed. "How old are you? You can't be that much older than me."

"Twenty-five," he said as if it was a relief to admit it.

"I'm almost nineteen," I said. "Is six years a big difference?"

He chuckled. "Yeah, Julia, I think six years is a big difference."

"Does it change anything?" I asked quietly.

"I don't know. I guess we'll find out." Parker raised his eyebrows at me. "Do you want to find out?"

I nodded slowly and he smiled.

"Me too," he said, and he sounded relieved.

I gave him a little wave from across the cab of the pickup and slid out the door. "Good night," I called.

"Sleep tight," he murmured back.

Just as I was swinging the door shut, he raised his hand to stop me. "Hey, statics tomorrow? You need the help, girl. If you do poorly on the test, you'll be knocking on the door of a D."

"Don't remind me," I groaned, and my heart dropped a notch or two.

"I'll help you," he said. "Tomorrow morning at ten."

"Do you know what time it is?" I complained.

"You've got less than nine hours. Get some sleep." And he leaned across the seat and pulled the door shut from the inside.

I felt somehow powerful slipping through the darkened halls of my dorm. I didn't meet a single person on my way to my room, and I relished the knowledge that I was alone with my thoughts and singular among all the sleeping girls around me. Parker was intelligent, a grad student, handsome, *older*. The importance of it hung across my shoulders as if I were draped in yards of heavy silk.

After staring at the ceiling for longer than was wise with a homework date fast approaching, I crawled out of bed and lifted my laptop out of the backpack that I had slung by the door. I curled back up under my sheets and propped a pillow against the side of the monitor so the light wouldn't wake Becca, savoring the fact that for once I had gone to bed later than her.

There was still no note from Thomas in my in-box, and I decided on the spur of the moment that I would be the mature one in this and put to rest whatever had come between us. I wrote him a nice, safe, ordinary message and pretended that nothing had ever happened. That I hadn't accused him in some roundabout way of having feelings for me or at the very least disapproving of me seeing other guys. It was an olive branch but not an apology, and although I knew I was being the tiniest bit malicious, I couldn't help including a short postscript.

Parker says hi.

cipher

PARKER BROUGHT MUFFINS AND COFFEE the following morning and acted as if having breakfast together were the most natural thing in the world. The morning had found me shy and uncertain, but by the time we staked out a secluded table in a far corner of the library, Parker's laid-back smile and casual manner had begun to set me at ease. Even if sleep had brought with it second thoughts for me, Parker was doing everything he could to show me that he had no doubts, no regrets. It was hard to stay uptight when he was so relaxed and confident.

I felt our age difference, though, when I tried to loosen up and follow his model of seemingly effortless acceptance of the situation at hand. It was impossible to know how to act. I got butterflies in my stomach when he leaned in close to point to something in my book. My palms were so clammy it was hard to hold a pencil. The laugh that I attempted to make light and carefree sounded hollow even in my own ears. Inexperience and apprehension collided to transform me into a stumbling, timid, inarticulate mess. And we were just doing homework together.

We were a page and a half into the first problem when Parker threw down his pencil, tipped back on two legs of his chair, and began to laugh.

I watched him with growing unease and tried to remember if I had said something amusing. When he continued to laugh—and I continued to have no clue what he was laughing about—I finally asked, "Something funny?"

"Not funny," he replied. "Cute." And he folded his arms across his chest like a self-satisfied cat snuggling down to watch my reaction to the mess he had just made.

"Cute?" I questioned, disliking his stance. It made me want to look behind me, to catch who was sneaking up on me before they shouted, *Boo!*

"You're being cute," he clarified, and it was obvious he wanted me to ask him *how* I was being cute.

I just raised my eyebrows.

"I've got you acting all bashful, Julia," he said with a hint of triumph in his voice. "You're nervous to be around me."

"I am not!" I defended hotly, knowing as I said it that I was beginning to blush.

Parker let his chair drop to the floor and put his forearms on the table to regard me with a smile. "Yes, you are. But don't worry—it's cute."

I opened my mouth to say something more, but I couldn't think of any retort that would be worth the breath used to utter it. It was a little mortifying to know that my emotions were so pitifully transparent. But at least Parker didn't find me pathetic; he found me *cute*. Was cute a good thing to be? I always considered cute to be strongly linked to all things fluffy and infantile. Puppies are cute. Babies are cute. Little socks with diminutive pink bows are cute. Eighteen-year-old college students should not be cute. I decided I was a bit offended.

"I'm not sure I want to be cute," I said with a little belligerence in my voice. I cringed. Tried to sound more mature. "I don't think I like to be referred to as cute."

"I don't think you have a choice," Parker responded, still smiling that unreadable half smile at me.

"Are you making fun of me?" I asked, and all the insecurity I felt turned my stomach so that the blueberry muffin that had left crumbs on my notebook started to feel sour.

Parker's face changed. His smile melted into something softer, and his eyes were big and serious. "No. I swear to you, I am not making fun of you." Then he leaned across the table and sealed his solemnity with a kiss so sweet and light that I barely felt the brush of his lips before they were gone. He must have felt like he had kissed a frog.

"So you kiss on the *second* date," I finally said when I had collected myself enough to realize that I should respond somehow.

Parker's rich laugh rang out again, and this time I was happy to have caused it on purpose. "That was hardly a kiss," he teased. "I don't think it counts. I think a real kiss has to be reciprocal."

"Hey," I shot back, "I wasn't ready—I didn't know you were going to kiss me!"

"So I have to ask your permission?" Parker assumed a beleaguered expression. "That's going to get really tedious."

I balled up the closest sheet of paper and threw it at his head. It bounced off his forehead and fell under the table.

"That was your homework assignment," Parker alleged disapprovingly.

"No, it wasn't. . . ." I pushed a few things aside on the table in front of me. The first page of the assignment was missing. "Oops," I said sheepishly. "I guess it was."

"Is that what happens to all your assignments?" Parker's tone had shifted ever so slightly to reveal that there was more to the question just beneath the surface.

I knew he was going to ask me about my less-than-fantastic performance so far in statics. It wasn't that I wasn't trying—most of the time I studied like a determined hermit—but with calculus and chemistry as well as psychology and philosophy for my gen ed requirements, I simply didn't seem to have room in my brain for a subject that left my mind in a useless state similar to wobbly Jell-O. The information just wouldn't go in. The pages of formulas and calculations on the way to a half answer that mattered less than the journey it took to get there became so confusing I could barely remember the objective. But I couldn't say all of that to Parker, who, in this moment at least, was less a friend and more the teacher's assistant of a class I was quickly failing.

This morning was so lighthearted and fun, I didn't want to go there. Besides, my fingers still rang with the faint resonance of a tingle from his unexpected kiss. So instead of responding to the serious slant in his voice, I pretended that I hadn't caught it and said, "You should see the origami birds I have hanging all over my dorm room."

"Quite the talent, are you?" he asked, still flirty, though the sober edge had not disappeared.

"There's more to me than my looks," I quipped and knew instantly that it was the wrong thing to say. It was an invitation for him to bring the conversation around to my other attributes. My mind perhaps.

He jumped on it. "Oh, I know there's more to you. I've always been attracted to your brain above all else."

I was trapped. Quickly I tried to come up with some way to divert him, some way to direct him away from the question I knew was burning on his tongue. Everything was so nice—I wanted to sip coffee with him and share the last muffin and laugh together, not dive into some intense discussion about why I was pursuing a degree in engineering when I was obviously struggling to pass the most basic entry-level class. He was going to ask me why, and I didn't have an answer.

We were quiet for a few moments, and I took the opportunity to rescue my homework assignment from its premature grave beneath the table. I carefully unfolded the paper and smoothed it flat with my hand, smearing the pencil as my damp palm grazed the numbers and lines. I sighed before I could stop myself.

"Statics is tough," Parker said sympathetically.

I knew that it was nothing of the sort. Sure, it was no walk in the park, but if I intended to graduate with a degree in biomedical engineering, it certainly shouldn't pose as huge an obstacle as it had become for me. It occurred to me for the very first time that I would probably not pass the class. Or at the very least, I would not do well enough to continue on this path I had so randomly chosen and then painstakingly laid out for myself. It was an unnerving feeling. A slipping, tumbling, falling feeling. How could I ever admit that I was wrong, that this future of my own creation was one I could not achieve?

Parker was watching me. I could tell he wanted to say something, but he didn't know what to say. He didn't want to offend me or hurt me or make me feel inadequate. I was aware that I should say something first, ease his discomfort, but I couldn't.

After a few more breaths in silence, he asked, "Why are you an engineering major, Julia?"

"I don't know," I whispered. I thought he would make me repeat myself, but he had heard.

He cupped his hand around the back of his neck and rubbed it as if he was tense. He made a sound like a low grunt and said, "Do your parents want you to be an engineer?" I didn't think he would be able to say anything to make me laugh, but that did. Parker looked confused. "Or your parents *don't* want you to be an engineer and you're doing it to tick them off?" he guessed with grasping inaccuracy.

"Parker," I said, "I don't have parents."

There was a shocked stillness as if all the air had been sucked out of the room, and I regretted my bluntness. "It's okay," I continued more gently. "My mom left when I was nine, and my dad died three years ago. I live with my grandmother."

While he processed this new information, I steeled myself for the troubled questions and sappy condolences that always followed when someone learned of my situation for the first time. This was exactly why I avoided the topic as much as I could—I hated the way I changed in people's eyes when looked at through this deplorable perspective. I wanted to pin a sign to my chest that said "I am more than a product of my past."

I was so far down the road of self-preservation that when Parker spoke, it hit me like a slap in the face.

"Bummer," he said unceremoniously.

I swallowed. In my three years of wearing the badge of an orphan I had never received such a response. I was still sifting through my emotions when a laugh bubbled up from somewhere deep inside, and against my will I began to giggle, a breathless, infectious laugh that gripped me until tears gathered in the corners of my eyes.

At first, Parker watched me a little apprehensively, but before long we were laughing together and didn't stop until we were both spent.

When it was over and I felt tired and content, I crossed my arms on the table and laid my head on them, regarding Parker with amusement still lining my eyes. "No one has ever said anything like that to me."

He raised an eyebrow. "Was it the wrong thing to say?"

"No, I think it's the best thing anyone has ever said to me."

Parker licked his index finger and drew an imaginary line in the air. "Score one for Parker."

"Ha-ha, you're funny," I groaned.

"I'm so suave, so cool. . . . I can say 'bummer to be you' to a girl, and she thinks it's poetry."

I rolled my eyes at him. "Hardly. I'm just thankful you didn't ask me if I was in counseling—"

"Are you?" he cut in.

"*No,*" I said pointedly. "And I'm not some wacko or charity case or wrecked for life."

"So there," Parker chimed firmly. He continued before I could reply, "But you still didn't answer my question. I'm sorry about your parents, and I'd love to listen if you're willing to talk sometime, but I want to know why you're an engineering major."

I had almost forgotten that my choice of degree was what had brought us to this point in the first place. For a moment I balked, but then I heard Parker's response ring in my mind again and I was gripped by the thought that I had nothing to lose by telling him the truth. It's not like I was keeping some huge secret or about to reveal devastating personal information. It was just embarrassing to admit that my aspirations were little more than pipe dreams. An ideal me in an ideal world of my own invention.

"I wanted to be different," I said at last, avoiding his gaze. "I scored highest in math and sciences on my ACT. When we got the results, our school guidance counselor had printed out lists of the careers that would best fit our strengths. I can't imagine being a doctor or a nurse. I'm not a huge animal person, so veterinarian was out. I don't want to teach. . . ." I sneaked a glance at Parker, and he wasn't looking at me as if I were crazy. "Engineering is so . . . respectable, exclusive, a little exotic. It screams *distinctive*, know what I mean?" I stopped. I didn't realize I was holding my breath until my chest felt tight, and I wondered anxiously why Parker wasn't reacting.

He wasn't going to blurt something out this time. I could tell he was trying to formulate exactly the right thing to say. I was a bit unimpressed when he finally asked, "Do you want to be an engineer?"

"Yes," I said without thinking. "No. I—I don't know. I don't really know what I want to be, but I have to choose something, right?"

"Not now," Parker argued calmly.

"Yes, now. I'm in college, I'm a big girl, and I have to make decisions about my life—my future." I sat up straight, and my back was so rigid it didn't touch my seat.

Parker kept pressing me. "You're a freshman. Go undeclared for a while. Take some classes and decide what suits you."

"No," I said quickly. "I started this and I'm going to finish it. I'm smart enough."

"I know you are." Parker leaned forward, pulled my hand across the table, and covered it with both of his own. "You're incredibly intelligent."

I didn't want to be defensive, but I couldn't stop myself from asking, "So why do you think I can't do this?"

"I think you can," Parker explained. "I just don't know if you really want to."

"I want to," I said without thinking.

Parker exhaled. "Does it make you happy?"

"What do you mean?"

"I mean, does it satisfy you? When you're working through a problem—even though it's hard and miserable and tedious—does there come a point when it clicks, when you feel content simply knowing that you're doing what you were born to do?"

The answer was an easy no, but for a moment I searched my life for a time—any time—when I had felt what Parker described. It was unsettling to find that I couldn't think of a single thing in my past or present for which that rang true. I had spent my whole life waiting for that awareness, that acknowledgment of *This is me. This is where I fit. This is who I am.* And Parker had just shown me that my search was not over. I was not an engineer. For a fleeting second, it made me want to cry.

Parker saw my expression and didn't wait for me to answer. "I'm not trying to talk you out of a degree in engineering, Julia," he said, pressing my hand beneath his own. "I just want you to do what makes you happy."

I shrugged because I didn't know what to say.

"I'll help you pass this test," he offered supportively.

Managing a smile, I said, "Let's start with that. I need some time to think about what you've said before I drop out of statics."

"That's a relief—who would I sit by if you bail on me?" Parker joked. He gave me a wink and graciously closed the conversation by pulling the book in between us. "We've got less than a week. What are you doing every waking moment?"

He had a way of making me laugh, and I was thankful for the diversion. Whether or not he had crumbled my plans with a few well-placed questions, I had to stay the course until I could see a more discernible road ahead of me. A part of me wanted to forget that we'd ever had this conversation, but somewhere hidden inside there was also a muted relief, a part of me that knew he was right even as I wished he were wrong.

I pushed it all out of my head as I reached for my pencil and leaned over the book with him. I focused on every word he said. If nothing else, I would pass the test. The rest would sort itself out later.

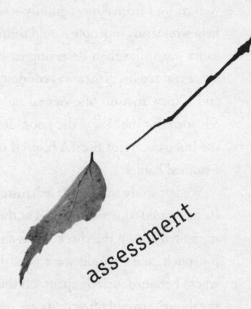

assessment

I HAVE NEVER WORKED HARDER in my whole life than the week that Parker helped me prepare for the test. Romance had absolutely nothing to do with our frequent study dates, and a little of the old Parker—the harsh, demanding, brusque Parker—resurfaced to push me to the height of my potential. I didn't even mind when he was hard on me because for some reason it made me feel like we were getting somewhere, like I couldn't expect results without a little blood, sweat, and tears. No pain, no gain, right?

While I worked, Parker corrected papers and took periodic breaks to show me where I was going wrong or how one of my formulas was improperly used or off track. We usually studied in the library. Once, when someone I vaguely recognized as a statics classmate walked by, I froze almost guiltily—we had been spotted. I couldn't help wondering if people would think I was trying to earn my grade some way other than deserving it. But as I caught my classmate's eye, I realized his glance was condescending rather than accusatory, and I knew that no one viewed me as competition. They actually felt sorry for me. I was the poor, delusional little girl who needed the intervention of the TA himself just to pull off a passing grade. I studied harder.

We left study sessions as exhausted as if we had just run a 10K. Parker would squeeze my hand at the door of my building and give me a tired kiss on the cheek. I was always too numb to even register his touch, and I would wave good-bye and stumble to my room, where I crashed, utterly spent, on the bed. However, as I fell asleep, the thought would often cross my mind that these days with Parker had made me care for him more than dinner dates with getting-to-know-you conversation and my hair done just so.

The day of the test, Parker was behind the podium in the lecture hall giving stoic instructions. I tuned him out and went over the formulas that I had worked so intently to cram into my mind. Parker had sent an e-mail to the entire class earlier in the week outlining exactly what we could expect the test format to be, what we could take into the exam, and what would be required of us. I memorized the information as if it were a Bible verse from my youth and without every word in its proper place I would not receive the coveted gold star sticker. Needless to say, I felt the few minutes before Parker handed out the test were best spent mentally reviewing.

I was at the end of a row, and when he handed me a stack of tests to pass down, Parker gave me an almost imperceptible suggestion of a smile. I saw it. It was enough.

The test was one sheet with three problems on each side. Every problem contained a drawing of a different stationary system and arrows indicating where force was being applied at various points in each system. It was my job to calculate the forces acting on the system and answer the handful of questions that accompanied the problem. I had practiced a dozen of these over the course of the last few days alone. I was ready. Taking a deep breath, I opened my blue book and began to write.

I was the last student to leave the room. As I gathered up my belongings and descended into the theater to hand Parker my test, I decided that being last wasn't necessarily a bad thing. I had been meticulous in my attention to detail. I had done well. I told myself that I had passed with flying colors.

When Parker took my test, he gave me a hopeful smile and a wink.

I smiled back to show him that all was well and I was confident. He didn't say anything and I didn't either. It felt too strange to be consorting with the teacher's assistant after an important test. He must have agreed because he turned to add my paper to the stack neatly collected in a printer paper box and didn't turn back.

I wasn't offended and in fact nearly floated out of the lecture hall because I was becoming more and more convinced that I had done just fine. The conversation that I had had with Parker a few days ago suddenly seemed less threatening, and I felt my shoulders straighten as I thought, *I can do this. I will be an engineer. I just need to apply myself a bit more.* With each step, the ground felt more stable beneath me.

Becca was flopped across her bed with a book when I walked in. Although I couldn't make out the title to know for sure whether she was reading for school or pleasure, I thought about teasing her that this was a rare sight. But I bit my tongue because I wanted her to ask me how the test had gone, and I figured a mild insult—no matter how accurate—was a poor way to initiate a conversation. Instead, I said a cheery "Hello," and she grunted a response as she continued reading her book.

Wanting to talk, I sat down at my desk chair with a weighty sigh and crossed my right ankle over my knee to unlace my hiking boots.

Becca, only a few feet away, ignored my obvious plea for attention.

Pulling off the boot, I sighed again.

Becca turned a page.

When my hiking boots were side by side on the floor, I tried another tactic. "Are you hungry?" I asked talkatively. "'Cause I'm starving. I think I'm going to microwave some popcorn—you want some?"

Becca looked up at me for the first time since I entered the room. "Huh? Popcorn?" It clicked. "Yeah, sure, popcorn sounds good." And her gaze dropped back to her book.

We weren't allowed to have microwaves in our dorm rooms, so I stepped into my slippers and padded down the hallway to the little community room. It was empty except for the girl who had done my hair the first day of classes. I cursed myself silently for not remembering her name. She was reheating a plate of something in the microwave, and she smiled when she saw me clutching my flat little packet of popcorn.

"Hi, Julia. I'll be just a minute," she said. "I haven't seen you around for ages."

"I've had tons of homework," I replied almost apologetically. Her genial smile made me regret that I had so little time to pursue friendships.

"Oh, that's right," she said, and her eyes got just a tad rounder. "You're an engineering major, aren't you?" The way she said *engineering* made it sound as if I would single-handedly do something miraculous and life changing for all mankind. Either that or sprout a third eye. I gave a slightly uncomfortable nod, and she continued. "You guys are so beyond me—I could never do what you do." She laughed good-naturedly. "I still count on my fingers!"

The microwave pinged and went dark. Turning away from me, the girl pulled the door open and stuck a finger in a plate of lasagna that looked like leftovers from an expensive restaurant. As if reading my thoughts, she glanced over her shoulder at me and said, "My boyfriend took me to Mario's last night. I told him it was too nice, but—" she shrugged—"he insisted."

"I'm sure you're worth it," I said, liking the fact that her smile broadened with my poor attempt at a compliment.

She collected her lasagna from the microwave. "It's hot enough. The microwave is all yours."

I tossed the popcorn bag in and waved good-bye.

She was almost gone when she suddenly hooked an arm across the doorframe to poke her head back in. "Hey, a bunch of us are having a movie night in my dorm room tonight—some chick flick I'm sure," she said, arching her eyebrows. "You can come if you'd like."

The invitation was so thoughtful and out of the blue that I struggled to find the right thing to say. I took too long.

"Oh, it was mean of me to even ask, wasn't it?" she murmured with a sad shake of her head. "You are way too busy, aren't you? I'm sorry. I know you engineers have it way worse than us early childhood development majors. We shouldn't rub it in."

I forced a smile as she disappeared, hurt not by what she had said but by the sincerity with which she said it. This distinctiveness that I longed to wear as a mantle of my own importance and worth seemed arrogant and cheap when someone so kind looked at me with admiration that I had done nothing to deserve. I decided the world would be a better place with a few more of her and a few less self-important professionals.

My mood had sunk a bit by the time I headed back to my room with a steaming bag of buttered popcorn. But I was still excited about the test and ready to share my enthusiasm with someone, even if it was only Becca, who wouldn't understand and probably wouldn't care. I tried to shake off the dusting of remorse that had settled over me after my community room encounter and marched into my room determined to have a nice chat. We had been able to talk in the beginning; there was no reason why Becca and I shouldn't be able to have a pleasant conversation now.

When I walked in the door, Becca was slipping into her coat.

"Oh!" I couldn't stop myself from sounding surprised. "I thought we were having popcorn."

"Sorry, Julia. I have to go out." Becca pulled a knit hat over her auburn spikes and gave me a rueful half smile. "But, hey, I'll take some for the road." She grabbed a cup off her desk and dug it into the bag of popcorn, spilling a blond shower of kernels on the floor at my feet. "Oops!"

I didn't say anything as I watched her sling her backpack over one shoulder and grab the door handle.

"Have a good afternoon!" she called. "Oh, and your grandma phoned. I wrote the message on the marker board because it didn't make any sense to me." The door swung shut.

I spent the next fifteen minutes lying on the bed and eating popcorn. When the popcorn bag was decimated and my mouth sore from too much salt, I finally felt I had enough energy to read Grandma's message. Swallowing a rush of self-pity and trying to remind myself that I was above Becca's petty jabs, I pulled myself almost groggily from my pillow and stepped over the pile of popcorn that she had left scattered across the floor. I ticked off Parker, Thomas, and even the girl from the community room in my mind and counted them as friends. I didn't need Becca and her moody self-sufficiency.

The marker board hung next to the mirror by the door, and Becca had used up the majority of it to scrawl: *R U coming to Thanksgiving on Sunday? The Walkers want to know. . . .* Beneath it she had offered her own commentary: *Julia, does your g-ma know that turkey day is two weeks away?*

Although her comment would normally have rubbed me the wrong way considering the mood I was in and the way I currently felt about my less-than-affable roommate, all Becca's foibles were forgiven as I read and reread Grandma's message. Thanksgiving. I had completely forgotten. It was like receiving the best kind of present: an unexpected one.

The Walkers had been celebrating Thanksgiving two Sundays before the actual holiday weekend for as long as I could remember. Once I had overheard Mrs. Walker explaining to my grandmother that she got sick of cooking two turkeys only six weeks apart every year—Mr. Walker was Canadian and wanted to celebrate Thanksgiving with his fellow countrymen in October; Mrs. Walker was American and insisted on observing the November holiday. Somewhere along the line she put her foot down, declared a Walker family Thanksgiving, and from that point on devoted her oven to a fifteen-pound bird only once a year.

When Dad died and Grandma and I lost all semblance of a family structure, the Walkers had enfolded us in their unusual tradition with graciously open arms. Actually, it was hardly a matter of charity—Grandma became the official baker for the event and brought baskets of her homemade rosemary rolls and fresh pumpkin, pecan, and Dutch apple pies. Everyone was better off because of our inclusion.

And now, thinking of hot apple cider and the noise and bustle of the Walker house as we got ready to feast, I almost cried with homesick relief. I hadn't grasped how much I missed my grandmother. It was a bittersweet, nostalgic feeling to hold her in my mind and come to terms with the fact that I had not seen her since I left for college. I suddenly missed my attic room in the tiny farmhouse with an almost painful ache, and I remembered the smell of our kitchen and the way the wind hummed in the living room windows as if I were standing in my home this very instant. *Home*. The word was warm and thick and comforting in my throat even though I could not make myself pronounce it. I wanted to go *home*.

It was Wednesday, and I had two more days of classes before I could leave. With the assurance of something so sweet and familiar dangling in front of me like an unfulfilled promise, two days of classes seemed like an eternity. The thought flitted across my mind that I could just go home now, e-mail my professors and tell them that I was sick. After all, I hadn't skipped a single class yet. But just as quickly as I considered it, I dismissed it. As excited as I was to go home, I hadn't completely forgotten the victory of today. I wanted everyone to be able to see me as a successful engineering major. I wanted to be thriving and blossoming and . . . *whole*.

I resisted the urge to pack a few things—to lay out a sweater or two on my desk to remind me that I would be going home soon—and convinced myself to work hard for a couple more days. My calculus and chemistry homework was done for Thursday, and since there had been a test in statics, there was no assignment for Friday. That left philosophy and psychology, and I almost laughed out loud because for once my load was fairly light. I decided my two gen ed classes could wait awhile before I gave them attention, and I grabbed my laptop to e-mail Parker my happy news.

I found an e-mail from Thomas instead.

For a moment, I was shocked that he hadn't even crossed my mind when I thought about the Walker Thanksgiving. After all, Thomas had once been the most important Walker family member in my life. With Parker becoming so much more than I ever imagined he would be and Thomas continuing along a silent path that all but erased him from my everyday thoughts, I hadn't needed to hold my old friend in that place in my heart that seemed ever vacant. He was slowly fading from my life. However, as I opened his message, I smiled with a hint of wistfulness and realized that everything was behind us now. I looked forward to seeing him—I would actually be able to talk and laugh with him like we were the dear friends of long ago instead of the fumbling, what-might-have-been strangers of today.

Thomas's e-mail was benign and ordinary, and as I read the first paragraph, my heart rose because all was well in the world. Parker was mine, I would be an engineer, and Thomas was my friend again. When I got to the last few lines, I had to reread them three times before I accepted that I was truly reading them right.

> Are you coming to Thanksgiving? I know we've been e-mailing, but it would be great to see you in person. We have a lot to talk about. If we were younger, I'd make you cross your heart and hope to die, stick a needle in your eye. But I guess now that we're old and mature I'll just say please. Please come, Julia.
>
> Looking forward to seeing you . . .
> Thomas

I couldn't begin to assess his motives. Had he written anything like this only weeks ago, I would have run all the way home without even pausing to put on my coat. Now I found myself wanting to turn back the clock, to forget that I had ever read such a baffling message. Surely Francesca would be there, lighting up Thanksgiving as she had for the previous two years. What could Thomas possibly want to say to me that was important enough to run along the lines of begging? What could he want to talk to me about with his perfect Francesca at his side?

I knew that I was being ridiculous, that something inside me was reading far more into the situation than I should have, but I couldn't help seeing a little too much intensity in his words. A little too much emotion. He wanted me home too ardently, and it made me hope for things I had given up hoping for long ago. I wished that I could close the lid of the laptop and pretend I had never read his words.

Maybe I could go home and do exactly that: pretend I hadn't seen his e-mail. I could be normal and happy and even evasive, making sure that I was always around the family and letting Thomas know that there was nothing he could say to me that would make any difference in my full, successful, and content life. Maybe if Thomas saw me so independent and assured, he would abandon whatever it was that he so desperately wanted to talk to me about.

Even as I thought about the ways I could put off Thomas, another part of me was stirring to the memory of what I had wanted for so long. This was *Thomas*. My confidant, ally, protector, savior. He knew me better than anyone had ever known me, including my own father. Thomas had been with me when Dad and I finally accepted that Janice wasn't coming back. More significantly, Thomas had been with me when I finally accepted that my dad wasn't coming back. We had history. I half hated myself for thinking it, but whatever he wanted to talk to me about was obviously charged enough to carry the weight of many emotions. Maybe the significance of all we shared was enough to change things between us now. Now—because I was a woman instead of a child.

But I was getting ahead of myself. Maybe Thomas wanted to consult me about various romantic schemes for his proposal to Francesca. Perhaps they were past that point already and would clutch hands lovingly as they asked me to perform some contemptible rite in their wedding like standing by the guest book or handing out little silver vials of bubbles as everyone gathered around their getaway car. I cringed just thinking it. And then, I reminded myself, the most logical scenario was that he only wanted to reminisce with the friend who knew him better than anyone else ever had. Sometimes you just need to be known.

With a deep, intentional breath, I steadied my furiously tilting mind and determined to put Thomas aside. I would take things as they came when I was home for Thanksgiving. I would stop obsessing about something I could never predict or know and focus on the good that was right in front of me.

Clicking on New Message, I stopped myself from replying to Thomas and instead wrote Parker a flirty note thanking him for his help. *I'll be gone this weekend*, I typed, not bothering to explain why. *What are you doing Thursday night?* I was already looking forward to seeing him.

homecoming

PARKER ACTED A BIT STRANGE when I told him I was going home for Thanksgiving. At first I wondered if he was hurt because I wasn't extending him an invitation. I almost giggled when I thought of bringing Parker home to meet my grandmother—I had a hard time envisioning that scenario even months down the line. It only reaffirmed for me that I was not ready for it now, and I never once seriously considered asking him to come.

However, with or without an invitation, I was confused and disappointed that what had been so comfortable between us as we studied together had once again become a bit timid and halting. I had expected it from myself—I still felt small and undeserving beside Parker—but I had not expected it from him. Parker had seemed so at ease with himself—and, more to the point, with us— that I had thought we were past the awkward introductory stages of our fledgling relationship. But on Thursday night, somewhere between the takeout kung pao chicken and the fortune cookies we had ordered from the Ginger Garden, it became clear that I had misread Parker's curious behavior.

It was only when Parker asked the one question that had been poisoning the space between us all night that I finally understood.

"So," he began, lifting the last egg roll from a pagoda-shaped box and holding it up for my consent.

I nodded.

He took a bite and continued. "So, this Walker family Thanksgiving . . . are they old friends of the family?"

"Something like that—we're neighbors," I said and was on the verge of explaining how my friendship with Thomas had sort of brought us all together when the source of Parker's peculiarity suddenly seemed clear. He had read Thomas's name on the e-mail that day in study group. He was wondering if this Walker Thanksgiving would include a certain *Thomas* Walker. I had to suppress a surprised smile at the thought. Was Parker feeling threatened?

I didn't dare say any of my thoughts aloud for fear of offending him, so I took a more moderate approach. "I've always loved the Walkers. I'm an only child, but they have this big, beautiful, crazy family—there's always something going on."

"Lots of kids?" Parker asked.

I nodded. "Five. There's Maggie—she's the baby—then Emily, Jacob, Simon, and Thomas." I stole a glance at Parker as I said the last name. He had been watching me and looked quickly away to busy himself by rearranging his chopsticks. When he didn't say anything, I went on. "Thomas is six years older than Simon so the last four are still pretty young. I think Maggie is eight."

"So Thomas is about your age," Parker asserted casually.

"A little over two years older," I confirmed. "We were good friends." I waited for Parker to say something, to bring up the e-mail that in a roundabout way had brought us together. When he didn't, I decided to make it easy for him. "Hey," I said as if it had just occurred to me, "I think you e-mailed Thomas once! You're practically friends with him too."

"Oh, is he the e-mail guy?" Parker acted as if he were just now putting two and two together.

"One and the same."

Silence stretched between us once again as Parker tried to settle on the best course of action from here. I let him take his time as I selected a fortune cookie and cracked it in half to extract the little piece of prophetic paper. *You will have good luck in relationships* was typed in fading ink on one side. The other side contained a single word in Chinese. I ignored both and rolled up the paper so tiny and tight it was the size of a small, white bean. I waited for Parker.

Finally he said, "Are you done?" and motioned to my plate.

A part of me relished the attention and Parker's obvious discomfort, but the peacekeeper in me didn't really want the conversation to be over until it was resolved. However, he had obviously moved on. "Yes, thank you," I replied, trying to keep any disappointment hidden beneath my voice.

He stacked my plate on top of his own and got up to take them to the kitchen. We were sitting on pillows around the coffee table in the living room, so when he began to clear things away, I pulled myself up and joined him because I didn't want the distance of an entire room between us. I surveyed the takeout boxes and, deciding that there were not enough leftovers to save, piled them all together with our used napkins and empty soy-sauce packets. I crammed everything into Parker's already overstuffed garbage can while he loaded the dishwasher.

The room felt taut, as if the tension between us could be plucked like a steel guitar string and resonate deep and sad throughout the house. I would have done anything to alleviate it if only I could think of the right thing to do.

In the end, it was Parker who once again made everything okay. The kitchen was clean, and he flipped the light off so we could go back into the living room to watch the movie we had rented. We reached the doorway at the same time, and instead of letting me walk through it, Parker took a step with me, put his hands on my shoulders, and turned me to face him so that my back was against one side of the doorframe and his pressed to the opposite. He leaned into the wood and studied me, one foot in the kitchen, the other in the living room. "Did you date Thomas, Julia?"

It was much more direct than I had expected him to be, and while I was thankful that we were dealing with it, I found that I was also uncomfortable going into detail about my history with Thomas. "No," I said.

Parker heard something more beneath it. "But you wanted to? He wanted to?"

"I wanted to," I admitted slowly. "Thomas was there for me when no one else was. I guess I sort of fell for him because he saved me in a way."

Parker looked sad. "Julia," he began, shifting his weight forward so that his face was inches from my own, "he didn't save you."

"Yes, he did—"

"No, he didn't," Parker interrupted. "You're tough and determined and strong. I've seen it in you—you don't need saving."

It was what I had always wanted to believe about myself but what I had always known was nothing more than a carefully constructed facade. Had I changed? Was I who Parker thought I was?

Parker studied my face for a moment, then closed the space between us, resting his hands on the doorframe above my head. "You . . . don't . . . need . . . saving." He punctuated each word with a soft, inviting kiss on my lips.

I wrapped my arms around his neck. "I don't?"

"No. It's one of the reasons I'm so drawn to you."

We were quiet for a moment, and he slid his arms around my waist so that we were pressed together. "Do you still have a thing for Thomas?"

I laughed and it wasn't at all forced. Standing here with Parker—with the words he said to me and the way he looked at me—how could I want anything else? "Are you crazy?" I asked, looking directly into his gunmetal blue eyes.

"Promise?"

"I promise."

"Then I'll let you go home for Thanksgiving," Parker said with a little affected condescension.

"You're so *gracious*," I murmured, and then I covered his mouth with my own.

A part of me was reluctant to leave Parker for the weekend, but when Friday afternoon rolled around, any hesitation was replaced by a soaring excitement that I was going *home*.

I threw some clothes and toiletries into my laundry basket and unenthusiastically added my backpack to the top of the pile. I couldn't go an entire weekend without doing homework, yet I was loath to take it along when I had so few hours with my grandmother. "If there's time," I told myself, knowing that there wouldn't be time and realizing that I would regret it come Monday.

The road home required all of two turns, so I set my cruise control on sixty-two. When I met the odd late harvester ambling down the road on its way to a field of dry corn, I honked and passed it with a wave and a smile. I had told Grandma to expect me around suppertime, and she was making my favorite: homemade vegetable beef soup stocked with fresh vegetables still crisp and new from her own garden. She never overcooked it, knowing that I loved my veggies with a little firmness in them, and she argued that the second day of soup was always better than the first because the flavors had simmered together but nothing was soggy or overdone. I had to stop myself from overriding the cruise control and weighting the gas pedal with my foot on more than one occasion.

I had been gone for only a couple of months, but somehow I expected everything to be changed. When I crested the hill above our farm, I held my breath in anticipation and was surprised to see that all seemed to be exactly as I had left it. The grove of maples, elms, and oaks flanking the house on the northwest side of the property was nearly bare, and I could see the brown leaves blanketing the ground almost two feet thick in some places. The crops in the surrounding fields were mere remnants of their earlier bounty, and Grandma's garden was nothing more than vacant, black earth. Other than the fact that what had previously been green was now brown, everything was the same. I couldn't decide if it was comforting or disheartening.

Grandma must have seen my car from the window over the sink because as I pulled into the driveway, she came out of the house. She was wearing a tan dress with her red gingham half apron tied around her waist. There was a towel tucked into the apron at her side, and she was drying her hands on it as she watched me drive up. She was smiling at me with her lips pressed together, and although I couldn't tell for sure from this distance, it looked as though she choked back tears. I did.

"You're here," Grandma said when I stepped out of the car and enfolded her in a hug on the front sidewalk. It was a soothing statement, an acknowledgment that wherever I may be after this moment in time, for now at least I was home.

I swallowed a sob and smiled broadly at her. "It feels good to be here. I missed you."

"I missed you, too," she whispered as if it were a secret. "I've been thinking about getting a computer so I can do that electronic mail thing with you."

I giggled at the thought of my grandmother trying to navigate the World Wide Web. "Maybe we should just call each other more often," I suggested.

"Good idea," she agreed. "I'm too old to start thinking about all that stuff. Do you know Ellie tried to talk me into getting one of those new convection ovens? What would I do with all those buttons?"

It was a natural and happy feeling to be joking with my grandmother on ground that felt so much a part of me that I was sure I was more myself just standing on it. Even on the front porch I could smell the soup and the fresh bread baking, and somewhere in the back of my mind I tried to convince myself that life would be better if I just never went back. The engineering college at Brighton was a world away from here. It was a thought I wouldn't even seriously consider for a second, but being wrapped in the solace of my home was more than a little intoxicating—I felt warm and safe and drowsy in the dearest, most satisfying way.

"I washed your sheets so they'd be nice and fresh," Grandma was saying as we made our way into the house, "and there're peanut-butter cookies in the cookie jar and a jug of that chocolate milk you like in the fridge."

"Grandma!" I chastised tenderly. "You didn't have to make me cookies or buy me chocolate milk."

"I know," she said, waving away my words as if bothersome flies buzzed around her head. "But I wanted to. Go put your stuff upstairs. Supper will be ready in a couple of minutes."

It looked like Grandma hadn't touched my bedroom other than to clean it every few weeks. Even the empty bottle of perfume that I had left on my dresser because I liked the shape of the curving glass had not been moved an inch. I touched a few things as I walked around the room, letting my fingers brush against the dangling beads of my lampshade and the stuffed bear on a little chair in the corner. The bed looked smaller to me somehow, and I lay down on it to make sure that I still fit. As always, my feet rested a few inches from the edge. I curled up on my side with a sigh, taking in the air of my home and exhaling it slowly through my mouth as though cleansing something deep within.

I waited for Grandma to call me down to dinner, but minutes passed and she didn't. The sounds of her setting the table drifted up the stairs, and I knew we were ready to eat, but still there was no request from the kitchen. It dawned on me that she would not call me down until I came on my own. She saw me as a guest. A wanted guest, a beloved guest, but a guest all the same. It was no longer my job to set the table. It was no longer her place to tell me it was time to eat. Supper would wait until the guest was good and ready.

A fist had closed around my heart by the time I descended the steps into the kitchen. I breathed shallowly, reminding myself that this was the natural course of things: girl grows up, girl moves out, girl gets life outside her old life, and life moves on. We were simply participating in the round, and this was nothing to get emotional over. And yet there was something in me that wanted to cry— the bitter of the bittersweet seemed slightly overpowering in this moment when I felt very alone in the world.

Grandma didn't seem to notice that anything was different. "Does your room look okay?"

I cringed because although I knew the comment was nothing

more than a reflection of my grandmother's expansive gift for hospitality, it was also what the manager of a hotel would ask his paying guest.

"It looks great, Grandma," I said, looking over the table and seeing there was nothing left for me to do. "I could have set the table," I offered.

"You work hard enough at school," Grandma scolded. "Relax when you're home. It takes me two minutes to set the table."

"Well, I get to clean up then," I asserted, trying to find somewhere to fit in this new dynamic.

Grandma regarded me for a second. "We'll clean up together," she finally said. "It'll give us a chance to talk."

I acquiesced.

The meal was wonderful, and everything was just as I remembered it. Grandma's vegetable soup was thick and full of tomatoes, and I shook pepper on it until the surface was dusty with black. I had two bowls, and when I had scraped what I could with my spoon, I took the buttered crusts of my bread and dragged them along the bottom and sides until everything was smeared clean.

"I love cooking for you!" My grandma laughed. "It's so much more fun than cooking for one."

I looked at her forlornly, and she realized her mistake instantly. "No, no, no," she cautioned. "I'm not trying to make you feel guilty. Nothing in all the world could make me more happy or proud than having you go to college and get your degree." She peered into the soup pot and assessed the leftovers. "Don't you worry about me. I cook for different people in the church twice a week—shut-ins, new moms, people who are sick. . . . I've got the house to take care of, and there's Prayer Circle on Wednesdays and Ladies' Night Out on Thursdays and church twice on Sundays." She leveled me with a serious look, leaving no room for discussion or debate. "Julia, I've got *lots* to do."

"It just feels funny," I said. "We're supposed to take care of each other."

"We are taking care of each other," Grandma declared. "We are taking care of each other by letting God work His will out in our lives."

The certainty with which she said it made me feel sheepish. I wasn't letting God do any such thing in my life and had in fact let Him go so ignored in my heart and mind that I had nearly forgotten I was supposed to believe in His existence. It seemed strange to be thinking of such a childish fairy tale when my life had become so significant, so grown-up.

Grandma must not have noticed that I had frozen a bit because she cheerfully began to push everything to the far side of the table so she could make room for her Bible. Family devotions were another thing I had almost forgotten about, and it made me feel the tiniest bit grimy and exposed—like I had done something mildly shameful and was about to get caught—as she opened her Bible now. She would read and then she would want to pray, and she would ask me if I had anything weighing down my heart. I quickly ran different possibilities through my mind and then dismissed them all as hurriedly as I thought them. What could I say that was neither too revealing nor trite?

My thoughtfulness was mistaken for concentration, and when Grandma was finished reading aloud, she said, "It really makes you think, doesn't it? How can God make beauty from ashes?"

I stopped myself from saying, "Huh?" and nodded sagely instead. It looked like she wanted to say more, like she wanted to discuss this passage with me, so I jumped in before she had a chance to dig deeper. "I have a prayer request."

"You do?" she asked, leaning forward slightly.

"I had a big test in statics on Wednesday, and I studied like crazy but it was really hard. . . ." I trailed off. "I'm just hoping I did okay."

"Statics? What's that?"

I was relieved that I had diverted her from more Bible talk. "It's one of the required classes for my engineering major," I explained. "It's mostly formulas and math and applications." I stopped when I saw the slightly awed look in her eye. Grandma had completed the eighth grade and been unable to attend another single day of school as there were baby brothers and sisters to take care of and a farm to run. She had been needed at home. "It's no big deal," I hastily clarified. "I just hope I did okay on the test."

"Oh, honey, I'm sure you did," Grandma assured me, patting my hand. "But we will definitely pray for that."

She folded her hands and prayed right then, and I gave up trying to pay attention after a moment. God felt like an estranged acquaintance, someone I had once known marginally and, after learning more about Him, now had no desire to know. Someone who was far less than He had purported Himself to be. But He meant so much to Grandma that I was silent and still and smiled sweetly at her when she was finished and we were cleaning up the dishes together.

"How is life at school going?" she asked.

I had to search myself for a moment to find the answer. It had been awful at first but was looking up now, and as I thought about Parker and the test that I had nailed, I found that I could tell her with almost complete honesty that it was going very, very well.

"It was hard at first," I said, "but I think I'm really getting the hang of it."

"Are you making good friends?" The same question was insulting from Thomas, but it was simple and straightforward from Grandma—there was only loving consideration behind her words.

For once, it was easy to know how to answer. I couldn't tell her that friends were hard to make when my classes absorbed nearly every minute of my time, but I also couldn't lie to my grandmother. I would walk the delicate line in between. "There are lots of great people in my classes, and I really like my roommate, Becca." I *did* like Becca, I told myself, and it struck me as funny that she still believed that my mother was a cordon bleu chef. I laughed and covered it up by saying, "She's really funny."

Grandma was drying dishes, and she looked at the plate in her hands as she carefully asked, "Any *special* friend?"

The way she said *special* left no doubt as to her meaning. I debated with myself whether or not I wanted to tell her about Parker and finally decided that it wouldn't be a bad thing to at least warm her up to the idea. If we stayed together, I didn't want him to come as a big surprise. "Well," I said, equally as carefully as she had phrased her question, "there's this one guy. . . ."

She smiled at me optimistically.

"I don't know him very well yet, but he's nice and handsome and very, very intelligent," I said, trying to offer just enough information without eliciting questions I wasn't ready to answer.

"He sounds nice," Grandma mused.

"He is," I stated. "He's in engineering also."

I watched her struggle to find something else she could say or ask that wouldn't be considered too nosy or intrusive. I didn't want her to worry or think that it was more than it actually was, so I promptly added, "We're not really dating or anything. We're just getting to know each other."

Grandma looked me straight in the eye. "I'm glad," she said. Then, because she was my grandma and because there was no one else to say it, she included, "Be careful."

I returned her gaze very sincerely and said, for her benefit only, "Don't worry. I will."

The rest of the night flew by as Grandma and I laughed and talked in the living room, having so much fun remembering that we actually took out the old Reebok shoe box that contained the photographs of my youth. There were hundreds of pictures inside—so many that Grandma had knotted an old tie around the box in order to stop photos from spilling out. We had to pull at the knot for what seemed like forever before it finally gave, and when the pressure of the tightly wrapped cloth was no longer holding the lid in place, a handful of photographs did indeed slip lightly to the floor.

Grandma reached for the one nearest her. "Oh! Look at this. . . ."

It was a snapshot of me and a half dozen or so kittens that populated the farm every spring. There was one perched on my shoulder and one in each of my hands. Two more were climbing over my crossed legs, and a little orange tail poked out from behind my back. They were lovely multicolored barn cats, the kind of litter that makes you marvel at how one mother could produce a coal black, a snowy white, and a variety of calico and striped offspring all at the same time. I used to pretend that at the very least they had to rub off on each other inside the womb. Surely the white kitten's paws were gray from being curled against her charcoal-colored brother.

"They're so cute," I cooed, a smile in my voice. "Do you remember Butter?" I asked, pointing to the suede kitten that could have passed for Siamese.

"Of course. How old were you in this picture?"

I took it from her and studied it for a moment. "Eight?" I guessed. "Nine? It was before I got glasses but after I broke my arm," I said, indicating the scars along my elbow that marked where the pins had gone.

We must have remembered at the same time because Grandma reached for another picture without a word, and I laid the photo with the kittens aside. It had been taken the week after Janice left, during the time when everyone still tried to console me with unexpected ice cream cones, carry-out pizza picnics in the park, and lapfuls of adorable kittens. It hadn't worked but not because I didn't appreciate their efforts. Instead, all the attention and fuss made me feel guilty that I didn't actually need consoling. I didn't miss Janice all that much. My heart broke a little with the remembering because I realized that it had been too much to ask of a nine-year-old.

"Here," Grandma said, handing me another.

I found myself peering at my dad and grandpa standing next to the antique John Deere tractor that they had spent years restoring. There was an undisguised pride in Grandpa's shoulders as he stood with one arm resting against the tall, deeply treaded wheels. Dad, standing beside him with his hand on Grandpa's other arm and looking very young and attractive, had a boyish grin on his face.

I laughed. "They look so handsome," I commented, tracing the line of my father's form in the picture.

"I remember when they finished it," Grandma murmured. "They were like little boys with a new toy."

"Where is the tractor?" I asked, returning the photo to her.

"We donated it to the county historical society when your grandpa passed away. They drive it in the local parades and use it during Heritage Days when everyone dresses up like pioneers." Grandma shrugged. "A part of me would have loved to keep it, but after Abram died, what would I have done with it?"

I suppressed a little sigh of disappointment, reminding myself that it was just a tractor.

"Don't worry," Grandma consoled. "There's a brass plaque on it that reads 'Restored by Abram and Daniel DeSmit.'"

Hours passed as we sat on the floor and sifted through all those dusty memories. Some of them were unfamiliar, even though I saw my own fawn-blonde head and too-big eyes staring out at me. It was as if a different little girl had taken my place and lived my life for a while, and I was surprised on more than one occasion to see myself in surroundings that I simply couldn't recall.

"Where is this?" I asked, holding up a photo that had Dad and me centered in front of desolate, rolling hills with horizontal tones of pink, green, and purple.

"The Badlands," Grandma said after glancing at the picture. "The three of us went there on our way to the Black Hills one year. Don't you remember?"

I shook my head. "I remember the Black Hills but not the Badlands."

"Come on, Julia," Grandma said encouragingly. "We were driving down Interstate 90, and your dad saw the turnoff for the Badlands and he just took it. We didn't plan on going, and we both complained all the way. . . . You really don't remember?"

"No," I admitted.

"It was the best part of the trip. We all said so."

I wondered how many other "best parts" of my life I had forgotten.

All evening we filled the farmhouse with our laughter and blinked back reflective tears—sweet, welcome tears that made me feel full and happy—on more than one occasion. We shared a beautiful night talking and smiling and remembering.

There was only one photo that made me feel anything other than contemplative and able to accept who I was and where I had been. I turned that picture facedown beside me as soon as I recognized it.

We were cleaning up the box of photographs when my hand brushed the back side of the picture I had tried to ignore. Grandma was busy struggling to make neat stacks, and she didn't notice when I palmed the snapshot and slid it deftly into the back pocket of my jeans. It was a perfect fit, and I could feel the stiff and smooth reminder of its presence when I stood up. I decided Grandma would never miss it, and if she did, she would assume it had been misplaced in one of our many long and messy strolls down memory lane.

"Good night, Grandma," I said, giving her a hug and a kiss when the pictures were back on their overlooked shelf. She was on her way to her room, and the lights were off for bed save the little bulb above the stove.

"'Night, honey." She hugged me back. "Sleep well in your own bed."

"Oh, I will," I assured her and mounted the steps to my room, feeling at peace with the world. My heart and head, never mind my stomach, were full, and I felt strong and capable of facing Thomas in a day. I felt grounded in myself, and though Parker wasn't with me, I wore his words about me and tried to remind myself of what I looked like, of who I was, when seen through his eyes. It made everything seem different.

As I slipped out of my clothes for bed, my thumb hooked around the back of my jeans and felt the firmness of the photograph I had taken. I hadn't forgotten about it, and I pulled it out expectantly and sat down on the edge of the bed. Tucking one bare leg beneath me, I hunched over the picture so I could study it.

The photograph showed Janice standing next to a hospital bed wearing a red floral print dress and white sandals. Her hair was short and bobbed and perfectly done, and she was clutching a small bundle wrapped in a mint green blanket. You couldn't see my face— the soft white cap I was wearing had fallen over my eyes—but you could see four of my tiny baby fingers wrapped around the edge of the blanket.

Homecoming was written on the back of the photo in black ink, and the pen had raised the picture on the other side so that I could run my thumb over the indentation and read it written backward. There were no other notations—no dates, no explanations, no list of the people in the picture or even my name. It was almost as if the event depicted had been momentous enough that it needed no further clarification.

On the surface it was a pretty picture. Dad had focused it just right, and the lighting was soft and complimentary to the tones in my mother's hair. The colors had once been bright and vivid, though faded now, and I knew that in most baby books it would have made a stunning memento of a day that goes down in a family's personal history as one of the most unforgettable.

It was frighteningly ugly.

Janice looked like she could have stepped from the pages of a parenting magazine with that sweet little bundle lying in her arms, a slim figure that hardly revealed the baby was even hers and a broad, sparkling smile on her face. Never mind that her smile reached no further than the upturned corners of her mouth. Her eyes were dull, blank, and weary, but there was something in them that also smacked of fear and desperation. Even with her arms wrapped around me, there was something in the intensity of her look that begged someone just beyond the camera to free her from this burden, to stop making her hold this wiggly baby that her eyes revealed she didn't want.

I lay down on my side on the bed and held the picture above me. Searching for hate or resentment or anger inside myself, I studied her face until I could see it etched on the back of my eyelids when I closed them. I found I felt none of those things for her. Instead, I couldn't help but be overwhelmed by pity for the young woman in the picture. She had failed in so many ways.

But what could I expect? She had been only nineteen.

great
expectation

THE NEXT DAY was filled with baking and comfortable silence. Grandma and I had said all there was to say to each other in the rushing landslide of conversation on Friday, and by Saturday we were content to simply be in each other's presence.

I helped her roll out piecrusts and knead bread as her radio played soft music in the background. It was old-time gospel from a local AM station, but I didn't mind the twang and vibrato because it sounded like my childhood. I remembered the words to more songs than I cared to admit, and I marveled at the fact that I had a hard time recalling a formula for statics but could remember with startling accuracy a song that I hadn't sung or even heard in years. It made my mind seem a little foreign, a bit wild and unexplored. What else hid in the depths?

I got up early for church on Sunday because I knew Grandma hoped that I would go with her. Still yawning, I pulled a dress from the stash of clothes that had been left behind when I went to college and descended the stairs determinedly. Grandma was already having a cup of coffee in the kitchen when I walked through on my way to the shower. I murmured a sleepy good morning and kept going so I would have time to prepare answers for a few questions I knew would come up today.

We hadn't talked once about my church attendance now that I was no longer living at home, but I knew my grandma was aching to know that I was continuing in the faith she and my father had tried to lay as a firm foundation beneath me. I was thankful for their efforts—I knew they were only trying to do what they believed was best for their daughter and granddaughter—but I was unconvinced as to the merit of their belief. God Himself had been alarmingly absent in my complicated life, and I felt that I owed Him nothing. I suddenly smiled thinking of Brandon and our many religious conversations. It had been a very long time since he had crossed my mind, and as I allowed myself a moment to reminisce, I couldn't help but conclude that we would be better suited for each other now. But I loved my grandmother too much to communicate all that angst and discontent to her so bluntly. There had to be something I could say that would be in between a flat-out lie and the potentially hurtful truth.

As I scrubbed berry-scented shampoo into a foamy crown, I

determined to tell Grandma that I was extremely busy and had not yet found a church home in Garret. Brighton was not a religiously affiliated school, but Garret was a distinctly Christian town peppered with churches that ranged from mainstream to eccentric. I could have worshipped in a modern building with theater seating and a band that rivaled any secular group with their shaggy hair, ripped jeans, and advertisement-worthy T-shirts. Or I could have pinned my hair in a bun beneath a little white handkerchief and sat on the women's side of a congregation that looked as if it had stepped right out of the late 1800s. I had seen both groups getting out of their cars in the parking lots of their respective churches as I drove past on my way to Starbucks every Sunday morning. It was hard to imagine finding a place in either extreme. I prepared myself to tell Grandma that I was still searching for the right fit.

But I never had the chance to defend myself.

In spite of the fastidiously constructed expression that I donned as I marched to the bathroom, something in my face must have alerted Grandma to the struggle that it was for me to look even marginally excited about joining her at church. She'd had half an hour to construct her response, and it was delivered with down-to-earth straightforwardness.

"You don't have to come to church with me, Julia," Grandma said when I emerged from the bathroom all primped and ready. She was pouring me a cup of coffee and didn't look up when she continued, "God is seeking you out, and I'm willing to trust His timing. I don't need to have you beside me in the pew today."

I wasn't ready for this approach, and it threw me way off-kilter. A part of me was thankful that the pressure was off, but another part of me wavered between feeling abandoned (Grandma was willing to let me go?) and uneasy (God was seeking me out?).

But I couldn't let Grandma see my agitation, so I said, "Don't be ridiculous. Of course I'm going with you." I almost said, *I love church*, but thankfully the words stuck in my throat, and I never had the opportunity to pollute the air with such an obvious lie. Instead I said, "I want to be with you as much as I can this weekend."

"Well, honey, you're always welcome. I just don't want you to feel obligated." She offered me the coffee and laid her hand against mine when I took the mug. "I gave you to God a long time ago."

As if I were a possession to be passed from hand to hand. But Grandma meant it sweetly, and I knew that in her mind I could receive no higher compliment. I tried to take solace in that knowledge, and because she was so sincere, I even muttered a little comment to her God. "Maybe I could believe in You if only You weren't so distant."

I didn't get a reply. I didn't expect one.

Church was more or less boring. I held the hymnal for Grandma and myself and stared at the navy blazer of the man in front of me as we passed from verse to verse. I found that I remembered the hymns as well as I recalled the gospel songs from the radio, and the words came as easily as if I had repeated them only yesterday.

I wondered at what point I had gone from a little girl with unquestioning belief in something I had never felt or seen to an almost grown woman who saw God as just another in a long list of seemingly harmless deceptions that parents use to keep their children in line. How was He any different from Santa Claus, the Easter bunny, or the tooth fairy? Be good, brush your teeth, do as you're told, and be rewarded with something temporary and breakable and trite. I could only remember the odd Christmas present, the rabbit I got for Easter one year, and a quarter was hardly a good exchange for the tooth that left me with a gaping hole in my mouth for months. I didn't expect anything from God but equally disappointing party favors.

When the offering plate was being passed and the somber stillness of the room eased, I allowed myself to look around. There were faces that I recognized, but most people had slid into obscurity in the years following my dad's death and become relative strangers. They still spoke to and adored my grandmother, but a moody, perplexing teenager was a slightly less inviting acquaintance to maintain.

No one who caught me looking at them bothered to smile, though a few whispered something to their significant others, and I knew that at the very least I was a peripheral object of mild interest. I couldn't be too upset that it seemed as if they had forgotten me as easily as I had put them out of my own life, but I was still a little disappointed. I reminded myself that teary, insincere reunions would have only made me bitter, but it didn't stop me from looking for a friendly face.

The offering plate had reached me, and I passed it on to Grandma, watching her slip a check into it that I was sure had been written out for more than she could afford. I couldn't help but feel a little resentful, and I looked beyond her down the aisle to muse that I hoped everyone else was stretching themselves as far as I knew she was.

The Walker family was sitting across the center aisle at the very end of the bench. Maggie was the only one who had seen me, and she was waving with just her fingers. They bounced up and down excitedly, and I smiled when I saw her mouth form an exaggerated *Hi*.

I mouthed it back and gave her a wink.

Next to Maggie sat Emily and then Mr. and Mrs. Walker followed by the three boys. Thomas was on the end.

My heart caught just a little when I saw him, and I had to remind myself that whatever he wanted to talk to me about would have no effect on our newfound friendship. I was happy now and at the beginning of a relationship that seemed very worth my time, and there was nothing—*nothing*—Thomas could say that would change any of that. Even as I tried to convince myself, my heart registered that he looked sad, and I wanted to wrap my arms around him. I looked away shakily, half wanting to tell him to leave me alone.

As we stood to sing the doxology, I couldn't help feeling that something wasn't right. I tried to glance back at the Walkers, but the arc of the pews as the congregation stood shielded them from my view. Only if I leaned over the bench in front of me could I catch sight of them again. I wasn't willing to do that. Mentally, I walked down the aisle and tried to remember how they sat, what they wore. I counted seven people and it hit me. Francesca was not beside Thomas.

I caught one last glimpse of the Walkers as the postlude played, and as far as I could see, Francesca was not among them. But Fellowship Community was a massive congregation for our small town—almost five hundred people filled the pews on any given Sunday—and I could have easily missed her somewhere in the crowd. It hadn't seemed like anyone other than Maggie had noticed me, and it was plausible to imagine that I, in turn, had simply overlooked Francesca. Or maybe she wasn't feeling well. Maybe she had stayed home.

Watching their backs retreat from the sanctuary and rush to the coatracks to gather their things, I could almost hear Mrs. Walker chiding everyone to get a move on; there was a turkey in the oven and a million things to do. Our hellos would have to wait a few hours until Thanksgiving officially started at two o'clock in the afternoon. It was just enough time to make us ridiculously hungry for the delectable feast that Mrs. Walker had slaved over for days but not late enough to make us cranky and irritable.

Grandma and I hurried home behind them to bake the pies we had prepared and change clothes for the afternoon.

We walked over a little earlier than expected, but Maggie had been waiting for us. When we emerged from the path that cut through the grove in between the two farms, she came tripping down the front steps and threw her arms around my waist. I was holding a shallow cardboard box with a pie in each hand and almost dropped them both.

"Julia!" she screeched, looking up at me expectantly. "Why don't you visit us anymore? I haven't seen you in *so long*."

I kissed the top of her brunette head as I tried to recall the last time I had seen her. Surely it hadn't been a year. . . . "I missed you, Maggie. But school is so busy—"

"That's a *pathetic* excuse," she chastised.

I had to suppress a grin because she was no longer the slightly chubby, silky-skinned toddler who had curled up on my lap to watch *Dora the Explorer*. There were little gold earrings in her ears, and I could already hear the whine of preteen posturing in her voice. She was only eight, but her older sister, Emily, was knocking on the door of boy-girl parties and the wonderful world of makeup. Apparently Maggie had gotten in on the action a bit before her time.

"Sorry, Maggie," I confessed. "I have no excuse. I'm a terrible friend."

"You're not a terrible friend," she conceded. "But don't go away for so long *ever again*." She poked me in the side twice, emphasizing the last two words with all the melodrama of a little princess. Everything about her betrayed her elite status as the baby of the family.

I laughed. "Okay. I won't go away for so long *ever again*."

Grandma had ascended the porch steps in front of us, and Mrs. Walker had met her at the door. "Hi, Julia!" she called over Grandma's head. "Welcome home!" Then she put a hand beneath my grandmother's arm, and they ambled into the house, their heads bowed together, chatting cheerfully in the entryway.

I don't think they heard when Maggie leaned in and said in a too-loud whisper, "Francesca isn't here today, and I'm *so glad*. You're *way* nicer than her. She treats me like I'm seven."

Torn between shock and amusement, I nodded and let her take one of the pies out of my hands. Deciding it might be interpreted as condescending, I resisted the urge to tell her to be careful and watched warily as the Dutch apple pie tilted at an alarming angle. But I kept my mouth shut, wondering why the remarkable Miss Hernandez wasn't here and secretly relishing the knowledge that I was the favorite. As I crossed the threshold of the Walker house, it was hard not to smirk just a little that Maggie liked me better than Francesca. *But it's not a competition!* I rushed to scold myself. *I don't want Thomas. She can have him.*

The house was warm and humming and infused with the rich aromas of Mrs. Walker's handiwork. There was a no-television-on-Thanksgiving rule, so there was something upbeat in the CD player and people were scattered around the great room. I tried not to look too obvious as I craned my neck to search out Thomas, but he was nowhere to be seen. *In the basement pining after Francesca*, I concluded. I ignored whatever emotion that thought tried to push to the surface.

Pulling off my coat, I focused instead on the Walker home. A bright and spacious kitchen gave way to a dining room that was less a room and more a sweeping curve in the wall filled with an enormous harvest table in front of a bay window overlooking the grove. From there the ceiling arched dizzyingly to match the pitch of the roofline, and the room opened up graciously to include a fireplace with a stone mantel, a sitting area around a flat-screen television, and a pool table beneath a low, antique, green-glass light in the far corner.

As I set my pie on the counter and returned Mrs. Walker's tight, sincere hug, I marveled a bit at the surroundings and questioned my youthful attraction to the Walker family. I couldn't help wondering if part of their appeal had been the luxury and comfort of their home. When I was younger, I never really thought of them as rich or of myself as poor. Seeing everything now, it hit me that we were indeed polar opposites.

"Is there anything I can do?" I asked Mrs. Walker, forcing myself to focus on the present, on the woman right in front of me who had been, at least in some small way, like a mother to me for those few years of my life.

She was examining me intently but smiled when she said, "I don't think so, honey. The table is set, the potatoes are mashed, and the turkey is about to be carved by my husband. . . ." Mrs. Walker raised her voice a bit at the end, and when Mr. Walker glanced over his shoulder from his perch on the arm of a chair in the living room, she pinned him with a meaningful look.

"Time to carve the turkey already?" he asked as if on cue.

Mrs. Walker just smiled at him.

He hoisted himself off the chair with a theatrical sigh, and she gave his arm an affectionate little squeeze as he walked past.

"Hi, Julia," he said, pausing to give me a quick hug. "It's good to see you. You look great!"

I gave him a discomfited smile, but when he was out of earshot, Mrs. Walker refused to let me off the hook and instead echoed his sentiments. "You *do* look great, Julia."

"Thanks," I stammered, succumbing to a full-on blush. "I've been doing my hair differently."

Mrs. Walker touched my cheek, and my breath caught at the tenderness of the action. "Your hair is pretty, but I wasn't talking about your hair. It goes deeper than that." She lowered her voice just for me. "You look happy."

"I am happy," I said softly.

"I'm glad." She nodded once and patted my cheek gently before bustling back into the kitchen. "Not like that, Jonathan!" she admonished boisterously, mocking her husband's carving efforts. But there was laughter in her voice.

I crossed my arms around myself and watched them for a moment, wavering a bit between undying love and commitment to this beautiful, exceptional family and slightly jaded skepticism because they were just too perfect. I would have never fit into this family as anything more than the mildly misfit friend, and I allowed myself to dwell on Parker and his addictive idiosyncrasies for a moment. It hit me that I was happy because I had finally given up on trying to be something that I was not.

We were all gathering around the table when I saw Thomas for the first time. He emerged from the basement looking tired and cheerless, and he walked with his eyes glued to the floor. I took a deep breath; smiled at him as a dear, old friend; and waited for him to look up. He didn't.

There was an unspoken seating arrangement, and when Thomas took his spot next to me, he had to acknowledge my presence. A smile drifted across his face, and I realized that he was surprised to see me. I was a bit taken aback at his seeming indifference after he had beseeched me to attend, but I couldn't help feeling sorry for the dullness in his gaze. I touched his arm in a display of solidarity and friendship, and something like gratefulness flashed behind his eyes.

The seven Walkers sat arranged around Mr. Walker, who was at the head of the table by the expansive window. I was beside Thomas, and Grandma took the spot next to me. Then came Mrs. Walker's parents, Mr. and Mrs. Martin, who were both nearly deaf but cute and wrinkly and old in a way that made you love them simply because they had known so much life. Rounding out the table were Mrs. Walker's only sister and her husband. They had never had children and insisted on being called Uncle Matt and Aunt Kathy even by me.

I studied the table after everyone sat down and tried to act completely normal and not at all perturbed that I sat next to Thomas instead of Francesca, who had filled that particular space with striking grace and beauty for the last two years.

It wasn't until we were done praying and the platters were being passed that Thomas finally spoke. "I'm glad you came, Julia," he said, passing me the sweet potatoes. They were glistening with butter and brown sugar, and I helped myself to a heaping spoonful.

"I wouldn't have missed it for the world!" I said, trying to communicate my contentment and utter disinterest in anything he might have to say to me that was even remotely different from the just-friends mantra that he had perfected over the last few years.

Thomas was silent for a minute as he selected a still-warm-from-the-oven roll and handed the basket to me. "I'm sorry I haven't e-mailed you for so long." He stole a glance at me out of the corner of his eye. "My modem was broken." An obvious lie. "Did you get my e-mail from a few days ago?"

"No," I said brightly. Another obvious lie. "I haven't checked my e-mail in a while." Sitting next to him, without the dazzling Francesca in between, I couldn't help wondering what his motives were, why he looked so sad. I decided I didn't want to know. *Drop it*, I begged him silently. *Just let it go. Don't tempt me. Don't make me want you. Don't use me as a confidence boost after a painful breakup. I'm happy now—don't mess that up.*

"Oh" was all he said, obviously disappointed.

I decided he was on the verge of revealing a hint of what he wanted to talk to me about when the conversation around the table broke in on our little private chat.

"Where's Francesca?" Aunt Kathy asked loudly. Her mouth was slightly agape, and her eyebrows knit together in confusion.

The last two Thanksgivings had seen Aunt Kathy and Francesca hit it off like long-lost friends. They had giggled and made plans to go shopping together for Christmas, and Uncle Matt even switched places with Francesca last year so she and Aunt Kathy could talk and gossip unhindered. I had slipped out after dessert with a pounding headache and resolved never, ever to come back. Funny how those sorts of resolutions never keep. Funny how I would have actually *preferred* to have Francesca sitting beside me this year.

Mrs. Walker shot Thomas a look, but he was staring at his plate. She filled in diplomatically. "Fran couldn't make it this year."

My ears perked up. Fran? Pet name? Or was there a little bitterness in the tone of Mrs. Walker's voice?

"What do you mean?" Aunt Kathy exclaimed, completely clueless to her sister's sensitive attempt to bury the topic. "Francesca's practically family! She should be here."

"She was busy," Mrs. Walker offered, rather tight-lipped.

"Too busy to drive twenty minutes for a home-cooked meal with *family?*"

Thomas cut in. "Actually, Aunt Kathy, Francesca and I are taking a break for a while."

Aunt Kathy looked dumbstruck. "But—"

"Kathy, let it go." Mrs. Walker's voice left no room for another word on the subject. "Who still needs potatoes?" she added, holding up the casserole dish as if it were a trophy.

Maggie caught my eye from across the table and gave me an ambitious wink.

I pretended I hadn't seen her, feeling troubled that at least one person around the table was hoping I would step into Francesca's now-empty shoes. They were heels. I was more of a hiking boots kind of girl.

Aunt Kathy seemed mildly offended, and it cast a cloud over the rest of the meal. Mrs. Walker countered her sister and wore her cheerfulness like a distasteful responsibility, and though every word she said and every smile she forced was happy and light, there was a sense of martyrdom seeping through her spirited veneer. Everyone else seemed caught somewhere in the middle, and I ended up feeling just plain depressed that Francesca's absence had more or less ruined the first Thanksgiving I had looked forward to in two years. I silently berated Thomas for either breaking up with Francesca or doing something stupid enough to make her break up with him. Their separation was obviously making everyone miserable. Well, except for Maggie.

After the dessert had been served and everyone gratefully left the table to escape to some corner of the house, Thomas finally made his move. I had gotten up to clear the dishes, and when I reached for his plate, he grabbed my wrist.

"Can we talk?" he asked quietly, and his fingers loosened on my skin so that he was encircling me but not touching me. It was as if he was afraid to make contact.

He looked so sad and desperate that I abandoned my earlier strategy of avoiding time alone at all costs. Thomas had been there when I needed him; it was only right that I was here for him now. "Of course." Though I tried to keep my voice blithe, it was burdened with the depth of emotion I felt for him. I couldn't say no to him and he knew it.

"I'll meet you downstairs in a few minutes." He got up from the table without looking at me again and disappeared down the staircase at the far end of the great room.

I brought the stack of plates I was holding into the kitchen and set them next to the sink.

Mrs. Walker was rinsing dishes, and she looked up when I added them to her pile. "Talk to him, Julia, would you? He's so sad. . . ." Her eyes betrayed the muddle of emotions that she felt. There was something in her that resented Francesca for some reason, but I could also see that she wanted her son to be happy, even if happiness was Francesca.

I touched her arm, thankful that for once I could do something for her. "I'm going to. He's waiting for me downstairs."

"Oh, thank goodness," she whispered urgently. "Get out of here—we'll take care of the kitchen."

The basement was exactly as I remembered it, and I had to shake my head to clear the cobweb of memories and emotions that came with this life-laden place. I hadn't been down here in years. Thanksgivings with Francesca had sent me straight home after dinner, so it had been over two years—back when Thomas was still preparing for his first year of college—since I had been surrounded by the road signs, patched couches, and incense-scented milieu of my old hangout. I took a moment to breathe in the air.

Thomas was sitting on the couch, and when I was able to register his presence, I moved to sit in the love seat against the wall. He patted the space beside him. I barely even thought about it before I sank down next to him.

We stayed there for the span of a few heartbeats, Thomas studying the carpet and me studying him. Finally I shook off some of the heaviness and managed to say, "Hey, Thomas, what's going on?"

He gave his head the slightest shake and looked up at me as if from a trance. "Isn't it obvious?" he asked at length. "Francesca broke up with me."

I didn't want to feel a rush of hope, but I couldn't stop it any more than I could forget that Thomas had saved me when no one else would. *Parker*, I reminded myself. *Brighton, engineering, Parker* . . . Thomas was my past. I was living my future.

"I'm sorry," I said eventually, quietly. "What happened?" It seemed like the right thing to say.

Thomas sighed almost angrily. "She dated a guy for a long time before coming to college. They were supposed to get married, but she broke off the relationship when she met me." He stopped to rub his face with his hands. "I was going to ask her to marry me, Julia, but she said she needed to find out if she still had feelings for him. She said she didn't want to spend the rest of her life wondering what if." He stopped as abruptly as he had started.

I appreciated the fact that this was probably the first time he had tried to explain it all to anyone. The bitterness his mother felt was shallow enough to confirm that her version of the story started and stopped with Francesca breaking up with her son for some unexplained and indiscernible reason.

I tried very hard to be objective and said, "What does that mean? Is she getting back together with her ex-boyfriend?"

"I don't know," Thomas said forlornly. "I don't know what it means. I'm just supposed to leave her alone for a month while she finds out if she can't live without me. She says there's a difference between being able to live with someone—theoretically you could make yourself live with anyone—and not being able to live without them." Thomas turned to look me full in the face. "Do you understand that? Do you get the difference? Because I think it's just semantics."

I thought about it for a moment. Being able to live with someone versus not being able to live without them. I decided I couldn't speak from experience on that one. However, I could tell Francesca a thing or two about living without someone after you knew with all your heart and soul that you could never, ever do such a thing. I had lived without my father. I had lived without Thomas. I had survived.

"I don't know, Thomas," I finally said. "I guess it makes sense that she would want to be absolutely sure before making a lifelong commitment. . . ." It was the wrong thing to say. Thomas looked at me as if I had just slapped him in the face. Frozen, I didn't know what he wanted me to do, so I just sat there waiting for him to make the next move.

I had almost given up on our hopeless conversation when Thomas spoke again. He wasn't looking at me, and his words were so quiet that I could hardly make them out. "That's not all. Francesca thinks that I have an unresolved relationship in my past."

The room went still. I held my breath and waited for him to continue. When he didn't, I cautiously filled in the gaps. "With me?" I asked, the words barely making their way past my lips.

"Yeah." His response was equally as soft.

My mind made one last frantic attempt to hold on to Parker and all I had built for myself, but it was useless. My heart was screaming, *Do you? Do you? Do you? Am I unresolved? Do you have feelings for me? Do you love me the way that I have loved you since you smiled at me over a stolen stop sign on a glacial winter night?*

He answered me as if my thoughts had been whispered in his ear. "I don't know." He repeated to himself, "I don't know."

And then, because he saw the hope in my eyes or because he

needed to know for himself or because he knew he could never go back to Francesca without saying in utter truth that there was no one else, he put his hand on my face. I could feel the lingering imprint that his mother's hand had left there only hours before, but when Thomas touched me it was different. He considered my cheeks and my forehead and my lips, and when he brought his gaze to my eyes, they collapsed somewhere beyond my reach. He leaned in toward me, and whatever defense I had built against him had been so obliterated that I met him in the middle.

We paused, and the exhalation of his doubts danced with my own timorous hope for the split second before he kissed me. It was the merest gasp of a kiss, the slightest glancing touch, and then he pulled me to him hungrily. I responded with all the longing, all the trapped and wretched waiting of the years that I had loved him. We kissed and held and drank each other in desperate, reckless gulps, and when I was ready to cry with the fullness of the ache that I had felt for so long, Thomas pulled away.

He covered his mouth with his hand for a moment, and his eyes were unreadable as I struggled to regain the air that he had stolen. I reached for him, and his hand left his mouth to catch my own while he filled the room with a laugh that left me reeling.

"Oh, Julia!" Thomas swung my hand like a delighted little child. "We're still best friends!" He gave me an exuberant kiss on the cheek. "That was like kissing my sister!"

free
fall

A FLASH LIKE LIGHTNING sparked through my soul as Thomas smiled at me with triumph and relief blazing in his eyes. He was oblivious to—or intentionally ignoring—the feelings that were dripping from my face like phantom tears that I had yet to cry.

I wanted to hit him. I wanted to take all the frustration and even rage that I felt for him and contain it in my closed fist, give it back to him so that I didn't have to hold it pressed to myself anymore. But as quickly as the emotion surged, it ebbed and flowed out of me like a wave falling back into the immensity of the sea. I was left on the dark, empty beach—cold and wet and in pain.

I tried to say, *I have to go*, but my mouth was incapable of speech, and in a haze of numbness and shame, I pulled my hand from his and staggered from the couch.

"Julia?" Thomas sounded surprised. "Where are you going?"

I didn't answer or look back or even acknowledge that I had heard him, and when I mounted the steps to leave, he didn't move to stop me.

"I had to know," he said.

I kept walking.

"I'm . . ." I thought he was going to say *sorry*, but he didn't. Maybe he knew what he had done, and he silently hated himself. Or maybe he was already thinking about Francesca and was relieved that I was simply going to walk away. Whatever he felt, when my argyle socks were all he could see of me, I heard him say, "Good-bye."

It felt irrevocable.

Somewhere inside me a backup generator began to run, and it powered me through the great room when I was sure that there was not a hope in the world of acting even marginally normal. I managed to return Maggie's hug, smile gratefully as Mr. and Mrs. Walker said polite good-byes, and even nod when Mrs. Walker furtively whispered in my ear, "Is he going to be okay?" The fact that my bottom lip was tucked between my teeth seemed to be lost on her.

Only Grandma noticed the current in the air around me, and she joined me at the door as I slipped into my shoes. "Julia, what's wrong?" her voice was low and warm.

I stopped her as she reached for her own shoes. If she spoke to me like that again, I would fall entirely to pieces, and I was sandbagging furiously against just such a flood.

"You don't have to come with me, Grandma," I croaked, choking a bit on the first words that I had uttered since inviting Thomas to break my heart by whispering, *"With me?"*

Her eyes invaded mine, and I tried to make the upward turn of my lips look convincing. "I'm just tired. I need to get back to school. I'm so behind. . . ." I pulled my jacket off the antique coatrack and gave it a hard shake as if to beat off a fine layer of dust—the very residue of air from the Walker house—though none existed. I slid my arms into it, happy to have something, anything, around me.

Grandma was still searching my face, and I didn't want her to find what she was looking for, so I put my chin against her shoulder as I hugged her and said, "Please stay and enjoy the afternoon. It would be such a waste for you to go home. I'm going to pick up my things and leave. I'll be gone in five minutes."

I knew I hadn't convinced her, but when she sighed, I also knew that she would comply with my request—even if it was against her better judgment. "I don't know what happened, but—"

"Shhh, Grandma, just don't. Nothing happened." I blinked hard, then pulled away and smiled at her. "I'm fine. See? I love you and thank you and I'll see you soon." The words tumbled out almost mechanically, and I quickly asked her God to let her know that I meant them with every ounce of my being even if it didn't sound like I did.

Outside, the air was cold and sharp, and everything seemed to have edges that I hadn't noticed before. The crunch of dry leaves beneath my feet was raucous and harsh, the naked trees were vulgar and exposed, and the breeze that had formerly held the fresh, clean scent of impending winter was biting and cruel. I hurried from the

Walker house half afraid that someone would come after me, that they would all find out what had happened. The thought spurred me into a jog, and I tripped over the uneven earth with my hands crammed deep into my pockets and my head tucked heavily against my chest.

Grandma's farmhouse was so quiet and empty it felt like a tomb. I rushed around in the shadows, not bothering to turn on the lights as I stuffed clothes, toiletries, and the odd book into my backpack. It was obvious that when I arrived back at Brighton I would realize I had left something behind, but I didn't care.

Before anyone at the Walker house could think twice about my departure, I was gone. I didn't buckle my seat belt or turn on the radio or look once at my speedometer. I drove. It was a reflex action, and anything else would have required me to move—to move my arm, my eyes, my mind, or my heart. I was imploding, falling into myself because the alternative would require me to think or feel. It was like curling into a tight, small ball and taking shallow breaths to stave off nausea. *If I am still, if I don't move or breathe, I'll be okay.* Occasionally a thought would rise to the surface, and I'd wish for less than a heartbeat that I had never come home for Thanksgiving. As quickly as it entered my mind, I would push it almost violently away and return to a state of immobility. I was anesthetized.

It wasn't like I planned to go to Parker's apartment, so when I pulled up in front of his place, I was almost surprised to come out of my trance and find myself there. But it felt wholly right, and as a tear finally slid like a token offering down my cheek, I had to stop myself from throwing open the car door and rushing into the comfort of Parker's arms.

I gripped the steering wheel to ground myself and found the capacity to think logically still hiding somewhere in my shaken mind. Parker couldn't know what had happened. He had been apprehensive of my visit home in the first place; in some impossible way he had doubted Thomas and my ability to read him. If Parker knew about the kiss, if he knew that I let it happen and that I was crushed by the outcome, it would change everything.

Acting completely normal and unchanged was almost too much to ask, but I couldn't stand the thought of returning to my dorm room alone. Becca would be there full of questions, or worse, she would be gone. Or worse yet, she would be there and *not* be full of questions. Each scenario left me cold. And, I reasoned with myself, I needed a little tenderness right now. I needed someone to hold me, to look at me as if I was worthy of time, attention, maybe even love.

I erased the tear from my cheek with the tip of my finger in gentle, sweeping strokes. The skin could not be red from pulling, and my eyes could not be bloodshot. I blinked a few times and took deep breaths through my nose and practiced a quick smile in the rearview mirror. Digging in the cup holder, I found a stick of gum and popped it in my mouth as I smoothed honey-flavored balm on my lips. The result was almost natural. I looked fine. Maybe a little tired. Maybe a little hollow behind the eyes. The long drive would excuse that. Parker wouldn't suspect a thing.

The clock on the dashboard read seven-thirty, and I wished aloud that Parker would be home. Home alone, I amended. Lights glowing in the living room had already informed me that someone was there, but I knew I could hardly count on it being Parker. I had told him I wouldn't be back until late Sunday night and that I would not see him until Monday at the earliest. I crossed my fingers as I walked up the sidewalk.

Parker opened the door before I had a chance to knock. "Julia!" he exclaimed. "What are you doing here?" He was wearing his coat, but his shoes were untied and he was holding a nearly bursting garbage bag.

"I came home early," I said with a shy smile and a shrug. "I thought I'd stop by for a minute since it's not too late."

Parker put his hand around my neck and pulled my head toward his so he could kiss my forehead. "I'm glad you're here. I just have to take the garbage out." He held up the bulging bag and explained, "Garbage day tomorrow. Go on inside. I'll be right there."

I let myself in and hung my coat on the hook, kicking off my shoes with a sigh. I had been right to come here. Just being near Parker made Thomas's basement seem very small and very far away. But even that tiny thought made my stomach pitch, and I hurriedly pushed it out of my mind.

No one else was around as far as I could tell, so I sat down on the couch to wait for Parker. There was a football game on TV, and I stared at it blankly for a minute before finding all the color and noise and movement irritating.

I looked around the room. The coffee table had been pulled close to the couch, and I put my feet up on it just as I was sure Parker had been doing only minutes before. There were papers scattered across the table and weighted down with Heineken bottles—two empty and one half full. I picked up the bottle with beer still in it and sniffed. It smelled like yeast. I remembered my dad once saying that too many people drank to forget. It sounded good. I took a gulp.

"Julia!" Parker reproached from the doorway. "You're not old enough!" He winked at me playfully.

"Are you going to stop me?" I retorted, taking another swig and trying not to grimace.

He laughed. "Nah. It's warm anyway. You finish it." He shrugged off his coat and stepped out of his shoes, then bounded across the room to jump on the couch beside me. "Chug, chug, chug," he teased.

I gave him a wry look and complied.

"Hey, I was teasing," he said soothingly, taking the now-empty bottle from my hands and adding it to the others on the table. "Was Thanksgiving that bad? I mean, my family's messed up, but I thought since you don't have one it couldn't be too terrible. . . ."

"Ha-ha," I muttered, rolling my eyes at him. Then I mustered up the courage to lie to his face and said, "Thanksgiving was nice. I'm just glad to be back."

"I'm glad you're back too," he announced and leaned in to give me a kiss.

I shrank, wondering if Thomas still lingered on my lips somehow, if Parker would know that I had kissed someone else in my absence. But the kiss was a brief peck, and if Parker noticed my hesitation, he hadn't read anything into it at all.

"So, did you have fun?" he asked.

"It was great to see my grandma," I answered, trying not to add more lies to the one I had already told. "And the food was good."

"Better than my spaghetti?"

"Never," I assured him though I nodded as I said it.

He pinched my arm playfully, but I brushed his hand aside and laid my head on his shoulder.

"You into the game?" Parker inquired.

"No."

"We don't have to watch it," he said. "I'm a Vikings fan—but don't tell anyone." He switched off the TV.

I didn't want to talk or be serious or do anything other than sit in silence, and the only way I could imagine that happening was if he finished watching the game. I had wanted to rest my head on his shoulder and close my eyes and just be still, listen to the sound of him breathing beneath the announcer's play-by-play, but I didn't know how to convince him that I actually wanted to watch the game after I had stated that I wasn't interested in it. I had ruined it for myself, so I said, "What do you want to do?"

He was quiet for a moment, as if considering his choices. "Actually," he finally admitted, "I want to talk." His pause told me he already had a topic chosen. After a few heartbeats he said, "I was hoping you'd tell me about your family."

"I've already told you all about my grandma," I replied, struggling to keep the frustration out of my voice. I didn't want to talk.

"Not your grandma, Julia. You said you'd tell me about your parents sometime." Parker dropped his shoulder carefully and eased away so I had to sit up and look at him. There was a gentle expression on his face, and I couldn't help but be touched that he genuinely wanted to hear my story.

The floodgates were about to burst open, so I said hastily, almost harshly, "Not tonight, Parker. I'm not in the mood."

He looked slightly taken aback, but he gave in without a fight. "Okay," he said after a pause. "No football game, no talking . . . what *do* you want to do?"

I felt bad that I had come here to use him for comfort and was now being difficult. It crossed my mind that I should just tell him about my dad—he was a beautiful person to talk about—but I simply couldn't muster up the energy. My gaze floated unenthusiastically around the room as I tried to come up with something fun or witty or interesting to say, but I was so heartbroken and uninspired. I wondered if I should just leave.

And then my gaze stopped on the papers littering the coffee table, and it registered for the first time what they were. My head whipped toward Parker, and he realized that I had identified what was on the table.

"Oh no, no, no," he said instantly, leaning forward to quickly gather the papers into a pile. "Not now."

"Yes, now," I said doggedly, grabbing for the papers even as he swept them out of my reach.

"You can wait like everyone else. Do you think you get special treatment because the TA has a thing for you?"

I nodded emphatically and without thinking climbed onto his lap to get access to the papers he was holding above his head. He rapidly lowered his arm to the floor and let the stack drop. He grabbed my wrists and held them tight.

"Those are our statics tests, Parker," I protested. "I could use a little good news right now."

Parker didn't question why I needed good news, and he didn't let his gaze drop from mine for a single second. He held my eyes carefully and said nothing while his grip tightened on my wrists and his eyes tried to communicate without words. It was only after he had stared at me so intently, so gravely, that I finally understood. Something in my face clicked, and he knew that I knew.

"Julia," he began softly, "it's okay, really. It's just one test."

"I failed?" I whispered falteringly, though I already knew the answer to the question.

"Not by much," Parker jumped in, trying to salvage at least some of my pride. He didn't understand that pride was such an insignificant corner of the whole picture.

The pressure of all that lay concealed in my heart was too great to hold. I didn't sob or make a noise at all, but the tears I had been collecting for months, even years, began to spill down my face too quickly to count.

Parker didn't seem alarmed as I sat on his lap and cried. Instead of trying to talk me out of my sadness, he pulled my head onto his shoulder and wrapped his arms around me. "It's okay," he consoled, stroking my back and scattering kisses on my head.

I didn't touch him or hug him or reach for him. I just sank into his embrace and let him hold me up because I didn't think I was capable of doing it on my own.

When I had soaked his shirt with my tears and was aware enough of myself to be horrified by the pathetic display he had just endured, I pulled myself from his embrace and slunk humiliated from his knees. "I am so sorry," I breathed, not daring to look at him.

"Don't be sorry," Parker said, catching my hand so that some small part of us was still touching. "You don't have anything to be sorry about. I know how much you wanted to be an engineer."

Earlier he had assured me that it was just one test, but when he spoke of me as an engineer in the past tense, I knew that it was over.

I couldn't do it. I had given it everything I had, and I had failed. Failure seemed to be a bit of a theme for me on this day that I would have given a year of my life to erase. If before I had felt like I was falling, now I lay past the point of pain, splayed across the ground.

"No, Parker, that was . . ." I couldn't even think of a word to encompass how mortified, how despondent I was about the scene I had just made. All pretense—the cool and collected image I had refined for myself—had been obliterated in fifteen minutes of wet, messy sobbing.

Thomas and the test faded to the background as I came to terms with the fact that I was back to square one. I was no better off than I had been when I was a little girl wondering where I fit in a family without a mother, or a teenager in a world without my father, and now a woman without . . . *anything*. Not even a sense of who I was or should be.

I couldn't look at him, and I didn't know what to say, so I repeated my earlier attempt at an apology. "That was so . . . *awful*. I am so sorry."

He reached across the arm of the couch to grab a paper towel from the end table. It was covered in unidentifiable crumbs, and he shook them onto the floor before handing the crinkled napkin to me. "Here," he offered kindly.

I cleaned myself up, hiding my face in my hands for a moment under the guise of wiping away my tears. After a shaky breath, I balled the paper towel tightly in my fists and got up to leave. I still hadn't looked at Parker once since he told me wordlessly that I had not passed the test. As I crossed in front of him, I glanced furtively at him out of the corner of my eye and tried to give him a wry smile.

He was studying me, and when he met my gaze, he put his legs up on the coffee table and would not let me pass. "You're not going anywhere," he informed me. "If you think you can deter me with a few tears, you've got another thing coming."

I didn't know how to respond, but I didn't have to because Parker stood up to block my path. He cupped my face in his hands and examined me as if trying to burn in his memory each and every freckle and line. "You can cry with me," he said faintly.

When we kissed, I knew that there were too many emotions behind it. Sorrow and disappointment and anger assembled eagerly beside longing and desire—a legion of pent-up aches and loneliness. I needed him like a drowning woman gasping for air, and he responded to my intensity with equal passion. It was mindless and foolish, but neither of us made any move to stop, and though the occasional spark of consciousness rose to the surface, I was either unwilling or unable to pay attention to it.

At some point he took my hand and led me to his bedroom.

I followed.

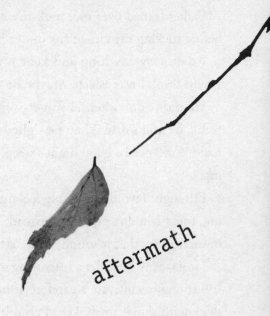

aftermath

LATER PARKER GAVE a humorless little laugh and said that we should definitely use protection next time.

The room spun, and the nausea that I had been restraining for hours lurched into my throat so I could not speak or breathe. *"Next time,"* he'd said. I pressed my eyes shut because I had never planned on there ever being a *this time.* I was lying on my side and he was behind me, running his fingers down the length of my arm. My mouth was dry and forming words that he could not see and I could not distinguish. It wasn't until I had repeated them cease-lessly for longer than I could remember that I finally realized I was whispering, *Oh, God, oh, God, oh, God.* . . . It may have been a prayer. Or a curse.

Parker leaned over me, took my hand, and kissed each knuckle before tucking my closed fist under his chin. "Hey, you okay?"

I didn't say anything and kept my eyes tightly shut. Maybe he would think I was asleep. Maybe he would leave me alone.

He didn't do either. "I forget sometimes that you're only eighteen," he said softly. Then he sighed heavily and gave me back my hand. "You need a good night's sleep. You'll feel better in the morning."

I thought I would probably feel much, much worse in the morning, but I couldn't say that. Instead, I managed to clear my throat in such a way that it sounded like affirmation.

He gave my shoulder a reassuring squeeze. "Good," he whispered, still trying to cultivate a carefree atmosphere though the room was thick with things unspoken. I couldn't imagine what he wanted to say to me when words were so foreign to my petrified mind that I couldn't form a single coherent thought.

Parker rolled onto his side away from me, and in a moment I felt him cover my bare arm with the sweater we had discarded.

I dressed and left in silence.

It was impossible that I was drunk, but the drive to my dorm room was an erratic mess of embarrassing proportions. I blinked and swerved and shook my head to give myself just enough perspective to keep the car between the curb and the yellow line. My hands were shaking, and I looked down at them as if from a great distance and realized that the rest of me was shaking too. I was cold. My teeth were chattering.

When I stepped from the car, it was dark and clear. There was no one in the parking lot, but the stars were a million prying eyes. In the silence and the stillness my body finally rebelled, and I vomited until there was nothing left inside me. I was void of tears, so my stomach had responded to the need to empty myself of something, to create an escape for some of the crushing horror that threatened to consume me. It didn't help. I was still being devoured. Trembling, I touched my face and neck with ice-cold hands. It felt like somebody else's face, somebody else's hands. I wondered if death was this glacial and tremulous.

But whether you want it to or not, life goes on.

If there is anything that I will take to the grave as certain, it is that life goes on. It isn't true that whatever doesn't kill you only makes you stronger—sometimes you are left as little more than the most fragile, defenseless shadow of the person you once were, broken and insubstantial and weak and lost—but whatever doesn't kill you does leave you vulnerable to another day. Your life—or what's left of it—will go on. That is not always necessarily a good thing.

My life went on though I didn't really want it to. Monday morning came on the heels of Sunday night just as it has since the beginning of time. I got up and got dressed and went to class because it was what I was supposed to do. I imagine I looked exactly the same. I sat in the same spots in the lecture halls and wore the same jeans that I donned at least a few times a week, and I was, for all intents and purposes, the same Julia that I had always been. Except that I wasn't.

I didn't blame Parker or Thomas—or anyone for that matter—and when I thought of seeing Parker in statics, instead of wanting to attack or avoid him, I was plagued by a need to apologize to him. I had to say sorry to someone—the desire for pardon, for someone to say that I was absolved, that I was *forgiven*, was as desperate inside me as the impossible wish that I had never gone to Parker's apartment in the first place. One could never happen; the other was a possibility. The hours between waking and statics found me anxious and weary.

Parker was waiting for me in statics, and he held out his hand as if to steady me when I stepped next to him to take my seat. He couldn't very well hold my hand in front of the entire statics class, but I could see in his eyes that he had to touch me somehow, and because I didn't hate him, I placed my hand in his. For a moment, he squeezed.

"You look tired," he commented gently.

"I am," I replied. My voice sounded far away, as though I were calling up from the bottom of a deep well.

He didn't say anything for a while, just watched me as if he could glean the right response from the tilt of my head or the pallor in my cheeks. I was thankful that he didn't ask me if I was okay. "You know," he finally started, "we may have gone too fast. Let's slow things down a bit, Julia."

It seemed way too late for such a feeble sentiment, but I nodded because it was what he wanted me to do. Then I whispered, "I'm sorry." I meant it with all my heart, and I said each word with gravity and an earnestness that was so solemn as to be grim. I opened my mouth to say it again, but Parker smiled. It was the wrong reaction entirely. I looked at him, wounded and confused.

"You don't have to be sorry!" he said. "It's not that big of a deal. . . .

Sure, it happened earlier than I would have anticipated, but . . ." He shrugged. "What are you going to do?"

He was a stranger to me. I did not know him and probably never had. Looking at him with a half smile on his face and an almost mischievous glint in his eye, it crossed my mind that I did not want to know him. But what can you do when nothing turns out the way you planned? when you don't know what to do or where to go? You cling to what you *do* know, even if it is not what you want. Even if he is not *who* you want.

Parker was patient with me for a couple of weeks.

He was thoughtful, conscientious even. He sent me flowers once. The bouquet was simple white daisies with a yellow ribbon in a clear glass vase, and it hurt me a bit to look at them. It was apparent that in Parker's mind I was being a little ridiculous, a little immature because I was reacting so strongly to something that was simply the natural course of every adult relationship. He was indulging me, though it was against his better judgment, and I decided I should be thankful that at least he hadn't run the second I became so withdrawn. I guess it was hard for him to understand that my one mistake with him was just the icing on the cake, the slip of hand that tumbled my castle of cards to a dismal, chaotic wreck. I felt like a little girl sitting among the mess and picking up cards one by one, trying to figure out where I went wrong.

I gave up entirely in my engineering classes and attended only because it was habit and because it was a sufficient place to wonder where I would go from here. Maybe it would be a good idea to get a job for a while and just figure out what I really wanted out of life. Maybe I could take Parker's advice and start over next semester with a course load of classes that actually piqued my interest. But what I really wanted to do was crawl in a hole and close my eyes until everything faded enough that I could live without shielding my face. Everything felt too much—too bright, too loud, too intense.

One night in early December, Becca and I were actually in our dorm room at the same time getting ready for bed. The room was calm, and though I couldn't explain why, I suddenly wanted to talk to her. Something compelled me to reach out of the trance that I had been in for weeks.

Becca hadn't gone home for the Thanksgiving break and was so anxious to do so in a week that she had already begun packing for the monthlong Christmas holiday. A toothbrush poked from her mouth as she folded and refolded a blue sweater, then threw it on top of the open suitcase at the foot of her bed.

We hadn't said much to each other as the semester drew on, and I found that I didn't quite remember how to begin a conversation with her.

I tried. "Are you going to have enough clothes left for classes next week?" I meant it to sound teasing, but my tenor wasn't right.

She glanced up quickly as if I were being sarcastic. "Of course," she mumbled around the toothbrush, barely pausing to look at me.

I could hear her sucking from across the room, but I hardly even bothered to notice anymore. Becca had an odd habit of chewing on her toothbrush long after she had brushed her teeth. It was just one of the many quirks we each possessed that had accumulated into a mountain of grievances we held against each other.

I really wanted to ask her advice about something, so I pressed on though she didn't seem interested in conversation. "You must be so excited to go home."

"Mm-hmm . . ." Becca sighed, pulling a stack of jeans from the shelf in her closet. She added it to the growing pile in her suitcase. It landed with a dull thump.

"Are you still undeclared?" I asked as if it had just occurred to me. "It's been so long since we've talked. I don't even know if you've chosen a major."

The slump of her shoulders made it evident that I was irritating her by continuing to talk. We had reached a sort of unspoken arrangement: we could cohabit tolerably by staying out of each other's way as much as possible, but we admitted our differences and gave up trying to be chummy or close. Apparently I was breaking the tacit code. I didn't say anything else.

Taking a cup from her desk, she dropped her toothbrush into it. After a deep swig from her open water bottle, she said, "Yeah, I'm going with social work."

"Social work," I parroted. "What made you decide that?"

Becca raised an eyebrow at me. "Because I liked the classes." She turned back to her halfhearted packing. "You have to make a decision at some point," she said offhandedly.

"I'm dropping out of engineering," I said out of the blue, surprising even myself. I hadn't admitted it to anyone yet, not even Parker—though he had deduced as much.

For the first time in a long time, Becca leveled me with a straight stare. She held my gaze for a moment before asking simply, "Why?"

"It didn't feel right." I shrugged, struggling to be nonchalant.

"What does your boyfriend think of that?" she asked, tipping the lid of her suitcase closed. "May I turn off the light?" she added.

"Sure." I answered her second question so I had time to formulate a response to her first. She flicked the light off, and the ensuing darkness was leaden and absolute as my eyes adjusted to the change. I heard her crawl into bed, and I followed her lead. "Parker is more a friend than a boyfriend," I said into the shadows because I didn't want to admit that Parker didn't know about my decision. And because I felt the slight need to defend—something inside me flinched when she referred to him as my boyfriend.

Becca was quiet for so long that I was sure she had decided to pretend she was already half asleep. But her breathing wasn't even, and she eventually said, "He sure seems like a boyfriend."

I didn't say anything.

The bed complained noisily as Becca turned over, but she had rolled toward me instead of away. Her voice sounded close when she spoke again. "What are you going to do? I mean, if you've dropped engineering, what's your major?"

"I don't have one," I confessed abruptly, the words longing to jump off my tongue.

"Oh. Well, hey, no big deal. You'll figure it out."

Encouragement from Becca's lips made me smile in spite of myself. At what point had we switched places? When had she become so collected, so together? When had I become such a directionless mess?

"Yeah . . . ," I said, drawing out the word. "My schedule is obviously complete for next semester, so I guess I'll have to change all my classes. . . ."

"What will you take?" Becca asked, and I could hear her stifle a yawn.

I tried to give the question my full and complete attention. Math and the sciences had spilled out of my veins when I had realized how utterly defeated and useless they left me. I was almost too embarrassed to try again. What if I failed? On the other hand, I always had to fight and wrestle my way to a good grade in the humanities. I loved to read but not to analyze. I loved to write but only personal correspondence and the infrequent and often mortifying journal entry. My options seemed pretty limited. Becca was waiting for an answer. "I don't know," I finally offered weakly.

"Well, you have to have *some* idea," Becca chided as if I were holding out on her.

"Not really," I countered. "Maybe I should just get a job while I sort things out." It was a hesitant suggestion, a careful statement that was more a question than anything. I was looking for approval or guidance or at the very least a little advice, even if it was poor advice. It had once been Becca's specialty.

But she took my casual disclosure as the absolute truth. "You're *quitting?*" she asked, her voice croaking on that odious word. I could see her silhouette in the dim light glowing from between the shades. She was sitting up rigidly and staring in the direction of my bed.

"No, absolutely not," I quickly assured her. "I'm just . . . *brainstorming.* . . ." To be honest, dropping out didn't sound like an altogether horrible option, but Becca was a little too excited by the possibility. Had I become that unbearable of a roommate?

"Oh." She flopped back onto her pillow, turning away from me this time.

I found I didn't really want to talk to her anymore either, and I rolled to face the wall.

After a moment she shot over her shoulder, "I guess you could always go and intern under your mother. That would be fun . . . living in the city . . ."

I bit the heel of my hand while I tried to come up with something to say. In the end, I didn't have it in me to lie anymore, so I muttered, "Becca, my mom is not a chef. I think she's a waitress."

The hush from Becca's side of the room was tangible. I wouldn't have blamed her if she didn't say another word to me, pathetic fraud that I was. As it turned out, she wasn't going to let me off the hook that easily. "Julia," she started and her voice was cool, "I'm not even going to ask. But, girl, you have *issues*."

She didn't know the half of it.

nineteen

ON DECEMBER 10, I turned nineteen years old. No one but the resident director at the end of the hall knew it—I hadn't told a soul—and when a bright sign festooned with ribbons and a couple of sagging balloons was hung up on the strip of corkboard next to our door. Becca tried not to notice it. She had begun to completely ignore me, and I didn't try to win her over because I would have done the same thing if the roles had been reversed. Her contempt for me was matched only by my own disgust for myself.

But she couldn't avoid the gaudy sign as she left for class in the morning, and she was civil enough to read the bold, red message out loud. "'Happy birthday, Julia,'" she mumbled, but I couldn't tell if she meant it or if she was merely repeating what the poster proclaimed.

"Thanks," I said softly. She was already gone.

Grandma had sent a package, and she left a message on my voice mail. I was in the room when the phone rang, but I pretended that I wasn't around because I didn't have the heart to talk to anyone. The small package she had sent was sitting neatly on my bed—I hadn't unwrapped it when it came in the mail a few days earlier, adhering to the conviction that birthday presents were meant for birthdays, not the day before.

As the telephone rang in the background, I used my car key to rip open the packing tape on the squat cardboard box. There was a card tucked in a baby blue envelope on top of a milky white square of crocheted yarn. I put the card aside, feeling incapable of reading about my grandmother's love, and lifted the blanket out carefully. The folds dropped open, and the blanket spread from my chest to pool like spilled cream on the floor at my feet. It was thick and soft, and my fingers disappeared in the gentle shimmer of an exquisite pattern. The design was so intricate that I could hardly identify where Grandma had started and stopped—the wool moved and shifted like a strong current beneath the surface of still water.

I held the blanket to my face. It smelled of Grandma and home and a newness that was clean and unspoiled. I wrapped it around myself and curled up on my bed, knowing that countless hours and days and even weeks of my grandmother's life twined around me like a tender embrace. It took my breath away.

Skipping chemistry was not a conscious decision, but Grandma's blanket was so warm and comforting around me that I fell asleep where I lay. When I woke up, a twinge in my stomach reminded me that I hadn't eaten breakfast, and I was shocked to glance at the alarm clock beside me to see 11:17 blinking in monochromatic green.

I sat up slowly and pulled the blanket tight across my shoulders. Grandma's card was still waiting patiently at the end of the bed, and I reached for it halfheartedly. Sliding my thumb under the corner of the envelope, I tore it open, leaving a mess of jagged edges. The card depicted a mountain scene and was from one of those boxed sets on display at any pharmacy or dollar store. I had received cards from the same set for every birthday the last four years running, and something about the familiarity of it made me want to cry. I avoided looking at the card and instead tipped it upside down so the twenty-dollar bill Grandma always stowed inside fell into my outstretched palm. It was just enough for lunch and a little birthday present for myself.

An hour later, as I left Wal-Mart clutching my purchase in a flimsy plastic bag, I wondered at how I could consider such an item a gift.

The bathroom was empty at twelve-thirty in the afternoon— everyone was in class, at lunch, or napping—and I pushed open the door to the stall at the very end. Within seconds a tiny pink plus sign appeared in the first window of the slender plastic stick just as I knew it would. Though I had hoped I was wrong, though I had prayed to the God of my youth to spare me this one grief, the test was merely a confirmation of what I had slowly become sure of in the days and weeks after the night I came home from Thanksgiving. There was a certain relief in knowing beyond a shadow of a doubt.

No more worrying, wondering, or waiting. No more false hope. No more denying it. I was pregnant.

I wrapped the test in toilet paper, thankful that at least I had the bathroom to myself. Pushing it to the very bottom of the garbage can, I felt fear and shame crawl across my skin like a cold northern breeze on a hot fall day. Any strength I felt was fading quickly in the threat of the long winter ahead. I crossed to the lineup of sinks and tried to wash some of the guilt from my hands. Soap and water were not enough to clean what felt dirty in me.

Bundling myself in mittens and a long scarf, I wished I could tuck Grandma's blanket around me instead of the stiff parka that was hung over the back of my chair. But of course, that was a ridiculous sentiment, and I zipped the unyielding coat with fumbling fingers and started absently down the stairs to wander in the chill December wind. There was no intent to my roaming, no destination I could discern, but my body needed to move, to distance myself from any closed space that afforded my fears easy, unobstructed access to my heavy, tortured heart.

The sky was gray and sagging against the weight of innumerable skeins of unfallen snow. A cool dampness infused the air—the fragrance of frost, sinuous and raw—and hung in misty exhalation among the barren twigs of sleeping trees. I turned my palms outward at my sides and let the almost-winter afternoon poke fingers of insufficient blessing across my stooping frame.

I walked until my eyes were bright with cold and thought about how grateful I was that my dad would never know all I had done. Who I had become.

Once, before he died, he had caught my hand in his and held it almost harshly against his chest as if nothing could convince him to ever let it go. He knew then that he was very sick, and we made jokes when his hair began to fall out from chemo because we wanted to believe that it would grow in again when the cancer had left him. The illness had become him and was as inseparable from his body as the blood that tried unsuccessfully to fight and restrain. He knew he was dying. It made him despair of ever saying all he wanted to say to me, and often a moment would grab him so that his heart could not beat again until he had told me what he needed to tell.

"You were not a mistake, Julia," he whispered to me that day.

The sun was shining, and it was hot and iridescent outside, making the ground float inches above where it was supposed to be like the mirage of an oasis across the scorching desert sand. I was wearing a blue bikini with white flowers beneath a tank top and cutoffs. My feet were in flip-flops, my toenails painted the color of cotton candy, my hair tied in a ponytail at the nape of my neck. There was a beach towel slung across my shoulders. I was young and innocent and naive. He was older than his years and weathered and dying. It had never once crossed my mind that I had been a mistake. He had most likely struggled with that thought every day for the last sixteen years.

"I wanted you from day one," Dad murmured, searching my face as if what he said would change my life forever.

I shifted from one foot to the other, wiggled my thumb as it lay trapped beneath his skinny hands. "I know you love me, Dad," I said because his gaze was unnerving. He was going to tell me a secret that I had always known deep down, and I didn't want to hear it. "I'm going to be late," I added quietly, apologetically.

My plea went unobserved.

"There is a big difference between an unexpected surprise and an unwanted one," he pressed on, pleading with me to believe him. "Don't blame yourself for what happened between your mother and me. You were the one beautiful thing that came out of it all." He was blinking now, remembering.

For the first time ever I allowed myself to think of how it must have gone, what Janice must have said to him. I didn't want to know—a part of me wished I could ignore it always—but now that he was talking, I couldn't stop myself from picturing her. Had she cried? Had he? Did he propose to her the moment the words crossed her lips or did he run? Were my grandparents opposed to the idea? Two wrongs don't make a right!

Then a thought exploded through me like lightning charring a rotten tree: had he begged her to keep me?

Dad had caught up with me in the mudroom, and I could feel heat creeping through the old, poorly sealed door. I could kiss him on the cheek, pull my hand from his, and walk into the sun, where everything could be forgotten or at least buried beneath the scent of tanning oil and lazy conversation with Thomas. Or I could ask him and make him tell me the truth. *Did she want me, even a little?*

"I love you too, Dad," I whispered, touching his cheek with my lips and turning from him.

He had squeezed my hand before he let it go.

Now, as I walked in the stillness and the cold, the beginning of a life inside me, I didn't regret never asking him that question. I didn't want to know the answer. It was enough to understand that he had wanted me. Though it felt like someone else had the thought and offered it like an inheritance to me—something I could not refuse—I discovered that I wanted this baby. I hoped it was enough.

Whether it was subconscious or intentional, I found myself standing outside Parker's duplex. His truck was in the driveway instead of out back beneath the carport, and when I touched the hood, it was still warm through my frosty mitten. I knew it had been a long day for him already—Tuesdays and Thursdays were even worse than the Monday, Wednesday, Friday routine—and I almost walked away without knocking on the door, without repeating the conversation that had played in my mind since I first suspected that I was pregnant.

But I didn't have much time. Christmas vacation was five days away, and when I went home, I did not plan to come back. At the very least, Parker had the right to know that he was going to be a father. Something inside me shrank at the thought, realizing that though Janice had given birth to me, it would be fraudulent to call her a *mother*. Maybe Parker would be like Janice. Maybe he would have no desire to be a father, good or otherwise. But either way, he deserved to know.

When Parker opened the door, a shadow fell over his face, and he seemed to force an uncertain smile at me. His attention and consideration were waning as I became more and more remote, and though he deserved credit for sticking it out to the best of his abilities, I knew he was ready to cut his losses and move on from me. I wasn't angry at him. I was just sad for us.

"Hi," I said, and there was sympathy in my voice because he didn't know what was about to hit him.

"Hi," he imitated. We stood there for an awkward moment before he took a step back from the door. "Would you like to come in?" he finally asked, though it did not sound like he hoped I would comply.

"I would," I said, taking a step toward him as he made room for me on the threshold.

Two of his roommates were spread out across the living room, doing homework on opposite couches. I could hear voices coming from the bedrooms, and a woman's laugh indicated that she was the fiancée I had never met. The apartment was bustling. There was no way I could say what had to be said in here.

I turned to Parker as he eased the door shut. "Actually, Parker, would you mind taking a walk with me? We should talk."

To say that he appeared relieved may have been a bit of an over-statement, but he grabbed his coat hurriedly and ushered me out-side. "I was thinking we should talk too," he said when we were on the front step. He must have seen his opportunity to put an end to all of this, and he took my elbow and steered me past his truck to go back the way that I had come. "I've been meaning to call you," he said.

"I've been meaning to call you," I echoed.

We walked in silence for a block as if his roommates would spy on us and we needed to be sure we were alone before we could truly be honest. When the duplex was out of sight behind a row of evergreens and a split-rail fence designated the beginning of Swallow's Nest Park, Parker stopped. "Sit, Julia," he suggested, though it sounded more like a command. He moved to curl his arms around me and lifted me onto the splintery fence so our eyes were level. His hands rested on the wood on either side of my hips, but he did not touch me again in any way.

"Parker," I started before he could say anything. "I—"

"No, Julia," he interrupted. "I need to say something first."

"But—"

"No buts." He leaned down and let his head fall between his shoulders, and I could see the top of his head. It was apparent that he wouldn't let me talk first, so I waited for him to speak. After a few deep breaths that collected in a foggy mist over my lap, Parker began. "I don't want you to think that I used you."

It was an introduction that left no room for speculation about his eventual conclusion.

"I really liked you." Parker looked up quickly and amended himself. "I really *like* you. But ever since . . ." He shrugged. It wasn't like he needed to fill in the blank. "Everything is just *different*. I think I was right in the beginning. You're too young for me." He pushed off from the fence and kicked at the root of a tree that was bubbling through an enormous crack in the pavement. "Julia, you're only eighteen."

"Nineteen," I corrected without thinking. "It's my birthday today."

His eyes shot to mine. "Oh, I am such a jerk. I can't believe it's your *birthday!*"

A wry smile was all I could conjure up, but my heart truly did go out to him. I should have been a fond memory in the annals of his life, but from this day forward and forevermore I would be, at best, never far from his mind and at worst, an enduring black spot of guilt and regret.

"It doesn't matter," I consoled him. "I've never been big on birthdays anyway. Besides, I knew that this—" I motioned from myself to him and back—"couldn't go on."

Parker sighed. "I really am sorry. You're . . ." He struggled to find the right word. "Well, you defy explanation, Julia." He smiled at me sweetly and closed the space between us to place a gentle kiss on my mouth. "I really do hope everything works out for you."

"Same to you," I murmured, placing my hand on his shoulder.

He obviously felt magnitude in the weight of my touch and looked at me a little warily as he asked, "Was there something you wanted to say to me?"

My eyes dropped to the broken sidewalk, but my fingers curled into the flesh of his arm as if I knew I would have to hold him there. I bit my bottom lip until it was numb in the icy air, and when I looked up at him, I could see that he was as innocent and unsuspecting as a child before a momentous revelation. *I'm sorry, honey, but Santa Claus isn't real. We're moving away because Daddy has a new job. Your mommy and I are getting a divorce.* It hurt so much to tell him; I mouthed the words twice before I could give them voice.

Parker stared at me incredulously and followed my lips with his eyes.

"I'm pregnant," I croaked.

He recoiled as if I had slapped him with every ounce of my strength. "What?" he spat out, though it was shock and not anger that hardened his voice.

I didn't want to say, *You heard me,* because it seemed abrupt and unkind, so I said nothing. I held his eyes with my own because the truth was apparent, and I didn't have to repeat myself for Parker to know that it wasn't a ploy or a game to keep him when he had just said good-bye.

"I don't understand," he muttered, stepping away from me, though distance wouldn't change anything. "It was just *one time*."

"It was enough," I said quietly, and my voice filled the space between us and not an inch more.

Parker clenched his hands into fists and pushed the bony knuckles into his eyes. He rocked forward on his toes and then back to his heels, and if we'd been on a football field, I would have considered him a formidable opponent—he looked ready and able to annihilate anyone in his way.

I moved to slide off the fence and go to him, but the fierce angles of his body belied muscles that were taut and ready, and I didn't want to startle him out of whatever stronghold his mind had escaped to.

When the silence had stretched to the point of snapping, I forced myself to try and calm the storm that was swelling inside him.

"Look, Parker," I started feebly, "you don't have to do anything. I'm not asking anything of you." I hadn't planned on saying more, but words stumbled over my tongue on their way to escape. "I don't want you to marry me or pay child support or anything stupid like that. I just wanted you to know. I felt like you should know. I couldn't walk away without giving you the chance to . . ." I couldn't finish the thought. I had no idea what I wanted from Parker. But something uncoiled inside when I said all I had come to say, and I slumped on the fence, dropping my arms beside me to stop myself from falling.

Parker let his hands release their hold on his eyes, and he studied me for a moment. "You're keeping the baby?" he asked, his voice a mix of contempt and disbelief.

I hadn't considered anything else, so his question left me disoriented and confused. "Yes," I replied finally.

He stepped up to me and gripped my arms in his powerful hands. Something in me had called him to take charge of the situation, and he held me now like a little girl who didn't understand what was happening and needed to be told what was best for her and everyone involved. "Look, Julia, we need some time to think. Go home and get some sleep. We'll talk tomorrow. You're not making sense, okay? We need some time and distance. . . . We'll figure it out." Parker said the last part to himself, but he gave me a little shake and squeezed my arms so hard it almost hurt. Then he turned abruptly and started down the sidewalk heading away from his apartment. He broke into a jog after a few long strides, and when he disappeared around the block, he was running.

I just watched him go.

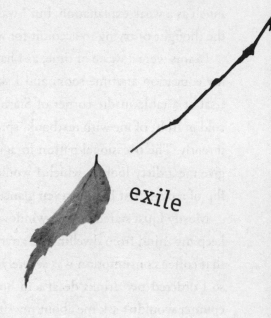

exile

I packed my car a bit at a time, taking small loads of things to fit like the pieces of a complicated puzzle in the trunk of my little two-door sedan. Every time I left the dorm, I took something with me so that one day I got up and looked for a clean pair of jeans and found my closet nearly empty. It stunned me. I hadn't realized how quickly the transition out of this life was happening.

My half of our shared room had always been sparse, but Becca noticed the slow erosion and left me a note on our message board. *Moving out?*

I scribbled a messy *Yes* underneath her words, and she didn't ask anything more, either in person or via the marker board. It kind of bothered me that she was willing to accept my departure without so much as a weak explanation, but I was also grateful. I couldn't bear the thought of trying to account for why I wasn't coming back.

Exams were a waste of time, as I had no intention of continuing my education anytime soon, and I skipped them entirely. Instead I sat at a table in the corner of Starbucks and let vanilla lattes go cold in front of me with textbooks spread awry as if I were studying intently. The occasional patron foraging for an empty table would give me a dirty look to which I would respond with a halfhearted flip of a page that I hadn't even glanced at once.

Mostly I just stared out the window at passing traffic and tried to keep my mind from dwelling on anything. I had heard somewhere that coffee consumption was severely frowned upon in pregnancy, so I ordered my drinks decaf and hoped that Connie behind the counter wouldn't ask me about my sudden switch.

Someone had also once commented that pregnant women have a certain look, a glow that is unmistakable. I couldn't help questioning if all my subversion was rendered ineffective because of my own body quietly proclaiming my condition. It was an awful thought. I was betraying myself. Whom could I depend on if I couldn't even trust myself?

The steady evacuation of campus had begun on Wednesday. As students completed their last exams, shouts of relief and triumph punctuated the halls, and cars began to disappear from the parking lots.

I had called home when I knew Grandma would be gone for her Bible study and left a message on the answering machine telling her that I would be home on the weekend. There was a part of me that was so anxious to leave I could hardly stop myself from jumping in my car and driving away without a single look over my shoulder. Another part of me—a much larger, more insistent part—was seized with an undulating, nauseating horror at the very thought of going home and explaining to my grandmother that I wasn't going back. Explaining to her *why* I wasn't going back.

It had been a lonely few days of watching and waiting, and the only reason I stayed close to my dorm instead of living in my car or roaming around various public haunts was because I was holding my breath for a phone call or a visit from Parker. He had run away from me on my birthday and hadn't come back. While I could forgive him if I never saw him again, something in me knew that it wouldn't be right if everything just ended so unceremoniously. I believed there was more to him than that, and I gave him every opportunity to deliver on his promise that we would work everything out.

We had to be out of the dorms by six o'clock on Friday night, and when my watch said 5:59, I slung my backpack over my shoulder and walked out of my room for the last time.

Becca had left the day before and had actually stopped to say good-bye and wish me well in a voice that bordered on sincere. Maybe she was just happy that she would have the room to herself next semester and any well wishes were meant for her own happiness. Either way, it was nice to leave her on relatively cordial terms, all things considered, but as I slept in the room by myself for one final night, I succumbed to feelings of utter failure and recounted almost sadistically all the mistakes I had made. I collected them in a dismal little pile in my mind—a derisory altar to the god of my own demise—and practiced the apologies that I would make if I were a better, stronger person.

The one apology that haunted me more than any other was the one that I would never get to make to Parker. I had waited as long as I could, and he had remained silent, secreted away someplace where he tried furiously to either forget my existence or unravel a way out of this mess. There was nothing I could do but walk away and hope that someday he would forgive me, and we would be able to think of each other with something less excruciating than crushing remorse.

But as I walked away from Brighton on that dark, cold evening in December, I found Parker's truck huddling beside my car in the abandoned parking lot.

I could see him hunched over the steering wheel, looking straight ahead, and I watched him for a moment, waiting for him to notice me. When he didn't, I dropped the backpack on the hood of my car and tapped on the passenger window of his truck with just the tips of my fingers.

His head swung around as though I had shattered the glass, and he stared at me blankly before reaching across to open the door from the inside.

"Hi," I said softly, sliding in and shutting the door behind me with the tiniest click. There was a basic and understood need to be gentle.

Parker didn't respond at first, just went back to his original position clutching the steering wheel and staring out the windshield as if he were navigating icy roads in the middle of a blizzard. Indeed, as I looked out the window I noticed that it had begun to snow, and tiny, frozen flakes drifted aimlessly in the slight breath of a breeze. They were uncertain and few in number, and I followed Parker's gaze to watch them consider the earth beneath them only to swing upward on a gust of air and alight somewhere different entirely.

After studying the developing snow for longer than was comfortable, Parker reached into his back pocket and pulled out his wallet. Still not looking at me, he fingered through a number of bills and extracted a sizable stack of cash. He folded the wallet and put it away, then tapped the money on the dashboard and doubled it in half so that it was a bulging green square.

"Here," he said, thrusting the money at me as he continued to stare at the snow.

I was completely bewildered. "What?" I asked slowly. My hands didn't move from my lap.

"Take it," Parker insisted, pushing it at me again and looking at my face for the first time. His eyes were inscrutable.

"No, Parker." I shook my head. "I told you I don't want your money. I'm not taking that." I folded my arms across my chest.

"Take it. It's enough for an appointment at the clinic. You can get this taken care of over Christmas and be back by next semester. Nobody has to know."

"I'm sorry." My mouth went dry, and I felt each word as if it were cotton on my tongue. "I can't do that."

"What, now you've suddenly got morals?" Parker challenged. But in spite of his ugly words, his eyes were desperate, and I could see that he was more distraught than angry. "Just get it over with, Julia. Don't let this ruin our lives."

That was it—he thought if I had this baby it would ruin his life. Maybe he envisioned me showing up on his doorstep someday, my arm around a towheaded two-year-old and my hand outstretched for something he didn't have to give. Maybe he imagined a wife and children in a life that was worlds away from here and how they would react if one day a teenager came knocking at his door to proclaim, "I am your son." I had known that this would change my life forever, but I hadn't taken the time to appreciate how much it would affect Parker, too.

Gripped by a need to mourn with him, I stretched out my hand and laid it gently on his arm.

He mistook my motion and slid out from under my touch to press the wad of money into my palm. Taking both of his hands, he closed my fingers around the cash and held me tightly. Seizing my gaze with his own frantic eyes, he made an appeal. "Julia, I know how much you loved your dad. What would he say if he were alive? What would he want you to do? Would he want you to give up everything? ruin your life?"

I bit my lip to stop a sad smile from passing over my face. Parker knew nothing about my father. "You don't understand . . . ," I murmured.

And then, because my dad had borne my shame before—had forgiven me and blessed me and loved me in spite of myself, had seen hope in something hopeless—I haltingly told Parker my story of the chick. I still didn't understand it, but I longed to make him realize that no matter how ugly this was, it wasn't consequentially the very end of the world. I wanted to prove to him that maybe this too could be something more than the misery it seemed to be.

Parker didn't interrupt me, but he let my hand slip from his and turned away to look out the window again.

When I had stumblingly, inarticulately said everything I could think to say, there was silence in the truck. The snow was falling more readily now, and it collected in wispy ribbons of white along the edge of the windshield and began to fill in the cracks in the sidewalk beyond. Each flake was hard and bitter, hitting the windows and the hood of the pickup with an indifferent little thump, almost as if each flight from heaven was a separate kamikaze attack. Parker's truck was running and the heater was on, but I couldn't help shivering.

The money was still in my hands, and I realized with a start that as I talked I had rolled it into a tight little cylinder and was turning it like a spool in my fingers. Suddenly self-conscious, I smoothed each bill against my leg until they were all flat and neat again, then offered them humbly to Parker.

He glanced at my hand and ignored my offering as he said, "Why did you tell me that? What in the world makes you think that some stupid chick you killed over a decade ago has anything to do with what is happening *right now?*" He slammed his hands into the steering wheel with the last two words, punctuating the air with his frustration and emphasizing that, as far as he was concerned, nothing was more important than focusing on the present so that the future could unravel itself without the shackles of past mistakes.

My heart sank because I realized that he didn't want to try to understand. He didn't want to know me or work through this or find comfort in a memory that meant so much to me. He wanted to be rid of a problem and then do everything in his power to forget that it had ever existed. If I had any hope for tenderness or understanding, it was crushed.

"I just wanted you to know," I said, trying not to choke on the words. "You asked about my dad. . . ."

"Well, Julia," Parker said, turning suddenly to me. Any of the earlier despair in his voice was replaced by a cool fury that made me lean backward into the door of the truck. "I think your dad got such a kick out of that lame story because it is so painfully obvious as to be stupid. Don't you see the lesson in it? Don't you get it? *Let go*."

His eyebrows arched as he reached for my hand and crumpled up the bills inside of it. Shoving aside my arm, he crammed the money into my coat pocket in a flurry of crinkled paper and pent-up aggression. He zipped it closed, giving the bulging pocket a couple of harsh pats. "Let go, Julia. Don't hang on to this so tightly that it ruins your life. Let go and start over. I'm going to." He stopped brusquely and then added almost as an afterthought, "And get out of my truck."

I reached shakily for the door handle and wondered at how hands that had held me so gently could be so icy and hard. "Good-bye, Parker," I said so low it was almost a whisper, hoping that I could make it to my car before he saw how profoundly he had hurt me.

"You bet it's good-bye," he shot back. "I don't want to see you or hear from you ever again. If you're not mature enough to handle this like a woman, you're on your own. You are *not* dragging me down."

Parker smashed the clutch to the floorboards with his foot and turned the ignition key though the engine was already running. It made a horrible, piercing screech, and he cursed furiously. "Get out, Julia," he said again, directing his rage at me. "And for your own good, grow up."

I tumbled out of the truck when he put it in reverse and swung the door shut as he pulled away. He left in a rush of squealing tires and exhaust, and I knew if I ever saw him again, it would be too soon as far as he was concerned. I was shaking almost uncontrollably and had to lean against the car to try and catch my breath in great, shuddering gasps.

I was the solitary living silhouette in a parking lot that had been all but abandoned. A lone exile in a place where there would be no one to hear me cry. But I wasn't crying. There was warmth radiating from my cheeks, and something like a hot and liquid horror was melting me from the inside out . . . but I wasn't crying. I couldn't. He hated me and I could hardly blame him. I hated myself. Tears were for remorse or sorrow or overwhelming joy. I was none of the above. I was trapped. Though I could take care of everything so easily, though I could erase any future need he or I may have to explain the folly of our youth, I wouldn't do it. I *couldn't* do it.

I yanked the zipper, thrust my hand into my pocket, and dug out each and every bill as if it were a live coal. The notes felt dirty to me, as if Parker were trying to pay me somehow or buy his own absolution. With a sense of growing urgency, I threw them from myself, and they spun in the air and drifted to the ground, carrying the weight of his regret and anger, carrying the pardon that he would not receive. They dropped onto the powdery asphalt without a sound, littering the thin lace of newly fallen snow. I didn't stop to count, but I saw a few fifties at my feet and more twenties than I cared to tally. I decided the price of my forgiveness was more than a few hundred dollars.

part 3

lighthouse

EVERY LIGHT ON THE MAIN FLOOR of the farmhouse was on when I swung my car down the long gravel driveway. The snow had been working itself into a frenzy of white that was beginning to resemble a blizzard, and through the swirling fog of flakes, the sagging little house glowed like a transcendent beacon of warmth and welcome.

It had taken me much longer than it should have to drive home, and I knew Grandma was sick with worry and busying herself with anything to take her mind off every horrible scenario that was steadily wrapping a stranglehold around her heart. The lights were a purposeful distraction. I could just see her marching from room to room, flipping switches and pulling chains on the single bulbs in the mudroom, pantry, and above the stove. As if light could drive away her fears. As if the brilliant glow from every window could lead me home—a veritable lighthouse on the whitecapped sea of prairie.

Grandma was so wrapped up in whatever she was doing that she didn't see my car pull into the yard. I was halfway up the steps before she appeared in the doorway. There was a look of quiet amazement in her eyes, almost as if somewhere deep down she hadn't expected me to come home, and she found it both startling and wonderful to see me walking up the stairs. She watched me for a moment, a smile just beginning to crease her face and set a sparkle in her lovely eyes.

I didn't smile back, though I tried, but I held the look she gave me and etched it in broad, sweeping strokes across my memory so I would never forget it. It was hard not to be melodramatic, to think that I would never see it again.

When I was within arm's reach, Grandma said, "Julia, I was so worried about you." There was only a trace of the worry that she must have felt lingering in her quiet voice.

"I'm sorry, Grandma," I said, cringing at what I considered to be unjustified love and concern in her voice. "I should have called you, but I didn't want to stop for anything."

"You did what you had to do. I'm just glad you made it *home*." She lingered on the word for a moment, savoring it as if the farmhouse only became a home when it was *us* instead of just *her*. Then she reached out and wrapped her arms around my shoulders. Ushering me into the entryway, she helped me out of my coat, murmuring mostly to herself the entire time. "The Weather Channel says we're in for the biggest storm of the year. . . . They've already closed down a stretch of Interstate 90 west of Blue Earth. . . . It's been snowing here for hours. . . . I hate it that you had to drive in that—"

"It was okay," I interrupted. "The roads weren't so bad until about a half an hour ago. By then I could practically see home."

Grandma glanced around for a moment before understanding my gentle rib. She laughed. "It looks pretty ridiculous in here, doesn't it?"

The truth was, the kitchen felt like an inquisition room. My grandmother was hardly a fierce inquisitor, but my own guilt clung heavily, and it was hard not to see everything against the backdrop of the things I had to say. But I squinted a bit and shielded my face to tease her, managing a feeble smile when I noticed that even the little trail of lights in the china buffet was lit. "Is the oven light on?" I questioned jokingly, breaking into a full smile in spite of myself when I realized that indeed it was.

"I have a reason for that one!" Grandma defended. She swept her arm at the counter beside the stove, indicating the pans of cinnamon rolls that were rising there. "I was going to bake them tonight instead of waiting until the morning." She laughed expectantly, waiting for me to goad her on.

But the momentary cheer had passed. The smile slid off my face abruptly, and if my shoulders didn't visibly slump, it sure felt like they did. On any other night, I would have come back with some cheeky comment, and we would have laughed and teased until she offered to pop some popcorn and brew a pot of coffee. We would have settled into the kitchen chairs to play seven-up or some other card game with a name we could never properly remember, and talk until Grandma commented, "It's way past my bedtime!"

But tonight I felt like my heart was anchored back in the parking lot at Brighton, weighted down amid all the tainted money I had discarded. Buried under the snow. There was a physical tug at my chest, and I repressed the urge to rub my breastbone with the heel of my hand, wondering how a heartache could actually make your heart ache.

It was my plan to tell Grandma the truth in the morning. I wanted a good night's sleep behind me, and I wanted Parker's hateful words as far away from me as they could get. I had hoped that the morning would bring a little perspective, a little relief to the heaviness that threatened to pin me to the ground. But Grandma knew something was wrong. She could read me like she read her garden, knowing just when everything below the surface was ready to be brought up.

When I was younger, I would spend half the summer checking to see if the carrots were done. I would single out the greens of one little plant, glance around surreptitiously to make sure Grandma wasn't watching me, and expose the root, only to find that it was thin and white—and ruined now that I had unearthed it. Grandma, on the other hand, would wake up one morning and announce, "The carrots are ready." We'd arm ourselves with baskets and begin the harvest. Every year they were perfect and crisp and golden orange, even though the date of harvest sometimes varied by weeks depending on the amount of rain and the daily highs and lows. The carrots were never so big that they were woody and overripe nor so small that they hadn't reached the peak of their flavor. Just perfect. And just as Grandma could sense it in the earth, she could sense it in me—there was something right below the surface.

Grandma didn't waste any time. "Julia, what's wrong?" She pulled out a chair from the table, and I all but fell into it. Never taking her eyes off me, she angled into her own chair and reached across the table to put her hands where mine should have been. I was clutching my fingers in my lap, wringing them out of sight, and I didn't reach for her. She kept her hands in front of me, an offer that would not expire. "You look sick, honey. What happened?"

Now that I was blinking in the brightness of the overly lit kitchen, I knew that I couldn't hide it, not even for one night. My only regret in telling her now was that I had no introduction, no way to ease into the words that would hurt her in ways I could only imagine. There was nothing I could do to diminish it or make it less painful to hear. I couldn't think of a single thing to say other than the truth.

Staring at the table, I willed myself to utter the words. They came almost as if they had been waiting eagerly behind a locked door and toppled out hurriedly when the latch was released. "I am pregnant," I said, surprised at how elemental it sounded, how the baby could already be so much a part of me that I began the sentence with *I am*. It was so much softer when contracted, so stark when divided. As if the words stood back-to-back drawing unavoidable consideration to themselves—denoting the depth of importance in the word that followed, cautioning a move from shallow water.

I had half expected the lights to flicker or for Grandma to gasp in shock and anguish. Neither happened. In fact, the room was so still and motionless that I felt I could hear the pulse of electricity in all the glowing bulbs. Grandma's hands were still flat on the table in front of me, and I studied the crescent curve of white on each neat nail, wondering if those fingers itched to slap me just a little. I wouldn't have blamed her one bit. A part of me wanted it. I looked up, ready to show her that I would accept the discipline, that I needed it and deserved it.

Instead, when my eyes met hers, the compassion on her face dealt me a blow I wasn't expecting. Anger, frustration, disappointment, bitterness, revulsion, dismay . . . I could have accepted any of those. I wasn't ready for sympathy.

"Oh, sweet girl," Grandma breathed, and I could almost hear her heart break with the words.

Sweet girl? My throat was tightening—it wasn't right for her call me that. And it only became harder to breathe when she lifted herself out of the chair and came to stand beside me, pulling my head against her chest and stroking my hair as if I deserved comfort instead of condemnation.

I wanted to push her away, to say it again so that she grasped what I had done and how I had wrecked my own life and hers. Maybe she hadn't heard me properly. But she was warm and soft and smelled of lemon dish soap and cinnamon—clean yet mild and earthy. I couldn't push her away if I wanted to. I let her hold on to me.

Grandma's heartbeat drummed a steady, soothing rhythm against my cheekbone, and I could feel words echoing in her chest though I could not make them out. She wasn't talking to me; she was probably praying to God. I was actually reassured by the thought—maybe He could clear a path for me. Though the house was bright, I couldn't see a single step past the very next one I had to take, and even that was uncertain. Anything beyond sleeping in my own bed tonight was lost in complete darkness, and I couldn't begin to imagine where I was supposed to go from here. I would have felt isolated but for the wrinkled arms around me and the words that I knew were for me. I put my arms around her.

"This is not the end," Grandma said, repeating herself as if cooing to a howling newborn even though I wasn't crying. "This is not the end. This is not the end."

It seemed like a strange thing to say, but with every repetition she drove a tiny seed of hope farther into my heart. I almost didn't want it there—hope is not a promise, merely a wish, a yearning for something that may never materialize—but it sank down deep where I could not extract it and began, even in that moment, to put down fragile roots.

It was the hope that scared me most of all, and only when I had felt it tremble inside me did I begin to cry.

nativity

GRANDMA AND I WERE TRAPPED inside the house for two and a half days. The snow fell inch by inch and hour by hour, and from the windows we watched it pile up on frozen fence posts as if it were a complicated dance performed just for us. It didn't bother us that we were more or less prisoners in our own home; we actually appreciated the time alone as we tried to sort things out according to our own best intentions. Strangely, we didn't really even talk that much about it. We simply spent time with each other, feeling our way around the room again now that we were no longer two but three. Now that everything was different.

Occasionally Grandma would offer me a bit of advice on how to care for the baby growing daily inside me. Her suggestions were never backhanded, never intended to harm or ridicule, and I gathered each fragment of wisdom as if it were of incalculable worth and followed it to the letter. I began to sleep on my side, avoided crossing my legs, renounced my coffee addiction entirely, and obediently chewed the vitamin C tablets that Grandma set beside my milk glass at every meal. If she would have advised me to say a hundred Hail Marys or do some long-since-banned penance, I would have submitted myself on bended knees. I almost wished to be Catholic just so I would have something tangible to *do*.

But the fact that she didn't kick me out of the house because of my heinous and soon-to-be-visible sin didn't necessarily make me feel at peace about anything. There was a lapsed churchgoer in me that knew I deserved hellfire and brimstone, a sobbing confession and the righteous judgment of God and my community. It was like waiting for the ax to fall. I wanted to tell someone else, to get it out in the open so somebody would respond the way they were supposed to. If a public renunciation of self would restore some sort of calm to the restlessness that made my fingertips itch and my pulse race just a beat or two too high, I ached to get it over with.

However, on Monday morning when Mr. Walker finally made it over to our yard with the plow secured to the front of this John Deere tractor, I smiled at him and waved from the front porch. I struggled tenaciously to act as if everything in the world were as right and pure as the snow that had made the view from our window a wonderland. The truth was, the very thought of telling him made me want to crawl into a hole and die. I held my breath and tried to be normal when Grandma and I invited him in for a cup of coffee and a slice of the apple cake we had made on Sunday when it became clear that church was less than a shadow of an option.

"Did you two fare okay in the storm?" Mr. Walker asked, licking caramel sauce that had dripped off the cake from his spoon.

We nodded optimistically, and if we looked weary at all, it was easily ascribed to being cooped up for so long.

"It was kind of fun," Grandma commented. "I haven't seen a storm like that for years."

"Well, the snow isn't going anywhere until January at the earliest. Have you seen the forecast? We're going to have one crazy-white Christmas!" Mr. Walker sounded thrilled at the prospect.

I mimicked the smile I saw on my grandmother's face.

Christmas was a week away and—not for the first time in my life—I wasn't looking forward to it. Holidays with Dad had always been off-the-wall affairs replete with birthday cakes for Jesus at Christmas and the ubiquitous white bunny in a basket overflowing with green paper grass at Easter. I got one four years in a row until the rabbit hutch beside the garden shed was filled to overflowing, and we had to put ads in the paper to rid ourselves of the many offspring. There had been an extravagance to everything when Dad was around, and though in retrospect I could recognize that he felt trapped into somehow trying to make up for the many failures that he thought had forever wounded our family, there was a certain charm in our lavish celebrations.

The year after Dad died had been a very quiet Christmas. He had been gone for only slightly over two months, and Grandma and I simply didn't have the heart to commemorate him the way we should have. He would have wanted us to put on Grandma's old gospel records or *A Country Music Christmas* and drink far too much eggnog and be a little decadent in spite of ourselves. We couldn't do it.

That somber first holiday alone set a pattern for us, two lonely ladies that we were, and try as we might, we could not rid ourselves of the solemnity of an occasion that reminded us of the meagerness of our family. I was the only daughter of an only son, and there was a sort of palpable regret in Grandma sometimes, almost as if everything inside her lamented the fact that she had never had more children—that I didn't have aunts and uncles and cousins to bear some of the desolate burden.

For my part, I had never longed for an arching family tree. But I did begin to dread certain holidays with a quiet dismay that made me wish we could simply gloss over that particular date on the calendar and get on with life as normal. The more minor days were fine—Thanksgiving, Memorial Day, the Fourth of July, Labor Day—because we were always invited somewhere for those celebrations. But people drew lines around their families for the important holidays, tenderly pulling each other in and politely closing doors around themselves to protect the sanctity of those moments alone. I didn't blame them one bit. Dad and Grandma and I had done the same.

This year, with the world tilted off its axis and my own body as unfamiliar to me as an unexplored wilderness, Christmas simply seemed irrelevant. When Mr. Walker reminded me of it, I checked out of the conversation around the table and tried to make myself focus on the details: a present for Grandma, cards for a few people whom I always sent cards to, a tree. . . . A tree? I glanced over my shoulder into the living room and realized that there was no Christmas tree in front of the bay window. I had no deep love for the holiday, but it seemed wrong to go through Christmas without a tree.

"Got a little cabin fever?" Mr. Walker asked, startling me out of my reverie. He put his hand on my forearm and smiled warmly at me. "You should get out of the house."

"I'm sending her out this afternoon," Grandma conceded. "We need some groceries."

Mr. Walker gave my arm a squeeze and pushed back his chair. "Well, if you get bored, Francesca is spending Christmas with us and seems a little desperate for female companionship."

I waited for a shiver to accompany his words, but they evoked no such emotion in me. I had known Thomas and Francesca would get back together, and now I just didn't care. It was as insignificant to me as if they were virtual strangers. Which I decided they were.

"Thanks for the invite," I said courteously, but I didn't offer a word more. He could interpret my intentions however he chose.

Mr. Walker settled a suede cap on his head and pulled down the fur-lined earflaps. He tapped his fingers to the edge of the hat and gave us a little nod. "As always, ladies, thank you for the hospitality."

Grandma gave him a warm smile and came around the table to dissolve some of his phony obsequiousness with a hug. "Have a very merry Christmas, Jonathan."

"You too, Nellie. Julia."

After he was gone, Grandma and I donned our winter gear and

headed outside to dig out the car. Turned out, Mr. Walker had already done the job for us. We stood on the driveway for a moment, looking at the swells of white and the steely clouds that threatened even more snow and feeling a little useless and lost.

Finally Grandma said, "I made a grocery list. Do you want me to come or would you like some time alone?"

"Well, do you want to get out of the house for a while?" I asked, not daring to say that I really wanted to be by myself.

"I've got lots to do here," Grandma assured me. "You just go."

I was undeserving of such understanding, but I nodded gratefully and accepted the piece of paper and small envelope of cash that she gave me. "I'll be back soon," I promised.

Value Foods was so packed with people stocking up on necessities that I got the second-to-last shopping cart in the whole store. The aisles were traffic jams of mothers chasing energetic toddlers who were reveling in the freedom of being somewhere other than the stifling four walls of all-too-familiar homes. There were at least a dozen people waiting at the meat counter, and the dairy case had already been emptied of the pound blocks of butter Grandma liked to use for baking.

I tried not to get annoyed and made substitutions whenever I came across an item on my list that had sold out. It actually seemed appropriate somehow to have such a hodgepodge holiday. I had to settle for chicken instead of the traditional Cornish game hens that Grandma prepared for our Christmas feast. Low-fat eggnog because the regular cartons were already gone. Margarine substituted for butter.

At the checkout, I counted the cash that Grandma had given me and waited for the final amount. When $36.57 flashed on the till, I realized I had enough and asked the girl behind the counter to add a Christmas tree to my bill.

"They're pretty picked over," she warned me. "But they're cheap— $19.95," she said as if it were the steal of the century. Without waiting for me to change my mind, she typed in a lengthy code from a laminated piece of paper that hung on corkboard beside her. "Do you need help getting it strapped to your car?"

"No," I said, handing her exact change. "I'll manage."

"Hey, it's up to you. Have a merry Christmas!" she called after me as I slid the handles of four plastic bags on my arms and grabbed a gallon of milk and juice in each hand. I was about to wish her the same, but she was already helping the next customer.

I wrangled the groceries into the passenger seat of my car and drove it over to the side of the grocery store where there was a makeshift lattice fence around a handful of snow-laden Christmas trees. The boughs of each tree were wrapped in twine so they looked skinny and imprisoned—wrestled into a straitjacket in some satirical comment about the absurdity of such a commercialized holiday—and I studied them for a moment before walking up to the smallest one and grasping it by the trunk. It only came up to my nose, and the top branch was spindly and crooked. I knocked the bottom against the pavement a few times, and snow fell in a shimmer of frosty silver around me. The tree still looked pathetic. I wanted to grab my car keys and cut through the twine so I could see what it looked like without the ropy shackles, but I knew I would never be able to get it home unfettered. It would have to do. I didn't really have a choice.

I crammed the tree in the backseat of my car with the short stump on the floor and the last few inches of evergreen sticking out the open window behind my head. It wasn't pretty, but it worked, and as I navigated the parking lot more than a few people smiled at me and waved as if my little tree and I were part of some sort of quirky Christmas miracle.

It had been my intention to go straight home, but when I drove past the used-books store on the corner of Main and Hedgerow, I found myself stopping almost against my will. My mind flickered to all the money that I had left in the snow at Brighton, and a drop of regret poisoned the well of my soul when I imagined what I could have done for Grandma with that kind of money. I had always tried to get her meaningful Christmas presents, something that would please her the way that my dad's perfect gifts had always delighted and amazed. But I hadn't been given his innate ability for gift giving, and my well-intentioned but usually off-the-mark presents were unimpressive and predictable. A glass pitcher, a new set of baking pans, fancy rose-scented soap and lotion. I hadn't given a single thought to what I wanted to get her this year, but I had to assume that this might be my last chance to pick some-thing—*anything*—up.

The store was stuffy and smelled of dust and mothballs and old books. It was a sweet, familiar smell. I had been a patron of the narrow rows for as long as I could remember, always looking for something popular or interesting—a jewel that someone had over-looked and left as a modest treasure for me to find. I had never found anything even remotely precious. Apparently people held on to their treasures.

Mr. Fletcher, the owner, was sitting behind a low desk against the wall nearly obscured from view behind stacks of books that he was evaluating and pricing. He was the only person in the store, and he barely looked up when the bells above the door chimed. His watery eyes took quick note of me as he said, "If you need help, you know where to find it."

I had heard him say the same thing more times than I could count. I had never asked for his help.

I went straight to the religion section and thumbed through books on the only faith that Mason acknowledged: Christianity. Once, I had unearthed a translation of the Bhagavad Gita and had made it to the second chapter (*"When the mind constantly runs after wandering senses, it drives away wisdom, like the wind blowing a ship off course. . . ."*) before Mr. Fletcher wondered at my silence between the aisles of books and found me reading the "beautiful, haunting, and poignant" core text of the Hindu tradition.

He had whipped it out of my hands before I could finish a particularly arcane passage about "vanishing into God's bliss" and censured me for not telling him that I had found it among the sanctified texts he fastidiously arranged and rearranged. Someone had obviously slipped it into his store as a joke, though he took it very seriously and seemed to question with grave, milky eyes behind bottle-glass spectacles how much damage such a book had done to me. I was twelve, maybe thirteen. I had found it incomprehensible and lovely. Nothing more.

No such volume existed there now, and all I could find were tired copies of Janette Oke books nestled between the odd commentary and various parenting tomes. I touched the spine of one and wondered if someday soon I would reach for parenting wisdom from a complete stranger. From someone so utterly and impossibly removed from me and my situation that I would have to weigh each suggestion against my life and decide whether or not it held value for me. I hoped I would not have to depend on such abstractions.

There was nothing for Grandma in the religious section.

I wandered through cookbooks, fiction, and even children's literature before I crossed through poetry on my way to the door. I hardly even slowed down to skim the titles, but a thick book with tattered binding that had begun to roll away from the spine caught my eye. It was a muted gray-green with gold filigree that had faded to a dull glow. There were flowers with red petals climbing the sides and wrapping around the cover in a repeated pattern of cultivated lushness. Had the book said anything other than *The Complete Works of John Donne*, I would have walked away. Instead, I carefully opened the cover to read the price Mr. Fletcher had penciled in. Twelve dollars. I would have paid much more.

My father had actually been the John Donne devotee in our home, quoting the occasional line from a sermon or a poem though he was no literary mind or even very well read. But something about Donne had grabbed Dad in his high school days, and he had often proclaimed his undying loyalty to a man as godly and yet as allusive and honest about his own doubts and shortcomings as the seventeenth-century Anglican priest. Dad called him an Elizabethan David—a wicked, fallen, broken, but *seeking* man after God's own heart.

I knew that to place such a lovely volume in Grandma's hands—a book that would have been enormously meaningful to her son—

would be the finest gift I had ever given her. I flipped past the memoir and chronology of Donne's life to the contents, where I found among the poems of his first collection the verses that Dad had particularly loved: "A Hymn to God the Father." I read it three times, wondering at how such fear and sin and repetition of transgression could end in forgiveness. How it could end in "I fear no more."

I paid Mr. Fletcher with a twenty from my pocket and watched as he counted out the bills for my change. He peeked at the book a few times as if reluctant to part with it, as if he had changed his mind about the price or had never intended for it to end up on one of his shelves.

When I mentioned it was for my grandmother, he seemed to resign himself to letting it go, and as he handed me eight dollars, he said, "Did you see the inscription inside the back cover?" I shrugged and he gently took the book from me and turned to the last page. There, in slanting calligraphy, I read: *For my esteemed friend, D. Scott Braddock, from your friend G. Adolph Erni. Christmas 1884.*

"This book was a Christmas present over a hundred years ago," he said. I could tell that in his mind it lent the book a certain weight, a history that made its value far more than the twelve dollars I had just paid for it. I couldn't help feeling a bit guilty, like I had stolen it from him somehow.

"I didn't realize," I began falteringly, about to return the book though I hated to part with it.

Mr. Fletcher saw my hesitation and thrust it into my hands, waving me out of the store. "Give it to your grandmother. I hope she enjoys it."

It was a gruff thing to say, but he didn't mean it that way. I thanked him very earnestly as I turned to leave. He received one of the first real smiles I had mustered up in the last several weeks, but it was lost on him—he already had his head buried in another book.

Though it wasn't snowing, I carefully tucked the heavy volume into my coat. Mr. Fletcher hadn't given me a bag, and I hardly dared to ask him for one in case he changed his mind and decided he wanted to keep the book.

In the car, I rearranged the groceries into three bags and wrapped the fourth around the book, folding and refolding it until it was a tight, waterproof bundle. Although I was already hoping that Grandma had wrapping paper at home, I knew I probably wouldn't be able to wait until Christmas to give my gift to her. The very thought of surprising her was so stirring that I could almost be convinced as to the merit of the holiday I had only minutes ago dwelt on with dread. I hummed along with the radio on my way home.

"A tree!" Grandma exclaimed when she came out to help me unload groceries. "I had completely forgotten about getting a tree this year!"

"I thought it would be nice," I said meekly, hoping she wouldn't consider me presumptuous in my purchase.

"Oh, it is nice," she murmured, touching the tip that was sticking out the window. "I love how a pine tree makes the whole house so fragrant." Grandma stroked the needles for a moment before turning back to me, an exuberant expression on her face. "Let's do Christmas tonight, Julia!"

"Tonight?" I echoed hesitantly, though I couldn't think of a single reason not to. Besides, the book hiding beneath the driver's seat was a convincing argument in her favor.

"Why not? We'll turn on some music and have some fun in the kitchen for the rest of the afternoon; then we'll put up the tree, eat too much, and laugh the night away."

It was a fine thought. I grinned at her. "Merry Christmas," I said.

She clapped. "How fun! How spontaneous!"

The rest of the day was such a rare pleasure that I had to stop from time to time and make myself genuinely appreciate it, take it all in. It was as if we had been given an invaluable few hours of freedom—freedom from our fears, our obligations, our own worries, and our unanswerable questions. It was as if we had been given a gift that we hadn't asked for but immediately realized was the only thing that we truly wanted. I wanted to shout with the lightness of it.

When we had eaten every Christmas delicacy we could conjure up and when Grandma's records were tired from being played and replayed, we turned off the music and the lights in the kitchen and brought the tree in from the porch. I had shaken off as much snow as I could, but when we had the tree rooted firmly in the stand and cut through the twine with a steak knife from the kitchen, the boughs fell in a shower of freezing droplets. We giggled in the glistening cascade, enjoying the sprinkling baptism of icy water.

The tree itself was fat and charming, and the one bare spot only made us love it all the more. We strung colored lights around it and garlanded it with paper strings I had made when I was a little girl. There were glass ornaments from my grandmother's childhood tree and a wooden cowboy with arms and legs that moved from when my dad was a kid. The final touch was silver icicles that hung on tiny hooks and twirled daintily in the slightest breeze. Grandma sat with her back against the couch, directing me where to put them so that the tree was resplendent in glimmering light.

"I love it," she pronounced as I placed the last icicle. "I could sit here all night."

"Me too," I whispered, joining her to gaze at the finished tree.

We sat in silence for a moment before she said, "The only thing it's missing is presents."

"Not for long," I teased, hopping up from the floor to retrieve my hidden treasure. We had been so busy that I hadn't even bothered to ask for wrapping paper or find a more suitable covering for it. The book was still unfittingly adorned in a Value Foods bag, but I thought it looked mysteriously satisfying—there was no accounting for the value of what lay inside.

I returned to the living room with a barely concealed grin on my face and found Grandma placing a bundle beneath the tree.

"Caught!" she said with a laugh. "I wanted you to think Santa brought it."

"I don't think I ever believed that."

"No," she consented. "You were far too wise to be fooled with such nonsense." It sounded like a compliment, but there was something in the tone of her voice that carried the slightest resonance of regret.

I ignored it. "You go first," I said, sitting cross-legged on the floor in front of the tree and offering her my sad-looking parcel.

"Lovely paper," she cooed, stroking the plastic bag and giving me a bit of a sly look.

"It's all the rage right now, Grandma. You really should try to stay current with these things," I kidded, straight-faced. "Oh, be careful," I added as she turned the bundle over in her hands. "It's fragile."

She gently unwrapped the plastic bag and eased it off the book with a little sigh of anticipation. It was something she did every year, this show of eagerness to make me feel like I had nearly taken her breath away with such a thoughtful, caring gift. I had never warranted it before, but when she realized the book that she held in her hands, her eyes really did widen slightly.

"Oh, Julia, what a beautiful book," she breathed. "Your father . . ." She couldn't say any more.

It was a joy to see her sincerely appreciate something I had given her. "I just stumbled across it," I confessed, feeling that I had misrepresented myself a bit. It wasn't like I had thought of the gift myself; it had sort of hopped off the shelf at me. *It* found *me*.

"Oh, but I just love it. I don't know that I'll understand a single word that's written in it, but I do love it."

I laughed. "Of course you'll understand it. You're the wisest woman I know." The words sounded a bit strange in my ears, but I realized as I said them that I really did mean them. When I thought of her life, of all she had done and endured, I could think of no one who had lived her days with as much insight and wisdom.

"Here," I said quickly, trying to defuse the strange feeling in the air from a compliment that came too close to serious introspection, "look at the inscription in the back."

Grandma read it with delight in her face, and we flipped through a few passages, laughing at ourselves when something was particularly obscure or complicated. I didn't show her the poem of Dad's particular interest, deciding I would save it for another day as it felt too serious, too burdensome, for such a night as this.

"My turn," Grandma finally said, laying the book aside and collecting the package that I had watched her place beneath the tree. "We were on remarkably similar wavelengths when we selected Christmas presents this year," she observed with a smile.

The parcel in my hands was obviously a book, thinly veiled by a layer of red wrapping paper with gold-flaked poinsettia leaves. It was large and heavy, and though I suspected a parenting book of some sort, I could hardly imagine what psychologist would have the resolve to stick with such a tiresome, overdone topic for so many pages. I tried to cast an enthusiastic look at Grandma before sliding my finger under a fold in the paper.

Before the paper was completely off, I realized exactly which book it was. The worn corners and overstuffed pages were familiar even when I first held them in my hands, imagining that they belonged to some mundane modern volume. But when I could see various papers and mementos peeking out from between the pages, I had to acknowledge what it was even though I could hardly bring myself to believe it.

"You're giving me your Bible?" I asked, and my voice was much quieter than I intended it to be.

"I want you to have it," Grandma said, almost as if she knew she would have to talk me into keeping her most treasured possession.

I was baffled. "But I have a Bible."

"I know, but I wanted you to have this one." Grandma leaned over and lifted the Bible from my grasp so she could take my hands in her own. "Julia, I never parented a daughter, and if I had, her teenage years would have been twenty years ago. I don't know what to do with a nineteen-year-old now any more than I knew what to do with a fifteen-year-old a few years ago when your dad died. I feel like I have failed you in so many ways."

"Grandma—," I tried to interrupt, but she squeezed my fingers as if warning me to let her finish what she had to say.

"We're going to make it through this—I know that for sure—but I've never been much of a preacher, and I've never been one to take control, so we're going to work our way through this together. This—" she inclined her head at the Bible lying beside us—"is the best road map I've got. You need it now. I want you to have it."

I glanced down at the imposing book softened by the collection of devotionals, prayers, flyers, musings, and keepsakes sticking out at all angles. She saw me looking at them, and when I opened my mouth to protest again, she cut me off by saying, "I want you to have it *all*. You called me wise earlier and I know that's not true, but I know you will find some wisdom in there. I don't want to withhold anything that just might help in some small way along this journey. I don't want to hide anything from you if it might be able to cast a little light on the coming days."

I was speechless. It was the most excessive gift of self I had ever received, and I absolutely did not know what to do with it. Grandma was offering me her heart and soul, her spiritual journey—what could be more intimate? I wasn't sure that I even wanted what she was so freely offering, but it was such an extravagant bequeathal that I felt humbled and small beneath the great love and immensity of it. In the end there was nothing I could say but "Thank you."

"You're welcome," she said, and she gently laid her hand against my forehead.

It was a strange thing to do, as if she were testing my skin for the telltale, radiating warmth of a fever, but as she touched my head, I understood her hand was laid on me in blessing. Her palm was cool and soothing against my skin, and I pressed myself into it almost against my will as a part of me even now balked against her unfathomable kindness. Who was I to deserve her hand so tender along my brow?

The room was still and glowing with the lights from the Christmas tree. Grandma held her hand above me in the silence, and I couldn't help but imagine December next year, a baby in my arms. My breath caught in my throat. There was a swell on the horizon, a fathomless, deepening wave that would surely consume me in a torrent of blue. I was to be dashed against the rocks. What could I do but sit there with my eyes closed and let myself slowly, clumsily accept her gift, her love, her blessing? Her promise of light.

last

threads

I BEGAN TO CARRY GRANDMA'S BIBLE with me everywhere. It was a security blanket of sorts, a survival manual that I had not yet opened nor tried to understand, counting on the hope that when I truly needed it I could whip it open and some resounding truth would ring forth with unmistakable clarity. The Bible was my backup plan if my own resourcefulness managed to fail me.

However, Grandma had never intended for me to use her treasured book as my ace in the hole. Her amusement was indulgent at first, then waning, and finally it ripened into a quiet disappointment that propelled her to confront me one morning at breakfast.

"You know, Julia, you should actually try reading it." She pointed a forkful of scrambled eggs at the book that lay idle beside my plate.

I started to say, *I do* but stopped myself before I could lie to her face. "I know," I murmured instead. It wasn't as if I didn't know the old stories. It wasn't as if I had never read the book. Was it really necessary to read and reread such a tedious and seemingly incomprehensible collection of children's stories?

Grandma read my mind. "I know you know the stories, but there's a lot more to the Bible than you remember from Sunday school."

She rarely chastised me, so when she did, the obligation I felt to honor her was tenfold what it would have been if she had been the type to nag me constantly. "I don't know where to start," I finally admitted, willing to do whatever she suggested.

That one comment started a tradition in our little family. Every morning I would come downstairs for breakfast and find a slip of paper on my plate. Between the flowery border of a three-inch square piece of stationery I would read my assignment for the day: sometimes a couple of chapters in a book I had to look up in the table of contents, other times a few verses from various books that kept my fingers jogging over the parchmentlike paper for over an hour. I was surprised to find that I could remember the Old Testament books in their proper order thanks to a rap song we had learned in Sunday school when I was nine. The New Testament books, on the other hand, were less familiar, and no matter how hard I tried to keep them straight, I kept mixing up First and Second Corinthians with First and Second Chronicles.

To say that it was immediately rewarding would be a lie. At first

I read and reread passages trying intently to glean wisdom and help from the ancient words. Later I got bored and found it hard to focus, dwelling instead on the possibilities of my future: getting a job, finding day care for the baby, maybe moving out of the farmhouse so Grandma wouldn't have to regress to the stage of her life that she had left behind decades ago.

When I went to my doctor for the first time, he sternly reminded me of the possibility of putting the child up for adoption, and the thought consumed me for days and eliminated any ability I had to silently read my Bible. I sat with the book open but utterly unused, and I deliberated and argued with myself until I realized that I could never do such a thing. It didn't matter how beautiful, honorable, and possibly even better for the baby that self-sacrificing act might be. I didn't have the courage. I wasn't strong enough. I didn't need to bury myself in Bible passages to know that one truth.

Though I considered myself rather weak and irresolute in regards to the pregnancy, when it became public knowledge that I wasn't going back to school after Christmas break, I found I had reserves of strength that took me completely by surprise. Maybe my steely forbearance through whispers and stares was a direct result of the overwhelming conviction that I was doing the right thing. This child was not a mistake. My own actions, my recklessness with Parker, had been a dire lapse in judgment—a sin, to use the language that I was beginning to become reacquainted with—but to call the child an error was as abhorrent to me as the thought of ending the life I had so carelessly begun.

I couldn't help but wonder if my dad had felt the same way. It seemed he was a shadow just behind my shoulder, fading against the light I cast each time I turned to catch him hovering over me. He didn't whisper to me as some otherworldly apparition or my own personal guardian angel, but as I walked the same path that he had taken, he reminded me of things—of the fierceness with which he'd loved and protected me every day of my own mistaken life. I understood the depth of his love against the backdrop of indiscretion and the well-intentioned but cruel assumptions of people who believed they knew what was best for the child who was already so inexplicably dear and loved.

In the first few days, I simply smiled and ignored nearly everybody. I went to church with Grandma the Sunday after the gossip had spread like a ditch fire in the fall—rushing through each blade of grass and licking every green thing dry until nothing but ashes remained—and sat still and resolute beneath the onerous weight of conviction and disapproval.

No one knew that I was pregnant, but they did know that I would not be going back to school after Christmas, and there was plenty of speculation about why. Maybe I had been caught up in the party crowd, falling prey to drugs and alcohol. Maybe Brighton wouldn't take me back because I had confirmed myself to be slothful and stupid and had been kicked out. Whatever the reason for my departure, it was surely juicy and scandal worthy, and though I wished I could have proven them wrong, the truth was probably worse than their malicious assumptions. I dreaded the day that the whole truth would come out.

It would be unfair to say that everyone was as cold and charred as I, in my cynical imagination, envisioned them to be. One sweet woman actually wrapped me in a fervent embrace and said absolutely nothing while she held me as if her grip alone would protect me from every possible sorrow. She knew nothing of my trouble, and yet she touched my cheek as she walked away and offered nothing more than the solidarity of her arms. I had to blink back tears.

The Walker family was in Florida when the rumors began to fly, but I had given Grandma permission to fill them in on the entire situation before they left. They would keep my secret, and I didn't blame her one bit for wanting to tell them—our families had been friends for far too long to let something so consequential be discovered in the trickle down of a vicious small-town rumor mill. But in a way I wished I could have been the one to tell Thomas. It would have been awkward, painful even, but I felt able to take full responsibility for myself, and though I knew things could never be patched up with us, I wanted him to know that I was strong now. Or at the very least, aware of myself: my own strength, my immeasurable weakness.

Almost as if my body was unwilling to let me forget that very weakness, it had begun to rebel against me. My mornings became a nauseous affair where a thing so small as walking down the stairs into the kitchen brought on a wave of seasickness so intense that I had all but sworn off food and movement between the hours of seven and ten. I was on the verge of adding *opening my eyes* and *breathing* to the ever-growing list of nausea-inducing activities.

But every day when midmorning rolled around, the sickness left nearly as quickly as it had come, and I found myself energetic and eager for any activity that would make me feel healthy and human again. Usually I bundled up against the cold and fought my way through snow so high it washed over my knees and took the long walk through the grove to meet the mailman as he crept by around quarter to eleven.

"Morning, Julia!" he would call with a smile, standing beside a brown station wagon with a U.S. Postal Service magnetic sign slapped on the door. He always waited for me if I was still trekking up to the road and gave me the rubber-banded bundle of letters and flyers with a conspiratorial wink. Bushy white eyebrows poked out from underneath his stocking cap, and I always had to suppress a giggle when he winked and made them do a little caterpillar dance. He was a gentle man and kindhearted. When I accidentally let it slip that I was having a baby, he touched my hand as he passed me the mail and promised he wouldn't tell a soul. He didn't judge me or turn away from me, but he gave me a look that nearly broke my heart. *I* wanted to comfort *him*.

One early January morning, I walked up in the snow and he was lounging beside his car as if he had been there for hours.

"Got some bills, Julia," he called as I got closer. He said that nearly every day.

"Good, Eli; we like bills." It was my standard reply.

"Got a Wal-Mart flyer," he added.

"Keep it," I said. "I know what they have at Wal-Mart."

He laughed. When I broke through the snow at the edge of the road and stepped onto the asphalt with a huff, Eli waved an envelope almost happily in the air. "Got a letter today too."

My breathing was a bit labored from the exertion of climbing through the clinging snow, and I cocked my head at him as I puffed in and out. "Who's it from?" I asked, struggling a little to make the words come out normal.

"No return address." Eli sighed. "Maybe it's a love letter!" He blurted the words out merrily, then blushed to the whites of his eyebrows as he realized what he had just said to an unmarried, pregnant teenager. "Er, um . . . I . . ."

It hurt to see him so embarrassed, and I quickly jumped in. "Maybe it's a belated Christmas card. I love Christmas cards!"

"Yeah, that's it, a Christmas card."

As I accepted the collection of mail, I gave him a full, toothy smile to let him know that any slip of the tongue was instantly and entirely forgiven and forgotten.

He smiled back a bit uncomfortably and offered me a little wave and a nod as he hopped back into his car.

I stood on the edge of the highway by the mailbox and looked down at the modest farmstead below. Traffic was slower than one car every few minutes or so, and when the improvised mail truck was gone, the road was quiet and the air was still. Winter has a sound all its own, and without birdsong or buzzing insects or a breeze in the grass, I could hear the ethereal creak of snow on snow and ice on ice. The outbuildings were dark and empty and covered in untouched snow like a child's toys abandoned in a sandbox for years. Roofs sagged beneath the weight of all that whiteness and leaned heavily on tilting walls as old men with burdened backs rest precariously on canes. It wasn't a sad sight, merely tired. The farm looked as if each year of existence had slowly chipped away at the optimistic belief that everything would turn out all right in the end, that happily ever after is the bookend to every story. I realized, as I stood there, that I would never have the fairy-tale ending. But weary buildings with a lifetime of living etched in their aging walls offered their own sweet perspective. A life that seemed attainable.

Forgetting about the letter, I started slowly down the plowed driveway, avoiding the hard-packed, icy ruts and throwing my arms out for balance when my boots skidded over a patch of frozen slush. It was peaceful and solitary, and I didn't turn around when I heard a car in the distance, waiting instead for the interruption to fade into the expanse of far-flung horizon. But as the engine revved closer, I glanced surreptitiously over my shoulder and watched an apple red SUV turn at our mailbox. It was the Walkers' Suburban.

I took an unbalanced step to the side of the driveway and watched the vehicle inch its way toward me. Thomas was at the wheel, and I tried to swallow the dry air in my mouth when I saw the reluctant droop of his head, as if someone were pushing him forward against his will. It struck me that though I had been brave and almost eager when speaking to him was little more than a hypothetical, with his vehicle creeping down my driveway, there was nowhere I would rather be than miles away from where I was. I scanned the Suburban for his brothers and sisters. For Francesca. He was alone.

He pulled next to me, and I watched his window hum down smoothly. Watched the glass steadily withdraw into the door instead of watching him. We stayed like that for a moment, me exposed and chilly on the side of the gravel driveway, him wrapped cozily in the warmth radiating from the cranked heater. Uneasiness snaked between us like a live current.

Finally, with a palpably forced cheer, he said, "Would you like a ride?"

I looked at his face and saw my own discomfort and apprehension written in his hesitant gaze. "Where?" I asked slowly, because I couldn't imagine going anywhere with him.

He gestured at the house, and I raised a cautious eyebrow at him.

"Look, I was just hoping we could talk for a minute. Do you have a minute, Julia?"

It was hard not to let a self-deprecating smile crease my lips. What did I have if not bottles of time lined up as yet-to-be-filled days and years that stretched endlessly before me? "Okay," I said because it was the only conceivable response. "But I'll walk."

Thomas lifted one shoulder as if to shrug and took his foot off the brake. I watched him coast down the incline and pull up to the garage door.

Following gingerly in the tread left by the mammoth SUV, I tried to imagine what Thomas hoped to accomplish by showing up unexpectedly. I didn't know what to say to him—or how to prepare my mind or heart for whatever *he* hoped to say to *me*—and I couldn't begin to presume that I knew why he was here. It wasn't really fear or even regret that gripped me as I walked and waited, just a reluctant hope that everything could be forgiven between us even if it was never forgotten. I resolved to seek peace.

By the time he had turned off the SUV, stepped out, zipped up his coat, and walked a few paces to stand in the dim, gray shadow of the ramshackle chicken coop, I was only feet away. Expectant.

"I thought you were in Florida," I said, eager to at least start on safe ground.

"I was. We got back late last night." Thomas scuffed his feet at the snow.

Though I instantly regretted thinking it, I couldn't help but remember the tilt of his head and the suddenness of the smile that had caught me all those years ago. If I took only a few steps backward, I would be in the very spot where I had first laid eyes on Thomas.

"I bet it's nice in Florida this time of year," I tried, attempting to be natural.

"Very nice," he echoed. His brown hair had been lightly sanded with blond in the ten days of their vacation, and his skin was tanned and smooth.

I studied the side of his face as he gazed over the barren fields, and I glimpsed a curve of white skin just above his ear—bare and cool and intimate—hidden in the shadow cast by the straight angle of his hair. It struck me as almost indecent. I looked away quickly, feeling like I had seen something that I should not have seen.

He turned to glance at me and misread my blush to mean that I was ashamed of the pregnancy he obviously knew all about. "I'm sorry about . . . ," he began, and I saw crimson start to creep up his neck too as he tried to backpedal out of an impossible situation. "I mean, I'm not *sorry*. I just . . . I heard about . . . it must be very . . ."

"It's all rather indescribable," I offered carefully. Thomas still looked sick to his stomach, so I continued, "I'm okay—really I am."

"You look okay," he said tentatively and then cringed at the implication in his words—the expectation that I would have been tent-sized already or at least haggard. Not bright-eyed and blushed from the cold. Not like myself.

I understood how he felt every time I looked in a mirror. Shouldn't something unmistakable have changed in me? Shouldn't it be possible to read what lay before me like a scarlet letter emblazoned on my chest? We had all read the book in English class those many years ago. We knew the price of stupidity . . . or at least of getting caught.

We stood in the snow and the silence, and I spent more time wondering what Thomas was thinking than concentrating on my own thoughts. I imagined he wanted to ask me who the father was, wanted to confirm his suspicion that the "jerk TA" from statics was everything he had tried to warn me he would be. I couldn't admit that to him.

Instead, when the lack of words became almost tangible in the air between us, I presented the answer to a less-burdened question. "August," I said as if he were waiting for me to say it. "The baby is due in August, so I suppose I have a few months yet of looking pretty . . . *okay*." I had meant to say *normal*, but the word seemed somehow irrelevant.

Thomas nodded slowly at me. "August is a long time away." He made it sound like everything could be the way it had always been between now and then. Like the stork would come and deliver the baby near the end of the summer, and until that point I could just be myself, live my life as though nothing had changed.

"How's Francesca?" I suddenly asked, compelled by a need to shift the conversation off myself.

He looked at me sharply, as if I were picking a fight or pressing a wound, though I had only said it because I could think of nothing else to say. "She's fine," he answered after a moment. "We're back together."

I actually smiled. "I'm glad, Thomas," I said and was mildly surprised to find that I meant it quite sincerely.

He still studied me with a bit of a guarded look, but a smile made a quick sweep over his face as he must have realized that I meant him no harm. "You know," he said bravely, "you are very much like her. She reminds me of you. Or you remind me of her."

I tried to take his summation as a compliment. "Say hi to her for me, okay?" I blurted out, astonishing even myself. It was little more than a courtesy, but I couldn't believe that I had the civility to say it.

Thomas must have appreciated the miles we traveled in those few words, and he quickly changed the topic again lest we find ourselves taking steps back instead of forward. "Did you get my letter?" he asked.

"Letter?" I shook my head. "I didn't get a letter from you."

Thomas reached for my hand and pulled a yellow envelope from the stack of mail in my loose grip. A flyer slipped from the bundle and fell to the snow at our feet. He picked it up with a flourish and returned it to me without giving me back the envelope that he had grabbed.

"You *did* get my letter," he said with an edge to his voice that was a little too light, too carefree.

If I had thought before that he'd come to patch things up with me, I knew now that his visit was to explain whatever he had written in that letter. The relief playing at the corners of his mouth was unmistakable. A part of me wanted to wrench the envelope away from him and rip it open, to hastily read what he didn't want me to see. But I wasn't five and I wasn't about to make a scene, so I tried to keep my voice even as I asked, "Do I get to read it?"

"It doesn't say much," Thomas assured me. "Anyway, I wanted to say it to you in person, and now I can." His words hung for a moment before dissolving into little puffs of evaporated air. I could smell the peppermint gum in his mouth as I watched the struggle behind his eyes when it struck him that he would have to say those things now. He shifted nervously on his feet, knowing that I was waiting. That I expected to hear whatever he had penned in the card he refused to let me read. Now.

I waited.

Thomas cleared his throat. "I just . . . I wanted to say that you were a good friend." He said it quickly, though I didn't think it was a lie. There was something about our friendship in that note.

I looked at him unblinkingly.

"And that I'm sorry about anything that I ever did to hurt you. I didn't mean to hurt you." It must have been too much of an admission, for he added, "If I hurt you."

"You did," I confirmed, because I needed to say it to him. "You did hurt me." And then, since I could hardly blame him for all that had happened, I said quietly, "Apology accepted."

He had been looking at the ground, and when he heard the earnestness in my voice, he lifted his eyes to give me a sheepish smile. "Thank you. I had to hear that from you."

"Was there anything else in the letter?" I asked, still feeling like there had to be more to it for him to wrench the envelope from my hands as if he regretted ever sending it.

Thomas gave me an impenetrable look before sliding his thumb under a loose corner of the envelope and ripping an ugly gash in the buttery yellow paper. There was a blank white card inside, and as he took it out, I longed to snatch it from his grasp and know what he had written. But it was probably better not to know. I folded my arms across my chest and watched as he tipped the card on its side and caught something in his outstretched palm. He clutched it for a moment in his closed fist before holding his hand out to me.

When I paused, Thomas nodded, and I extended my arm to accept his little gift. He put something cold and tiny on my fingers, then curled my hand around it and squeezed my fist in his own warm grip.

I pulled my hand from his and studied his diminutive present. It was a cross painted with a cheap, bronze-colored lacquer that had aged rather unattractively to a rusty green. I didn't recognize it at first.

Thomas obviously saw my confusion because he jumped in to clarify. "It's from that card, Julia. The one Janice sent you when your dad died . . . ?"

"We burned the Twenty-third Psalm," I remembered aloud.

"Yeah, and the cross fell into the mud and I picked it up."

"And kept it?" I asked incredulously.

Thomas laughed a little at himself when he admitted, "It felt weird to throw it away. It's sacred somehow, you know?"

I didn't know what to say.

He must have anticipated more of a reaction from me because his arms hung awkwardly at his sides, angled and rigid, as he studied me. "I just wanted you to have it," he muttered. "Don't think that I think it means something, because I don't. . . . I mean, the *cross* means something, but I'm not trying to . . . be profound. . . ." He trailed off. "I just thought you might want it."

Although whatever power Thomas had once had over me was now little more than a dim and quickly fading spark, it still hurt to see him so self-conscious and uncertain. As if waking from a sound sleep, I roused myself and rushed to smooth things over, pushing my own reaction to his unsolicited gift deep inside. "It's nice, Thomas. I'm glad you gave it to me."

"You are?" he sputtered. "Because I almost didn't give it to you. That's why I'm here—I thought you might be angry with me."

The anger I had felt toward Thomas had diminished when the reality of my own imploding life had taken center stage. A letter with a cheap, old cross was not enough to rekindle any emotion more potent than defeat, though I could hardly say that out loud. I suddenly felt very tired and could not stop a weary sigh from escaping my lips.

"I'm not angry," I said. Then I wrapped the cross in my fist and waved it at him with what I hoped was an intrepid, even optimistic, smile. "Thank you."

He hunched his shoulders and thrust his hands deep into the pockets of his coat as he murmured a shy "You're welcome."

And that was it. There really wasn't anything left to say. The space between us was rich with good-byes and the soft and resonant click of a firmly closed door. A small part of me wanted to put my arms around him one last time, but instead I leaned back and made a tentative move toward the house. He fell in step beside me. We remained in our own thoughts as we walked to his Suburban, and I waited politely for him as he opened the door to hop in.

He climbed into the driver's seat and started the SUV, holding the door open with one hand to give me a sweet, sad smile. "Bye,

Julia." It was clear that he wanted to say more. The words fought on his tongue and he opened his mouth and closed it again, but before I could say a quick good-bye and end the conversation, he pressed on. "Good luck with everything, okay? And, hey, I want you to know that—"

"Thank you, Thomas," I interrupted. "It was very nice of you to stop by."

He looked for a moment like he was going to continue his thought, like he wouldn't be able to put the transmission in reverse without saying everything he had come to say, but then he rubbed his fingers roughly over his lips and forced a smile at me. "Take care, Julia."

"You too," I said.

I didn't watch him drive away.

Grandma met me on the porch with an old cake pan full of leftovers for the cats. She raised an eyebrow at me when she saw the Walkers' Suburban pulling out of our driveway, but I touched her arm to say, "Later," and she didn't ask. I retreated into the stillness of the house and watched through the glass in the door as she descended the steps. I could hear her call loudly across the yard for the cats, and I traced their movements as they emerged like lithe, shadowy phantoms from every nook and cranny.

When my coat was on the hook and my boots had been discarded on the drying rack, I stood in the kitchen and felt the tarnished little cross pull me down with a weight that was impossible for such a tiny object. It was as if those small, intersecting lines were etched with the story of my life, a tale so bent and burdened it seemed impossible to set it right—to straighten what was crooked, to smooth the rough places.

I thought of Janice, and though it was unanticipated and unexplored, I gave myself over to the longing that I had for her even after all these years. When—*if*—she heard about my pregnancy, would I get another card? Would she sign it *Yours truly*? For a moment I imagined what it would be like to see her. Maybe I could write to her. Or e-mail or call. Maybe I could find a way to carve a different ending for at least that part of the story.

Maybe I wouldn't have the courage.

When Grandma came into the house, she stomped her feet on the rug in the mudroom and yelled happily, "Julia, the sun broke through the clouds when you went into the house! You should see it out there—it's bright and shining, and the snow is sparkling like diamonds! Come outside for—" She broke off when she saw me lying on the floor in the living room.

I was on my stomach with my arms curled under my chest and the cross still clutched in my white-knuckled hand. My head was turned to the window. She came over to me and, without any prompting or fuss, lay down quietly with her head next to mine. Our noses were inches apart.

"What's going on?" she asked gently.

I opened my mouth to speak, and my voice cracked around a sob. "Grandma, I can't." The words were less than a whisper. They hung like torn spiderwebs in the air between us.

Her eyes softened, and she reached out to lay her palm on my cheek. "You can't what, honey?"

I closed my eyes. "I can't do this. I'm not strong enough. I'm not good enough. I don't know how to be a mother."

Grandma stroked my cheek as she lay beside me, our bodies

stretched out like offerings on top of the green shag carpet. "Shhh . . . ," she murmured. "I know it's hard. I know you're scared. It's okay to be low."

My eyes flew open, and I squinted at her though my head ached with the effort of seeing. "Low? Grandma, I am so far down, there is nothing left beneath me. I *am* the bottom. I *am* what lies beneath. Where can I possibly go from here?"

A tear slipped off her nose to match mine already darkening the carpet. "I don't think you have to go anywhere, Julia," she whispered. "You turn around. You look up."

I rolled over onto my back and stared at the ceiling. Let the tears drip down my temples and into my hair. I wanted to hope. I wanted there to be something beyond waiting for the next closed door, empty promise, heartrending good-bye. "I'm looking up," I said quietly.

"There's nothing else you can do." Grandma rolled onto her side and tucked herself around me, curling an arm over my stomach and twisting her ankle through mine. She pulled me close and put her mouth beside my ear. She began to pray.

seeking

SOME DAYS I IMAGINE I can feel my baby pirouette inside me.
An arm sweeps across curious eyes, a leg arcs and stretches before
curling close to a warm little body, and a heavy head nods in sleep.
It is nothing more than a fantasy, for though I know she does that
even now, I also know that I will not be able to feel her explorations,
her very exhalations, for at least another month yet.

I know that I should not treasure her so extravagantly as this.
That every woman who has ever struggled to get pregnant within
the encircling embrace of a loving marriage will soon find me
obscene, will beg God or her doctor or her husband to tell her
why an undeserving child like me should be blessed with life while

her own arms—capable, mature, eager, stable, willing—go empty. Maybe they will look at me and hope against all hope that I will offer her to them—a gift so opulent and dear that we will both spend the rest of our lives loving and hating each other with an almost frantic, secret devotion that both blesses and grapples with envy and doubt. Two mothers sharing one child. Two mothers, wishing they could have been the one to do both—to give birth and to give the child a life.

I will do both to the best of my ability.

One morning over breakfast, it struck me with all the weight of a life-changing epiphany that I am a mother. Or at least an almost mother. I found it strange to imagine myself as such, and though I have spent my life trying to assemble and arrange all the parts that would form a whole me—a healthy, happy, honest representation of who I truly am—that one role seemed more foreign and somehow more real than any other part I have yet tried to play.

"I am a mother," I said out loud, listening to how the words filled the room with indefinable meaning.

My grandma looked at me with a peculiar expression on her face.

"I am a daughter and a granddaughter," I continued. "A high school graduate, a college dropout, a lover of all things green. I am a bookworm, a poor conversationalist, and a bit of a card shark." Grandma smiled at that one, and I grinned back. "I think I am a poet at heart. A hard worker and a recent realist. I am . . . I am . . ." I stuck a fingernail between my teeth, trying to capture the essence. Trying to think of more.

Grandma pulled my hand out of my mouth and held it. "You are a new creation," she said with conviction.

The words were full and brimming with anticipation—mysteriously striking, even exotic. I held them as tenderly as an extraordinary treasure that I could not yet fully appreciate and rolled them around in my heart and mind before trying them over my tongue.

New creation.

I am a new creation.

There is a little contract tucked in the front cover of my Bible where I keep a growing list of the things I will commit myself to do, a list that collects and names what I always wanted my mother to be and that I promise my child I will try to be for her. It's the "how to" of my endeavor to be a new creation, to be more than I ever imagined I would be.

The first thing I wrote down is *a good cook.* Since penning the phrase I have devoted myself to becoming my grandmother's apprentice in the kitchen. Only two weeks after cleaning and chopping every vegetable, stirring pots of soups and sauces she had already created, and shadowing her every move between the fridge, stove, and sink, I made my very first beef stew while Grandma read in the living room. It was a pretty near approximation to the perfection she achieves. A little too bland maybe. A little too thick. I figure I have years to get better.

Somewhere near the top of the list I have also written *fun.* Jumping in puddles after a spring rain sort of fun. Remembering and repeating every silly knock-knock joke from the inside of Laffy Taffy wrappers sort of fun. Once, shortly after Janice left, Dad made pancakes for us on a Saturday morning and fashioned a smiley face out of chocolate chips on top of mine. I was probably too old for that sort of thing, but I remember it fondly anyway. It was a game to try to capture a mini kiss of chocolate in every bite. I look forward to having that kind of fun. To making her laugh.

Grandma cringes a bit when I refer to the baby using the feminine pronoun. She says I shouldn't set my heart on having a girl, that it's not a good idea to call the child *she* until I know for sure that that's what the baby is.

It's not so much an expectation as it is a feeling. I can't claim to know anything about the baby inside me, but I can't help the fact that I just know deep down that I will have—that I already do have—a daughter. I won't be disappointed if the doctor pronounces some day in August, "It's a boy!" But I will be very surprised. I already feel like I know her.

And the thought—or hope—that she is in fact a *she* has prompted another thing on my growing contract: *encouraging*. One more trait that I wish had been used to bless me when I was a little girl. And, being honest with myself, an attribute that I still wish I could be the beneficiary of today.

My dad was an amazing cheerleader, my advocate, ally, and friend, and my grandmother should be sainted for the depth of her patience and love, but there is a part of me that always wished for the confirmation of a mother. Not just someone to tell me that I was pretty—though I intend to tell my daughter every day of her life that she is absolutely, unequivocally beautiful—but someone to recognize my worth as a daughter, a young woman, a someday mother, a person. Someone with whom to feel a part of that never-ending bond of almost immortality—you go on from me and she goes on from you and on and on and again and again until God comes back to complete the round.

He is on my list too.

I wrote *Godly* with a capital *G*, though I hardly know what it means. *Like God* was my first attempt at a definition, but Grandma informed me that no one is like God. I had chained myself to an unattainable goal. *Becoming* like God, she instructed, is a slightly more realistic pursuit. It implies a long road, a journey alongside a friend who becomes more dear and beloved with each step taken together. It is the expedition of a lifetime, not a four-hour flight. A two steps forward, one step back dance that allows me to make mistakes as I learn His moves, His will, and His direction for my—until now—achingly directionless life.

The thought stirs me.

Janice left, my father died, and Grandma will follow. Who is my constant? Who will walk with me when everyone else has faded to the background, to a place where they exist in little more than carefully preserved memories? There is something inside me that knows beyond every rational and irrational doubt that I was not meant to walk alone. That He longs to stand beside me.

There is a verse in Matthew that says, "Ask and it will be given to you; seek and you will find; knock and the door will be opened to you." I wrote that verse on a piece of paper, and I taped it to the mirror in my bedroom. I read it every day, and believe me, *I am seeking*. I don't know yet if it's true, if everyone who seeks finds what they are looking for—finds that He will walk beside them—but I do know that seeking is better than waiting. I can feel Him just around the corner.

It's a different kind of longing.

About the Author

NICOLE BAART was born and raised in a small town in Iowa. After lifeguarding, waitressing, working in a retail store, and even being a ranch hand on a dairy farm, she changed her major four times in college before finally settling on degrees in English, Spanish, English as a second language, and secondary education. She taught and developed curriculum in three different school districts over the course of seven years.

Teaching and living in Vancouver, British Columbia, cultivated a deep love in Nicole for both education and the culturally inexplicable use of the word *eh*. She became a Canadian citizen for the sole purpose of earning the right to use the quirky utterance.

Nicole wrote her first complete novel while taking a break from teaching to be a full-time mom. She is also the author of hundreds of poems, dozens of short stories, a handful of articles, and various unfinished novels.

The mother of two young sons and the wife of a pastor, Nicole writes when she can: in bed, in the shower, as she is making supper, and occasionally sitting down at her computer. As the adoptive mother of an Ethiopian-born son, she is passionate about global issues and works to promote awareness of topics such as world hunger, poverty, AIDS, and the plight of widows and orphans. Nicole and her family live in Iowa.

turn the page for an exciting preview
of the sequel to

After the Leaves Fall

humility

IT'S NOT THAT I EVER had delusions of grandeur or even that I think I'm better than anyone else, but there is something about donning a tag that says, "Please be patient; I'm a trainee" and asking, "Would you like paper or plastic?" that is uniquely—even brutally—humbling.

Paired with a blue canvas apron cinched tight across my expanding waist, the plastic name tag positively screamed from my chest and made me frighteningly conspicuous at a time in my life when I longed for anonymity like parched earth wants for rain. *Cover me,* I thought the first time I dressed in the awful ensemble. Standing alone in my room in front of a mirror too honest to disguise the profound hideousness of it, I felt more exposed than if I had been wearing a skirt that barely covered my floral-print panties. "Oh, God, if You love me at all," I breathed, "cover me."

"You look cute," Grandma commented diplomatically when I sulked into the kitchen moments later. But by the glint of a smile in her eye I knew that *cute* was a euphemism for *ridiculous*. "Just don't tuck your shirt in, Julia. It won't . . . you know . . . look too . . ." She fluffed her fingers around her midsection, and flour poofed in little clouds about her hands like smoke from somewhere up a magician's sleeve. She cautiously, encouragingly, raised an eyebrow at me.

I looked down to see the petite crescent curve of my belly pressing against the knotted apron strings. Startled by what I saw, I sucked in impulsively. It disappeared—the growing evidence of *her* disappeared—a flat shadow beneath a fold of cerulean. "That's the best I can do," I said dolefully. "We have to tuck our shirts in. It's part of the dress code. And—" I reached into the front pocket of the apron and produced a thin, mustard yellow tie—"we have to wear this."

Grandma almost burst out laughing but allowed herself only a restrained little chuckle. "You know, I see those kids in Value Foods every week, but I never really noticed the uniform. Is that a clip-on?"

I nodded bleakly and snapped the clip at her, alligator style, before affixing it to my starched collar.

"It's crooked, honey." She wiped her fingertips on a towel and left the bread dough that she had been kneading to circle around the worn oak table and face me. She tugged at the obscene bit of fabric, pulling it this way and that before tucking it under the top of my apron and stepping back. "There." The word sounded almost portentous to me—definitive.

"I'm going to be late," I croaked, clearing my throat self-consciously. "Don't wait up for me. I'm helping out with a restock tonight. They're going to train me how to record inventory. . . ."

Grandma pursed her lips at me knowingly and spread her arms in understanding. I walked heavily into her embrace. "I'm proud of you, Julia," she murmured into my hair. "It's really not that bad, is it?"

I didn't want to be melodramatic, but I couldn't drown the sick feeling that was rising past my chest and into my throat, where it sat threateningly at the back of my tongue. *They'll see me,* I thought. *They'll judge me.* But I said, "You're right—it's not so bad. It's just that all the high school kids work there. I'll be the oldest person besides the manager. . . ."

"You only graduated last year," Grandma reminded, trying to cheer me up. "You'll probably even know some of the employees!"

Great, I thought.

But she was doing her best to be helpful, and I managed a wry smile because at the very least she hadn't said, "You'll have so much in common with them!" The disappearing smoothness beneath the straight line of my apron guaranteed that I would have absolutely nothing in common with my coworkers.

"Well," I said, pressing my palms together and trying to force a little enthusiasm into my voice, "I'd better go or I'll be late."

"Wouldn't want that your first day on the job!" Grandma followed me into the mudroom and gave my back a little pat when my coat was zipped up and my hand was on the door. "It's going to be just fine."

"I know," I replied without blinking.

She watched from the door as I drove away, but the sun was already a memory on the horizon—a thin ribbon of purple, little more than a bruise left by the imprint of orange—and I'm sure all she saw of my departure was taillights. It was better that way. I hated the thought of her seeing how I strangled the steering wheel.

Value Foods was far from the worst place in town to work. There was the packing plant, the egg plant, the paint factory, and a wide assortment of hog farms, cattle farms, dairy farms, and goat farms, where my skin could absorb a variety of rancid smells that stayed with me even after multiple showers with lye soap and industrial-strength hand cleaners. The grocery store was tame compared with the rest of the job market in Mason, and in truth, I was lucky to get the job. I needed something full-time, with benefits, and as much as I hated to admit it, Mr. Durst, the manager, was from out of town and wouldn't mind that my pregnancy would progress like a neatly drawn life cycle in a full-color science textbook before the entire town. What was my personal scandal to him? In fact, when I warily mentioned that I was almost four months pregnant in my job interview, Mr. Durst looked at me as if to say, *So what?* He did ask, "Will it interfere with your ability to perform your job?"

I assured him that I would be able to scan boxes of cereal and bag oranges well into my third trimester if not up to the day I delivered.

He grunted and handed me a uniform from out of a stack on the desk behind him.

"Do you want to know my size?" I wondered out loud, holding the standard issue pants, shirt, and apron gingerly.

"Small, medium, large, extra large," was his only comment, and indeed, when I located the tag inside the shirt it read *medium*. For a while at least.

"Start with that," Mr. Durst instructed. "We'll get you more later."

Training was an evening job since, for most people, the hours after suppertime were reserved for baths and play and television, not grocery shopping in our conservative little town. When I drove into the parking lot at seven o'clock, it boasted only a dozen cars or so, and though I was tempted to pull close to the door and save myself the trek through the below-freezing temperature, I dutifully drove to the back of the lot, where the employees were supposed to park. I yanked my hood up over my head and stuffed my hands into my pockets, running the whole way across the empty parking lot with my apron flapping against my knees.

The store was overly bright, and someone had turned the elevator music just a tad too loud. A little grocery cart corral at the beginning of the first aisle was stacked with carts, and only one checkout lane was open.

The cashier, someone I didn't recognize, was sitting on the counter right beside the red-eyed scanner and blowing a green bubble of fluorescent gum so big I was afraid it would pop and get stuck in her eyebrows. She sucked it in when she saw me and gave me a bored wave, beckoning me over with a flick of her wrist.

"You're Julie, right?" she asked, and though there was no hint of unfriendliness in her voice, I cringed when she called me Julie.

"Julia," I corrected, trying to sound upbeat.

She just stared. "Okay, whatever. You're late, by the way."

I twisted my watch on my arm and consulted the face again, though I had already checked it twice since driving up. "It's a minute to seven," I argued.

"Clark—he's the assistant manager—insists that we be at least ten minutes early for every shift. Better if it's fifteen minutes; he'll forgive you if it's five. But you're late."

"Nobody told me that," I said and regretted how whiny it came out.

She shrugged. "He's waiting for you in the back room."

"Thank you," I said and started off past the registers. It was a small thing, the thank-you, but it endeared me to her the tiniest bit.

As I was walking away, she offered, "Never sit on the counter." She drummed her fingers on the laminate surface beside her thighs as if to illustrate her point. "But if you're going to, make sure that Clark is in the back room. He'll kill you if he catches you."

I smiled and made a mental note of the name on her tag. *Alicia.* And below that: *2 years of faithful service.*

The back room of Value Foods was little more than an extended storeroom. The walls were cold, concrete blocks, and the shelving was stark and unattractive, the ugly sister of the sleeker, more appealing units that graced the aisles of the store and made things like Ho Hos actually look appetizing. There was a dingy bathroom near the loading dock and a sprawling metal desk that served as a break room at the far end of the elongated hall. Both locations were barely illuminated by naked lightbulbs that fought valiantly to dispel the dismal shadows and lost miserably.

When I used the bathroom after my interview, I'd thought about telling someone about the one burned-out bulb above the sink. But standing over the corroded fixtures and browning drain, I acquiesced. Crummy lighting actually improved the overall impression of the entire back room.

Thankfully, I knew I wouldn't find Clark amid the boxes and gloom. Opposite the break area at the far end of the passage was a duo of glass-fronted offices. The one on the left—the office with two actual windows to the outside world—was Mr. Durst's. The other office I had been told belonged to the assistant manager, Clark Henstock.

The light was on in his office, and he was looking at me through the glass.

I walked briskly toward him, trying to hold a capable look on my face that was both professional and eager yet not at all forced. Though no reflective surface played back my features and told me so, my face felt like it was locked in a grimace. I licked my lips, tried again, and finally abandoned the feeble attempt at confidence. The door to Clark's office was open, and I stepped up to the threshold, stopping in the doorframe to say, "I'm Julia DeSmit. You must be—"

"Clark Henstock," he said, clipping off each separate syllable with a virtually militaristic accuracy.

I almost said, "I know," but I managed to hold my tongue and was grateful for it when he tossed a pen at me. It came out of nowhere, and my hand shot up almost of its own accord. Against all odds, and probably for only the second or third time in my life, I made the perfect catch. The Bic thumped satisfyingly in my palm, and a grin unpredictably and embarrassingly sprang to my lips.

"Caught it." I laughed and immediately felt like an idiot. Wagging the pen lamely, I shrugged one shoulder as if to shake it off and dropped my arm to my side.

Clark assessed me for a moment before stating coolly, "I need you to sign a few papers." He turned to the table against the glass wall overlooking the storeroom and arranged three documents in a perfectly straight row. "Here, here, and here." He pointed when I stepped up to the table.

I signed my name three times, and each signature looked different from the last because I had to lean closer into Clark to reach the far papers and my body couldn't help avoiding his as if we were propelled together magnetically.

Although I half expected him to comment on it, he merely swept up the documents when I was finished and sank in his cushy chair. Swiveling toward a paper-laden desk, he tucked my papers into an open file and dropped it in a box by his feet. Then he looked at his watch and said without turning to me, "It's 7:04. You're late for work. Next time make sure you arrive on time."

It was impossible not to cringe, but I forced myself to bite my tongue and stay put, awaiting further commands. Clark remained with his back to me, and I determined to be as quiet and enduring as the sweetest of saints. Clasping my hands in front of me, I studied the back of his head while I practiced patience.

His hair was dark brown and noticeably thinning. On a man with a deeper skin tone, Clark's hair loss might not have been so pronounced, but Clark was white in a way that excluded any speculation of diversity in his family tree. The chalkiness of his scalp peeking through sad little patches of scraggly hair was unnecessarily unattractive. Not that Clark was ugly. He was just trying a little too hard to maintain the coif of his youth when he was obviously pushing forty. *Shave it off,* I thought. *Embrace your age.*

Almost as if I had spoken aloud, he whipped around to face me. "What are you still doing here?"

I managed to mumble, "Waiting for instructions."

Clark's sigh was a barely concealed groan. "Take a little initiative, Miss DeSmit. Be a problem solver. I'm not here to babysit." And he spun back to his computer.

I melted out of the office and wandered over to the break area, where I shed my coat and hung it over a folding metal chair. It was suddenly very cold without my winter parka, and I wrapped my arms around myself, hurrying out of the storeroom lest Clark turn to see me dawdling and fire me on the spot. Deciding my best course of action would be to ask Alicia what to do, I cut through the aisles and nearly collided with a boy who was almost a full head shorter than me.

"Oops!" He laughed a little too heartily. His yellow tie was crooked at his throat, and his stiff apron was stained with what looked like darkening blood from the meat counter. The thought nauseated me. "Sorry!" the boy exclaimed, wiping his hands on his apron and extending an arm to me. "I'm Graham. You must be the new girl."

"Julia," I muttered, taking his hand though it was almost painful to do so. His fingers were warm and soft.

"Nice to meet you, Julia. You'll like it here. It's a good job!"

While he looked too young to be working anywhere and his enthusiasm was slightly overkill, it was hard not to smile back when he was grinning in my face. "Glad to hear it," I commented vaguely, hoping that a response wouldn't encourage him too much.

"Alicia is the shift manager," Graham went on as if he intended to take me under his wing.

I rolled my eyes at the thought of yet another person on the rung of managerial staff at Value Foods.

"No, no, she's nice," he hurried to explain, misunderstanding my expression. I started to explain myself, but he continued, "Denise is a bit of a bear sometimes, but Alicia lets us leave early for our breaks sometimes."

I gave him a little nod and took a small step back to disengage myself from his unsolicited conversation. "I'll keep that in mind," I said, slowly backing away.

But Graham followed. "Hey, I'll walk you to the front. It's almost my break time anyway, and I can introduce you to people as we go."

"Graham, I—"

"Oh, it's okay, really. I don't mind at all." And though he could just barely peek over my shoulder, he took my elbow and steered me down the aisle as if he were some elderly benefactor and I a little girl.

I tried not to sigh as I allowed myself to be led through the store. Graham would release me long enough to let me shake the outstretched hands of my coworkers, but as we continued to the checkouts, he would manage to take up his paternal position again. There was nothing malicious or inappropriate in his gesture, and because he elicited genuine warmth in everyone we met, I did everything I could to be friendly and fine with whatever social particulars made him comfortable. I couldn't escape the feeling that much of my life from now on would be molding myself to fit snugly against other people's ideas and ideals. It was safer there where I could blend in, where I could be smooth and seamless and hidden—predictably contrite for my situation and newly flawless in my efforts at virtue. It made my head ache with inadequacy.

Value Foods wasn't an enormous store, but by the time we passed nine packed aisles and started through the produce section to the front, I had met half a dozen employees. All of them teenagers. None of them particularly enthused to see me. I was just the new girl—and an old one at that.

I peeked at my watch when we got to the front and waited patiently while Alicia finished with a customer.

An older man with what looked like a brand-new overcoat paid for his bottle of wine with a crisp twenty-dollar bill while Alicia grinned at him as if he were the single most interesting person she had ever met. She waved and watched him walk away, and he was halfway through the first automatic door when she finally turned to focus her attention on Graham and me. The easy turn of her lips sunk immediately, and she clicked her tongue as if to chastise us. "It's quarter after seven," she said.

"I know." I didn't offer any more because I was already becoming well aware of how things were done at Value Foods. Arrive on time, do your job, and stay out of Clark's way. I was just about to add Alicia's name beside Clark's when the sternness left her face and she shrugged.

"Whatever." She pointed to a mop bucket waiting in the sectioned-off lane beside hers. "We mop the store every few days on a rotating schedule. You're new, so you get the honors tonight. Produce section and freezer aisle. Just remember to put up the Wet Floor signs. We don't want a lawsuit." Alicia craned her neck for a moment and scanned the store. Seeing the coast was clear, she hopped back up onto the counter and squeezed a little dab of hand sanitizer into her palm, working it in as if it were a luxurious cream. "And, Graham," she added, looking up, "you only have ten minutes left on your break."

"Yup," he said cheerfully and waved exuberantly at us as he started away. "Have a good time, Julia! It was nice to meet you!"

I gave him a halfhearted flick of my fingers and ducked under the plastic chain to grab the mop bucket. "Is he always that happy?" I asked Alicia.

"Yeah, 24-7," she confirmed. "He's fourteen, you know. I don't remember being that cheerful when I was fourteen."

It occurred to me that I should banter, keep up this little conversation and make a friend. But the apron strings were cutting into my waist, and my head was already beginning to throb from the fluorescent lights and the music that must have been standard issue in the eighties for every doctor's office, elevator, and shopping store in the country. Maybe an instrumental version of some Michael Bolton or—heaven help us—Chicago song. All I could think was, *I have to listen to this for four hours?*

"Start at the back and work your way up to the front," Alicia instructed. She watched me unhook the chain and pull the mop bucket out into the aisle. "You know how to work that thing, don't you?" Her hand pulled an imaginary lever. "Just put the mop head in that slot and pull—"

"Yes, thank you." I quickly nodded, though I had never used a mop before in my life.

"Okay. Have fun." Alicia returned to rubbing her fingers.

I began to back slowly down the aisle past the fruits and vegetables and bins of nuts. The bucket was heavier than it looked, and I was so focused on maneuvering it that when the mister started over the lettuces I jumped out of my skin and knocked a grapefruit from a mountain of Ruby Reds. It plopped right into my bucket and splashed dingy water on my shoes. Had I a foul mouth, the moment was ripe for a string of curses that may have actually been deemed warranted by most people.

But I bit my lip instead and rolled up my sleeve to fish the grapefruit out. It was slick with brown water and probably bruised, and because I didn't want anyone to buy it, I stuck it in my apron pocket intending to pay for it later. I almost laughed in surrender when I saw the caricature of pregnant roundness protruding from my belly.

Mopping wasn't as bad as I first imagined it would be, and the monotonous motion actually felt more like a workout than a menial task. Sweep to the left, sweep to the right, swish in the bucket, squeeze. I wouldn't go so far as to say I enjoyed it, but the solitariness of such drudgery was a definite bonus. None of the other employees approached me even once.

With my hand on the grip of an oversize mop and the smell of dusty water at my feet, I had a few stolen moments of indulging in the what ifs-of my life. What if I had stayed in college? What if I had never gotten pregnant? What if things were different between Thomas and me? The list could go on forever—past recent mistakes and on to long-ago losses—and though I wanted to indulge in a little self-pity, I didn't because Grandma expected more of me these days. I pushed those thoughts out of my mind and, with a self-deprecating smile, mopped with all the heart of a born grocery store employee.

The store itself was dead, and the occasional customers who did brave the abandoned aisles walked quickly and clutched bulging coats around them as if this was the last place they wanted to be. Often they carried just a single item—a loaf of bread, a gallon of milk. At least two people besides the man in the overcoat stopped to peruse the wine section.

When a woman walked past me, I only looked up because her footsteps were so heavy. Her back was toward me, and she was wearing a jean coat with faux fur at the wrists and collar. Long, dirty blonde hair hung in a ponytail, and though I couldn't see her face, there was something about her that seemed too old for such youthful hair. She glanced over her shoulder, and I quickly dropped my head, not wanting it to seem like I had been staring at her. I heard her leave then, and because there was something about the sad slant of her back that tugged at something deep inside me, I watched her approach Alicia.

I had made it almost to the end of the aisle, and I could see and hear everything that went on between the two of them. The woman laid a half gallon of milk, a bag of pretzels, and two carefully chosen Braeburn apples on the counter.

Alicia barely looked at her and didn't even bother to smile, much less flatter her the way she had wooed the man with the wine.

For her part, the woman kept her head down and her hands in her pockets as if she was almost apologetic about her presence in the store.

"Four dollars and three cents," Alicia said when the last item had been scanned. She turned to put the groceries in a plastic bag while the women dug in her pockets.

She produced four crinkled one-dollar bills and spread them out self-consciously in front of her. Passing them to Alicia, her hands returned to her pockets to find the change. She probed and poked, and though I was supposed to be looking at the floor, I could see her fingers thrusting at the fabric and coming up empty.

"Do you have a take-a-penny jar?" the woman asked quietly.

Alicia stared at her. "No."

My hands went to my own pockets, but the pants were brand-new and the only thing I found was lint.

"How much was it again?" Her voice was so soft I could barely make out the words.

"Four dollars and three cents," Alicia repeated matter-of-factly.

The woman dug a bit more, and I wanted to yell at Alicia, *Just let her have it. I'll pay you later!* But I put my hand on the mop instead and looked down. I didn't want the weary woman to think that anyone was witnessing her shame.

I didn't realize I was holding my breath until I heard her say, "I guess I'll have to leave one of the apples."

When I exhaled, I felt them both look up. Fortunately, I was half turned away from them, and the splat of my mop on the floor disguised the tail end of my wheeze.

"Whatever," Alicia intoned.

Buttons were pushed and cash register tape whirred, and within moments the woman was gone.

"Sheesh," Alicia said, catching my eye. "Seriously, it was like three cents. Can you believe some people?"

"No, I can't," I said, but she didn't catch the arrows in my look.

I finished the floor with an almost vicious energy, but by the time the front doors were locked and we were ready to start restocking shelves, I had all but forgotten about the woman. Though she nibbled at the corners of my mind, it was easier not to focus on her. And even downright soothing to allow myself the thought that at least one person had it far worse than me.

have you visited
tyndalefiction.com
lately?

Only there can you find:

+ books hot off the press
+ first chapter excerpts
+ inside scoops on your favorite authors
+ author interviews
+ contests
+ fun facts
+ and much more!

Sign up for your **free** newsletter!

Visit us today at: tyndalefiction.com

Tyndale fiction does more than entertain.

+ *It touches the heart.*
+ *It stirs the soul.*
+ *It changes lives.*

That's why Tyndale is so committed to being first in fiction!

TYNDALE FICTION

CP0021